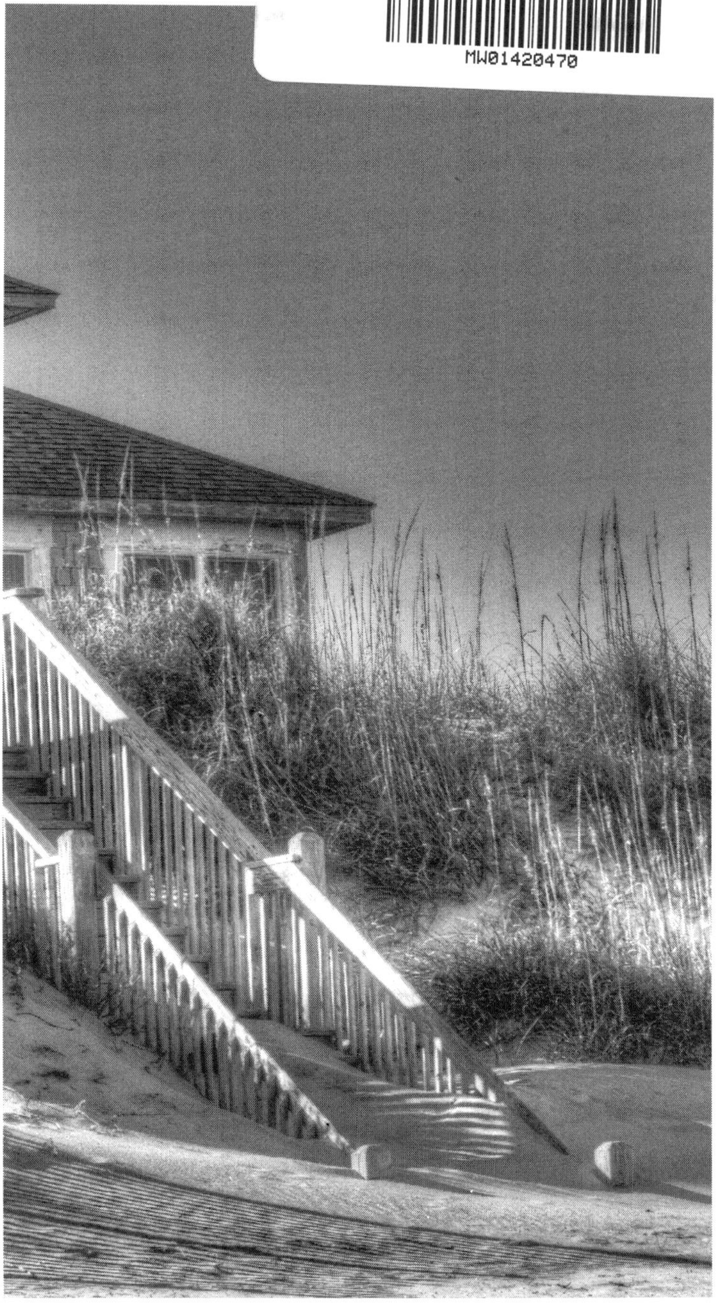

*CHANGING TIDES*
Published by SAPELO PUBLISHING
Copyright © 2023 by Veronica Mixon

All rights reserved.
Except for use in any review, the reproduction or utilization of this work in whole or in part in any form by any electronic, mechanical or other means, now known or hereinafter invented, including xerography, photocopying and recording, or in any information storage or retrieval system, is forbidden without the written permission of the publisher.

This is a work of fiction. Names, characters, places and incidents are either the product of the author's imagination or are used fictitiously, and any resemblance to actual persons, living or dead, business establishments, events or locales is entirely coincidental.

Printed in the USA.

# CHANGING TIDES

VERONICA MIXON

*To my husband, with everlasting gratitude for your belief in me, your undying love, and your enduring trust in my ability to tell a good story.*

# CHAPTER ONE

*Katelyn*

"THERE'S A SERGEANT Thacker to see you." My assistant, Jennifer, stood in my office doorway. Her face flushed with concern and a touch of curiosity.

"I don't know anyone by that name." I grabbed my purse. "I'm late. Ask Melinda to help him."

"He's a uniformed police officer. And he's asking for Owen Landers's mother."

Black squiggly lines swam in my periphery, and I gripped my desk.

Jennifer stepped aside, and a man in a dark blue uniform ducked through the opening. His shoulders drooped as if posture was the last thing on his mind. His puffy brown eyes held remnants of dread.

I braced for the inevitable hit, as you do at a stoplight when you glance in the rearview mirror and see a car racing forward. "Owen?"

"Yes. But your son's not hurt." He waved a palm toward my desk chair. "Maybe you should sit, Mrs. Landers."

I heard my mother's voice in my head. This is going to be bad. I tightened my grip on the edge of my desk. "Where is my son?"

"In the hospital."

"Hospital?" My head spun like I was half-drunk or fighting the flu.

He stretched his arm across my desk as if to catch me. "The hospital's just a precaution. Your son suffered a few scratches. No broken bones. No stitches." He rounded my desk and clasped my hand in his, patting it like my grandmother had when she turned a pinch of dough into a biscuit. Three quick taps. "A bystander pulled your son from the Porsche in time."

The room hushed. It was as if the air, the lights, and the officer hung in suspension, waiting for further explanation. "In time for what?"

"Your husband, Adam Landers, died at the scene. I'm sorry for your loss."

"Ex-husband." The words escaped my lips before I could grab them back. "We're divorced." I pressed my hand to my mouth. My mind felt pushed and compressed. "Adam's dead?" I should cry. I wanted to cry. To weep for Adam. But I had no tears left for him. Still, the officer's news emptied me. Owen would be devastated. "Which hospital?" I ached to touch my son. See him. Hold him. Comfort him.

He handed me a card. "Your son's at Children's Hospital. Can someone drive you?"

I must've walked out of Morgan Stanley and climbed into the passenger seat of my car, but I didn't remember taking those steps. When my mind resurfaced, Jennifer drove, and Arnold Palmer Children's Hospital loomed dead ahead. Questions bounced through my brain.

Where was the accident?

Did Adam die on impact, or did he linger in pain?

Did Adam's sister Vivienne know?

Who pulled Owen from the wreckage? I wanted to kiss that person's feet.

Then I remembered my text message threatening to haul Adam into court for breaching our custody agreement. My stomach lurched, and the bitter taste of bile coated my tongue.

Jennifer parked the Hummer, the only valuable asset Adam asked for in the divorce and didn't get. She grabbed our purses in one hand and my arm in the other.

"The police officer said he wasn't hurt," I said. "He'll be in the emergency room." I ran through the lobby, down the hall, and stared at the receptionist with beautiful silver hair and pink lipstick the exact color of her smock. "My son—" An uncontrollable tremble shook my body.

Jennifer arrived out of breath. She threw our purses on the counter and wrapped her arm around my waist. "Hang on, Kate." She spoke to the receptionist. "Ms. Landers's son was in a car accident this afternoon. Owen Landers, he's eight years old."

The pink lady nodded and typed something on her keyboard. Picked up her phone. "Owen Landers's mother is here."

I paced a five-foot circle in front of the pink lady's counter until a nurse in green scrubs walked from behind a pair of swinging doors. "Who's the mother of Owen Landers?" She looked from me to Jennifer.

"I am."

She settled her gaze on me. "We moved him to the second floor. Room 212. But you need to go to admitting—"

"Elevator's that way." Jennifer pointed down the hall.

I flew down the corridor, dodged a woman pushing a man in a wheelchair, and punched the elevator call button. The doors slid open with a rush of air. Jennifer and I jumped inside, and I pushed the second-floor button.

Owen's room was in front of the nurse's station. Inside, the only light came from a small lamp on the table beside his bed. And Owen slept. He wore a blue-striped hospital gown, a white sheet folded across his chest. And on his forehead, a small bandage, the only sign he'd survived a fatal accident.

Another nurse in green scrubs followed me into the room. "Are either of you the mother?"

"I am. Why is he sleeping?" No cuts. Only a bruise on his forehead. No blood. I ran my hand over his chest. "Is he hurt? The police officer said he wasn't hurt."

"The doctor gave him a sedative."

"Why? What happened?"

"I don't know. He just arrived five minutes ago."

She placed a clipboard at the foot of Owen's bed. "Dr. Sanderson is on rounds, but she'll be here soon. His paperwork states for you to go downstairs and sign the intake forms and give the admitting clerk your insurance information." The nurse rushed her words, clearly in control but not in an unkind way. A no-nonsense tone. It was one I recognized and often used with my customers.

"I'll go later. I'm not leaving my son." I smoothed curls from Owen's forehead and ran my hand down his arm. My fingers lingered on a scratch above his elbow, not bandaged. I eased the sheet off his legs and ran my fingertips over his feet. I counted his toes.

A few minutes later, an admitting clerk arrived with a laptop. I answered her endless questions and provided my ID and insurance cards. She finally left.

I repositioned a chair close to the bed, sat, and held Owen's hand, determined to be the first thing he saw when he opened his eyes.

A young woman charged into the room as if responding to a code blue. She stopped at the sink and washed her hands. "I'm Dr. Sanderson." She wore her knee-length white coat unbuttoned and looked to be in her early thirties. Her blonde ponytail and short black skirt might've swayed my impression.

"Why is Owen sleeping? Is he hurt?"

"He was agitated when he arrived. I ordered a sedative." Dr. Sanderson dried her hands, walked to the far side of the bed, and lifted one of Owen's eyelids. She seemed satisfied and plucked the clipboard from the end of his bed. "I've scheduled a child psychologist to examine Owen. I'll have to consult with him before he can be released."

My heart banged inside my chest like an unlatched screen door in a storm. "A psychologist?"

"Your son arrived inconsolable." Dr. Sanderson said the words as if they didn't rip out my heart. She made a note on the chart and put it back in place. She must've noticed my shock because her hazel eyes filled with compassion. "A sedative, in this case, is understandable. Owen witnessed his father trapped inside his burning vehicle. It must've been gruesome. Three seasoned paramedics were still visibly shaken when they brought your son into the ER."

"Oh, my God." I attempted to conjure the image of Adam inside his brand new silver Porsche 911 Speedster, burning. The picture refused to form. Not Adam. Movie star gorgeous, and easily the most handsome man I'd ever known—blond hair, cobalt blue eyes, wide open smile that showcased perfectly whitened teeth. Burning? I shuddered. Tried pushing away the image, but it tap-danced on the edge of my conscience, and I knew it would never completely disappear.

The no-nonsense nurse handed me a glass of orange juice. A whiff of antiseptic followed her hands. "Sip this. You'll feel better."

Dr. Sanderson touched my shoulder. "I'm going to keep your son tonight for observation. I'll review Dr. Cooper's report, he's the psychologist, and then we'll decide when Owen can be released."

I set the juice on the side table and held Owen's hand. "Sweetheart, it's Mommy. I'm here, baby. Mommy's here." I ran my fingers through his curls and kissed his forehead, his eyelids, his cheeks.

The doctor and nurse left.

"I'm going to step down the hall and grab a bottle of water," Jennifer said. "Can I bring you anything?"

"No, thank you." I had no clear idea of the time. "I'm going to stay with Owen tonight. You can drive my car home, but I should call my mom."

"I've already called Roslyn. She'll be here by nine o'clock." Jennifer removed a five-dollar bill from her wallet. "And the nurse said Adam's sister Vivienne called to check on Owen, so she knows. Is there anyone else I should contact?"

Owen would have to attend his father's funeral. "No. There's no one else I need to call." I gripped my son's hand and kissed his fingers. Tears welled in my eyes. I let them flow.

Four hours later, Mom arrived. She slipped into the room and mimicked the same rituals I'd gone through to ensure Owen was okay. She kissed his cheek and then turned her worried gaze on me. She placed her tote bag on a chair. "I stopped downstairs and bought you a Diet Coke. It's in the bag. I brought a few things you might need, a toothbrush, a comb."

Jennifer hugged Mom, whispered something I didn't catch, and gripped my hands. "I'm leaving, but I'm only a phone call away."

Mom folded me into her arms, and I clung to her, blubbering through a new wave of tears. "Adam burned to death, and Owen witnessed it." Even during the worst of our marriage battles, when I hated Adam to the core of my being, I hadn't wished him dead. The muscles in my thighs trembled, and I leaned against the bed frame for support. "Adam and Owen were on their way to a baseball game in Gainesville, even though Adam knew I'd made plans to take Owen to the rodeo in Kissimmee.

"When Adam didn't drop Owen at the bank at noon, I sent a text threatening to haul him back to court if he didn't have Owen at the bank by four o'clock. The car accident was my fault." I said it more to myself than to Mom.

"Adam flipping his car was not your fault."

"I knew the text would set him off—but I was livid and sent it anyway."

"Adam was driving." Mom wrapped me in another hug. "Today's your birthday, of course, you were angry. He ignored your child custody agreement which plainly stated each parent has the right to have the child on their birthday." She held me at arm's length. "You should come home."

I pulled away, found a box of tissues on the table beside the bed, and wiped my tears. "Orlando is home. The doctor said Owen was distraught when he arrived. She had to sedate him. And a psychologist has to examine him before they release him."

"After the funeral, come back to Savannah, let me help you through this."

"Mom, I can't discuss this now."

"Adam's death means the custody battle for Owen is over, and you have two beautiful homes sitting empty in Georgia. You have no reason to stay in Florida now." Roslyn, the fixer. She saw a problem and swooped in with a solution.

"The Barry House is Calvin's." My voice held a subdued, bruised note, and the space between my eyebrows and down my nose tingled. Any minute the tears would start to flow again. "Once Cal calms down, he'll want it back."

"Then spend the rest of the summer in Shell Hammock, at Spartina."

She opened the tote bag and handed me the Diet Coke.

"Spartina's the perfect environment for Owen after this nightmare."

Mom had never cared for Spartina, but she knew my grandfather's home held a special place in my heart. I could practically hear her lining up debate points in her head. Mom wasn't a we'll-cross-that-bridge-later kind of woman. She planned. She argued. She usually won. "You're a single parent now, and traveling three weeks out of four is no longer an option."

Her trump card struck the intended mark. My gaze locked on Owen. "I could transfer to another department." But at my management level, no positions would offer flexible forty-hour workweeks.

Adam's voice joined in the fray. *You're an analytical machine. Born without the mothering gene.*

"You've been running our family trust and working full-time at the bank for three years." Her voice turned soft and consoling. "You need to slow down."

It was an ongoing conversation Mom and I had at least once a week. But now she was right. I was all Owen had.

"Spartina's kitchen renovation is almost complete." Hope laced Mom's voice. "And the river's a magical place in the summer. Especially for a boy."

Memories of my granddad's summer home, afternoon breezes on the water, horseback riding, and kayaking trips to the island played like a film in my mind. "Owen's been begging for a horse." Thanks to my grandfather's inheritance, I could offer my perfect and peaceful childhood to my boy. No bad memories. Nothing to remind Owen of the horrors of today.

Vivienne swept into the room with two nurses in her wake. "Don't give me a lecture on visiting hours. I'm his aunt—" She spotted Mom, and her face froze, but then she zeroed in on Owen and rushed to his side. "Owen."

She leaned over the bed and spoke into his ear. "Aunt Viv's here."

I watched to see which Vivienne was in attendance.

The kind, sweet girl I'd known in high school kissed Owen's cheek. But inside that toned, petite body lurked another woman with a malicious heart and a mouth of venom.

Vivienne shook Owen's shoulder. "Honey, Aunt Viv's here. Wake up."

I leaned over the bed and gripped her hand. "Viv, Owen's sedated. The doctor wants him to sleep. Don't wake him."

She ran a loving hand down his arm and kissed his forehead. Then she turned. Her beautiful pixie face contorted into gargoyle ugly. "You." She stabbed her blood-red fingernail at me. "You killed my brother."

# CHAPTER TWO

*Katelyn*

Two Months Later

AN AIRBOAT WASN'T the strangest thing I'd ever seen on this barrier island on the Georgia coast. When I was ten, my cousin and I built a treehouse and spotted a three-hundred-pound black bear heading for the marsh.

Owen covered his ears. "Mom, why's that boat so loud?"

I pried his fingers loose. "It has an airplane engine." I recovered his ears with my hands and tried buffering the screeching whine of the boat's motor.

"Can it fly?" he yelled.

The driver came ashore, shot past a burial mound, and swung back into the sound. The engine powered down, the silence so sudden muted sound waves hung in the air.

I dropped my hands to my side. "No. An airboat doesn't fly. It's designed to skim over water or marsh grass like in the Florida Everglades." I couldn't remember ever seeing one on the Georgia coast. I considered the raised mounds to my left. "And I guess it can ride over land, too."

This swath of ground on the island's east end was protected land. Land my ancestors had meticulously maintained for the past seventy years. It wasn't a playground for some idiot with an amphibious floating toy.

I'd first noticed the boat when we set our anchor at the mouth of the creek. The driver kept his craft within my eyesight while we climbed dunes and skirted marsh grass lining the river. He'd been nothing more than an ill-mannered nuisance until we neared the island's eastern tip. Then he moved in, racing up and down the bank until he became impossible to ignore.

I refused to let him ruin our day. Kneeling beside Owen, I pointed to the shell mounds. "See those raised hills? That's where the Indians buried their braves."

Owen shifted his weight to his toes.

I grabbed his shoulder. "We can't move any closer than this sign."

He resettled on his heels and considered the four mounds. "Is this like the place where Daddy lives?"

"Kind of like that." I weighed my words carefully. I'd navigated weeks of therapy to get Owen to this point, agreeing to an afternoon away from the video games used like a drug to numb his emotional pain. "It looks different here because the Indians buried their braves standing up. That's why the hills are so high."

Owen hadn't mentioned Adam since we'd moved into Spartina, except for the nightmares. But screaming for his dad when he was half-asleep wasn't the same as casually mentioning his name in conversation. Was this progress? It seemed like progress.

He plopped on the sand and scooped a fiddler crab into his hand. "They look like white mountains."

"It's the sand and oyster shells." I snatched up a large white fiddler scuttling across the sand and encouraged the crab to crawl into Owen's hand.

"We own this whole island?" he asked for the third time in five minutes. "Even the mountains?" He glanced up, and his hat slid over his forehead.

I lifted the brim and swept curls out of his sapphire blue eyes. His dad's eyes. His hat was too big and completely covered his ears. It had been Adam's favorite. Owen never took it off. Even when he slept, he kept it on his nightstand. When he woke in the mornings, the hat returned to his head.

I glanced at the airboat and made certain it still floated in the sound. "The island belongs to us. No one owns burial grounds, but we are responsible for protecting them."

I motioned for him to stand. "It's getting late. We need to head back to the boat."

"Did the Indians fight?"

"No. The braves were hunters. A peaceful tribe." The airboat motor screeched, and I glanced over my shoulder.

Like a teen boasting a new hotrod, the driver accelerated, turned a donut, and flew across the marsh. Two donuts later, he spun back into the creek. Just a kid showing off.

"Do crabs bite?" Owen asked.

"They pinch." I dragged my gaze from the boat.

The fiddler crawled up his arm. "It's okay. He won't bite you."

Most of the barrier islands were state owned. The airboat driver might not realize this land was private. I kneeled beside Owen. "Hey, I'm going to try and flag down the guy in the boat and ask him not to drive near the Indian mounds. You wait here." I walked toward the water and waved my hands over my head.

The boat pulled to a stop and idled ten yards offshore. I motioned for him to wait and sprinted forward.

The driver gunned his motor, mowed over a patch of

marsh grass, then crossed the tip of the furthest burial mound and circled back to the middle of the sound.

Irritation swelled like a prickly ball in my chest. Even if the driver thought this island belonged to the state, he had no right to destroy the land. I walked backward and kept my eye on the boat. Owen met me halfway with an index finger stuck in each ear.

I fished my cell from my jean pocket. A patrol boat could be in the area. I held my phone high and spun a slow circle. No bars. My mother-son fantasy imploded into pragmatism. It was time to go home.

The airboat's engine kicked up a notch, and the boat glided into the mouth of the nearest inlet—an inlet that led straight to us.

I hugged Owen to my side. The guy's taunting no longer seemed childish, and I considered my options. If we walked the riverbank, our skiff was ten minutes away. Taking the cow trails through the brush meant walking for twenty. Twenty minutes of Owen complaining about being hot and thirsty. Twenty minutes of slogging through hundred-year-old vegetation.

The driver raced his engine.

Owen tugged my arm. "That boat hurts my ears."

Twenty minutes of my child not being subjected to a jerk.

I pointed west. "It's cooler walking under the trees than the riverbank."

"Is that boat going to follow us?"

Minimize his anxieties, and the nightmares will recede. Therapist theories always sounded simple until one had to put them to practical use. "Nah, he's just goofing around. His boat's probably new, and he wants to see how fast it turns."

We started up the path, and I used both hands to rip a hole in the wall of moss and vines.

Owen pulled his cap low and walked through my opening.

I stepped in and let the vegetation fall back in place. Moss-draped limbs and vines the size of my thigh hung from trees bowed and bent from years of coastal winds. The tangy ocean breeze mixed with the heavier earthy scent of the river and enveloped us in a cloud of mist. It was like stepping into a flora sauna fully clothed.

The airboat's rumbling engine grew louder. But we were hidden behind a curtain of green, and I took a moment to get my bearings. We were at least a quarter mile from our boat. I added ten minutes to my estimate and slung my arm over Owen's shoulders. "Tide's going to turn soon. We need to hustle."

We slogged up an old trail that wound through high ground still used by deer and wild hogs. If my memory held true, we'd end up in an oak hummock.

Owen scampered around me, his arms swinging wide. "Can we camp here? Have a bonfire and put up our tent under this tree?"

The distant whine of the engine filtered through the trees. "We could." The boat wouldn't follow us. Why would he? "But camping on the beach would be better because we'd have a breeze to keep away the sand gnats." The whine of the motor grew faint, and my shoulders relaxed. Get a grip, Kate. This isn't an island survival show. I searched for another trail I remembered that headed south.

"I want McKenzie to come to our campout." Owen picked up a stick and used it as a slashing sword for vines, twigs, moss, anything within his reach.

"McKenzie lives in Florida."

"Aunt Vivienne would bring her if I asked." He lifted a palm frond off the ground and stopped to watch a frog hop into a pile of leaves.

"We'll see." I urged him forward. "You'll meet new friends at school."

He turned away and swiped his stick at a vine. "I don't want new friends. I want McKenzie."

Squirrels chattered. Birds chirped. No engine rumbled. Whatever the airboat driver's issue had been, he was gone. "Hey, you want to check out my old treehouse?"

"We have a treehouse?" Owen pumped a fist in the air. "Suh-weet!"

"It's on the way. Follow close behind me because we might see snakes—maybe even an alligator."

His eyes grew wide with excitement, and I hoped enough fear to keep him from dawdling. We reached the end of our trail and looked out over thirty yards of open pasture bordering the river.

"Where's the treehouse?" Owen jumped flat footed over a limb. I shoved down the thought of a rattler lying in wait. "It's a little farther up, closer to where we anchored our boat."

"I can have a fort with a treehouse lookout." Owen was like the kid who discovered a pile of Christmas presents a week early and dreamed of the possibilities. "And you will have to say the password to get in." He danced in front of me, his face animated, his cheeks splotchy.

"Secret password, huh?" From this vantage point, I could see the river. The tide had already turned, and I estimated fifteen minutes before the water in the creek vanished, leaving behind mud and oyster beds. Our skiff couldn't be more than five minutes south. No problem.

"Passwords are cool," I said. "My cousin and I used to have a special code word to get into our treehouse." I reached for Owen's hand.

"What was the code?" His fingers slid away, and he darted forward. The boy had one speed—mach.

I followed at a jog. Ten steps in, the crank of a motor

stopped me midstride. "Owen, come back." It was as if we were wearing trackers.

Owen slid to a stop and glared at the driver. "Why's he following us?"

I ran full throttle and pushed Owen behind me. "I have no idea." What did this guy want?

The shrill of his engine grew closer.

Owen peeked around my waist. "I hate that boat," he yelled over the motor's whine.

"Yeah, I'm pretty sick of him too."

I squinted against the sun, made out the registration numbers on the side of the boat, and committed them to memory.

The driver turned a one-eighty and zigzagged back the way he'd come. He'd traveled twenty yards before I remembered the camera on my phone.

Owen's hand crept up my forearm. "I'm glad he's gone."

"Me too." I wanted to find our skiff and get off the island. "The treehouse isn't far. You want to race?"

"Sure."

"See that tallest pine tree?"

Owen crouched into a running stance. "Yeah."

"Whoever gets to the tree first wins all the ice cream."

"The whole carton?"

"The entire gallon."

We crossed the open field in less than twenty seconds.

"I get all the ice cream. I get all the ice cream." Owen did one of his fist pump jigs.

"I think it was a tie."

He stared me down. "You didn't tag the tree." His expression was as serious as a banker turning down a loan. "You gotta touch the tree, Mom."

God, he was cute. "Yeah, yeah. Nana probably bought plain vanilla anyway." I searched the area for a trail leading toward our skiff, picked my way around a decaying oak stump, then turned back and lifted Owen. "Come on, let's get a move on. Our boat's up ahead."

"What about the treehouse?"

"It's in an old oak near the river's edge, but we won't have time to check it out today."

Our trail ended at the bank of the river. It was an area I knew well, but nothing about the open space looked familiar. A new wooden platform floated near the bank, and the path leading west had been cleared of every vine, brush, and fallen limb.

Owen started up the new trail.

"That isn't the way to our boat." I turned a three-sixty and compared the native land with the cleared. This much work had taken considerable time. Time nobody would spend without reason. Poachers wouldn't build a dock and clear-cut this much land for a few deer.

"What's down that way?" Owen pointed to the open path.

"An old sugar mill." A group of five buildings—all of them in disarray. I couldn't fathom why someone would clean land they didn't own.

I grabbed Owen's hand. "Let's go."

He lifted the tail of his t-shirt and wiped the sweat from his face. "How much farther to the treehouse?"

"Keep your eye on the monster oak up ahead." Branches of the stately tree swept the ground. "The floor is wedged into the middle."

Owen took off in a fast sprint and hooped a yell. "It's humongous." He scurried three steps up the ladder. "We've no time, sweetie. Tide's heading out. You can climb the tree next time. "

"I just want to look."

He shot up two more steps, and the crack of splitting wood drained the last of my patience.

"Get down." I pointed to the ground. "Now."

As if weighing the consequences, he dangled his foot

in space and descended at a speed that would give a racing inchworm more than a fighting chance. He ignored the last two supports, jumped, slipped on a pile of leaves, and popped up.

I turned his shoulders toward our skiff.

He stomped down the path, boarded the boat, and adopted the familiar I-wish-we'd-never-moved-here pout he'd practiced to perfection over the past two weeks.

Water rushed out of the creek at an alarming speed, but somehow, I dodged the sandbars, and we cruised into Three Cees Sound.

We passed the entrance to Canton and headed for Coulson River and home. Five hundred yards down, sitting smack in the mouth of the Canary River, sat the idling airboat.

# CHAPTER THREE

*Katelyn*

THE GUY I now thought of as the stalker slid his boat from the mouth of the Canary River and into the sound. I checked my phone for service. No bars.

Owen sat with his feet propped on the cooler, slouched into a contortionist twist that only kids seemed to manage without a muscle-pulling injury.

Confident my boat couldn't outrun an airplane engine, I locked my speed in at twenty-five knots and cruised toward Spartina.

The stalker kept a constant three-hundred-yard distance, then suddenly, peeled left and headed back in the direction of the island.

I spotted Spartina straight ahead, eased off the throttle, and breathed a sigh of relief. Then reconsidered. Did he know I'd reached home?

I noticed a fishing boat cross tied to our dock's piling. Not that uncommon in our laid-back community for locals to fish around a friend's jetty. I cruised alongside. The man driving the boat didn't look familiar, but I plastered on a neighborly smile. "How's it going?"

The boat, a thirty-two-foot Grady White was loaded with sonar equipment but no fishing poles. A short, stocky man wearing a black wetsuit climbed the stern's ladder, pulled off headgear resembling a miner's hat, and finger-combed his hair over a receding hairline. He stuffed a black diver's bag into the bottom storage compartment.

The other man slipped on a pair of dark sunglasses. He reminded me of a rangy bad guy in a Saturday Western, all arms and legs, and a scruffy beard. He positioned himself between his partner and me and flashed a lopsided grin that came across more anxious than friendly. This guy was creepy. Not his clothes or his snake-tattooed forearm or his movie villain smile, but something I couldn't put my finger on.

I motioned for Owen to come closer.

He ignored me.

I stepped sideways and put myself between Owen and the creepy guy. "You guys are blocking my lift."

The scary guy turned his head and looked at my dock as if he'd just noticed the empty rails. "I guess we are." He laughed, but the sound merged with his two-pack-a-day gravelly voice and came across as sinister.

Owen scuttled around me and leaned over the side of our boat. "Why do you have a light on your head?"

The man wearing the wetsuit kept his back to us.

"What's the light for?" Owen upped his volume, but the man didn't respond.

The scary guy walked to the captain's chair, took his time lighting a cigarette, then popped the cover to what looked like a GPS screen.

My spidey sense tingled—these guys were trouble. "I'd appreciate you moving on." I pointed to a group of dark clouds to the west. "I don't want to get caught in that storm."

His partner slammed a cargo door and began unwinding their ropes from my dock.

I kept my voice in the semi-friendly range. "Why were you guys diving under my dock?"

The driver glanced at his tight-lipped partner. "Just hunting for shark's teeth."

"Cool." Owen perked up. "Can I see one?"

He started his engine. "Sorry, kid. We zeroed out today."

Adam and I had shopped for boats one summer, and this rig, decked out with GPS, radar, and twin Yamaha motors, would retail at close to a hundred grand. Their diving equipment was first class and looked new. Maybe I was edgy after the stranger in the airboat, and my trespassing tolerance was exhausted for the day, but unless these two were mining for gold sharks' teeth, something didn't add up.

The driver shifted into gear, and I grabbed my phone and snapped a picture of the boat's registration number.

"Why'd you take that guy's picture?" Owen asked.

"Because I didn't believe him. I don't think they were searching for shark teeth, and I'm going to report them to the authorities."

"You mean the police?"

The hitch in his voice tugged my heart. I ran a calming hand over his back. Police never led to anything good in Owen's world. "It's nothing to worry about."

The Georgia Department of Natural Resources website listed all boats registered in the state. Finding this guy's name and the identity of the airboat stalker would be as simple as a couple of clicks on my laptop.

We set the boat on the lift and grabbed our gear just as the first roll of thunder rattled. We made a run for the house, but I'm not sure why we bothered. We were dirty and sweaty, and after slogging through the brush, our clothes smelled like they'd been used to bury a dead animal.

We made it to the deck and took off everything but our bathing suits. I turned Owen toward the back stairway. "We'll have ice cream after dinner."

"Yes." He pumped his fist in the air and darted up the stairs.

I couldn't shake my unease and turned the deadbolt on the back door. I debated setting the alarm, but we were home. We were safe. I sniffed the air, and the last of my anxiety evaporated. The house smelled like an Italian trattoria. My mother would never be confused with a Martha Stewart wannabe, but her pasta fagioli was manna from heaven.

I dodged the kitchen. My stomach grumbled in protest, but I wanted to soak under the jet sprays and find a few answers before relating our afternoon adventures to Mom. I stopped in the foyer and checked the front-door lock. Might be an overreaction, but the protective mama voice in my head whispered otherwise.

---

Showered and curious to research the owners of the two rogue boats, I made my way to the library. I loved the massive room. The antique furniture covered in worn tapestry, my grandfather's eclectic collection of sea creatures shoved indiscriminately among his favorite books. It felt like home.

I poured a glass of wine, settled in front of the mahogany inlaid partners' desk and located the DNR website on my laptop. I ran a search for the airboat's registration and came up empty. I found the photo of the dive boat on my phone and typed in the decal numbers. The owner's name and address popped onto the screen.

Calvin Thompson—AKA my estranged cousin. "Great." My head swirled, but I hadn't consumed enough wine to blame it on the alcohol. I closed my eyes and tried visualizing my blood pressure receding to a calm, base level—a Lamaze mind-over-matter trick I'd never quite mastered.

Proactive, Kate. Take control. First, call the sheriff and

determine if a trespassing complaint against the airboat is warranted. Second, talk to Calvin and find out why two sketchy men were diving under Spartina's dock. Third, stock up on chardonnay.

Mom walked into the library carrying a loaded supper tray. "Owen's eaten and is watching a movie. Black Beauty—big surprise." She gestured for me to move my computer over and set the tray on the desk. "He wanted to play a video game, but I won't be sucked into a match I can't possibly win."

"No one wins against Owen." The soup smelled of onions and garlic and a whiff of oregano, but my appetite had evaporated.

"Owen claims the red bumps on his hand are from a fiddler's pinch," she said.

"Could have been, he handled enough of them." I couldn't take my eyes off my computer screen. What could Calvin be hunting under my dock?

Mom fiddled with the silverware and unloaded the tray onto my desk. "The welts looked more like poison oak."

I glanced up. "Poison oak?"

"I doused him with calamine lotion and gave him Benadryl. He'll be fine. But what possessed you to traipse around Barry Island?"

Some things didn't change with time. "I want Owen to love the island as much as I do."

She placed a breadbasket on the table and leaned the empty tray against the wall. "I've never understood your fascination with that land. And you went alone. Why didn't you wait and take someone with you?"

I took a generous gulp of wine. The smooth buttery liquid against my tongue drowned the words poised on its tip. "I know every inch of the island. Why would I take anyone with us?"

"Owen said an airboat followed you everywhere you

went." She rested her hand on the desk, leaned in, not remotely fooled by my nonchalance. "What's he talking about?"

"The answer to that might take a while."

She settled into a green leather wingback, and her forehead creased into one long wrinkle. "You seem worried."

"What?"

"You're rubbing your chest. You're worried."

I dropped my hand and leaned my head against the back of my chair. "I need to talk to the sheriff in the morning."

"The sheriff?" Mom's tone rivaled a high school coach's bullhorn. "Why do you need the sheriff?"

I hit the highlights of our afternoon. To her credit, she only interrupted once for clarification.

"Why didn't you call the sheriff as soon as you returned?"

"Tomorrow's soon enough." I drained the last of my wine. The dull ache treading back and forth across my forehead was less noticeable. "Believe it or not, it gets crazier." I told her about our welcome home party.

"Could be some locals spearfishing," she said. "Spearfishing's illegal."

Mom waved a so-what hand. "Good reason they'd be tight lipped."

"And people spearfish in clear water, not a muddy river. These clowns claimed they were hunting for shark teeth." I printed out the registration sheet.

"People hunt for shark teeth," Mom said. "It's not that unusual."

I slid the DNR record across the desk. "This is the registration for the dive boat's owner. You think Cal has a new interest in shark teeth?"

Mom studied the paper, then placed both hands on the arms of the wingback and pulled in a long, slow breath as if she were readying herself for a yoga lesson. "Well, if my nephew's up to mischief again, we'd better find out what it is and quick."

I wanted to argue Cal's side, but if my cousin held title to the first-class rig, what were the odds he'd loan it to those two guys to hunt for shark teeth? What were the odds he wasn't involved in another shady harebrained scheme? And what were the odds he'd give me a straight answer if I asked?

My estimate was somewhere around a million to one.

"I'll have a talk with Calvin." I kneaded a golf-ball-sized knot in my stomach. "I wonder if moving back is such a great idea."

"You need a new environment. So does Owen." Mom pushed the bowl across the desk. "Your soup's getting cold."

"Owen's nightmares have escalated, and he's sullen most of the time." I picked up a roll, broke it in half, and added butter. "If I ask him a question, I'm lucky to get a grunt in reply."

"Owen's eight, Katelyn. Eight-year-old children sulk. It's their only power in a world of adults. Kids are resilient. He'll be fine."

I had no choice but to cling to the adage 'mother knows best'. I massaged my temples. "I don't have time for whatever scheme Cal's involved in."

"Talk to him. Find out what he's up to."

"He's still clutching his trust-fund grudge that Grandfather made me executor." I wondered if there was a Lamaze trick for guilt management.

"He didn't exclude Calvin from the will." Mom's tone mirrored my frustration.

"Spartina Bluff and the island are yours." Mom pushed the soup bowl another inch and motioned for me to eat. "This house and the surrounding land are not part of the trust. No reason for Calvin to hang around here."

"Calvin wasn't on the dive boat."

My mother responded with her trademark "tsk." They covered a variety of situations—disbelief, irritation, shame. When I heard it, I was never sure which lecture to expect.

"Family property means nothing to him," she said. Ah, irritation.

"Dad knew if he left Spartina and Barry Island to Calvin, that boy would sell both before the ground over your grandfather's grave turned cold." Her eyes flashed with indignation. "You inherited this estate and the island because you appreciate your heritage. Calvin never has."

The dull ache in my head ramped into a steady pound. I poked around in the drawer for a bottle of aspirin.

"Calvin gouged you on the price of Barry House." She lingered over the words as if each were a sentence in its own right.

I washed down three aspirin with a gulp of wine, not a good combination. "I paid Cal's price to keep the property in the family. In a few months, he'll cool down and want it back." I hoped so because Spartina and the surrounding sixty acres was all I could handle.

Roslyn spit out another "tsk." "When you see Calvin, tell him to keep his ruffian friends away from Spartina. I don't want Owen exposed to those kinds of people."

"Ruffian? Is that like a hooligan?"

"They could be pals from jail." She waved her hand around to make her point.

"Jesus, Mom." It took every ounce of self-restraint not to give her one of my teenage eye rolls. "Cal was sixteen and got caught with a dime bag of coke. It was county lockup. Let it go."

I decided between the aspirin and the wine I should eat. I took a bite of my roll, an herbed Tuscan. She'd baked my favorite, and I suffered a jolt of shame for giving her a hard time. "Okay. I'll call the sheriff about the airboat first thing in the morning. And I'll stop by Cal's on the way to the office and see what's going on with his boat."

Mom walked to the bar and looked through the herbal teas, reached overhead for a cup, and flipped on the Keurig. "Willie Schroeder's the new sheriff."

"Willie's the sheriff?" That was a name I hadn't heard in years. "What happened to Homer?"

"He retired. He and Susie moved to Sarasota."

She added a couple of raw sugar cubes to her mug. "Why don't you call Willie? It's not that late for a friend."

"A friend from fifteen years ago. I'm not sure Willie will be happy to have his Sunday evening interrupted." But my Monday schedule was packed. I could hit the highlights on the phone. It was worth a try. I found his number and dialed. My call went to voice mail, and I left a message.

"Call Calvin." Mom sipped her tea. "He'll talk if you threaten to hold up his money."

"I don't control the money." A clarification I'd made several times since my grandfather's death. Mom assumed as trustee and head honcho I could work out that trivial detail. "I follow the trust's parameters." I didn't add that without the upcoming loan re-structure, all trust payments—hers, Cal's, and the head honcho's—would be in jeopardy.

She sat back in her chair and plucked a roll from the basket. "Before Willie calls back, it'd be wise to know what's up with the dive boat. Might be something you need to contain."

Good point. I dialed my cousin's number. He didn't pick up—big surprise.

Mom began a recitation of Calvin's teenage shenanigans.

My cell phone buzzed, and it was the first time I could remember being relieved a sheriff was calling.

"Thanks for getting back to me so late," I said. "I had an altercation with an airboat today on Barry Island. Can I file a trespassing complaint on the phone?"

"I can write it up tonight," Willie said. "But I'd rather do it in person. Say forty minutes?"

I checked the time. It'd be better than rescheduling my morning. "Okay, your house or mine?"

"I'll come to Spartina. And Kate, I'm going to bring along a federal marshal. There might be more to your trespassing complaint than you realize."

# CHAPTER FOUR

*Nathan*

DEPARTMENT OF JUSTICE usually stuck to midrange hotels. Nathan crushed a cockroach scurrying across the orange shag carpet and stuffed three case files into his briefcase. But lodging options were slim in Montgomery County, a twenty-mile stretch of four fishing communities an hour south of Savannah.

Sheriff Willie Schroeder's courtesy call could net his agents a much-needed housing solution. He crossed the hall and pounded on Erica Sanchez's door, then remembered his captain's parting order—Lead from behind. It was her team first. Probably should have included her in the decision to question Katelyn Landers.

Erica opened the door. Based on her crossed arms and tight-lipped nod, her opinion of him hadn't changed in the past three hours. Her standard dress was supposed to be a white shirt, blue jeans and a navy windbreaker with DEA plastered in three-inch letters across the back. More often than not, Erica wore fatigues and army boots, as if affirming she was the resident badass. She leaned against the doorframe.

"Katelyn Landers visited Barry Island this afternoon and had a confrontation with an airboat." Nathan's tone came across sterner than he had anticipated and resulted in a lingering raised brow from his second-in-command.

"We have to bring Ms. Landers up to speed before somebody gets hurt."

Erica glanced at her watch. "You're going to meet with her tonight? It's almost nine."

"She's the one who called the sheriff."

She shifted and looked away. "Figures the princess would call Willie."

"Claimed she and her son were stalked by an idiot in an airboat."

Erica stepped back and half closed the door. "He was just trying to keep them safe."

Nathan grabbed the handle and held the door in place. "How would you know?"

She finger-combed her cropped red hair, a color Nathan figured was from a bottle or maybe a packet of Kool-Aid. "Because it was one of my guys."

"The airboat?"

"Yes."

He waited for an explanation. Surely she planned to offer one. He rotated two fingers in the air. "And?"

A kaleidoscope of emotions ran over Erica's face—embarrassment, annoyance, exasperation, cagey.

He rotated again.

She rubbed the back of her neck. "Took Johnston almost an hour to get Kate back in her boat and into the sound."

"Any reason you didn't notify me that Johnston had an encounter with Katelyn Landers?" Nathan didn't need a PhD in behavioral science to know Erica considered him a micromanager. She made a point to mention the differences in their leadership styles several times a day. "And when did we get an airboat?"

"I commandeered the craft before you joined the team. Boat arrived today." She stepped back. "It's all in the report I'm five minutes from emailing. And you weren't notified because I handled it."

"You didn't handle it very well. She's filing a complaint." Leading from behind didn't equate to coddling, but Nathan reminded himself that in her place, he'd resent having a federal marshal take over his team. "I'm going to send the family to Savannah. Ask to use Spartina Bluff as a base until we close the case."

Erica slouched against the door, a broad grin spread across her face. "I wouldn't count on using that fancy estate as our base."

"It's the perfect location to monitor the traffic on the island."

"Oh, I get your reasoning, but Katie's no pushover."

"I find citizens quite willing to assist law enforcement, especially if we're protecting their land." Nathan checked the time on his watch. "Sheriff and I are headed over. I want you to come along and soften the blow."

Erica blinked, then laughed deep from her belly. The kind of laugh people used when sharing an inside joke. Nathan wasn't on the inside, so he didn't feel obligated to join in.

Her laughter softened to a chuckle. "Well as much as I'd like to bear witness to you and the princess squaring off, trust me, I'd be no help. There's not enough water under that bridge."

Interesting. So the inside joke belonged to Erica and Kate Landers. Just how well did Erika know the Kate's family? He'd do a little digging on that point later.

"We brief the Chatham County sheriff in the morning at six forty-five. You can hitch a ride with me, and I'll fill you in on my meeting tonight with Landers on the way to Savannah."

"Can't wait to hear all about it." Still grinning, she closed the door.

Nathan checked his watch. Now he was running late. He hustled to his unmarked green Chevy, climbed inside, and reconciled that maybe it was best that Erica stayed behind. No matter what his boss believed, Erica Sanchez being a local might be a hindrance, not an advantage to their case.

He made the twenty-minute drive to the Landerses' estate in less than fifteen, turned off the highway and drove through a stately bricked column entrance with an inconspicuous Spartina Bluff marker. He contemplated the types of people who named houses. Old-moneyed families living in historic homes, new-money snobs trying to give the impression they were old money, silver-spooned yuppie types like Katelyn Landers.

He parked behind a brown SUV and took a flight of six steps that led to a pair of the largest doors he'd ever seen at a private residence. Spartina Bluff wasn't a home. It was an institution.

Sheriff Willie Schroeder stepped from the shadows and nodded a greeting. The sheriff was about Nathan's height, an inch or so over six foot. Nathan, described as tall and slender, would be considered plump compared to Willie. Willie yanked his jeans to his armpits and pushed the bell.

Nathan had expected door chimes or maybe a ringing rendition of church bells playing a few chords of a Beethoven symphony, but not Elvis's "Blue Suede Shoes." Someone in the family had a quirky sense of humor. He doubted it was the woman opening the door.

Willie took the lead. "Sorry to bother you this late, Mrs. Barry. Kate's expecting us."

She ushered them into a foyer that could be used as a small ballroom. Regal came to mind—the house and the woman. Nathan recognized Roslyn Barry from the pictures in her dossier. Noah Barry's dutiful daughter-in-law. A former Miss Georgia who was possibly more beautiful today than in her teen pageant photos.

Rugs covered the gray marble floors and appeared weathered, antique, and Persian. A crystal chandelier, a piece that would look at home in any European castle, hung from a mirrored dome and glistened against the floor-to-ceiling windows that looked to be leaded glass. He'd seen his share of millionaire homes, but nothing like this.

Katelyn Landers hurried down a winding staircase. Nathan mentally compared her to the slew of photographs in his file. He estimated she was every bit of her five-eleven registered height, but her weight looked closer to one twenty-five than the one forty listed on her driver's license. She paused on the last step and swept the foyer with stunning emerald eyes. She wore an easy, friendly smile.

Nathan stepped forward, his hand extended. "Marshal Nathan Parsi."

She gave his hand a quick shake, sidestepped, and drew the sheriff into a full embrace. "Thanks for coming, Willie."

Willie's cheeks blushed scarlet. "It's good to see you, Kate. Real good."

She led the group down a wide expansive corridor and into a crowded, cozy room that looked more in line with an upscale antiquity bookstore than a home library. He eyed mementos from every corner of the world crammed between books that appeared to have enough age to be first editions.

Roslyn paused at the threshold. "Kate, I'm going to check on Owen." She turned to the sheriff. "It was good to see you again, Willie." She met Nathan's gaze, then pulled the door closed.

Katelyn walked across the room and removed a diet cola from a bar refrigerator. "Can I offer you a soft drink, water?"

"No, thanks." Willie sat in a scuffed leather wingback flanking a massive fireplace.

"I'll take a water." Nathan sank into a worn brown sofa

that he'd bet a year's pay was Italian leather. Opening his briefcase, he located his red folder and positioned his cell on the side table.

Katelyn handed him a glass of ice and a bottle of water.

"Thanks." He patted the seat cushion next to his. "I'd like to tape our meeting."

She glanced at Willie. Her expression didn't hold fear, but a couple of wary lines did crease her forehead.

"I hope you don't mind." Nathan offered up a good-cop let's-be-friends smile. "Recording is easier and more accurate than taking notes."

She blinked a couple of times and added a few more wrinkles to her brow. "Federal marshals don't usually get involved in trespassing complaints."

"Schroeder mentioned you had an incident on Barry Island this afternoon." Nathan patted the cushion again.

Katelyn sat on the sofa's edge. "That's right."

He fished a small notebook from his pocket. "I'd like to determine if it has any connection to a case I'm working on."

He flipped a couple of pages. "I understand you recently inherited the island from your grandfather."

Katelyn tilted back a few inches. "Yes."

Nathan closed and placed his tablet on the side table. He needed her comfortable, engaging in regular conversation to obtain an accurate baseline. "What time of day did you encounter the trouble?"

She glanced at the closed notebook, and her shoulders softened. "We arrived around three thirty. I saw the airboat shortly afterward, no more than a couple of minutes."

Nathan poured water into his glass. "Sheriff says you and your son came by boat?"

"It's a barrier island. No bridge." Katelyn turned to Willie. "You know anything about someone clearing land and building a jetty on the south side of the island?" Nathan noted her cadence. No hesitations, fully in control.

Willie slipped his forefinger inside the collar of his knit shirt and pulled. "That's one of the reasons we're here."

"I'd like to clarify a few things before we talk about the dock." Nathan's response resettled Kate's attention back on him. "Would you describe your confrontation with the airboat?"

"Like I said, he showed up as soon as we arrived." She told the story of her afternoon confrontation in a calm, even voice. He purposely interrupted her several times for clarifications, and Katelyn repeated her answers concisely before continuing on without embellishment. A sign she told the truth. Other than a couple of quick glances at Willie, her eye contact was constant with Nathan. The color of her eyes varied between shades of jade to mossy brown each time she mentioned the airboat. She claimed the driver was young and unusually aggressive.

Erica, if she'd known, had left that part out.

Katelyn Landers's primary concern seemed to center on the airboat. Changes to her island were a secondary matter. She played the part of a naïve owner, gave the impression she didn't know why or by whom her land was being used.

"Anything else?" He picked up his notebook and pen, flipped a few pages, and made a quick note, then glanced up.

Annoyance had settled into the lines around her eyes and darkened her pupils. "Isn't an airboat stalking me and my son and someone building an unauthorized dock enough?"

He nodded. He could admit it was one of his men in the airboat, explain that she and her son came within fifteen minutes of witnessing a drug drop. But he couldn't chance her warning her cousin Calvin Thompson that the airboat was operated by DEA. He took a sip of his water and then slowly surveyed the room. "You also inherited this estate from Noah Barry?"

Her gaze followed his as if trying to see the space through his eyes. "Yes."

"Does anyone else live here?"

She glanced from Nathan to Willie. "Our caretaker, James."

"You have only one full-time employee in residence?" Much better than he'd hoped. The fewer people who knew his team was on the property, the better.

She looked at Willie. "What does my property manager have to do with a trespasser on Barry Island?"

By her terse response, Katelyn Landers wasn't accustomed to discussing personal business with strangers, especially law enforcement. "Ms. Landers. May I call you Katelyn?"

"Kate." She brought her drink to her lips. "Everyone calls me Kate."

"This is more than a simple trespassing issue."

Nathan pulled a stack of photos from his file and handed her an eight-by-ten. "Did you know about these improvements to your sugar mill?"

She placed her drink on the table and took the photo in hand. Textbook confusion swamped her face, slack mouth, furrowed forehead. She looked at Willie as if she expected her friend to intercede.

Willie's face remained as empty as a whiteboard wiped clean.

Kate drew the photo closer. If she faked her confusion, she was very talented.

The photo included a shot of five buildings that would soon topple to the ground. Except for one, the largest of the group, an old pack house. The color differential in the roof tiles gave the appearance of recent repairs.

"Were you aware of the recent modifications to your building?"

She rubbed her finger over the two-by-fours bracing the double entry doors. "This work wasn't approved."

"Anyone else with permission to make repairs or use your island?"

"No."

"How about before Noah Barry died?"

Her eyes softened at the mention of her grandfather. "My grandfather was bedridden and unable to speak after his stroke."

"Do you have another family member who might authorize repairs without your knowledge?" Nathan gentled his speech as if he understood her confusion. A funeral director's cadence, soft and much practiced.

"A family member?" Her vacant gaze drifted back to the photo. He pinpointed the exact moment Kate's suspicions shifted, tilted, and fell. Her eyelids fluttered, her breath shortened. Someone was uppermost in her thoughts. Was it her cousin Calvin Thompson, her caretaker James, or was it someone else?

"New trail, new roof on the mill." Willie chimed in right on time.

So far, Nathan was pleased with the sheriff's performance. Willie had laughed at the notion Katelyn Landers might be involved with drug runners. Nathan was fairly confident the sheriff didn't understand what a behavioral analyst did, but Willie knew about US marshals, and that was enough to secure an agreement that he'd be the pinch hitter in this interview.

Willie leaned forward. "A little odd, don't you think, that you wouldn't know about work on your island."

"Well, I didn't know." No doubt in her voice, just a hint of exasperation. "Not much goes on in this county without someone apprising the sheriff. I expected you to explain what's going on."

Willie, head down, eyes downcast, played his part and appeared appropriately shamefaced.

Nathan waited. Sipped his water. He was comfortable with silence.

After a full five seconds, Kate gave up on Willie answering and turned back to Nathan.

Nathan placed the photos of the sugar mill back in his folder. "Repairs on your mill were minor and wouldn't take more than a day or two. The Coast Guard, not the sheriff's department, patrols the waterways. And with the current political environment, the Coast Guard's focus is on the ports."

She shifted in her seat. "Exactly what is happening on Barry Island?"

Relaxing against the back of the sofa, Nathan decided to test Kate's compliance. "I'm heading up a DEA team who's followed a drug ring from Veracruz to the East Coast. It's a six-month investigation, but each time we get close to a bust they pick up and move on."

Kate's face drained to the color of sheetrock. "My island's being used by drug runners?"

"Yes."

"Why haven't I been informed?"

"I believe that's what I'm doing."

"Before now."

"Until now, there's been no need to involve you." He gauged her reaction.

"Why haven't you arrested them?"

"We were ready to move in three weeks ago, but they got word and dropped out of sight. Now it appears they've relocated and are using your island to break down and package."

She took a long, slow breath. "Well, what's your plan?"

"Bust them."

"When?"

"As soon as possible."

"Why are you waiting?" She barked her questions, one louder than the next.

Nathan couldn't afford for her to find her footing. "We should wrap the case in the next few days. Until then, you should stay off the island."

"That's not a problem." Some color had returned to her face, but her lips remained pasty.

"Due to your estate's proximity, it'd be best if you and your family stayed elsewhere."

Her body stilled, and her eyes darkened.

It was a reasonable suggestion, and with a home in Savannah and her mother's residence located only two blocks away in the city's walking district, easy enough to manage. "Is there a problem?"

"Isn't it a bit extreme to vacate Spartina Bluff? Barry Island's across the river." If Kate leaned any farther from Nathan, she'd be in a full back bend.

"You own another home in Savannah, three blocks from your mother's home that is adjacent to Forsyth Park. I see no reason for you to risk your family's safety by staying here."

"But my house in Savannah isn't furnished." Seeming to reconsider. "You're right. It won't be a problem. I'll make arrangements to stay at my mother's home until you notify us everything has settled."

"I appreciate your cooperation."

Kate rose, her foot pointed for the door.

"One more thing." Nathan stayed seated.

Kate's frown was immediate, followed by an unsteady sigh.

"I want to post a seven-man team on your property."

"Here?"

"The proximity of your dock to the island would give us an edge."

Her hand crept to her lips. She cut her gaze in Willie's direction, shook her head, and stepped back.

Nathan threw down his ace. "My request may seem somewhat unusual, but the sooner we close our case, the sooner your life will return to normal. And it would be an asset for our team to have clear visual contact with the island." Nathan offered an easy shrug. "I have a morning meeting in Savannah, but we could be in place by tomorrow noon."

Her face remained stoic, but he watched a mental debate play out in her eyes. A full pallet of faded pinks and whites washed over her cheeks. She crossed her arms and ran her fingers over her forearms. A form of self-soothing.

She glanced over the room, as if considering his request, then lifted her chin and gave a short, curt nod. "You can use the guest house over the garage." She walked to the bar and dropped her diet cola in the trash. "Marshal, why do you think this drug ring chose Barry Island?"

Nathan pocketed his phone. "Since your island's abandoned, it could be as simple as your land poses the least risk."

Her only reaction was to run her fingers over her forehead as if staving off a headache. All Kate's physical reactions indicated she'd been blindsided by the news a drug ring had taken over her island. He didn't get the buzz she was evading or lying.

But Nathan was very interested in how she'd handle her brand-new suspicions. He'd know soon enough if she'd zeroed in on her cousin. Calvin Thompson had a tail.

Kate went to the desk and scribbled on a piece of paper. She handed the note to Nathan. "My cell phone, my direct line at the Savannah office, and my mother's home phone number. It's unlisted."

"Thank you." He tucked the sticky note in his briefcase. Didn't bother to tell her that all the numbers were already in his file, and there was no such thing as an unlisted number to a federal marshal.

The double doors opened, and Roslyn stepped back into the library. She took one look at her daughter's face and stepped with purpose to her side. Nathan noted the mother-daughter bond was discernible and solid.

"One last thing." Nathan waited until Kate's eyes met his. "What's your family's connection to Juan Ignacio Cabral?"

"What?" Roslyn's shocked tone registered the exact time as Kate's puzzled, "Who?"

# CHAPTER FIVE

*Katelyn*

MOM VICE GRIPPED my arm, an unspoken warning for me to keep quiet.

"Juan Ignacio Cabral?" Marshal Parsi said the name again. "Does your family have a connection with his?"

"Juan Cabral was an old friend of my father-in-law's. He and Dad were college friends who kept in touch," Mom added a touch of condescension to her sweet southern singsong. "They shared an affinity for remote fishing resorts. Nothing more."

Parsi kept his questioning gaze on me. Every inch of his six-foot frame hummed. I'd been in enough boardroom showdowns to recognize he'd aimed the question in my direction.

"Do you consider him a family friend?" he asked.

"Kate's never met Juan," Mom said. "And I haven't laid eyes on him in years."

Parsi closed in a step. "Is that true?" There was something bristly under the surface—disbelief, misdirected irritation. It was hard to tell.

I wanted to see Mom's face, figure out why she'd overexplained my grandfather's relationship to Cabral. She seemed very quick to disown Cabral's friendship. But I refused to look away from the marshal and his unwarranted scrutiny. He gave me the uncomfortable notion he was peering into the deepest recesses of my mind, sifting through my darkest and innermost secrets. He could delve all he liked. I had plenty of secrets, none connected to a Cabral.

My grandfather graduated from college fifty years ago, which put this Juan fellow in his eighties. How could an eighty-year-old man be significant to a drug case?

I had nothing to hide. "I don't remember meeting anyone by the name of Juan Cabral. Why? Is my grandfather's friend important?"

A stare down with a US marshal seemed inadvisable. I dropped my gaze to a pile of mail stacked on my desk, stepped closer and flipped through several envelopes. I hoped he'd get the I'm-a-very-busy-woman message.

Mom inhaled an uneven breath, and I couldn't help glancing over. She gripped the back of a wingback chair so tight her perfectly groomed nails came close to puncturing the brown leather.

"You've never met Juan or his nephews?"

"Nope, never had the pleasure." I glanced at the grandfather clock in the corner. "It's getting late. If that's all, I need to check on my son."

"I'll be here at noon tomorrow with my team." Parsi turned with military precision and walked from the room.

"Thanks for agreeing to see us so late, Kate." Willie ducked his head and followed the marshal down the hall.

I followed them to the front door, locked up, and returned to the library.

Mom had switched from herbal tea to a glass of merlot. She swallowed a sizable gulp. "If you ask me, Marshal Parsi was a little full of himself."

I skimmed my hand over my lower abdomen trying to stifle my butterflies—butterflies that resembled a school of piranha nipping my intestines with quick, lethal bites.

"Why'd you get uptight when Nathan asked about the Cabral family?"

"Nathan?" She graced me with one of her iceberg-melting stares.

Inwardly, I cowered. But I dug deep and stared back. "Just answer the question."

"Don't make the mistake of getting friendly," she said. "Bad enough you're allowing his team to vacation in the guest house. My God, what were you thinking?"

Mom must have heard me agree to lodge Parsi's team over the intercom. What was I thinking? Maybe I could blame it on my splitting headache. "I'm worried Calvin's into something over his head."

"That's no reason to allow eight US marshals the run of your compound."

I laughed, and my brain banged against my skull. If I popped any more aspirin, the piranhas would draw blood. "It's a stretch, don't you think, to call a house with sixty acres of pasture a compound?"

Mom sank into the sofa, grabbed a pillow, and placed it behind her. "You think Calvin's involved with this drug ring?"

"God, no." I kneaded my forehead. "Surely not." My intestines were inflamed. I wanted to blame it on a virus, but … those penetrating brown eyes. Eyes that I would typically describe as lazy bedroom, but tonight more in line with heat-penetrating missiles, had pushed every intuitive alarm button I possessed. "I'd call Calvin again, but it's after eleven." Etiquette dictated nothing but emergency phone calls after ten o'clock, but texting was a gray area. I grabbed my cell and sent a message asking Cal to call me immediately.

During Parsi's hour-long interrogation, I examined and discarded the possibility that Calvin was the reason drug runners squatted on my land. My cousin often walked a thin line with the law. But drug running? No way. He wasn't an idiot.

"Did the marshal seem familiar to you?" The idea we'd met in the past swirled in my head the minute I shook his hand. "Parsi sounds Middle Eastern. Do we know him from somewhere?"

Mom looked at me as if I'd suggested she eat a raccoon. "Why in the world would we know a federal marshal?"

She had a point. I plopped on the sofa beside her and tucked one leg under another. "Okay, spill it. What gives?"

"What are you talking about?" She sipped her merlot. Hedging. She knew exactly what I was talking about. "When Nathan asked about Juan Cabral, you had a hissy fit."

"Don't be overly dramatic." She placed her drink on the table, picked up a Guns and Garden magazine, and thumbed through the pages. "After I explained that Dad and Juan were old friends, the marshal acted as if he didn't believe me. It irritated me."

Yeah, right. Irritation always turned Mom's voice a notch above a squirrel protecting her young. I nodded. Conceding all points was my only hope of ferreting the truth out of her. "How well do you know Juan Cabral?"

"Not well." I wasn't sure which was faster, her headshake or the flutter of her fingers running over her blouse. She tossed the magazine aside, rose, and walked to the desk. "Haven't seen him in years."

"I'm curious why his memory upset you."

"Don't be ridiculous. Why would questions about Juan Cabral upset me? I hardly knew the man." She stopped at the window and peered into the black sky. "We met when I worked part-time at Barry Real Estate."

"I didn't know you worked in Granddad's office."

"It was when your father was in Alaska. Before you

were born." Her gaze meandered around the room. She picked up her glass and downed the last drop.

"Any chance Juan Cabral is a drug lord?" I asked. Mom gave me a short, impassive once-over. "Juan Cabral was charming and handsome but no drug lord. Dad didn't associate with criminals."

"Juan and Granddad were close friends?"

She gave a half shrug. "Dad visited Juan in Mexico on occasion, and once or twice a year they traveled to remote fishing spots in Central and South America. They were two old friends with an expensive hobby." Mom walked to the sofa and sat. "I'm glad you agreed to stay at my house in Savannah. Your office is only a few blocks away. I'll schedule tennis lessons or golf for Owen to introduce him to boys his age."

"I'm worried about changing Owen's environment so soon. He's just beginning to think of Spartina as home."

Mom glanced around the room. "There's not a neighbor within a mile of this place. A drug ring is using the island. Those men are diving around the dock. I don't like you and Owen living here."

"The dive boat is Calvin's, and it was your idea for Owen and me to move back to Spartina."

"That was before I knew a drug ring worked across the river."

I eyed the stack of property appraisals on my desk and calculated the hours it'd take to get ready for my appointment with the Charleston appraiser. "Spartina's practically a fort. We have a good security system and an on-site property manager. No place safer." Maybe Mom's agitation had less to do with Cabral and more with the nearby drug ring. She was a city girl and had never enjoyed Spartina or Shell Hammock, the quaint fishing village down the road.

"Even the marshal said it's dangerous to stay here," she said.

"The marshal wants to use Spartina as a base for his team. We're in his way."

Mom shifted in her seat and rearranged the pillow behind her back as if settling in for a long chat. It was getting late, and I still had at least two hours of paperwork on my desk.

"You don't think the marshal believes we're in danger."

"No." I pinned her with a stare that left no room for further discussion.

She fiddled with the fringe on a throw pillow. "You don't think he believes we have anything to do with what's happening on the island?"

Meaningful stares rarely worked on my mother. "You and me?"

"Calvin."

"Cal's reckless, not stupid."

"I hope you're right."

I leaned over and took her hand. "Mom, please don't say anything to Owen about staying in Savannah for the next few days. I want to tell him at the right time. This change could agitate him."

She grew quiet, and I didn't interrupt her silence. After a few minutes, she let out a ragged breath. "Losing a parent is tragic. I remember how devastated you were when your father died. But children are resilient, and it's best not to over-pamper them."

A lump grew in my throat and made it impossible to speak. Sitting at my father's bedside during his peaceful passing hardly compared to Owen witnessing Adam's horrendous death. I rose and went to my desk. But I wasn't up to a verbal battle with Mom. And she meant well. "I'll see Calvin early tomorrow morning, then meet at your house around nine and explain to Owen why we'll stay with you for a while."

Mom agreed, and we hugged goodnight. I tried shuffling through the pile of correspondence on my desk, but I couldn't get past the possibility our family name could be linked to a drug bust. Calvin wanted to cash out of the business, but that was impossible until the company's debt restructuring was completed. Negative news would be a deal breaker for the banks. Any hint of our family being connected to a drug cartel and the bank would pull their offer to refinance the estate's nine Atlanta office buildings, and they might shut down our credit lines.

I'd have a frank discussion with Marshal Parsi tomorrow. If I gave his team the use of my guesthouse, I wanted assurances there'd be no mention of Barry Island when he made his bust. Not one word to cast suspicion on our family's name or Barry Real Estate and Development, a four-generation business that passed to Calvin and me with Grandad's death six months ago.

I opened a FedEx package delivered by courier containing an appraisal of company warehouses in South Carolina. I flipped to the estimated value and groaned.

We owned twenty-one warehouses stretched across coastal Georgia and South Carolina, each a profitable income-producing rental. This was the fifth appraisal of a property that had undergone extensive repairs, but according to the appraisal, the property's value hadn't increased.

The bank debt restructuring package I'd worked on for the past year required verification of our company's net worth, which equated to property appraisals. But the five appraisals I'd received all quoted less than forty percent of value on our books. Something somewhere was seriously amiss.

I shut down my computer, turned off the lights, and climbed the stairs to check on Owen. I opened his bedroom door and found him propped in bed, watching a Disney movie without sound.

"Why aren't you asleep?" I picked up his bedcovers off the floor.

He reached for his blanket. "I woke up."

"Watching movies keeps you awake." I found the remote and turned off the television. "Did you have a scary dream?"

"No."

I sat on the edge of the bed. Owen appeared relaxed, without body tension or evidence he'd been crying. "Was something bothering you?"

He shrugged.

I held my hand in the air and wiggled three fingers. "What can you do if you wake during the night and can't go back to sleep?"

He sighed the long-suffering exhalation of a kid wishing to be left alone. "Draw a picture. Write a story about my worry. Or come to your room." He slid down and rested his head on the pillow. "How many more days until my birthday?"

Deflecting was a technique Owen had mastered early. I fastened him with my best motherly stare.

He rolled his eyes. "Okay. I won't turn on the television anymore when I wake up. How many days until my birthday?"

I lifted his ball cap off the wooden chest on the nightstand and lifted the lid. We called it his worry box. The top picture was a car upside down in a ditch, flames lapping through the windows. He'd drawn this version of Adam's car accident three days ago. I had a sharp gut-wrenching urge to shred every paper inside, all the monsters chasing kids and small animals, every rendition of the car accident, wipe away every last gory picture in the box. But the therapist insisted Owen's memories were his to resolve, not mine. I longed to take him in my arms, promising nothing bad would ever happen in his world again. Instead, I tucked the blanket around him.

"Mom." He shook my arm. "How many days until my birthday?"

"Ten." I swept curls off his face and considered my afternoon appointments. Searched for a free hour for a much-needed haircut.

He rose up on one elbow. "Aunt Viv called. She's going to take me to Disney World for my present. She's coming to get me in two days."

"Your Aunt Viv called?"

"You were busy, so Grandma talked to her. You're supposed to call Aunt Viv back." He scratched his legs under his blanket.

I pushed off the cover, found the calamine lotion on the nightstand, and dabbed the liquid on the red welts covering his shins and ankles. "Do these burn, sweetheart?"

"No. They itch." He scratched his thigh.

I held his hand and squirted more lotion on the welt. "I'll speak to Aunt Viv, but this isn't a good week for us to go to Florida. Maybe after your birthday, we can plan a trip to Orlando."

His eyes widened. "But I want to go." He scooted to the top of the bed.

I twisted the cap on the calamine bottle, placed it on the nightstand, and wiped my hands on a tissue. "I'm sure you do, but I can't leave now."

"You don't have to." Tears pooled in his eyes. "You weren't invited—just me. It's my present."

My heart stumbled. "And it's a great present." I motioned him back under the blanket. "I'll talk to Viv, and we'll work something out. But it can't be this week."

"Aunt Viv said you'd say no." Owen crossed his arms like a stubborn miniature Buddha. "You don't like her because she's Daddy's sister."

"I like your Aunt Vivienne just fine." Which wasn't entirely accurate. I liked her. Once upon a time, I'd even loved her. But Vivienne regurgitated her pain over Adam's death in spiteful accusations.

"I hate you," Owen said in a calm, neutral voice, but his eyes were full of emotion. Anger. Hurt. Distrust.

My heart dropped like a two-pound sinker. "Well, that's okay." I kissed the top of his head. "I love you enough for both of us." Turning up the Sonos speaker sitting on his nightstand, I waited for soothing piano sounds to fill the room. Tears threatened, but they weren't solely from Owen's disclaimer of love. My entire day had been one fight after another. A group of bankers armed to the teeth with numbers would be much easier to navigate than my real-life dramas.

I placed Owen's room monitor on my nightstand. Found my phone calendar and searched for a free hour in tomorrow's schedule. No way around it. I'd have to delegate the haircut to Mom.

I showered, brushed my teeth, and dressed for bed, with my ex's voice whispering in my ear. Face it, Kate; your priority is your career, not your family.

When the bank loans closed and my property manager Joseph Lafferty returned from his month's leave, my life could revolve around Owen. I closed my eyes and let the tranquility of Bach filtering through the speaker lull me to sleep.

---

"Daddy," Owen's helpless cry blasted through the monitor. I jumped out of bed and flew up the back stairs.

Owen cobra-wrapped his arms around my neck. "Daddy couldn't find me." His breath was uneven, and his pajamas were damp with perspiration.

"It was a dream, sweetheart. Only a bad dream." I cradled him in my arms and rocked. The clean scent of his shampoo mixed with the medicinal odor of calamine. I kissed his head and his neck and assessed his keening on a scale of one to ten, ten being all-out terror. This episode fell somewhere in the middle, a four or maybe a five. Middle ground, the therapist had stressed, was progress.

Each snubbing sniffle nicked my heart as if blood oozed from the chambers and blocked me from taking a full breath. I couldn't stop Owen's nightmares, no matter how many trauma books I read or how many sessions with the therapist I sat through trying to understand my baby's hurt and confusion.

I rocked him until his body went slack and heavy. I tucked him in bed, and this time I remained by his side until he fell into deep, untroubled slumber.

By three o'clock, I'd given up on sleep, pushed past the nightmare worries and Calvin's harebrained schemes, and turned my attention to a problem I had a reasonable chance of solving. Who was this friend of Granddad's?

There had to be a link between the Cabral family and the drug ring. Otherwise, Nathan Parsi would have no reason to ask about the connection to our family. But surely Juan Cabral, now close to eighty, wasn't involved. Evidence that the relationship between Granddad and his friend was fishing and not drugs should be easy enough to prove. For the second time that evening, I rolled out of bed.

Pale moonlight lit my granddad's office. I stood in the doorway and breathed in my childhood's faint, sweet scent. Danish Davidoff pipe tobacco permeated the rugs and furniture. Memories of Granddad's booming laugh filled my head and trickled into my heart.

If my grandfather had spent time fishing in Mexico, his credit card statements would be the most logical place to find proof. I should be able to find charges from a lodge, boat rentals, and even fishing equipment. I remembered seeing Granddad's personal bills in a Bombay chest in the far corner of the room.

I began with the oldest invoices, skimmed through the pages, and found nothing about fishing charges. That didn't make sense unless Granddad charged the trips as a company expense. Maybe he'd entertained potential clients, and the records were on business statements at the office. I'd make a point to check in the morning.

I opened a small silver box on the top shelf and found Granddad's passports bound together with a blue rubber band. His most recent passport was in the safe, but these four had expired. These books listed trips to France, Belgium, London, one trip to Japan, and ten years ago, he'd spent a month in Australia.

My heart pinged at the memory. Granddad had invited me to join him, but Adam and I were trying to get pregnant. I'd recently accepted a promotion at Morgan Stanley—two logical reasons not to head off across the world for a four-week vacation. Now, I was sorry I hadn't made an effort.

The passports covered forty years, but there was nothing to indicate Granddad had traveled to Mexico or Central and South America. I opened the safe and checked his most recent passport. Not one stamp. Mom had been confident Granddad visited Cabral in Mexico, and they'd traveled Central and South America to fish.

I picked up my cell and searched my contacts for Ben Snider, the best private investigator I knew. Ben and I had worked together on several too-good-to-be-true investment vehicles for Morgan Stanley. If anyone could uncover the truth about Juan Cabral and Granddad, it was Ben.

## CHAPTER SIX

*Katelyn*

I'D TURNED THE mystery of Juan Cabral and Granddad over to Ben, and I focused on another problem disrupting my life—what my cousin Calvin was mixed up in. I stared at his thirty-three-year-old three-bedroom, two-bath ranch that he'd inherited when my aunt died.

Instead of sitting in my car, I should overlook Cal's three unreturned phone calls, knock on his front door, and invite myself in for coffee. But I couldn't ignore the warning whirling in my head that Cal's wife, Beth, might not know about her husband's new dive boat. Spill that secret and I could forget about getting his opinion on the island trespassers. I was confident I'd see it on his face if Calvin were involved in something shady.

I stifled a yawn and wished I'd taken the time to make a thermos of coffee before leaving Spartina. I hiked my skirt to my thighs and tried to find a comfortable position, an impossible feat in the front seat of the Hummer, a vehicle I hated. It was mostly because I owned one of Adam's impulse buys. I couldn't help believing if Adam had agreed to take the Hummer in our divorce settlement, he wouldn't have purchased the Porsche, and he'd be alive today. Instead, the judge awarded him our five-year-old Toyota Highlander, which Adam traded for a new Porsche a week after our final hearing.

A light drizzle fogged the windows. I found an old tissue and wiped the windshield. The kitchen light came on, and Calvin stood at the window sipping from a cup. Five minutes later, the garage door rolled up. I gave myself a pep talk, buttoned my jacket against the morning drizzle, and walked up the drive.

Cal, briefcase in hand, walked to his black Escalade. Seeing him was like looking at photos of Granddad and my father as young men: straight blond hair, brown eyes, a broad-shouldered swimmer's build. I walked into the garage.

Cal's eyes turned into razor slits. "What are you doing here?"

I closed the distance between us. "You'd know if you'd take my calls."

"I'm busy."

"With the dive boat?"

"What're you talking about?" His befuddled look didn't play. The corner of his left lid twitched. Calvin was a third-rate bluffer.

I reminded myself that conversations with Calvin could swing into screaming matches quickly. "I know you own the Grady diving around Spartina's dock."

"Old man might've left you the estate, but the river's public land." His mouth turned into an I-have-the-upper-hand smirk. "My buddies can dive anywhere they please, and there's nothing you can do about it."

"It's not the diving I'm worried about. It's what they're harvesting. Is it legal?" I turned my back to a green trashcan shoved into a corner of the garage that smelled of day-old shrimp and crossed my arms to appear in control. "What's in the black bag, Cal?"

"You get bored running the trust?" Cal's tone swung into a testy challenge; if he was hedging, he had a reason.

"Don't throw this back on me." I heard recrimination in my tone and pulled back. Accusations never worked. Begging had possibilities. "Cal, please. I'm all Owen has. And I can't work the hours and do the travel anymore. Our debt restructuring will cash you out and give me breathing room until all the properties sell. I need five more weeks. Keep whatever scheme you're working on under wraps for five weeks."

"Hey, the bank was your idea. So that's your problem."

"Untangling a trust isn't magic. I can't just wave a wand. If you're looking to cash out, this is the fastest way. And it'll more than make up for whatever piddling deal you've got going."

Cal opened his mouth. A lie wouldn't be far behind.

I held my hand up to stave off whatever comeback he had planned. "I know something's going on. And the Feds have the island under surveillance."

His head snapped back. His jaw worked back and forth like a cow chewing cud. "Old man also left you the island. Your land—your worry."

The back of my neck pinched, like someone tweezing the fine hairs one by one. I'd missed something somewhere, a word, a gesture. Understanding Cal's motives had slipped by me unnoticed. The estrangement between us left too many issues unresolved—Barry Island, Spartina, and me managing the trust. I started with the biggest problem. "The company's not as successful as you think."

He laughed a deep, guttural sound that wasn't from amusement. An outburst of pent-up, poisonous emotion.

I rushed on. "It's true. All eleven commercial office buildings were in disrepair when I took over after Granddad's stroke. Rental rates were abysmal. It's taken me three years to renovate and overhaul our Atlanta portfolio. Occupancy rates are now steady, but the company has debt. If you want to cash out, this bank restructuring is your best option."

Cal pointed a finger into my chest. "I want my money."

I swiped his hand away. "Then don't jeopardize our future." I had trouble keeping my emotions in check, causing me to talk too fast. But I had his attention. "And something weird is going on with the South Carolina warehouses. The appraisals are coming in wacky." I stepped back. This garage smelled like a sewer. "I don't need any more problems."

He honored my heartfelt plea with a bitter laugh, a harsh, ugly sound. "As far as I'm concerned, taking care of snags is why you're paid the big bucks."

Same old Calvin. "That's it. That's all you can say?"

"I have my own problems. The business, bank problems, and island are yours." His voice had an acrimonious edge that would fool most, but not me. Cal wasn't angry; he was worried.

"What's wrong?"

He opened the car door.

I grabbed his arm. "Talk to me." He tried shrugging me away, but I gripped his briefcase and drew him closer. "Tell me what's going on."

He wrenched his briefcase free and flung it into the backseat. "A couple of friends borrowed my boat. They didn't take anything that was yours." He put his hands on my shoulders and squeezed. "Katie, forget about it. They won't be back." He climbed into the driver's seat.

I grabbed the window, held the door open, and took a second to weigh my words and filter out the sore points. Granddad's booming voice played in my head. Katie-girl, family always comes first. Do what it takes to protect what's ours. "I can't help if you don't tell me what's happening."

"Stay out of my business."

One of Cal's shady deals was about to ruin my world.

The world I'd worked the past three years to rebuild. Memories of working sixteen-hour days, my marriage disintegrating, and weeks of travel without seeing my son rushed forward.

"Now you want me to stay out of your business?" The roar in my ears matched my voice. "Now that nineteen-year-old Amanda's not calling six times a day threatening to tell her daddy you're the father of her baby?"

Calvin's jaw clamped tight. "That happened two years ago. And it wasn't too long ago you were begging me to vouch for you in court."

I sagged against the car as exhaustion erased my fury.

"I've done everything you've asked. Signed all your papers." His tone turned softer and more heartfelt. "Let it go."

"Let what go?" I pushed off the car and looked into his eyes. Tried once again to reason with him. "The only reason the bank is willing to refinance millions of dollars of debt is because of our company's reputation. Our name. Bad press will be a deal breaker."

He stared straight ahead and white-knuckled the steering wheel.

"I'm going to let the Feds use Spartina as their base," I said. "In exchange, I'm going to require they keep our name out of the papers when they make their bust."

"Bust?"

"Yes, bust. A drug ring is using Barry Island." I stared into Cal's brown eyes and asked the unthinkable. "Your dive boat doesn't have anything to do with drugs, does it?" An unbelievable and incomprehensible thought shook loose in my head. I took a step back. "Cal, do you know Juan Cabral?"

Resolve hardened his face. "Never heard of him." He started his engine. "Move."

I backed up another step.

He slammed his car door and backed out of the garage.

I stood in his driveway, watched Cal's taillights disappear, and, along with them, all hope that he hadn't found another get-rich scheme.

## CHAPTER SEVEN

*Nathan*

NATHAN GRIPPED THE dashboard of Erica Sanchez's SUV. A Savannah morning traffic jam was not the time to ride shotgun with Erica at the wheel. Tires skidded, a horn blasted, and the crawling traffic reached a standstill. A white BMW idled at the crosswalk, waiting for a jogger to amble past. Smoke and the smell of burned rubber drifted from the car's back tires.

Nathan rolled down the car window, stuck his head through, and tried to see around the horse and carriage parked half a block away. Negotiating the morning traffic in downtown Savannah, a grid of historical squares combining homes, businesses, and public parks, entailed hair-pulling patience that would tax the biblical Job.

Erica banged her fist on the steering wheel. Her patience appeared more on the nonexistent level.

Nathan's phone signaled a text message. "Katelyn Landers just arrived at her mother's residence." He popped the glove box and set a magnetic cop light in place.

Erica whipped around the stalled lane and rode two tires on the sidewalk for six blocks. At Whitaker Street, she stopped in front of a sprawling Savannah gray brick surrounded by a porch large enough to host a three-hundred-person reception. Roslyn Barry's house was like a picture in one of those southern designer magazines, except for Kate Landers's Hummer sitting cockeyed in the driveway and the two police cruisers parked on the corner.

Nathan and Erica jumped from the car and hurried through the open double mahogany doors into a wide foyer.

"Kate." Erica turned left and sprinted down a hall like she'd done it a million times.

Nathan paused at the first room on the right and peeked into a formal living area overlooking the park across the street. Everything appeared neat and orderly. Roslyn Barry's dining room could sub for a period movie set with antique mahogany furniture, silver candelabras, and a sparkling crystal chandelier. An adjacent door led to a pristine white and chrome kitchen larger than his apartment. The back door stood open, and Erica and a uniformed policeman conversed on the back porch.

Nathan kept moving. At the end of the hall, French doors stood partially opened. He paused on the threshold and fixed his gaze on the papers, books, and broken glass littering the floor of a home office. A wide-eyed Kate Landers, vertical but just barely, leaned against a burl-inlaid desk holding an armload of books.

Nathan removed gloves and shoe covers from his jacket pocket.

Kate dropped an armload of books on the credenza. "Why are you here? I haven't notified the police." The wrinkles on her forehead reminded him of a friend's Chinese shar-pei."

He slipped a pair of blue booties over his shoes and entered the room. "A beat officer noticed the front door ajar at eight o'clock." Nathan perused the room as if responding to a city burglary call was an everyday occurrence. "When it was still open at eight forty, he called it in." He pulled on a pair of white latex gloves.

"Police officer?" Kate shoved a desk chair aside, stepped to the window, and searched the street. She wore a straight black skirt, a white blouse, and plain black shoes. Nothing showy, but somehow, she made the nondescript outfit look like a million bucks.

Katelyn Landers was close to perfect—maybe a little too perfect. It upset his synchronicity vibes.

Nathan studied the room's alarm equipment. "Was the security system engaged?"

"Yes. Mom's been at Spartina for the past two weeks."

With a glass-break device above the window and an infrared motion detector positioned over the door, the intruder had been talented enough to circumvent the system, or they knew the code.

Kate glanced at the grandfather clock in the corner. "Mom's late. She and Owen were supposed to meet me here thirty minutes ago." The worry in her voice held none of her take-charge tones from the night before. "She can't face this without warning," she added.

"Roslyn knows." Erica walked into the room, gloves in hand and shoes covered. She gave a curt, almost grudging nod in Kate's direction, then snapped on her gloves and squatted. She lifted the edge of a drawer and thumbed the file underneath.

Kate closed the distance in two steps and slammed the file shut. "Prying into private business usually requires a warrant."

Erica popped up and edged back, rubbing her neck.

Hands on hips, Kate stalked forward. "And how do you know my mother knows about the break-in?"

Erica's jaw clenched, she glanced through the window as if carefully shifting through her words to find the right ones. Nathan figured diplomacy to be a new experience for his second-in-command. "When we got word of a possible burglary, we sent a man to Spartina."

"What?"

Erica looked on edge, but Kate was livid. Kate held the upper hand in this relationship.

"Marshal Parsi," Kate said, "Last evening, you failed to mention that Agent Sanchez was part of your team." Kate's sarcastic undertone mirrored a parent chastising a child for lying. "Would either of you care to explain why a federal marshal and a DEA superstar responded to a possible robbery?"

"Is this a robbery?" Nathan asked. "Because if it is, the thief didn't know squat about antiques." He pointed to the credenza. "Those jade animal carvings look genuine and old." He nodded to a chest in the corner. "Egg under that glass dome looks like one of those Faberge pieces. Oil paintings and tapestries are on every wall, all untouched."

Kate turned a slow circle, scanning the room as if considering what wasn't missing. "This is my mother's home, but as far as I can tell, everything of value is still here." She considered Nathan. "But why are you here?" Her tone held no anger, just bewildered confusion.

He knelt beside a black briefcase leaning against the wall. "This yours?"

Kate's questioning gaze moved to the case. "No."

"Your mother's?"

"I have no idea."

Nathan raised an eyebrow. His finger hovered over the briefcase lock, waiting for Kate's nod of approval. After a few beats, she graced him with a sullen chin lift. He popped the lid and pulled an address book from the side pocket. Standing, he thumbed through the pages.

Kate reached for the book. "Whose is it?"

He raised the book out of her reach. "Prints. You're not wearing gloves."

Erica stepped closer and peered over Nathan's shoulder.

He flipped to the front of the book and glanced at Kate.

"When was the last time you saw Calvin Thompson?"

"This morning."

Pleased that she'd told the truth, he asked, "Here?"

"No. His house." Same clipped tone, but she didn't waffle. She crossed an arm over her body and held the other in a protective gesture—a normal reaction if the realization of the break-in had begun to sink in.

Calvin Thompson was under surveillance, so Kate hadn't owned up to anything he didn't already know. But did she visit her cousin to warn him or get answers? And how did Thompson's briefcase end up in his aunt's library?

Nathan was still a few hours away from approval to tap Kate's phone—citizens with nothing more serious than a speeding ticket on their record took longer. His request to tap Thompson's cell had taken less than an hour, but it hadn't helped with the early morning conversation between the cousins. No novice regarding privacy protection, Calvin rarely used his personal cell. When he did, it was to order pizza or call his secretary at the port. And he never failed to remove the battery after a call.

Nathan lifted the briefcase and placed it on the desk. "Did your cousin have this case when you saw him earlier?"

"I think so."

"You think." Erica stepped around Nathan and stood in front of Kate. "You don't know? You don't remember? What?"

"He had a black briefcase. I can't say for sure it was this one." Kate reached to shut the lid.

Nathan nudged Erica aside and caught Kate's hand in midair. "Prints."

Nathan needed to provide Kate with a reason to cooperate if he wanted answers. "After Calvin left you this morning, he went to a diner on Abercorn. His car's still in the parking lot, but your cousin's nowhere around."

Kate's shar-pei wrinkles made another appearance. "How do you know my cousin's not with his car?"

"Because I had a man tailing him. Your cousin managed to lose him." Thompson giving his man the slip, then ransacking his aunt's house, and leaving so abruptly he forgot his briefcase was interesting. Not enough for an arrest, but if he added the dive boat ownership, it was enough to bring Thompson in for questioning. And Kate was their best chance of finding him.

Erica's phone buzzed, and she turned her back to take the call. She barked an okay and pocketed her cell. "The forensic team's five minutes out. Wayne's in route with Roslyn and Owen."

"Who's Wayne?" Kate asked.

"One of my guys," Erica said.

"Why's he bringing Mom and Owen here?"

Nathan's gaze swept the room. "We need your mother to look over the house. Make a list of any missing items." He wasn't exactly lying. Calvin had searched for something, he needed to know what.

"Owen can't come here," Kate said. "Uniformed police still terrify him."

"I assumed you'd want him with you." Surprise echoed in Erica's voice.

"You assumed?" Kate leaped forward like she was spring-loaded. "You have no right to assume anything about my son."

Erica's skin flushed close to the shade of her Kool-Aid red hair.

"You can take your son home." Nathan softened his voice. "But we'll need your mother to stay."

"I'm not leaving my mother to deal with this alone. I'll have my assistant pick up Owen." She turned to Nathan. "I can't find the landline and left my cell in my car."

"This room needs to be processed." Nathan placed his hand on the small of Kate's back and gently led her into the hall. "It's best if you don't add more prints." He handed her his cell.

She explained the situation to her assistant and asked her to pick up Owen. Her fingers constantly moved during the phone conversation, pushing her hair from her face, straightening her shirt collar, and smoothing her forehead. She was shaken, an understandable response to finding her mother's home burglarized, but Nathan's gut said there was more to her unease.

Kate handed him his cell, then glanced out a picture window in the living room. A beige four-door sedan pulled to the curb, and she rushed for the front door.

Nathan followed but lagged on the porch, taking the opportunity to assess the family dynamics. He needed to get a handle on Kate, a woman who might be the best con artist this side of Tijuana.

She wrapped Roslyn in a hug. "Mom, I'm so sorry. The intruder trashed your library, but it doesn't appear that anything important is missing. As far as I can tell, the rest of the house is untouched."

Roslyn visibly relaxed into her daughter's side. "Thank God."

Kate pulled her son close and tousled his hair. "Everything's fine." No way Kate's fake smile fooled her mother, and based on her son's face, he wasn't buying it either.

Nathan had firsthand experience with family felons and their secrets. And while Nathan had been innocent and unaware of his brother's terrorist leanings, it'd be a stretch to assume Kate shared the same blindness to her family's connection to a cartel drug lord. Katelyn Landers's record was so clean she practically squeaked. Records that spotless didn't generally play true in a family of crooks.

"Erica's inside," Kate said to her mother.

"Erica?" Roslyn didn't bother to hide her surprise.

"Seems she and the marshal work together. Something he forgot to mention last night." She was too far away for Nathan to read the nuances in her expressions. "They want you to look over the house and note anything missing."

"Why are the marshal and Erica here and not the local police?"

Kate turned and sized up Nathan. "Now, that's an excellent question."

Owen tugged Kate's arm. "Mom, can I go see Aunt—"

"Not now, sweetheart. She's working. Maybe later." The smile on Kate's lips was so tight her nostrils flared. "Mom, why don't you go on in? I'll meet you inside once Jennifer arrives to pick up Owen."

Roslyn walked up the drive and gave a terse nod to Nathan before walking through the door.

Kate leaned against the sedan. "A friend of mine's going to take you for ice cream. She's bringing her niece."

"A girl?" Owen groaned.

Nathan smiled. He remembered when girls still had cooties.

A light blue Toyota Corolla swung into the driveway. The woman Kate called Jennifer rolled down the window and spoke to her boss. She introduced Owen to a towheaded little girl, and he climbed into the back seat. The Corolla caught a break in the traffic and pulled onto Whitaker Street. A black sedan sped forward and all but kissed Jennifer's back bumper.

Kate fast-tracked for the street.

Nathan flew off the steps and caught Kate's arm before she made it to the curb. "It's ours."

"Why's he following Jennifer?"

Nathan grappled for a reasonable excuse that wouldn't cause more conflict.

Wayne stepped forward. "Erica's orders."

Nathan blew out a breath. Great. The two words guaranteed to start a war. "Erica said not to let the boy out of our sight," Wayne said.

Kate held her hand in the stop-talking position. "Erica Sanchez makes no decisions affecting my son. Ever. Understand?" She stomped up the drive.

Nathan gave her a mental salute. He was certain she was on her way to give the same order to Erica, a conversation he wasn't about to miss.

# CHAPTER EIGHT

*Nathan*

NATHAN MANAGED TO catch up with Kate halfway down the main hall. They turned a corner and came face-to-face with the man he knew to be Cedar Haynes. Nathan extended his hand. "Mr. Haynes."

Family attorneys were never a cop's best friend. Due diligence had shown this one as an engaging man currently romantically involved with Roslyn. So far, Nathan had found him to have no connection to their case. Decked out in a light blue seersucker suit, the guy looked stuck in a 1950s' time warp, a Jimmy Stewart lookalike sporting a cleft chin.

"Roslyn called me," Cedar said as if sensing Nathan's curiosity.

Kate buzzed Cedar's cheek. "Have you seen Erica Sanchez?"

"In the kitchen talking to your mother. I need a word with you."

She continued down the hall. "If it's about the warehouse appraisals, I'm working on it."

Cedar took a quick step, caught her hand, and held her in place. "No, it's something else."

"I'm sorry, Uncle Cedar, but it has to wait." She barged into the kitchen and homed in on Erica. "Why do you have one of your men following my assistant?"

Erica barely spared Kate a glance. "Because she has Owen."

Erica sat with Roslyn at an oval breakfast table in front of a window with a garden view. A uniformed officer stood on the back porch talking on his cell.

Cedar made himself comfortable in the chair adjacent to Roslyn.

"What difference does it make if Jennifer has Owen?"

"A drug ring's taken over your island. And a drug boat's diving around your dock." Her tone indicated her answer hit below the no-brainer level, and just in case Kate missed the jab, she adopted one of her pithy facial expressions that Nathan had come to dislike.

Kate's eyes widened, but her mouth remained firmly closed.

"And your cousin is now on the run," Erica added for no good reason.

Nathan leaned against the counter and studied the group. Roslyn's face was flushed but otherwise unengaged in the conversation. She busied herself folding a napkin in a small, then smaller square. Spotting someone's anxiety didn't explain the why, just that something had caused discomfort. Roslyn's demeanor had changed since entering the house.

Cedar sat stoic, a beacon of support—an attorney's normal and expected response.

"Someone broke into your mother's house." Erica used her pen to point down the hall. "Trashed the library but left the valuables." She leaned forward. "Calvin's briefcase was mysteriously left in the library, and he just happens to own that boat diving under your dock. I don't want Owen unprotected until we break this case."

Kate stiffened and seemed to grow by three inches. Nathan stepped forward, pulled out a chair, and sat. He slid Erica's notepad closer, the top page appeared blank except for a couple of lines scribbled at the top. "A jade box is missing? That's it?"

Kate tilted her head, leaned over her mother, and tried to view Erica's notes. "Nothing else is missing?" Her voice was filled with doubt and relief in equal measure.

Roslyn's shoulders ratcheted up around her ears. A spot on the table suddenly held her interest, and she vigorously rubbed her napkin over the blot.

The officer on the porch called out, and Nathan turned to look in his direction—a group of three walked through the back gate lugging black oversized leather cases. A woman and two men made up the crew. One of the men carried three clear cellophane bags that Nathan recognized as coveralls.

Erica pushed away from the table. "I'll get forensics started." She opened the door and led the group through the kitchen and down the hall.

Nathan turned to Roslyn. "What was in the missing box?"

She kept her eyes downcast and didn't answer for a few seconds. "A few old letters, some pictures."

"Nothing more?" he pressed.

"A pendant and matching ring." She didn't meet Nathan's eye.

Cedar leaned over, murmured close to Roslyn's ear, and then patted her leg. It was an intimate gesture.

By the squint in Kate's eye, Nathan assumed she didn't know her mother and the family's lawyer were more than old friends. As close as Roslyn and Kate appeared, it seemed odd the mother would keep that information from her only child.

"Who knows your alarm code?" Nathan removed a pad from his pocket and began writing.

"My housekeeper, Lila." Roslyn's voice was now softer than Nathan remembered. "Kate. Cedar."

Kate's gaze remained on the attorney. The man she referred to as uncle, but who wasn't.

Keeping his voice even but eyes trained on Roslyn, Nathan asked, "Did Calvin Thompson have the security code?"

"Not Calvin." Roslyn met his gaze and held. Based on the flickering glint in her eyes, she took umbrage with the question. "Cal's wife, Beth, has the code because she collects my mail when I travel." She amplified her frown and exhaled an irritated sigh. "I can assure you that my nephew and his wife have nothing to do with this break-in." From her tone, suggesting otherwise would border on harassment.

She was protective of her family. He got that. It'd be the same reaction if she were hiding something. "When was the last time Calvin visited you here?"

"Six months ago," Roslyn spoke decidedly. Odd she'd remember so quickly.

"And his wife?"

"They came together. Stopped in for drinks on the way to the club."

"Any reason your nephew might want something in the box?"

Nathan glanced at Kate. She looked in her mother's direction, but her eyes were elsewhere. Likely stewing over the possible reasons her cousin broke into her mother's home. Desperate for money didn't ring true. Family knew what was valuable, what wasn't, and, at a minimum, he would've snatched the Russian egg.

"I realize you found Calvin's briefcase in the library," Kate said. "But as Mom indicated, he can access the house with a key and knows the security code. If he visited this morning, technically, it isn't a burglary. And since we didn't report a robbery..." She glanced in the direction of the officer on the porch. "Makes the house being full of police rather strange." She gave the impression if the forensic team wasn't already on site, she would throw them all out. She'd kept her voice even, but the undercurrent was powerful enough to throw Nathan off his chair.

He mentally reshuffled his points. "I believe there's a connection to this break-in, the dive boat, and the drug ring on your island." Kate opened her mouth to speak, and he charged on. "We believe you and your family could be in danger if you stay here."

Roslyn's breath hitched.

"That's an asinine assumption." Kate's tone didn't hold the conviction of her words. "You can't know this break-in is connected to the drug ring. And how do you figure Cal's boat's connected?"

"It's the recovery skiff," Nathan said.

"The what?"

"Thompson owns the recovery boat that picks up the drugs." He waited and let his statement settle. Interested to see if the news surprised the group.

Roslyn's visceral signs leaned more to shock— shortened breath, staring into space.

Cedar casually leaned against the back of his chair. But his tight jaw and nervous finger tap on the table were giveaways Nathan's words brought discomfort.

"I thought the drug ring was using the island." Kate reached for a napkin, wiping away a light sheen of perspiration above her lip.

"The island's used to prepare the contraband for distribution," Nathan said. "But the initial drop is in front of your dock." He gave Kate time to decipher his words, then said, "You have a mile of riverfront with minimum boat traffic. A perfect drop point for a crabber or a shrimper."

"Shrimpers and crabbers fish offshore, not the river," Kate said.

"They cruise by your channel, coming and going from their home docks."

Kate's face didn't change, but several emotions zipped through her eyes. Primarily fear. Fear was a difficult state to pin down. A diverse emotion that appeared different on everyone. Nevertheless, it was recognizable when a person witnessed fear on a face.

Was Kate's fear generated from the DEA suspecting her cousin dealt drugs or that the authorities suspected her family and she'd be guilty by association? "I've secured a safe house. We can move your family this afternoon."

"What?" Kate's tone had all the notes of genuine shock. "Are you crazy?" Her words bounced around the ceiling.

Cedar cleared his throat and leaned forward. "Exactly why are you proposing a protective detail?"

No surprise the attorney would try and intercede. Actually, more surprising he hadn't spoken up sooner.

Nathan closed his notebook. "A drug cartel's camped out on Ms. Landers's land." He stored his pen in his jacket pocket. "Her cousin's already missing."

"No, he's not," Kate said. "Just because he didn't show up for work and you can't locate him doesn't mean he's missing." She spoke as if speed alone would make her words true.

Cedar settled back in his chair, seemingly satisfied for Kate to lead the argument. An attorney who didn't rise to a debate garnered a second look.

"And"—Nathan looked at Roslyn—"if your mother's right and the person who trashed her library isn't Calvin Thompson, then the perp is quite adept at surpassing security alarms. Staying here isn't smart. Until we know what's going on, I'd want them somewhere safe and protected if it were my family."

Kate pushed away from the table and stood. "I don't

need you to protect my family. I can afford to hire guards."

"You don't want to depend on rent-a-cops to protect your loved ones from a drug cartel," Nathan said.

Roslyn reached for Cedar's hand. He patted it absently.

Kate's expression turned flat as if her interior light had extinguished. "But wouldn't the drugs get wet if a shrimper dropped them in the water?"

Nathan had wondered how long before the idea would register. "Canister's sealed." Nathan tapped his wrist. "Like a dive watch."

Roslyn's face turned pasty, but Cedar Haynes's only tell was a slight flicker of his eyelids.

Kate's breathing grew shorter and choppier. Not hyperventilating, but getting close. "Calvin wouldn't put my family in jeopardy," Kate said.

"Your cousin knew you didn't live at Spartina; the island was all but deserted." Nathan let his statement hang.

Erica walked into the kitchen and stopped just inside the door.

Kate glanced at Cedar. He cleared his throat. "It seems a long shot to think a break-in at Roslyn's home in downtown Savannah has anything to do with whatever's happening on Barry Island."

"I don't agree, Counselor."

Kate gave a decisive head shake. "I don't believe Cal's involved with a drug ring."

"Your cousin's in it up to his eyeballs," Erica said. "And until we make the bust, you should steer clear of Spartina, the island, and now even this house."

Roslyn's gaze oscillated from Erica to Nathan and landed on the attorney, her expression demanding him to intercede.

He sat forward, eyes calculating, but offered no further comment.

Nathan couldn't get a read on the guy. Haynes was a well-respected pro bono defense attorney for the poor, privy to drug rings, gangs, and low-life crooks. He'd understand the risks, and Nathan had hoped the attorney would lend vocal support for a safe house.

"If Calvin's the perpetrator," Kate said, "why haven't you closed your case?"

A reasonable point Nathan didn't care to address at the moment.

Kate cocked her head. "Because you don't know for sure." She nodded knowingly. "That's it, isn't it? Calvin owns the boat, but that isn't sufficient to make an arrest stick. You're fishing, hoping I'll say something that will incriminate my cousin." She shot Nathan a look that would melt tungsten steel. "Well, let me assure you that will not happen. If a drug ring's using my island, I expect you to arrest the trespassers. Now. Today."

"We're not interested in the minions working your island," Erica said. "And the how and when we arrest perpetrators isn't your concern."

Nathan sighed. Subtle and Erica—never will the two meet.

Nathan jumped in. "Barry Island is your land, and you have a right to expect law enforcement to protect it." He gave everyone a moment and allowed tempers to cool. "We can identify the crew working the island, but Erica's right, we want their boss."

Cedar leaned forward. "In other words, you have no idea who's running the show."

Time to ease off. Nathan needed Kate's cooperation. "We don't see your cousin as the kingpin. But he knows who is. I want that name and am willing to make a deal."

Kate shook her head. "Doesn't make sense. Why would Cal sell drugs?"

"Money," Nathan said. "And a lot of it."

"Not enough to risk ruining his life." Kate shook her head. "Cal just wouldn't take that kind of chance."

"Yes," Nathan said. "He would, and I'll explain why."

She leaned against the counter and crossed her arms.

"In every illicit organization," Nathan said, "the primary goal is to acquire money. They also need money to operate. South Carolina has zero regulation on the money transfer businesses."

Kate lifted a shoulder. "What's that have to do with Calvin?"

"Savannah's within spitting distance of Charleston," he said. "Muling cash across state lines is child's play. Last year, eight billion dollars was wire transferred out of South Carolina, most of those funds laundered and untraceable."

Understanding flitted across Kate's face. "You're following the cartel's money trail. That could take months, possibly years."

"We don't think so," Nathan said. "We're very close to taking this group down."

"And your answer is to stick my family somewhere out of the way until you figure out how to close your case?" Kate's eyes flashed with stubbornness closing in on rage. "You're basing this on a few isolated instances. You assume the cartel's a threat to my mother, son, and me, but you have no proof."

"After today, are you willing to take chances?" Nathan's voice matched hers in volume, a notch above professional. He squashed his temper. "Our team's lost two agents trying to shut this ring down. I refuse to risk civilian lives."

"I'm not willing to shove my family off to a hidden location indefinitely while you meander over my estate and stumble onto a way to close your case. We are law-abiding. My family isn't going anywhere."

Nathan folded his hands on the table, breathed, and

retrieved his bearings. "You think the Cabral family cares that your family is respected and law abiding? They know Calvin isn't. You and your family are expendable. You don't want to get in their way."

Kate kneaded her forehead. "It makes more sense to send Mom and Owen on vacation." She looked at her mother. "I have some business dealings that can't be put off. But I can join you in a few days."

Roslyn's gaze slid past Kate, over Nathan, landing on Cedar Haynes. "I agree we shouldn't stay here. We can travel for a few weeks with Owen out of school."

"The safe house would be more secure." Nathan wasn't one to give in, but by the look on Kate's face, arguing would net him nothing. "But it's your choice. If you don't leave with your mother and son, the safest place for you is with my team at Spartina." He wanted eyes on Kate. All he needed was for Calvin to contact her once to get his location, and he'd close this case.

"I need to think." She walked out the back door.

It was midmorning, and the summer sun was already ablaze. Through the window, Nathan leaned to one side to gain a clear view of Kate.

A group of red finches descended on a feeder and ignored her as she walked past. She continued through the back gate and disappeared.

No matter. Five minutes ago, Nathan received a text message. The approval to tap Kate's phone had come through. He clicked the icon on his cell and hit record.

# CHAPTER NINE

*Katelyn*

I HEADED STRAIGHT FOR my Hummer and grabbed one of the rack phones out of the glove compartment. Ben, my private investigator, had been right. In his opinion, if federal marshals asked about family connections to a drug cartel, a tap on my phone was practically assured. Ben was ex-FBI and had an extra dose of skepticism. But since I had no idea what he would find while exploring Granddad's past, I'd agreed to the precaution. With Parsi's suspicion of Calvin, and Erica, the DEA superstar, showing up, my twenty-minute side trip to Walmart seemed a smart choice.

I checked my personal cell for Ben's number, keyed it into the new rack phone, and scanned the front yard. Too many cops milling around to have a private conversation. I headed for the back garden.

I faked interest in the neighbor's bird feeder, made sure no police were within hearing distance and placed my call. Ben answered on the second ring. I gave him the Cliffs Notes version of my morning and instructed him to put everything else on hold until he found Calvin. Two officers walked out of the house and through the back gate. I said a hasty goodbye, palmed my throwaway cell, and ran a hand over my racing heart.

Buying and using an untraceable phone wasn't the

same as buying an untraceable gun. I had the right to privacy; I wasn't doing anything illegal. So why did my heartbeat mirror a three-mile run on a treadmill? I skirted an outdoor bench and opened the kitchen's back door.

Erica leaned against the wall of ovens observing Parsi questioning Mom at the kitchen table.

"You said the missing box held old letters, a few pieces of jewelry, and photographs," he said. "Photographs of whom?"

I'd wondered the same thing. I eased the door closed and stood by the sink.

"Old photos of friends and family." Mom looked tired. Her eyes were rimmed in red, and her mouth pinched into a grimace.

"Can you be more specific?"

Parsi's commanding tone shot heat up my spine. This interview needed to come to an end. "Since my mother isn't planning on filing a complaint, I think we'll call it a day."

"I still have a few more questions." The marshal's voice clearly stated, "Butt out."

Cedar caught my eye and gave a quick shake of his head. I couldn't imagine why Cedar thought Mom should be subjected to Parsi's grilling. Something must've happened while I was in the garden.

Parsi scanned his notes. "The ring and pendant, why were they kept separate from your other jewelry?"

"I've always stored them in that box. The box locked, and I stored it in the bottom drawer of a locked desk." Mom adopted her hoity-toity voice. If the marshal took offense, he hid it well.

"Can you describe the jewelry," Nathan said. "Real stones or semi-precious?"

"Blue diamonds." Mom was matter of fact, but I must

have made a sound because she drew a navel-deep breath and pressed her lips together.

Until now, it'd been a mystery why Calvin would break in and take only a box. If the ring and pendant were blue diamonds—mystery solved.

"How big were the stones?"

Mom twisted her great-grandmother's ruby ring around her finger. "The pendant was around four karats, I guess. The ring smaller."

Nathan tapped his pen on the table a couple of times. "How much smaller?" His expression reminded me of one used by a husband grilling a cheating wife.

Mom shrugged. "Three karats, maybe."

"Jesus." My surprise echoed before I could stop myself. I tried to reconcile priceless jewels kept in a box in the library. The idea failed. Mom had a bank safety deposit box and a home safe.

A phone chirped, Nathan removed his cell from his pocket, scanned the screen, and slid it back. "What's your estimate on the value of the jewelry?"

"I've no idea." Mom rose, walked to the refrigerator, and removed a bottle of water. She swallowed a deep gulp without offering any refreshments to the group. Very un-Roslyn.

"How about the insurance value?" Nathan asked.

"They weren't insured." She took her seat and chugged the rest of her water like God's nectar.

I swallowed dry spit. Seven karats of blue diamonds—not insured and not in the safe.

Erica and Nathan turned to me in unison, as if it were up to me to explain my mother's illogical decision to leave valuables uninsured.

I searched and quickly discarded a handful of plausible explanations. I shrugged. I didn't think it was the answer they were hoping for.

"The robbers were probably startled." Mom jumped at

the sound of Cedar's voice. No easy feat reining in forty-year courtroom vocals. "They probably just grabbed the box and ran. Had no idea what was inside." Until now, Cedar had been uncharacteristically quiet. If that was all he had in his arsenal, he should stay that way.

Nathan checked his notes. "What about the letters? Something special about them?"

Mom dismissed the question with a "tsk." "They were letters from years ago. Mementos of my youth. I'm not sure why I kept them."

"What kind of box was it?" Erica's voice as terse and commanding as her boss's.

Mom graced her with the same look she'd given us when at seventeen we'd tried sneaking in at one o'clock in the morning using an empty gas tank as our cover.

Kudos to Erica. She didn't flinch.

Mom's coloring was pale, and her perfectly applied blush had turned into two rosy circles. She turned to Nathan. "The box was Chinese."

"Expensive?" Nathan nodded as if he knew. "It was a gift."

Mom had an extensive list of art and jewelry in the safe and appraisals of each piece. The knot in my stomach grew to a blazing baseball. Tension, like sound waves, swam in the air.

"All your other jewelry is insured?"

Mom met Parsi's gaze. "This is very tiring. I might remind you that what items I chose to insure is my business, not the business of the police or whatever you are." Now there was the woman I knew. And she was right; this was none of Parsi or Erica's business. Unless Mom filed a bogus insurance claim, whether the blue diamonds were insured was a nonissue for the police.

I slid into a chair beside Mom and took her hands in mine. "Is there anything you need from the house before we head out?"

She took back her hand. "No. I'm ready to leave."

"Sirs." A uniformed officer stepped into the kitchen. "Can I have a word?"

Erica and Nathan joined him in the hallway. Their mumbling filtered through the door, and I overheard the officer say the forensic team was packing up.

My phone vibrated, and I glanced at the message. "My assistant is on her way back with Owen. There's nothing more to do here."

"I packed last night, thinking we'd stay here for a while." Mom's words trailed off, and she massaged her temples.

"Spartina's only an hour away. I'll drive over and pick up your suitcase." I rose and searched the cabinets for aspirin.

"I planned to visit your Uncle Stanley's beach house in Florida for a few weeks. I'll go early and take Owen. You can meet us there."

I opened the container, shook two pills into her hand, and gave her another water bottle from the refrigerator.

"Thanks." She dutifully downed the pills.

"Going to your brother's only works if he agrees to accompany you," Cedar said. "I don't want you and the boy alone in a beach house in the middle of nowhere."

How had Cedar slipped into our familial picture without me realizing? "I agree. I'd feel better if Uncle Stanley was at the house." I knew my irritation at Cedar was misplaced and refused to give it weight.

"Good grief." Mom blew her exasperation. "Stanley has a full staff. We'll be fine." She closed her eyes for a moment as if collecting herself. Roslyn disliked weak women and resented being treated as one. She patted my hand. "I'll ask Stanley to join us if it makes you both feel better."

After Adam died, Owen and I spent a week with Mom at my uncle's beach house. Owen fell in love with Uncle

Stanley's three horses and mentioned returning more than once. I was sure he'd go with Mom without a fuss, especially if we scheduled a few riding lessons. "Clear it with Uncle Stanley, and I'll book NetJets to fly out of Savannah tonight."

"No need." Cedar checked the calendar on his phone. "I don't have to be in court until early afternoon. I'd rather drive them down."

Mom gripped my hand. "Promise me you'll come to Florida tomorrow."

Her urgency surprised me. "I have appointments in Charleston tomorrow, but I should be able to get away in a few days."

"You could work from Florida."

"With Joseph on vacation, work is piling up." If I was lucky and worked eighteen-hour days, waded through the pile of anemic appraisals, and wrapped up the loose ends on the debt restructuring deal, I could leave in two days. "Wednesday is the best I can do."

"I mean it, Kate. I want us all together until this is over." Mom's eyes stayed wary a moment longer, then she nodded a quick little snap. "Wednesday, then."

Clinging wasn't Mom's style, but she certainly melded into Cedar's side. I wasn't sure what was happening between them, but they seemed devoted. Mom didn't buy into the new share-all social-media mind-set, but not telling me of her new relationship with Cedar surprised me.

I had a quick mental debate and considered pushing everything on my calendar and going with them. But I was slammed. No time for impromptu trips to Florida or break-ins or drug deals or federal marshals or a backstabbing DEA agent. "Great. Then it's settled."

My sense of ease lasted for my sixty-second walk to the library to announce our decision.

"No." Erica slammed her hand on Mom's desk.

Plumes of fingerprint dust billowed in the air. "Everything is not settled, and I don't care what Nathan said. The safe house is manned and sitting ready. It's the safest option."

"Mom and Owen are going to my Uncle Stanley's." I looked around for Parsi, but he seemed to have disappeared. Other than an annoyance, Erica's temper tantrum hardly mattered.

"Nope. No deal." Erica began tapping keys on her phone. "You'll have to trust my way is best."

Everything inside me went quiet and still. Our past simmered in the ten feet between us. "Trust you? Never. Again." My hands curled at my sides. "And let's be clear, I don't need your permission. Telling you is simply a courtesy. Mom and Owen are leaving within the hour. Deal with it."

Erica snarled a low animalistic growl. That was new.

I swept past her and headed for the door.

"It's your family," she said. "If you don't care about Owen's safety—"

I whipped a one-eighty. Suddenly, I wanted to wrap my fingers around her throat and squeeze.

"Wait." Parsi stood in the doorway.

Desire to inflict pain must've been plastered across my face because he pushed past me and gave Erica a look that even I understood to be an ultimatum.

"Okay." Erica scanned the room as if she could see our past plastered on the green and burgundy striped wallpaper. "At least let our agents drive Roslyn and Owen down."

"Uncle Cedar's already volunteered."

"We'll need the address." Parsi palmed his phone.

When I didn't respond, he added. "Come on, Kate." His chide sent a stubborn streak up my spine.

He lowered his chin. "We don't know the who, what, or why of this break-in. Erica's right, don't take a chance on the safety of your family. I'll assign a security detail."

Erica slipped her phone onto the clip on her belt. "Calvin's gone under. Until we know the full picture, you'd be smart to agree to protection."

"I've got a two-man detail ready to roll," Nathan said. "They'll follow your family down to Florida. But there's a good chance Calvin will contact you, and you should be ready to talk him into surrendering."

The only thing they cared about or wanted from me was Calvin. Everything else was a smoke screen.

"You hear from Cal, and I better be your next call." Erica stopped riffling through the papers in Cal's briefcase long enough to point her finger in my direction. "If I have to chase him, he'll be sorry."

My desire to jump in and protect my cousin's legal rights had waned, but I rolled my eyes, lifted my chin, and pretended her threat hadn't sent my heart thumping. I couldn't wrap my head around Calvin's new home having bars. I had to find a way to save Cal and keep our family name out of the news. Calvin wasn't the only one walking a thin line. Without this debt restructuring, we'd all be facing financial ruin.

How did my life get so screwed so fast?

Owen flew into the room. "Aunt Erica!"

To her credit, Erica managed to catch him in midair and remain upright. She wrapped her arms around him, shut her eyes, and held tight.

The air in the room evaporated. I couldn't take a breath.

Owen's chatter registered in muted tones as if he were miles away. For his sake, I forced on a mask of humored indulgence and pretended each happy giggle didn't squeeze the vice crushing my heart.

# CHAPTER TEN

*Katelyn*

CEDAR POKED HIS head around the library door, spotted Owen with his legs wrapped around Erica's waist, and frowned. Suddenly, I felt much warmer toward Mom's new significant other.

"Kate, may I see you for a moment?" He waved for me to join him.

I was more than willing to take my leave from the happy reunion, so I followed him into the hall.

He grabbed my elbow and led me to the far window overlooking the garden. A cardinal bathed in the top bowl of a three-tiered fountain. I made a mental note to check the bird feeders before we left.

"Roslyn filled me in on your late-night visit." He kept his voice low, his eyes glued on Parsi standing in the foyer, talking to several uniformed officers.

Cedar leaned close to my ear. "Marshal Parsi's request to use Spartina as a base isn't anything to take lightly."

My focus of concern at the moment was shipping Owen off to safety. "Agent Parsi bunking in the guesthouse is a moot point since I've already agreed."

Displeasure slipped over Cedar's body like an overcoat.

I wanted to ask why he thought it a big deal, but Owen's giggles from the library caught my attention and drowned my curiosity. I wanted Mom and Owen on the road to Florida. Now.

"When I agreed to give the marshal access to Spartina, I planned for Owen and me to stay here with Mom." I tuned out the giggles. "I have an appointment tomorrow with the Charleston appraiser. If his appraisals on the South Carolina warehouses are close to accurate, our company financials are on the brink of ruin. And I can't rationalize the monthly rental incomes derived from the units if they're all in the physical conditions stated on the five appraisals I have on my desk. Joseph might be able to explain, but he hasn't returned my messages."

A streak of confusion crossed Cedar's face. Or maybe it was surprise or concern. It vanished so quickly I was left wondering if it was my imagination.

Nathan walked past and paused at the library door. "Let's roll."

Erica and Owen walked out of the library hand in hand. I smiled. I refused to concede that her relationship with my son bothered me.

Owen saw me and bounced forward. "Mom, can I ride home with Aunt Erica?"

I kept my smile unbroken. "Erica's working, honey." Astounding how normal a voice sounded through clenched teeth. "Why don't you find Nana? I think she's in the kitchen."

Cedar, bless him, took Owen by the hand and headed down the hall.

I followed Nathan and Erica to the door. "I'll meet you at the guest house in an hour. Keys are under the mat. Make yourself at home." I locked the door behind them, checked the living room French doors, and met the group in the kitchen.

Mom reset the alarm, and we left by the back entrance. We agreed to meet at Spartina, and Cedar and Mom headed for his Mercedes parked on the side street. Owen and I found the birdseed in the garage, filled both garden feeders, and headed out.

Navigating midafternoon traffic, while not as harrowing as the five o'clock gridlock, still crept. We crawled behind a trolley car for three blocks. We turned on Abercorn Street, and I couldn't delay discussing the Florida trip any longer.

Owen hadn't spent a night away from me in the two months since Adam's death. He'd accepted an overnight invitation from his Aunt Vivienne before we moved to Georgia, but a midnight phone call ended that visit. He wasn't clingy and barely tolerated my efforts to cuddle or hug. He just seemed to want me nearby. The therapist assured me his reaction was typical after losing a parent. I didn't mind; his need for me filled a place in my heart that had been empty for a long time.

I tapped his shoulder, interrupted his video game, and motioned for him to remove his earbuds. "Nana's going to visit Uncle Stanley for a few days."

"Can we go?" His face was a canvas of excitement. "We could go horseback riding on the beach again."

I feigned consideration. "She's leaving tonight, but I have to finish some boring work. You could go down with Nana, and I'll join you in a couple of days." I kept my gaze straight ahead but could sense him pulling back.

He stuck his earbuds in his ears and went back to his game. I gave him time to process the idea. We turned into Spartina's drive, and I tapped him on the shoulder, waited for him to remove his earbuds. "You'll need to grab your riding boots out of the mud room if you want to go with Nana."

He opened the door but didn't leave his seat. "If I go, will you call me every day?"

"Of course."

"Promise you won't forget?"

I leaned over the seat and took his face in my hands. "Forget you? Never. And you can text me or call if you get lonely. I promise to be there in two days."

"Okay." He beamed a full-out grin. "We can ride on the beach when you come. But I call Champ."

"Champ?" Champ was a sixteen-hand, eight-year-old gelding, full of himself and not the easiest of rides even for an experienced equestrian. "Maybe you could start with Beauty or Roman, leave Champ for next year after you've had a few lessons." I wasn't worried. My uncle, the proverbial mother hen, would never allow Owen to ride Champ alone.

Mom and Cedar rolled out the luggage Mom had stacked by the back door and offered a pit stop at McDonald's. Owen barely stayed in place long enough for a hug goodbye.

My family would be tucked safely away at my uncle's beach house in less than three hours. Owen would be happier than he'd been since we'd moved from Orlando. Whatever Cal was into, staying on decent terms with Parsi was the smart move if I wanted to keep my cousin out of jail and our family name out of the papers. A friendly tour of the estate would be a good place to begin our understanding.

I walked the short path to the garage, climbed a flight of stairs, and rapped on the door before entering the guest apartment.

Erica leaned against the counter in the galley kitchen, smiling, joking, and completely at ease with Nathan and a group of five men who could pass for an elite team of Navy SEALs.

A laptop sat on the bar separating the common area from the kitchen. One of the men tapped on the keyboard. He made a comment I didn't catch and pointed to the screen. Conversation ceased, and all eyes turned to the computer.

"Hey, Kate." Nathan threaded his way through his men. He didn't introduce them, and none looked up.

"Let's get started." He walked past me and opened the door.

Curious, I stepped behind the guy manning the computer. It took a second for me to recognize the screenshot was an overhead of Spartina and Barry Island. It looked similar to the Google Earth shot I accessed last week to show Owen.

"Kate." Nathan gestured through the open doorframe.

I took one last look and joined Nathan. "From here, it'll be quicker to head north, past the stables, and circle back around," I said.

He nodded, and we descended the stairs and walked down the gravel path leading to the barn.

The sun had set, but I'd purposely left the flashlight behind. The quicker the tour ended, the sooner I'd be on the road to Charleston. "Our barn's twelve stalls with two tack rooms. Another small two-bedroom apartment is overhead. Our caretaker's cottage is north of the stables, and we have a gardener's cottage farther down."

Nathan's sudden laugh had a condescending ring, but it was dark, and I couldn't see his face.

"Something funny?" I asked.

"You ever notice the wealthy say 'we' and 'our' when they mean 'I' and 'my'? You have stables, a caretaker, and a gardener's cottage. There is no 'we.'" He used air-quotes for "we."

"All the buildings and cottages are empty, except one home for my caretaker." I added air-quotes with "my." I turned right and began walking down the road to the main house.

He pointed to the open pasture. "Mind if we take a fast trip through the stables?"

"Barn's empty. I don't have horses or livestock."

"I'd still like a quick pass."

We walked side by side through the pasture in silence. Nathan used the flashlight on his cell, and I opened the paddock gate. Our arms bumped, and I jumped as if something had bitten me. He grabbed my elbow, and I could swear I heard him grin. I made a point of readjusting my blouse, and he dropped his hand to his side.

"Has your caretaker been with your family for a long time?"

At that moment, all the normal sounds of the night—frogs croaking, crickets chirping—hushed into complete stillness. Every pore in my body tingled.

"James has been with Spartina for twenty-six years." I pushed the stable doors wide enough to slip through, ran my hand over the wall, and located the switch. We shielded our eyes against the blaze of light. "His granddaughter's getting married somewhere up north. I think he said Maine." There were twelve stalls, six on each side, each one spotless. The normal fresh smell of alfalfa hay had been replaced with the heavy, oppressive odor of Pine-Sol.

"You don't have a housekeeper?" Nathan stopped and turned a full circle. "Spartina is a big place to handle on your own." He peered inside the first open stall.

I continued down the middle walkway. "Not if we live on the first floor and close the top two. Then I'll only need a weekly cleaning crew."

Nathan increased his pace and caught up. He poked his head into the tack room. Scanned the empty walls. "If you wanted a smaller place, why'd you move here?"

How could I put my longing to give Owen the happy and peaceful life I'd known as a child into words? "Memories. My best childhood memories are here."

He looked around the barn and nodded his understanding. "Do you have a security camera in this building?"

"No." We reached the last stall and backtracked to the open door.

"I'd appreciate a tour of your SITU."

I searched for a possible acronym. Blanked. "SITU?"

"Situation room." The realization he'd stumped me crossed his face. "Your security monitoring station."

I pointed in the direction of the main house. "Equipment's in a closet off the kitchen."

"Can I see it?"

It was late, and I needed to get on the road. "I'd rather do it tomorrow. I'll be back from Charleston by midafternoon."

"I'd appreciate seeing it before you leave." He ran a hand through his cropped hair. "My men are in a new environment." He stood three feet away, but his silky-smooth voice seemed whispering close. A pleasing, familiar sound somehow connected to my childhood. An impossibility since Nathan couldn't be a day over thirty-five.

Cedar's suggestion not to trust Nathan's motives hovered like a cloud over my head. I wanted to say no, insist he wait until my return. But standing in the empty barn, an invisible magnetism got in the way.

He cleared his throat and waited for my reply. "We chase bad guys." He seemed to think my delayed reaction was due to skepticism.

But skeptical wasn't what I was feeling. I mumbled my agreement and started for the house faster than safety allowed in the dark. I took care to stay in the lead and used the reprieve to remind myself that no matter how attractive and strangely familiar Nathan seemed, no matter how long it had been since a man had shared my life, the marshal was off limits. Completely. Absolutely. Off-limits.

I punched the code into the alarm control panel and escorted him through the kitchen and into an area the size of a walk-in closet. A wall of black-and-white screens showcased the view from fifteen perimeter cameras.

Nathan slipped past me. His body heat set off flutters low in my belly. Nathan didn't seem to notice. Focusing on each monitor, he tapped the last screen with his fingernail. "Your system's outdated by fifteen years, maybe more."

I stepped into the hall and headed for the kitchen. "A new system isn't high on my priority list."

"Newer monitors have split screens with remote monitoring capabilities." He followed me down the hall. "Are the bottom two screens positioned to pick up river traffic?"

"Yes."

"I'd like to have access to the SITU." The radio on his hip crackled with a muffled voice.

I shook my head. "There's no outside access to the monitors."

His raised brow and lowered chin reminded me of Roslyn when she'd caught me telling a fib. "This room was originally a standalone structure and can still be shut off from the main house," he said. Walking to the door leading into the main residence, he examined the threshold, then the casing. Pointed to the security sensor. "Shouldn't be a problem to bypass."

Now it was my turn to raise a brow. His familiarity with my home's floor plan struck me as more than a little disconcerting. Years ago, a renovation project incorporated the standalone kitchen with the main house, and my eccentric great-grandmother opted to leave the outside door in place. The fact that Nathan knew this historical tidbit gave me pause. I weighed my options. "I'll override the kitchen door and give your team access to the monitors, and that will also give you access to the larger kitchen."

He waved away my offer. "We'll take our meals at the guest house."

I scooted past him and unlatched the bolt that kept the outside door snug against the wall. "The garage apartment only has a two-burner stove and a small refrigerator. I'll be in and out for the next few days; it's no bother if your team uses the kitchen." If his men were camped out on my estate, an open area where they could come and go would allow me to chat freely, ask questions, and get updates on the case.

Nathan pointed his thumb toward the river. "Mind if we take a look at the dock?"

I started to refuse, then reminded myself of his promise that the sooner he closed his case, the sooner my life would return to normal. I motioned toward the French doors. "After you."

He radioed someone that we were exiting the house. I assumed to prevent us from being shot during our stroll to the river.

I fast-walked through the rose garden, past the pond, and headed straight for the dock. He kept up with ease.

"So how's this work?" I asked. "Your guys hang around the house and watch the island?"

"About sums it up."

"With binoculars?"

I was a step in front, but I heard his snicker. "Something like that."

"How many are on your team?"

"Counting Erica and me, twelve. Four are monitoring other areas."

"I don't see anyone hanging around."

"They wouldn't be very good at their job if you spotted them." He nodded in the direction of a live oak tree. "One's behind that tree."

"You saw him?"

He slanted his eyes in my direction and grinned. "I wouldn't be very good at my job if I hadn't."

I snapped my fingers. "Omar Sharif." My voice mirrored my disbelief as pleased with myself as if I'd just solved the last clue in Sunday's crossword puzzle. "I thought you looked familiar. At first, I wondered if we'd previously met. But that's not it. You remind me of Omar Sharif."

He rested an elbow on the railing, his smile full and wide. "Dr. Zhivago?" His mouth twitched. He shook his head.

I searched his face and compared the resemblance. "It's your eyes. Same body type. I think he might have been Egyptian. Are your ancestors Middle Eastern?"

His easy demeanor faded. He straightened. "Yes."

Once I spotted the resemblance, I couldn't stop seeing it, hanging in the corner of my mind like a hologram sliding in, then out. We leaned against the dock's railing and listened to the welcome surprise of a pair of dolphins blowing softly as they passed.

I sighed. "I've missed river nights."

It was my first time seeing him out of full marshal mode. His face was softer, his eyes darker—almost dangerous. The type of dangerous that told a woman she wouldn't have a chance against his charms. I ignored the fluttering bird in my chest. If I bought that ticket, there'd be no chance of a refund.

He planted both elbows and placed his back against the rail. "When we find Calvin, I'd like your help."

My imaginary interlude ended with a thud. "What kind of help?"

"Convince him to assist us."

A rush of heat swept my body. I pushed off the banister. "I need to get going."

I turned to walk up the ramp. He latched onto my arm.

"Protecting Calvin won't bode well for you." His tone a long way from silky.

I yanked my arm free and left him standing on the ramp.

# CHAPTER ELEVEN

*Katelyn*

NATHAN'S WARNING UNNERVED me, and I couldn't get the image of Calvin wearing orange cotton scrubs and plastic shower shoes out of my head. If Cal was part of this drug ring and I could convince him to cooperate, it might mean keeping him out of prison. But first, I needed a clearer understanding of Granddad's relationship with Juan Cabral.

How did Calvin get involved in the first place? Did Granddad and his fishing buddy meet stateside? Did Granddad take Calvin along on one of his fishing trips?

Mom thought my grandfather had visited Juan in Mexico, but his passport didn't agree. Mom said his passport should also have had several Central or South American stamps. But I found no entry stamps for those countries either. It'd bug me the rest of the night if I didn't check again.

I decided to wait and leave for Charleston the following morning, then went into my grandfather's office. I thumbed through his passports, but there were no Central or South America stamps, just like I remembered. I spent a few minutes plundering his file drawers looking for fishing resorts and found several European destinations and two in Australia. Something clicked, and I backtracked to a file labeled, Tacos, R.

An anagram?

Anagrams were a favorite pastime of Granddad's. I'd spent too many lazy Sunday afternoons working out his word puzzles to let this one stump me. He'd called it code breaking, like spies during the cold war—exciting stuff for a ten-year-old.

The Tacos, R. file was a four-part folder, complete with a map of a remote village on the water and directions to a building. An envelope stapled to the back flap held expired passports for Cecil Lucifer Cummings.

Based on exit and entry stamps, Mr. Cummings had taken a two-week trip to Costa Rica the summer I turned twelve. He'd also stopped over for a brief one-day visit to Uruguay. After which, he'd been a busy fellow with multiple trips to Central and South America. Cecil Lucifer Cummings was an unfamiliar name, but the photo was someone I knew well. It was a picture of my dead grandfather.

---

I juggled my large to-go cup of coffee, drove twenty minutes of back roads, and merged with the northbound traffic. I-95 at five in the morning was the Daytona 500 for semis. Charleston was two hours away. An unfamiliar ping sounded from my purse. I shuffled through my stash of new phones and said hello to Ben.

"Looking at the big picture, what's your foremost concern?" he asked.

"You've already hit a dead end?" When Ben reached an impasse, he returned to his source and tossed around theories until something clicked. Then he disappeared down an investigating rabbit hole to hunt. I'd played his "what-if" game dozens of times while investigating new investment opportunities for my customers at Morgan Stanley.

"My first priority is to find Calvin and keep him out of jail."

"How much do you know about your grandfather's business?"

His bumpy segue caught me off guard. I took a moment to recalibrate my thoughts. "Based on tax returns and audited financials, commercial leases are the sum of his business."

"Dig deep. Look beneath the obvious, and tell me what your gut says?"

He was on to something. "What've you found?"

He sighed. "Nothing I can piece together yet."

I was accustomed to Ben's annoying habit of doling out his findings like morsels of chocolate, allowing his audience time to savor his extraordinary detective prowess.

"Seventy-year-old companies have skeletons," he said.

I glanced at my purse resting in the passenger seat of my Hummer. I suspected Granddad's hidden bag of bones was the passports in the side pocket. "Okay, I've got another name for you." I felt the linchpin. The no-turning-back tipping point that couldn't be smoothed over, tucked under, or hidden away once the name left my lips. I inhaled a deep breath. "Cecil Lucifer Cummings."

"Cecil Lucifer Cummings," Ben repeated each syllable as if carefully making a note.

A dull pain settled inside my chest.

"Okay, I'll see what pops. My assistant sent three preliminary reports to the email address I gave you this morning."

Instructions to access Ben's off-the-grid account were on a slip of paper inside my wallet. I'd always believed Ben worked alone, tooling around town in his bright yellow Corvette. I sipped my coffee and pondered the idea he had a staff.

"You know how to spot a tail?" he asked.

I spewed liquid over the steering wheel. "What?"

"Your estate's crawling with Feds. Good chance they have a warrant that includes your landlines and cell phone, maybe even satellite coverage."

A warrant seemed pretty remote, one that included satellite surveillance definitely far-fetched. "Warrants require a judge. What reason could the marshal give to get a warrant on me?"

"Oh, I don't know. Maybe you're the land baron who owns an island occupied by a drug ring?"

Sarcasm was Ben's strongest rhetorical device. I glanced at the sea of headlights in my rearview mirror and rested my hand above a newly acquired stutter beat in my chest. "I'm checking out two warehouse properties this morning and have a lunch meeting with an appraiser. Fine with me if the Feds want to tag along."

"All the burners with you?"

"Burners?"

He grumbled a slew of words. The only two I caught were Sherlock and Barney Fife. "Throwaway phones."

"We're talking on one. The other two are in my bag."

"How many have you used?"

"Two. The one we're talking on, and I sent you three texts with one of the others." It didn't seem the time to chastise him for not answering.

"Where were you when you sent the texts?" he asked.

"Walmart parking lot and Spartina."

"Did you remove the battery after the Spartina usage?"

"No. I waited for you to respond."

His exasperated sigh crackled over the connection. "You can't use that phone again."

"Why?"

"Feds have that phone tapped."

Already weary of his suspicious nature, I clarified. "You're the only one who knows the number."

"Not if they have satellite."

I stewed on that for a minute. "How would they know I used the burner and not one of my neighbors?"

"If they have you under surveillance, they'd assume it was you using a burner."

I flashed on the fake passport, the dive boat, and Calvin's reaction to Juan Cabral's name. "I'll get rid of it."

"Keep it unless you need to disappear, better to appear stupid. Let's recap," he said. "Burners are for emergency calls, not for chitchat. If I don't return your call, there's a reason. We're not in high school, don't keep calling." His voice reeked condescension. "A compromised phone on your person means the Feds know your location. Same goes with your personal cell."

Any irritation from Ben's patronizing dissipated like ice water drenching a burning candle. "I'll remove all the batteries." I had nothing to hide, but the thought that someone might keep track of my movements seemed creepy.

"Removing batteries is a giveaway if they're monitoring your cells. You reach the point you need to lose a tail, and you're on foot, duck into a crowded store. Stash the phone under some merchandise and head out the back. If you're in a vehicle, speed up and stay out of sight long enough to toss the cell, ideally, in the back of a pickup heading in the opposite direction. Using a burner makes you suspicious. You get rid of a burner, and suspicion ups by ten. Make sure it's worth the effort."

I refrained from reminding Ben he was the reason I had throwaways in the first place. "I'll be more careful."

"Give them something to listen to. Use your personal cell for any call that doesn't matter."

I should label my phones to keep them straight. Use. Don't Use.

"I tracked your cousin's car to a diner," Ben said. "A cook taking a smoke break saw Calvin jump into an SUV. The cook recognized the SUV driver and fifty bucks gave up the name—goes by Snively."

"Bubba Snively. He's on the friend list I gave you."

"Yeah. Tracked him down. According to a talkative neighbor, Snively arrived home a little before eight with a man matching Cal's description. Besides a pizza delivery at 4:28, no one has entered or left the unit. I'll keep you posted." A click and dead air were the only clues Ben had hung up.

I was still stewing on Cal's bait and switch act when my cell chirped with a new text message from the Charleston appraiser.

—Emergency came up. Need to reschedule our lunch meeting.—

"Great." Looked like an early day in the office after all. I took the next exit and turned south for Savannah. My phone beeped, and I answered Cedar's call.

"Your Mom and Owen are settled at your uncle's."

"I appreciate you driving them down."

"No problem. I need a few minutes with you today."

A shudder of dread ran up my spine. An attorney asking for a meeting was rarely good news. "What's up?"

"Nothing we should discuss over the phone."

"Did one of the Atlanta buyers back out?" Three of our Atlanta properties were under contract. With the squirrelly warehouse appraisals, I couldn't afford more problems.

"My concern isn't real estate." Cedar's unwillingness to discuss business over the phone merged with Ben's warning that my phone was tapped. My dread thickened and spread like a morning fog. I quit pumping for details and agreed to a late afternoon meeting.

Twenty minutes later, I took the Savannah exit, spotted a Waffle House, and stopped for a much-needed coffee.

I settled into a booth and inhaled the smell of sizzling bacon. A perky waitress slapped down an empty mug and filled it to the brim.

I rattled off my standard Waffle House order, and she turned and faced the cook manning an eight-foot grill. "Mark order scrambled, hold the grits." I loved short-order-cook jargon.

I opened my laptop and used one of the burner phones as a hotspot to access Ben's secret email account. His report on Calvin held a few surprises—primarily that Ben could compile a detailed accounting of Cal's stock portfolio and bank accounts in as little as six hours. I noted increasing the security levels on all personal and company bank accounts.

According to Ben's report, Cal was broke. Not technically broke because he owned half the family trust, but his cash had dwindled to less than ten thousand. The hairs on my neck prickled. That couldn't be right. Cal and I received monthly stipends from the trust. He had a good job. His wife was a nurse practitioner.

Calvin's wealth, like mine, was mostly paper. But unlike me, he had no historical Savannah real estate to devour his savings. After what I had paid him for the family estate in Savannah, he should be flush with cash. I reviewed his stock statements. Over the past two years, Cal had liquidated every position and withdrew the funds in increments of nine thousand or less. But drawing out the money in small amounts would hardly matter, as the banks would notice the pattern and report the conduct as suspicious. I understood the DEA's interest in Cal.

My eggs and toast arrived, but my appetite had evaporated. Questions looped in my head like a song ditty that wouldn't shut up. Where had Cal stashed close to a million dollars in cash? Was Beth aware of the missing funds in her husband's accounts? I paid my bill and climbed back in the Hummer.

A chirp sounded, and I rummaged through my purse for the culprit.

"Where are you?" Ben asked. "In a Waffle House parking lot."

"Alone?"

"Yes. Why? What's happened?"

"I lost your cousin. He came out of Snively's building wearing shades and a black hoodie. He ducked into the parking garage."

Under no circumstances did Calvin ducking around in a black hoodie and sunglasses sound promising.

"I waited fifteen minutes, then followed him inside the garage." Ben's rhythm took on an automated tempo, similar to the male version of Siri, and grated my already stressed-out cranky mood.

"Snively's SUV is still in the assigned slot," he said. "No subject."

Subject being Ben's code for Calvin. "Is there more than one exit?"

"Not for a car." There was a pause. "The bottom floor has a half-wall." Ben's voice dropped off, and I heard the steady pounding of footsteps. "He must've jumped over the first-floor wall. Had another car close by."

"If Calvin had a car somewhere else, why'd he enter the garage?"

"Throw off anyone following." Ben sucked in some air. "Snatch something out of Snively's car—doesn't matter why. He's gone."

My adrenaline spiked at warp speed. Damn. "Did you run his credit cards?"

"No charges or cash withdrawals." Ben slipped back into his annoying computer cadence.

I racked my memory for any place Calvin might hide. "He must think the authorities are watching him."

"That'd be my guess. I'm going to have a chat with Snively."

Recognizing the familiar sound of dead air, I disconnected.

If Cal decided to bolt, would he leave Beth behind? No, I didn't think so. I dialed their home number. No answer. I called the hospital. The last I knew, she worked in CCU, maybe she worked the early shift. The nursing supervisor said Beth wasn't on the floor. I asked to have her paged and received a pithy lecture on using hospital pages—codes and medical emergencies only. I left my name and number.

I sat in my car with an overwhelming desire to have a sob fest. The phone in my hand vibrated, and Ben's number flashed across the screen. I put myself in emotional lockdown. "Any luck?"

"Yeah, Snively turned out to be a regular fountain of information. Seems your cousin's panting to talk to you."

That was doubtful. "He hasn't called."

"Told Snively you had a tail. Figured your phone's tapped. He's planning to lawyer up, then ask you to soft-pedal your DEA agent friend Erica Sanchez."

I put the throwaway phone on speaker, started the car, and headed for the office. "Did Bubba say why Cal needed a lawyer?"

"No."

"So Cal's with Cedar?"

"Maybe. Snively didn't know where Cal was headed when he left. I'm on my way to check out another friend's apartment. I'll head to the lawyer's place if your cousin isn't there. How soon before you get back to Savannah?"

"Change of plans. I'm fifteen minutes from my office."

"Does your office have a back door?"

"Yes. A direct entrance into my office."

"Unlock that door. If I find Calvin, you and your attorney will be lucky to get an hour before the Feds show up."

This time I disconnected. I called Cedar's house, cell, and private office line and left messages on all three. Then I called his assistant, Shirleen. She informed me her boss would be in court all morning and unavailable until midafternoon. Shirleen assured me she hadn't seen Calvin.

I got caught in Abercorn Street's morning traffic and came to a dead stop with my gas gauge flashing in the danger zone. I crept by a gas station, and I whipped into an empty bay. A blue Toyota and gray Ford Explorer pulled in behind me. An inkling of unease crept down my spine. I was sure both cars had been parked at the Waffle House.

The Toyota parked in front of the store. A man exited the car and went inside.

I stuck my credit card into the gas pump. The gray Explorer pulled in three pumps away, but no one exited the car. My already jittery nerves ratcheted up a couple of notches.

I finished filling my tank and merged with the cars heading downtown at the first break in traffic. Two minutes later, the guy in the blue Toyota whizzed by without a glance. I moved into the right lane and reduced my speed to forty, five miles under the limit. Vehicles paraded past in swift succession.

I glanced in the rearview mirror and located the Explorer behind an older model Cadillac. The windows were tinted on the Explorer, and I couldn't see the driver's face. My palms turned sweaty. I made a quick left on Liberty, then a right on Drayton. By the time I'd worked back to Bull Street, I'd lost sight of him—or her. I'd never been close enough to get a clear view.

I drove down Bull Street and parked in the private

space behind my office. Ben's yellow Corvette was nowhere in sight. I hustled up the metal stairs and unlocked my back door.

The Explorer was likely nothing more than a tourist sightseeing Charleston and Savannah. But to ease my mind, I tipped the blinds and scanned the area in front of our building.

A gray SUV rolled down the street and past our entrance. "Crap!" The vehicle circled the block like a stalking barracuda searching for prey. But it was mid-morning on Chippewa Square. The only options were slow, stop, start, and poke. There were twenty other parks in the historic district, and the same color Explorer with tinted windows hunting a spot in front of my building defied happenstance.

A white van pulled into the street half a block away, and the Explorer snagged the space. If he was my new shadow, from his parked position, he had no clear view of the back staircase.

# CHAPTER TWELVE

*Nathan*

NATHAN STOOD IN Kate Landers's kitchen, refrigerator door open, reviewing his options; bagels, English muffins, a gluten-free rice cracker the color of shoe leather, or a chocolate chip cookie. He snagged the tray of cookies from the middle shelf.

The mudroom door opened, and based on the casual chitchat wafting down the hall, his visit to Beth Thompson's would have to be pushed back an hour. Willie Schroeder entered the kitchen, twirling his black sheriff's hat and laughing at Erica's tales of city life in Atlanta. Willie caught sight of Nathan, paused, and shifted in place.

Erica motioned him forward. "You want a cup of coffee?"

"Sure." He glanced at the tray of cookies on the counter.

Nathan pushed the platter in his direction. "You saved me a phone call."

Transfixed in front of the built-in coffee system, Erica looked as lost as a kindergartner trying to solve eighth-grade algebra.

Nathan pointed at the green button, pushed it, and patted her shoulder. He placed a steaming cup in front of Willie. "How's Kate's surveillance going?"

"Smooth as Tennessee whiskey." Willie pulled out a stool and sat. He plopped four sugar cubes in his cup and stirred. "Pulled in a favor from the Charleston sheriff. His man picked up Kate crossing the South Carolina line at 6:17 this morning. Followed her for forty minutes before she turned around and headed back south. One of my cruisers caught her crossing back into Georgia about three hours ago. She was alone and took the Savannah exit. Figured if we got too close, Kate would spot a Montgomery sheriff cruiser, so I pulled my man off."

Willie peered over the condiment tray, fished a toothpick, and stuck it in his mouth. "She must've changed her mind about going to Charleston."

Nathan mulled that over.

Willie leaned in Nathan's direction. "I don't believe Katie has anything to do with the crew working on the island." He settled back against his chair and sipped his coffee. "Now, Calvin." Willie shook his head. "That one's slicker than snot. But Kate's a sweetheart, and just because a cat's got kittens in the oven, don't make them biscuits."

Nathan looked to Erica for clarification. Straight-faced, she nodded as if Willie had made perfect sense.

Nathan kept his voice neutral. "Kate and Cal have a bond, and we're counting on him making contact."

Willie adopted the face of a man wearing shoes a size too small.

"You hear anything on Thompson?" Nathan asked.

Willie crossed a foot over his knee. "Got a few locals that'd give up their sister for a dime bag. I applied decent pressure. Even rounded up a couple of dependable snitches." He blew and then slurped his coffee; the toothpick remained firmly in his mouth. "Nothing came of it. Nobody's seen or heard from Calvin."

Nothing in Willie's casual demeanor indicated he was

holding back information. "How about the marina," Nathan said. "Anything pop?"

Willie looked over the selection of cookies. "Couple of things. According to my wife's cousin Linda, who works in the sales office, a female brought in the paperwork three months ago to buy a decked-out Grady White with twin Yamaha 250 engines." He chose a double chocolate chip and removed his toothpick before biting off half. "The lady arrived before eight, her paperwork was in the name of Calvin Thompson, but she wasn't his wife. Joe, the owner, whisked the woman into his office. It was an all-cash, hush-hush transaction. He had Linda deposit fifty grand in the company bank account, and she saw him put another stack of bills in the safe. According to state records, Cal paid over a hundred grand for that boat."

Nathan made a note. "You get the woman's name?"

"Joe never said, and the purchase documents were already notarized, so Linda didn't talk to her."

"We can take a ride over," Erica said. "Have a chat."

Willie's foot slid off his knee with a thump. "If I bring a DEA agent to the marina, Linda's liable to be fired. She's already jumpy about telling me part of the cash went into the safe and not to the bank like normal."

"Tell you what," Nathan said. "You swing by and have a friendly chat. If Joe gives up the woman's name, we'll have no reason to follow up."

Willie's mouth firmed so tight his bottom lip disappeared.

Nathan thumbed back a couple of pages in his notes. "Owner's Joe Coffey, right? Lives on St. Simons Island?"

Willie laid his half-eaten cookie on the counter and gave a tight head bob.

"Boat paperwork appears legit?" Erica asked.

"Signed and sealed," Willie said. "Everything is in

Thompson's name, not his wife's. Calvin never showed his face." He stood, then picked up his hat. "You planning to use my men for any more surveillance details?" His voice no longer held a friendly vibe.

"We'll take it from here," Nathan said.

Willie fiddled with the brim of his hat. "For what it's worth, I don't think Kate's involved with this drug bunch." He faced Erica as if he expected her to chime in.

Nathan let the silence lie.

"I'll get back to you on Joe." Willie set his hat on his head and tipped the brim. "I'd appreciate being kept in the loop."

"We'll be in touch." Nathan stayed put and let Erica walk Willie out. He liked Willie well enough and thought he was a good man. But cartel money could buy a lot of good men. For now, the sheriff would remain a few feet outside the loop. He opened his laptop and noted two new reports in his inbox, one from the Florida detail, the other was Kate's phone log. He scanned Kate's calls. Consulted his notes and rechecked the dates.

Erica walked back into the room. "God, I'm starving."

"Got the impression Willie thinks we're railroading Kate," he said. "If I didn't know better, I'd say the sheriff's nursing a crush."

"Could be." Erica opened the freezer, removed a package of blueberry bagels, and placed one in the toaster. "In high school, over half the county was in love with Katie. Even I had a girl crush."

"A soft heart might be apt to give away privileged information," Nathan said.

"Locals think of the Barry family as above reproach." Erica brewed fresh coffee and sat across from Nathan. "Especially Kate. But Willie will hold up his end."

The smell of warm blueberries and coffee filled the air. Nathan gave in, rose, and took another bagel from the package. He plated Erica's, placed it on the bar, then popped in another. He rummaged in the refrigerator and found cream cheese and a tomato. "And you? You grew up closer to Kate than the sheriff. You think she's above the fray?"

Erica pinched off a quarter and slowly chewed. "I've seen her at her best and her worst. The princess is stubborn, sometimes even unreasonable, but anyone who believes Katelyn Landers has ties to the cartel is as crazy as a bat."

Nathan spread cream cheese on his bagel, sliced the tomato, and put a thin sliver on top.

Erica's mouth puckered as if she'd just sucked down half a grapefruit. "Tomato on a blueberry bagel? That's just gross."

Nathan took an oversized bite. Chewed. Wiped his mouth. "Kate's not playing straight. I don't have a clear read yet, but something's up."

"She's in full-court press to save Cal's butt." Erica's tendency to justify Kate's actions didn't stand up well for unbiased detective work. "And as usual, Calvin's in over his head," she added.

They chewed their breakfast with only the occasional bump of Erica's knee against the wall breaking the silence. The inability to infiltrate a new man into the cartel's ring was taking a toll on the team's mojo. But Nathan was confident something would break. "Kate's smart enough to be…what'd you call the ring leader?" Nathan said. "The Mack Daddy?"

Erica shook her head. "Kate's too smart to be a cartel Mack Daddy. Besides, she doesn't need the money or have a killer's instinct. Too soft."

"That's the point. Who'd suspect an enchanting southern lady?"

Erica's eyes locked on Nathan's. "Enchanting?"

"World's full of enchanting criminals."

The spark in Erica's eyes flattened out. "Even if I could wrap my head around Kate heading up the Southeast's largest drug ring, no way she'd use Cal. Cal has the social skills of a skunk. Nobody realizes Cal's a screwup better than Kate. And setting up Cal to take the fall on the dive boat doesn't wash for me. Kate kept her job at the bank and managed to oversee her grandfather's business for three years before he died."

Nathan brushed crumbs from his pants. "She traveled to Savannah at least twice a month during those three years."

Erica grunted her dissent. "Running drugs ain't no part-time gig."

Removing a napkin from a shiny copper tray, he wiped a dollop of cream cheese off the bar. "Kate's uptight and overprotective of her family, more so of her kid."

"Guilt's a strong motivator." Erica crossed her fingers. "Owen and Adam were bound tight."

"Why would Kate have guilt over her ex-husband dying?"

"Adam and Owen were on their way to a college ballgame on the day of the accident." Erica sat back in her chair. "It was Kate's weekend with Owen, but Adam blew her off. When he didn't drop Owen off at the appointed hour, she left a message on Adam's voicemail threatening to haul him back to court if he didn't drop Owen at her office within the hour." Erica's voice softened. "Adam had already pushed the judge one too many times."

She rose and carried her plate to the sink. Leaned forward and looked out over the river. "Adam was easygoing, but when Kate pushed, he saw red and turned as mean as a rattler. Police reports said he was traveling nearly ninety when he flipped his car."

"I saw the speed in the crash report but nothing about a voicemail."

"Vivienne told me." Erica opened a cabinet, tore a paper towel from a roll hidden inside, and wiped the water off the sink's counter. "Adam called his sister to complain about Kate on his way back to Orlando. Vivienne blames Kate for her brother's death."

"And you think Kate agrees? Shoulders the blame?"

"We're not exactly on speaking terms." Erica threw the paper towel in the trash. "But knowing Katie, that'd be my bet."

"Are you tight with the sister?"

"I'm Owen's godmother." She glanced away. "Vivienne keeps me in the loop."

Godmother was a surprise, but the explanation gave credence to Kate's underlying aggression toward Erica. "The phone call Kate made in the garden yesterday wasn't made from her cell phone."

It took a second before Erica's eyes flickered. "Kate has a burner."

"So it appears. We're cleared for surveillance on the home phone and personal cell. But unless the family suddenly converts to Islam and Kate begins surfing the Internet for directions on bomb building, it's not likely we're going to get satellite."

"If Kate's using a burner to communicate with Calvin, and we can't get satellite, we have no choice but to put a man on her full-time." Erica made the statement like it was a novel idea.

"No one's left." A sore point Nathan didn't mind thumping. On his first day with the team, Erica successfully argued that assigning a man to Kate was a waste of manpower. Not wishing to upend her authority, he'd conceded. He should've followed his gut.

"Kate must know where Calvin's holed up. He'll need money, food, human contact." The new information worked like Adderall on Erica's brain. Her pupils shrank, her speech turned rapid fire, and her focus drilled on one limited idea. "She'll lead us to him sooner or later. We've got to pull a man from the island detail."

"Everything's gone dark. We take someone off the island detail without eyes inside, we could miss a critical drop." Nathan texted the agent posted outside Beth Thompson's house and asked for an update. Nathan's cell buzzed a reply. "Beth Thompson's next on my list, and she's home. We snag her husband's location, I make him for a prime squeaker."

Erica snorted, her laughing grunt verifying Nathan's description. "Thompson will spill his guts inside thirty minutes."

Nathan walked to the back door and swiped through the photos embedded in Beth's surveillance update. "Thompsons live in a run-down house." He pocketed his phone. "And they both keep a low profile. The wife has to know her husband drained his bank accounts in preparation for this run. Doubt she'll be far behind." Nathan removed his hat from the rack beside the mudroom door. "Smart move to live under the radar."

"Wouldn't give Cal that much credit," Erica said. "Must've been Beth's idea."

"One other interesting item on Kate's phone log. At six thirty Monday morning, she called a private investigator."

Erica shrugged. "Probably something to do with your interview Sunday night."

He held the door open and waited until she walked through. "That thought occurred to me. I reviewed my notes, and nothing stood out except the Cabral connection."

Erica walked to the driver's side, but Nathan grabbed her arm and pointed to the passenger door. He slid into the driver's seat. "Investigator's name's Ben Snider."

"Could have something to do with selling the

company. Rumor is Kate made a few inquiries with hedge fund managers."

"Conducting legitimate business doesn't require a burner." He drove down the drive, wound through trees and pastureland, and waited for the front gates to open. "Innocent citizens don't use throwaway phones to talk to private investigators."

Erica drummed her fingers on her thigh. "I'm betting hiring Snider's related to business. But the burner, now that's all about Calvin."

Nathan thought there were too many unanswered questions to let the Ben Snider angle slide.

"We find Calvin," Erica said. "We need to hit hard and fast. Get the Mack Daddy name before Kate lawyers him up."

They had a file full of evidence against Thompson, and with Erica's DEA future hanging on closing this case, refusing to push for the obvious and pass Calvin off as the ring's leader spoke to her character.

Kate Landers might not fit the picture of a drug lord, but Nathan knew firsthand that things weren't always what they seemed. No matter what evidence the team unearthed, he was convinced Erica would never see Kate as their target. Erica had been assigned to the case because she was from the area and had contacts that would take another agent years to build. But in Nathan's opinion, Erica's past friendship with the Barry family was a hindrance, and he'd stated as much in his morning report.

They turned off I-95 and onto Abercorn. Turning left at Memorial, he took a back road into Thompson's neighborhood. Spotting his surveillance team a half block down, he parked in front of Beth Thompson's driveway. Nathan nodded at a female neighbor pruning her rose. She wore the biggest straw sun hat he'd ever seen.

The Thompsons owned a thirty-year-old, single blockhouse. From the appearance, not much of their expendable cash had gone into home maintenance. A yard, more brown than green, looked to be about a quarter acre in size. A hedge of overgrown azaleas stretched the length of the house and covered half the windows. Two scraggly potted palms flanked the front door, providing the only clue that the house was inhabited.

Erica pushed the doorbell. Thirty seconds later, she rang a second time.

Nathan stepped off the small front porch and looked toward a double window. A vertical blind moved, and then the front door opened. Nathan searched his memory bank for images of Beth Thompson. He had at least twenty photos of her in his file. None matched the woman standing in the doorway.

## CHAPTER THIRTEEN

*Katelyn*

I LET MY OFFICE blinds fall back in place and returned to my desk. Took a few deep breaths and tried tamping down my heart, leaping like jumping beans.

Keep busy until Ben and Cal arrive. I scanned my messages and noted Joseph Lafferty hadn't returned my four messages. Straightening a picture of Owen sitting on my desk, my fingers lingered on his sweet face. I missed that Owen, the little guy with the easy laugh and corny jokes. I squashed a smothering mom desire to call and assure myself he was really okay. Mom said she'd scheduled a morning riding lesson, and Ben and Cal could walk in any minute. So I sent him a quick text instead.

—How was your riding lesson? Are you doing any ring work? Miss you. Love, Mom—

The last phone message on my list was from Beth. She wanted to talk. Now. I dialed her home number, but she didn't answer. I called the hospital, verified she wasn't working, and left my name and number again.

I emptied my briefcase, removed the warehouse files I'd packed for my meeting with the appraiser, and began reviewing each record. I compared the report listing the improvements made to each of the six buildings over the past five years with the rental income reports. I tried in vain to justify the appraiser's anemic values.

An odd mix of emotions not easily explained except as intuition had served me well over the years. After my first flash of insight, I could often go back and trace the trajectory—how this thought or that observation or idea fused together and formed insight that cleared my confusion. At other times, my premonition was more of a hunch, a brilliant jolt that reached beyond conscious reasoning. This morning, the latter was the case. All was not as it seemed in my world.

In each file, the original purchase price of the properties, coupled with subsequent renovations, was antithetical to the appraiser's estimated value. And the amounts were far lower than could be waved away as a sloppy appraising job. None of the photos attached to the appraisals pictured new loading docks or showcased parking lots with state-of-the-art Neptune LED 680420 lighting packages. Millions of dollars of improvements charged to these properties appeared to be bogus. But the rents we charged for the properties were at the top of the scale. Didn't make sense.

I checked the back parking lot, verified mine was the only car taking up space, and walked across the hall to accounting.

Samantha, a tall redhead, ran our accounting department with proficiency and confidence that tilted toward smugness. She stood behind her desk clutching an impressive Brahmin purse I'd seen on sale at Saks for over four hundred dollars.

I stepped just inside her doorway. "I know you're probably headed to lunch, but I need several reports for an afternoon meeting."

She checked her watch. "What do you need?"

"Monthlies for the past three years on the South Carolina properties."

Her color faded, and every freckle on her face flushed. A nervous Samantha didn't sit well. She rested her Brahmin on her desk. "You cut your Charleston trip short?"

"Something came up."

She stared at me as if she expected me to explain further.

I waited.

She ran her hand up and down the handle of her purse. "The year-end summaries I gave you last week won't work?"

"No." My tone left no room for debate. "I want the details listed in the monthlies."

"Okay." She replied with all the caution of someone uncomfortable with the subject at hand. "That is thirty-six reports. I'll have to skip lunch." Samantha appeared quite deft at using guilt to get her way, but then I recalled she had three teenagers.

"Perhaps you could order in."

She gave me a look that might have been annoyance, but she was a hard woman to read.

I smiled. "I appreciate the extra effort. And since you're working overtime, pay for your lunch out of petty cash." I walked back across the hall and shut my office door. I had an itching desire to plunder Joseph's office but decided to put it off until everyone left for the day. I didn't plan to show my hand until I confirmed my newfound suspicion that someone in my employ had dirty hands. Perhaps more than one someone.

The unaccounted for millions dated before Granddad's stroke. On the surface, the idea my grandfather embezzled his own money didn't make sense. But I had a few ideas that Calvin could likely corroborate.

Right after Granddad's stroke, I upgraded our company's computer security, and Joseph and I were the only employees with access to all the files in each department. I entered my password and found and saved the same accounting reports I'd requested Samantha provide. I had no proof Samantha was involved in whatever was happening, but if she made any hurried accounting changes, I'd spot them. I couldn't imagine Joseph pulling off a scheme this size for three years alone. My four unreturned phone calls were beginning to make sense.

I paced my new office. The entire room was shades of brown; heavy masculine furniture, mahogany plantation shutters, Frederick Remington bronzes, and oak floors polished to a soft patina. Even the requisite Old World globe had turned the color of murky swamp water. Ordinarily, the room calmed my nerves and made me feel closer to my grandfather. A man who'd taken his inheritance, increased it threefold and lived an interesting full life. I had aspired to live up to his achievements. Now, I hoped I could find a way to dismantle his empire and stay out of jail.

My private line buzzed, and Cedar's name appeared on the screen. "I need to call you back."

I hung up before he could speak, grabbed a throwaway from my case, and dialed. He answered on the first ring.

"Is Calvin with you?" I asked.

"No, why would he be? Is this a new cell number for you?"

"Cal was on his way to visit you earlier."

"Been in court all morning. Haven't seen Calvin."

If Cal didn't go to Cedar's, he must've gone to his friend's place. So, where was Ben? I checked my call log. I'd spoken to Ben over three hours ago. Three hours was enough time to get Calvin here.

I tuned back into Cedar's voice and caught the end of a story depicting a courtroom debacle. "I'm five minutes from your office," he said. "Can I swing by?"

"Have you eaten lunch? I can order in."

"My afternoon's full, and I only need fifteen minutes," he said.

"Can you clear your afternoon appointments?" I couldn't stop the rush of panic in my voice. "I need your advice."

Silence. More silence. Did I lose the call?

"I'll make some calls." He disconnected. What was it with men and not saying goodbye?

---

Cedar breezed in without knocking, closed the door, then plopped onto my sofa with a sigh. "It was too late to cancel my afternoon appointments." He opened his briefcase. "But I can give you thirty minutes. And we already have a four o'clock on the books."

Out of soft drinks, I took two bottles of water from a bar hidden in the bookshelves. "What I need to discuss will take longer than thirty minutes. And I may need to cancel our four o'clock."

"I have early court in the morning." He checked his phone. "I can rearrange an appointment, cancel a lunch date and give you two hours tomorrow at eleven."

Tomorrow morning seemed a long way off. But it would give me time to snoop after everyone left the office and lay out my exact findings in a spreadsheet. I thought clearer when my numbers were in neat, straight columns.

I handed Cedar his water and sat at the other end of the sofa. "One problem can't be pushed to tomorrow. I have a private investigator looking for Calvin. He got a lead Cal was on his way to your house. That information has turned out to be bogus, but when we find Cal, we have to make a deal with the DEA and keep him out of jail."

Cedar twisted the cap off his water bottle and sipped. "If your investigator locates Calvin, we'll need to hear what he says before deciding to turn him over to the authorities. Might be smarter to keep him tucked away while we work out a deal. But don't count on Cal slipping by with no jail time."

"The Feds want to close their case," I said. "If Cal cooperates, you should be able to negotiate no jail."

"We'll play our hand, but this isn't a dime bag of coke. And don't speculate on Calvin ponying up. The boy's not stupid enough to turn on the cartel." Cedar's forlorn expression ignited the knot in my stomach.

He leaned forward as if sharing a secret. "If Cal's involved with the cartel and spills his guts—well, I wouldn't take bets on whether he'd live through a trial."

The dread circling me for the past twenty-four hours took root in my head and wrapped around my spine. "I never considered that possibility."

"Calvin will never get away without jail time, so put that thought out of your mind."

I managed to take a breath. "And if he's indicted, what would that mean for the company? Will the Feds tie up his business assets?"

Cedar slipped on his glasses. "Probably, which means the Atlanta contracts will stay in limbo."

Stunned, I waited for his guidance, an idea, something. "We have to close those properties. A balloon payment is due in ninety days." According to the appraisals, the South Carolina warehouses were all but worthless. The Atlanta office buildings were Barry Real Estate and Development's only valuable properties. I imagined my mother's shock when I announced half of Granddad's business was a sham.

"We can discuss all of this tomorrow," he said. "Right now, I need to go over something more urgent."

More urgent than filing bankruptcy and me signing three years of fictitious financials? Facing charges of bank fraud? My banking career flushing into Neverland? Nathan's last words whispered in my ear. "Help us put a criminal behind bars." Did that include me?

I inhaled a calming breath. Take one step at a time, Kate.

Cedar handed me a book and tapped the cover with his finger.

I read the title. "What Every Body Is Saying?"

He peered over his glasses. "My advice is to read, study, and memorize." He used his lecturing courtroom voice. "I did some checking. Nathan Parsi is ex-Special Intelligence and an accomplished linguist. But more important to you, he has a Ph.D. in behavioral science."

I swallowed dry spit. "Cedar, I need those properties in Atlanta to close. We have to find Calvin, and you have to do your magic."

"We'll work something out." He peered at me over his glasses. "Stay with me, this is important. The marshal has a Ph.D. in behavioral science."

"Why's that important?"

"Before Parsi joined the US Marshals Service, he had a top security clearance and probably worked undercover. I figure he chased terrorists."

"You figure?"

"File's sealed. My guy at GBI couldn't get past the first layer."

I wasn't surprised Cedar had inside contacts in Georgia's investigating bureau, just that he'd run a check on Nathan. "I don't see the importance of the marshal's service history."

"That's what I'm telling you. He's more than a US Marshal. He's a behavioral analyst."

I scanned the chapter titles in the book: Mastering the Secrets of Nonverbal Communication. Detecting Deception. The Mind's Canvas. I snapped the cover closed. "A behavioral analyst—isn't that like a psychologist?"

"You should be so lucky. This guy can read a minute flinch of your eyelids. Determine if you're lying, hiding something, or in the least bit uncomfortable. None of your secrets are safe."

"I don't have secrets." I flashed on the image of Mom's face when Nathan questioned her about the stolen box of letters and jewels and Ben's description of Calvin ducking out of the diner. It seemed I was the only one in my family with nothing to hide. I glanced at the side pocket of my purse, Granddad's alias passport practically flashing neon through the leather pocket.

I placed the book on the table, went to the window, and located the Explorer. "No offense, but I don't believe in hocus pocus."

"Hocus pocus?" Cedar's condescending scoff boomed off the ceiling. "Hocus pocus doesn't cost three hundred bucks an hour, which is the going rate for a BA."

I picked up my water bottle and swallowed a cold swig. The cool liquid squelched my growing desire to snap out a zippy comeback. Cedar took this stuff seriously, and he was trying to share his concern. Being wound spring tight was not an excuse for rude retorts. "Okay. Explain."

"You're aware of my winning record in court, right?"

Hard not to be when he mentioned it every time we met. "Your record is exemplary," I said. "You've won thirty-seven of your last forty-two cases."

"Right." Cedar flashed the smile of a proud teacher to his star student. "And you know why?"

"Because you're a genius?" I almost managed to keep the snark out of my voice.

He raised his hand in acquiescence. "True. But I have a secret weapon."

His eyes brightened. He adopted his closing argument face. I sat on the sofa and leaned back against the cushion. An oration was coming, nothing to do but listen.

He tapped the book. "I use the information in this to read my witnesses. Know when to push, when to back off." He brought his hand forward and back to demonstrate. "I've studied eight books on the subject, but this is the BA bible." His eyes twinkled like a self-help guru imparting secret knowledge. His expectant face waited for my comment.

I had nothing.

He leaned forward and lowered his voice. "I use a BA to select jurors."

"BA?"

"Behavioral analyst." He gazed heavenward. "Like Nathan Parsi."

"Are you saying that if I hired you to represent me in court, you'd pay someone three hundred dollars an hour to help you pick the jurors?"

He shot me a don't-be-absurd look. "No." He pointed a finger in my direction. "You'd pay him." He removed a prepackaged phone from his briefcase and laid it on the cushion between us.

I reconciled to check Cedar's monthly statements a little closer. I picked up the phone. "What gives?"

"It's a burner."

"I know what it is. Why are you giving me one?" I refrained from mentioning the one in my desk drawer and the two in my briefcase. I didn't want to give Cedar more reasons for an additional monolog.

"I'll give you a two-minute lesson on being in the Feds' crosshairs."

"That would be Cal. Not me."

"Federal marshals have made themselves mighty cozy at Spartina." His expression left little doubt he considered me naive. "If the marshal doesn't already have you under surveillance, he will soon."

The gray Ford Explorer on my tail stopped me from arguing. "I am being followed. I'm sure Nathan's hoping Cal makes contact."

Cedar shot me another one of his don't-be-absurd

looks. Those were a particular favorite today. "Don't assume your cousin's the marshal's only suspect."

"You're implying the Feds believe I'm mixed up with the cartel?"

"Not Erica, but the marshal. He doesn't trust you. I see it in his eyes." He smacked the BA bible. "I know the signs."

Before today, I'd have believed Cedar's idea was as loony as a Bugs Bunny cartoon.

He stood. "I have another appointment."

"I'll call you when Ben and Cal get here."

Cedar stabbed a finger in my direction. "Don't let the marshal catch you playing detective. Cal coming to you alone is one thing, but having a private investigator makes you look cagey."

"Cagey?" I gave him a Roslyn "tsk."

"Appears suspicious to hire someone to find your cousin when a federal agent has informed you they're looking for him." He pointed to the book. "And read the book and even the playing field. If you need me for anything you don't want the Feds to hear,"—he picked up the burner—"use this."

I rose to walk him out. "I'll be sure to carry it with me." Keeping all my phones straight would be tricky. Labeling them in code just to be safe didn't seem so far-fetched.

Cedar chugged the last of his water. "Call your investigator and tell him to hold off coming here. I'll work out a more secure meeting place. And you should plan to leave for Florida. Spend time with your son and mother until this blows over."

"As soon as we get Calvin squared with the marshal." And we discussed the dilapidated warehouses, bogus improvements, and the ramifications of my signing fraudulent financials for the past three years. "I'll leave right after our meeting tomorrow." My stomach burned, and even though I was starving, I knew it wasn't from a lack of food.

We walked down the hall and met Samantha coming out of her office. She gave Cedar a tight smile and handed me a file. I caught sight of Beth through the lobby window, wide eyed and scurrying up the steps. Cedar stepped to the side and let her pass.

She planted a hand on her hip. "Did you know Cal's wanted for questioning?"

Cedar shook his head, which I took as a warning to say as little as possible. I looked past him to the Explorer, still parked in the same spot. My day had turned busier than the corner Starbucks.

I waved a hand toward my office. Beth spun a half circle and marched down the hall. Maybe she knew Calvin was coming; her act could be a charade. I massaged the two-inch spot between my eyes. A migraine. A perfect cap for my perfect day.

# CHAPTER FOURTEEN

*Katelyn*

I SHUT MY OFFICE door, an unusual occurrence no doubt causing a few comments in the break room, and guided Beth to the sofa. She folded her full height, all six feet, onto the sofa and slung her leather carryall to the far cushion.

"I've been trying to reach you all morning." I placed Cedar's BA bible on the side table, then eased into an adjacent wingback.

In the past, Calvin's wife had downplayed her looks with oversized sack dresses and by arranging her long straight hair into messy buns. Today, her makeup was perfectly applied, and with a sassy new hairstyle eight inches shorter and three shades lighter framing her stunning gold-flecked eyes, she could pass for a Milan runway model. Hair wasn't the only thing Beth had shed; she was fifty pounds lighter.

She illustrated her new style with black ankle jeans hugging her long legs, five-inch wedge sandals, and a short yellow jacket showcasing what appeared to be newly acquired cleavage. My cousin's wife had upped her game.

She twisted a two-carat diamond solitaire originally worn by my great-grandmother around her finger. "Did you know Erica Sanchez is looking for Calvin?"

No idle chitchat. No, how are you doing? How's your son? Barry-style communication—getting to the point—was practically our family motto. "There are a lot of people looking for Cal, me included. Do you know where he is?"

She swept bangs from her forehead, slid her hands down her thighs, and leaned forward. An edge to her movements reminded me of a cheetah preparing to pounce. "Why do you want him?"

"Did Cal ask you to meet him here? He needs to talk to Cedar before Nathan Parsi finds him."

"Parsi?" Referring to her tone as indignant would be a mammoth underplay. "You're talking about the marshal who showed up with Erica? They claim Calvin's disappeared and don't believe I don't know where he is."

"Calvin didn't call, let you know where he was last night?" An itch of misgiving wound its way up my spine.

"Call me?" Her curt voice matched her expression. But doubt must've shown on my face because she shrugged. "We're separated."

"You're not living at Spring Street?"

"Not anymore." Her eyes were a beautiful golden brown, but I could see sadness in them.

"I saw Calvin at your house yesterday morning. He didn't mention you'd left."

"You came to our house?" A curious note seeped into her voice. "Why?"

"To discuss Barry Island."

"What about the island?"

"A drug cartel is using the land."

Beth didn't flinch, but she did tilt back a couple of inches.

"Didn't Erica and Nathan explain why they wanted Calvin?" I asked.

She shot off the sofa, knocking her shin against the coffee table. A Maya tribal mask toppled out of a wooden stand, but she didn't appear to notice. She stood three feet from my chair, hands at her waist, fingers digging into her hips. "Are you the one that told the police Cal's involved? Is that why they're trying to find him?"

"Of course not." I had to work not to let my frustration show. "I went to your house to warn Cal about the DEA's interest in our island."

"Don't you mean your island?" Her face might be flushed with anger, but her eyes held the pain of our past. However sleek she appeared, fear fringed her movements.

I softened my tone. "Cal didn't show up for work after my visit, and Nathan and Erica are convinced he's skipped town. I'm trying to find him before they do. If Cal's involved with this drug ring, he could go to jail. I'm hoping Cedar can make a deal."

Based on Cedar's assessment, I hesitated to promise anything more. "I thought we'd found Cal this morning, but something must've happened. I'm still waiting to hear back."

She stepped away and paced in front of the sofa. "We? Who's we?"

"I hired a private investigator."

"To find Calvin?"

"Yes."

Desperation, or a close cousin, slid into her eyes. "What proof do you have that Cal has anything to do with this drug business? Why do you accept he's guilty so easily?"

My head pounded, and my stomach churned. I needed aspirin, a Tagamet, and a case of Sauvignon Blanc. "For starters, the boat."

She sat on the far edge of the sofa, picked up her carryall, and hugged it to her body. "What boat?"

"The Grady White Calvin bought."

She shook her head. "We don't own a boat."

"Cal does. And Erica says it's used to recover drugs."

She hunched her shoulders but said nothing.

I couldn't imagine why she was here if Beth's visit wasn't on Cal's behalf. And I didn't buy the confused act. "Cal's boat retails for over a hundred grand. Title's clear, which means he paid cash. Hard to believe you were unaware that much money vanished from your accounts."

She glanced down. Her fingers twisted around her purse handle, and pink splotches crept from her neck into her cheeks. "We keep our finances separate."

I waited for her to say more. She didn't. "You don't know what Calvin does with your money?" Hundreds of thousands had been funneled out of his accounts. Could she be that clueless?

She straightened the tribal mask and ran her fingers over the smooth jade finish. "This is from Central America, isn't it? I've always wanted to travel." She gazed at the globe in the corner. "We've never been to Asia, Europe, Canada, or even Mexico. Cal claims we can't afford it. I don't believe him. Over the last two years, he was gone more than home. He has at least three phones. They ring all through the night." She faced me, her look imploring as if I could explain Cal's actions. "Who needs more than one cell phone?"

I adopted my boardroom poker face.

Beth drew a shaky breath. "I know he has another bimbo." She lifted her chin in a challenge, and I realized she was waiting for me to confirm or deny her suspicions.

"Doesn't matter." She swept her hand through the air. "I'm tired of Calvin's lies. Tired of his other women. I'm leaving him." She straightened her spine and slipped on a composed façade so fast it stole the denial poised on the tip of my tongue.

My soul recognized the kindred spirit of a woman living through infidelity. The denial. The self-blame. The hidden heartbreak.

"My mom lives in Alabama," Beth said. "Two months ago, she had a heart attack, her second this year. I'm taking her with me to Colorado."

"You're going to Colorado?"

"I've accepted a management position at a clinic in Denver. I want to be as far from Savannah and Cal as possible."

I heard a noise outside and went to look through the back door's window. Hoped it was Calvin, because this was his mess. But the noise came from two boys kicking a soccer ball down the alley.

The tension in my office was so thick you could chew it. I struggled and finally opened the latch on the antique window. Drew a long deep breath. The smells and sounds of summer assaulted my senses. Hot tar melting under the searing sun, confederate jasmine blooming on a trellis by the back stairs, and sounds of the tourists laughing their way through the park.

If Beth wasn't here on Cal's behalf, it was time to find out why she came. "You want a coffee or water? I have a nice selection of tea."

"Nothing, thanks."

I went to the bar. Chose a coffee pod and popped it in the Keurig. "When are you planning to leave for Colorado?"

"I was packing my car when Erica and the marshal showed up."

I carried my coffee to the sofa and sat beside her. "They said I couldn't leave town until they found Calvin. Can they do that?" She gripped my free hand. "Can they keep me in Savannah?"

"Did you tell them you planned to leave?"

"No." She released my hand to massage the space between her eyes. "I was scared to say anything. Erica peppered me with questions, and I couldn't think straight. Do you think I can leave?"

Her distress seemed sincere. Maybe she only wanted guidance. I patted her knee. "I don't know, but I'll call and ask Cedar." I went to my desk and picked up my phone. Remembered Cal's bank balances. "Do you need money?"

"I planned to ask you for enough to move." Her voice trailed off.

"I'll cut you a check." I put the phone down. This conversation might be better on one of the throwaway phones.

"I don't need money anymore." She wiped a tear with the back of her hand and sniffed. "I found a package in my suitcase lining."

I took a second to unravel her words. "You found money in a suitcase?"

"Yes." She extracted a tissue from her purse and blew her nose.

"How much?"

"Thirty thousand." Her whispering voice crushed the last hope of Cal's innocence.

"That's a lot of cash to keep in a suitcase."

She fisted a hand and covered her heart. "I told Cal I was leaving last week. He knew I'd find it when I packed."

Yeah, he's a regular Mother Theresa.

My call to Cedar went to voicemail. I hung up and sent a text asking for a callback. "Ben, my investigator, thought he had a lead on Calvin's whereabouts this morning. Cedar doesn't think Cal should come here, but I haven't been able to reach Ben or Cal to change the plan. I don't even know for sure if Ben's found Cal."

Beth fiddled with the zipper inside her carryall and then pushed the purse aside. She stood and drifted to the bookshelves, ran her finger across the bindings of the books. Turned and walked to the bar, studying the coffee and tea pods. Then she meandered back to the bookshelves.

The window overlooking the square worked like a magnet. I walked over and tilted the blinds. The Explorer had moved into a space two slots closer to my front door. "Have you noticed anyone following you?"

When she didn't answer, I glanced over my shoulder.

Her forehead was one giant wrinkle. "What?"

"I'm being followed. Marshal Parsi's probably hoping Calvin will contact me. Makes sense he'd take the same bet on you. Have you noticed a car hanging around your house or the hospital?"

A muscle ticked in her jaw. "No."

A woman, or at least someone with shoulder-length dark hair, sat in a white car across from the Methodist Church. All the other vehicles around the park were empty. I let the possibility go for now.

I finished my coffee and went to the bar to make another cup. God knew I didn't need the caffeine, but it gave my hands something to do while we waited for Cedar to call back. "If you leave for Colorado, Erica will assume you've run away with Calvin."

The book Beth held slipped from her hand and landed on the floor. "I'm not going anywhere with Calvin. My start date at the clinic is in ten days." She retrieved the book and shoved it back in place. "It's all the time I have to pack my mother's house, put it on the market, and drive to Colorado. I should've left two weeks ago."

I programmed the Keurig for a cup of tea, looked over my choices, and opted for the Zen green over the calm herbal. Finding my Zen sounded good right now. "Why haven't you already left?"

"I'm cashing out my 401(k). It's taking longer than I thought. But with the thirty thousand Cal left me, I can hire a mover and rent a place for Mom and me."

"You'll take a heavy penalty if you cash in your retirement."

"It's my only savings."

"You're not broke, Beth." My tea finished brewing, and I carried the steaming cup to my desk. "Cal has monthly payments from the trust fund." Since our real estate contracts were in jeopardy, I didn't mention his request to cash him out of our business.

"Cal gets monthly trust payments? How much?" Silence bounced off the walls.

It was an odd time for me to stick to my fiduciary responsibilities. But as an ex-banker, the threat of legal issues kept me from saying more.

Granddad only had two beneficiaries, Calvin and me. As trustee, I was required to remain faithful to his wishes and skirt any controversy that might lead to a lawsuit. "Our cash is tight, but the important thing is you and Cal are far from penniless. Once established in Colorado, I suggest you hire an attorney and protect your future."

Her golden eyes clouded, and she stared over my shoulder.

I'd lost her. "Do you understand how important this is? If you file for a divorce or even a legal separation, let your attorney know that Cal has a sizable inheritance in his future."

"I'm due in Colorado in ten days. If you're right and Cal's involved with this drug ring…" She held her face with both hands. "A nurse practitioner can't have a drug runner for a husband."

I checked Ben's secret email account—nothing new in the inbox. I sent a message asking him to call me before bringing Cal to the office. But they should've been here two hours ago if Ben had located Cal. "Do you have any idea where Cal might hide?"

"It's Cal, Kate." Beth's face twisted as if controlled by dark, ugly thoughts. "Any number of women would give him protection. Even a few of his poker buddies might risk it."

"I need names."

Her deep, sorrowful, humming breath went deeper than words. "I gave a list of names to Erica this morning."

"Give them to me." I grabbed a pen and pad from my desk and joined her.

"Chet Rincon, Scot Bishop, Bubba Snively." She crossed her arms and ran her hands over her forearms. "Amanda Hennessy might risk hiding him." Her eyes blazed, and her face, no longer pale, flushed with righteous fury. "Susie Clemons was proud as punch to inform me you handled the details of Amanda's abortion."

My neck went hot, and embarrassment rolled off me like beads of sweat. "Beth." Sadness, shame, and my plea for forgiveness settled inside the one syllable. I forced myself to look her in the eye.

Her pain made me so sad and tired that I wanted to slip off my seat and sleep on the floor. "I made a few calls and secured an opening in a private clinic. I'm sorry if you feel I betrayed your trust." I stopped short of attempting to justify my reasons. "I did what I thought was best at the time."

"Yes. I'm sure you did." Her deadpanned response did nothing to assuage my guilt, which I'm sure was her intent.

I returned the list to my desk and searched for anything to keep busy. I threw away my empty water bottle, collected my cup, and washed it in the bar sink.

Beth walked over and rested a hip against the counter. "I'm pregnant."

I stopped breathing.

Beth stared at the floor like a chastised child.

Could this situation get worse? She was three feet

away, and I wanted to hug and congratulate her on the baby. It was the right thing to do, but I just couldn't. All I saw was Calvin behind bars, Beth, and now an innocent child, living with a lifetime of scandal.

I stepped up and wrapped an arm around her shoulders. "It's wonderful news. I'm happy for you."

She reached for a napkin and wiped her cheeks. "I didn't know about the baby when I accepted the job." She moved away from me and wandered the room, trailing a finger over the back of a wingback. "I'd decided to stay and work on my marriage for the sake of our child. But this morning, when Erica said Cal ran drugs, I finished packing and stuck with my plan. I stopped here, hoping you might tell me Cal was innocent. But you agree with Erica." A tear leaked, then another, like a slow drip from a faucet that hadn't been properly turned off. "I won't raise a child under a cloud of suspicion. Savannah's a small town. A father in jail would be devastating for his kid."

A hot, tingling shame slid over my skin. This was the first time I'd considered how Cal's arrest would affect anything beyond me and our company's reputation. I moved to her side, put a consoling hand over hers, and allowed the idea of Cal's arrest to lie between us.

"I have to get to Colorado." Her voice gained control. "You have to help me."

Cedar's burner phone rang and saved me from responding. I answered and gave him a quick overview.

Cedar asked to speak to Beth.

I only heard one side of the conversation, but Cedar appeared to enter full witness preparation mode. Any response of Beth's over four words was halted for clarification. By the time she hung up, she'd given details on the last six months of her life.

"He said I could leave, but he warned if someone's following me, the Feds will know every move I make."

Until Nathan Parsi had Cal in custody, neither Beth nor I would be free of the Feds. The unfairness of us being swept into Parsi's net of suspects pricked a few holes in my moral compass. "We could go to Erica and explain why you're moving."

Beth returned to the sofa, laid her head on the cushion, and closed her eyes. "Is that what you think is best?" She looked ready to accept whatever I deemed appropriate.

"Erica might be more understanding if you told her about the baby. You don't look pregnant, and knowing Erica, she'd ask for proof, but a pregnancy test would suffice." I considered the idea, and tossed it around. "It'd be risky for her to trust you're playing straight and not running to Calvin. And blind faith isn't one of Erica's virtues, but it might be worth the chance. Even if she believes you, it's still probable she'll assign surveillance until they find Calvin."

"If the DEA follows me to Colorado and my bosses find out, I'll be fired." She leaned forward. Came close to sticking her head between her knees.

"Are you okay?" I hurried over, sat beside her, and rubbed her back.

"I'm all right." She inhaled a shaky breath.

She didn't look all right, but she was pregnant.

Maybe her gray color was from nausea.

I walked to the window, checked on my new friend parked in front of my office, and had a

Eureka moment. I turned and faced Beth. "Okay. I think I know how we can slip you out of town."

## CHAPTER FIFTEEN

―――――

*Katelyn*

I REACHED ACROSS MY office sofa and gripped Beth's hand. I tried giving her a we-got-this smile, but it was as if the walls of my chest had an internal tourniquet, and inhaling a breath seemed next to impossible. "You want a cup of green tea? I have one that supposedly calms your nerves."

"No, thanks." Her free hand moved over her stomach. "I'm not feeling well."

I gave her knee one last pat and went through it all again. I explained renting a car in either of our names would leave a trail the Feds could follow. But Pea, my sorority sister from Duke, owned a car dealership. She could sell a vehicle as a typical transaction. Holding paperwork could easily be passed off as business as usual.

I explained to Beth why the thirty grand she'd found in the suitcase should be left in the safe until we straightened out Cal's mess. Until now, she'd done nothing wrong, but crossing state lines with drug money might be questionable. Her glassy eyes were unreadable, but she handed over the cash.

The irony of me, a rule-following by-the-book girl assisting Beth in her quest to disappear, and then tomorrow expecting Marshal Parsi to believe I had nothing to do with Cal's disappearance or the company's shady business practices, wasn't lost on me. I massaged my temples and tried to alleviate the migraine lying in wait.

Beth picked up her water. She raised it ten inches before her shakes caused the liquid to slosh over the side. She set the glass back on the table. I suspected neither of us would pull this plan off without the benefit of liquid courage. I went to the bar, opened the wine cooler, chose a bottle of my favorite Chablis, and poured two glasses. After handing her a glass, I took a long-needed sip.

She kept her wine at arm's length. "I'm pregnant."

"You need something to steady your nerves. One glass of wine won't hurt the baby."

She studied the glass with the intensity of a jeweler seeing the Hope diamond for the first time.

I nudged her hand toward her mouth. "It'll be okay."

She took a cautious sip, then another.

I couldn't imagine why she accepted me as a medical authority. She was the nurse—I was a financial banker and a Lamaze dropout who believed withholding drugs during childbirth should be on Homeland Security's list of tortures.

One of my four burner phones buzzed. I checked the number and verified the area code before answering.

"This ducking-under-the-radar business is expensive," Peanut said, then rattled off two new phone numbers. "I've booked the rental. A gray Nissan Rogue will be parked in the alley behind a shop called the Twisty Sisters within the hour."

"I really appreciate this," I said.

"Tell me again why we're breaking the law to help your lying-no-good cousin?"

"We're not doing this for Cal," I said. "We're helping Beth. And we're not breaking the law."

"Yeah? Then why'd I spend over a hundred dollars on drop phones?"

"Drop phones?"

"I watch Hunted," she deadpanned. "I know the lingo."

I had no idea what she was talking about. "Using disposable phones is just a precaution. I think the Feds may have my home and office phones tapped."

"Katie-bug." Pea's voice reeked of misgiving. "Your Jesus complex has got to go. You're not on Earth to save the world. Your deadbeat cousin and his wife aren't your responsibility."

Peanut and I had been roommates and best friends in college, but caught up in our careers and family life, we'd drifted apart after marriage. We'd renewed our friendship over Facebook and our devastating divorces. "Beth and Calvin are my family."

Peanut sighed. "And blood trumps all."

"Cedar's going to help me sort everything out tomorrow. By this time next week, my life will be back to boring."

"Uh-huh. Well, so that you know, this little foray is costing you a week in St. Moritz."

I thought I sensed a smile, but I could be wrong.

"I expect daily in-room appointments with a hunky masseur."

Yeah, she was smiling. God, I missed her. "You got it." I was fairly sure my next request would push the bounds of our sorority sisterhood. I rubbed a sweaty palm over my thigh. "One more thing. Do you happen to have ten thousand in cash lying around?"

———

Beth and I chatted our way out of the office and down the sidewalk. Well, I chatted and kept a close eye on the white Chevy. All Beth managed was the occasional half smile when prompted. Other than ordering green tea instead of coffee at Starbucks, we followed the plan. We sipped and window-shopped the two blocks south to the Twisty Sisters Boutique. I opened the door, did a quick glance around, and didn't see the Chevy. I pushed Beth through the door, and a middle-aged clerk pounced.

"Can I show you ladies anything?"

I drew in air, stared into her expectant eyes, and little bubbles of hysteria in my throat popped. "We're just looking."

I death gripped Beth's shoulder and guided her to a dress rack against the back wall. Her face was a little pale and her mouth a little more firm than usual, but otherwise, she appeared almost normal. I held up a blue sundress the color of Owen's eyes, and the clerk oohed and aahed. I nudged Beth's side, and she threw her hand over her mouth right on cue.

"Oh, gosh." I scanned the store, pretending to look for the restroom. "She's pregnant." I zeroed in on the back door. "Needs fresh air." I dragged Beth five steps, held my breath, then pushed down the lever. I said a prayer of thanks, the alarm didn't sound. I pulled Beth into the alley.

"Do you want a glass of water?" The salesclerk stood in the open doorway.

I rubbed Beth's back. "No thanks. My car is parked around the corner. I think she needs to go home."

The clerk glanced from my face to the blue dress across my arm. I thrust the dress in her direction. "Can you hold this for me? I'll come back later."

"Sure. What's the name?"

"Kate Landers." I clamped my mouth. Probably shouldn't have used my real name.

The woman took the dress, gave Beth a pitying half smile, and walked back inside.

I spotted the Nissan Rogue parked two spaces down and opened the back passenger door. Fished keys from under the floor mat and handed them to Beth. "Give me your cell phone."

"Why?"

"Mobile phones have GPS tracking. You can't take it with you." I pulled a Walmart phone from my purse. "If you need to make a call, use this one. I've already put my number in the contacts. Don't call any of my regular numbers, and don't call anyone else you know on this phone." I mimicked Ben's instructions on the proper use of a burner.

We hugged goodbye, and she held on for an extra second before slipping behind the wheel. I tried to imagine what it would be like to be pregnant and muster the will to move across the country with an ailing mother. My opinion of Beth had changed dramatically today.

I waited until her taillights disappeared and then quickly disassembled her phone. I threw the receiver in a container of ice inside a delivery truck and the battery in a dumpster behind Leopold's Ice Cream Shop. I slowly strolled back to the office.

An empty red van claimed the Explorer's old parking spot. The white Chevy circled the square. When she passed me, she administered an impressive neck stretch, hit the brakes, and turned around in her seat. It took great restraint not to wave.

I stopped by the reception desk on the way to my office. "Where's Sandy?"

My assistant, Jennifer, tilted her head left and right until she nursed a muffled pop. "Sandy's at her third doctor's appointment this week." Jennifer offered a slow, humorless smile. "Sandy needs a job that doesn't require being present eight hours a day." If an eye roll could be conveyed in a person's voice, Jennifer had the tone nailed.

I saw where this conversation was headed and switched subjects. "Anyone come in while I was gone?"

"No." She turned back to her computer screen. "Everyone's left for the day, and I'm heading out. Will you be in tomorrow?"

"I'll be in around eight, but I have an eleven o'clock at Cedar Haynes's office, and then I'm leaving for Florida." Right after I spill my guts to Marshal Nathan Parsi.

My stomach grumbled. I remembered skipping lunch and my scrambled eggs were long gone. I returned to my office and called the Thai restaurant down the street.

While I waited for my food delivery, I sent another snotty text to Ben.

—Earth to Ben. Call.—

Then I compared Samantha's printed monthly reports to the ones I'd saved earlier and found no glaring discrepancies. Twenty minutes later, I sat at Joseph's desk, opened a container of lemon grass chicken, and stuffed a piece in my mouth. I stacked the warehouse files on the desk and thumbed through a multisection that rivaled War and Peace's size.

I fanned through the first half of the file and found none of the papers in date order—twenty years of records haphazardly stuffed inside. I pushed the chicken container to the corner of the desk and turned back to the beginning.

I flipped each page in the file, searching for a current lease on the warehouse. Instead, I found invoices, canceled checks, and brochures for loading docks and security systems. Entire sections of the brochures were underlined, and the same words were transcribed on attached invoices, a wonderful example of creative accounting.

I emptied drawers, pillaged file cabinets, and netted no leases. I sat back in my chair and dunked a soggy spring roll into hot mustard.

The bookshelves in Joseph's office held stacks of three-inch binders with thirty years of year-end statements and brochures. Joseph was big on full-color construction company brochures. I began clearing the shelves, stacking reference and accounting books in one pile and family photos and plaques from the Chamber of Commerce in another. I stared at eight empty shelves, and the burn that pooled like a bucket of gasoline in my stomach ignited.

My mind raced with all I had to accomplish before meeting with Cedar, but my body, definitely on a different schedule, sagged. I needed caffeine. I turned on Joseph's computer while my coffee brewed. Opened his document folder and stared at a blank screen. I tried scrolling, hit the control keys, opened his email, and found no history. Not one email. I opened an accounting program and searched for files and reports he'd saved. Nothing.

Joseph's computer had been wiped clean.

I opened the utility program, verified the hard drive hadn't crashed, and looked up the cleanup date. Friday—four days ago. My eyes rested on a family photograph sitting on the corner of Joseph's desk. The last time I'd seen my property manager, he'd mentioned his wife wanted to visit their daughter Jessica, or maybe Jessica planned to meet them somewhere. I couldn't remember the details. Either way, four days ago, Joseph wasn't in his office. Joseph wasn't even in Savannah. My mind went numb.

I needed a new plan. Maybe someone hacked the system, but why just clean Joseph's computer? I couldn't come up with a legitimate reason Joseph would have wiped his computer of all data. But there was one really good illegitimate reason. He was on the run.

I filed the books and papers back where they belonged. Stuffed a citizen of the year award between a book on the merits of investing in REITs and a picture of Joseph, his son, and a man I didn't know back on the shelf. I stood on my tiptoes and shoved the last book back in place, and hit something hard. Using the book in my hand, I fished out a four-inch-thick white binder he'd kept stored behind a set of accounting books. I opened the notebook, and a small thin black book fell to the floor.

I picked up the book: Journey, a James Michener anomaly and one of the few weighing less than ten pounds. I thumbed through the pages and noted a few words scribbled in the margin. None of them had meaning, I wrote them down anyway. A photograph slipped to the floor. A picture of Joseph with his arm around a woman in a wedding dress. She was smiling at another man whom I assumed because of his tuxedo was the groom.

The notebook neatly categorized Joseph's personal bills by month. No extra paper here. There was a section marked hospital. Bills for his wife's three bouts of ovarian cancer were neatly filed, each invoice in date order.

A phone buzzed. I glanced at the three burner phones I'd lined across the top of the credenza.

A text from Beth appeared on the screen of the third phone.

—1 hr from AL line. Tired. Stop 4 night.—

I texted back.

—Remember—Tk out phone battery.—

I refocused on the black book. What happened after Joseph left town that made him or a hacker delete every file on his computer? If he was on the run, why wait to delete incriminating computer files and leave so many compromising hard copies in the files?

His computer records might be toast, but Joseph was a pack rat. I could recreate most of the missing computer records if I used the twenty years of property records he'd left behind, county websites, and Samantha's accounting reports. I opened the first bulging file, separated the pages in date order, and discarded the duplicate copies. I was convinced Joseph was a tree hater.

At ten minutes to ten, I put the last file back in the drawer and forwarded a copy of my spreadsheet to Ben's secret email account. I had no doubt the mainstay of our family business was laundering money. I tried to register the emotions bombarding my system, but they were all over the place. Surprise. Dread. Distrust. Sprinkled with a heavy dose of fear.

I returned to my office, poured the last bit of Chablis into a glass, and drank every drop.

Bottom line—Barry Real Estate and Investment received bogus rent money from bogus companies and charged off bogus renovations completed by bogus construction companies. Our family business was a carefully constructed lie that could easily pass a routine bank perusal or an IRS audit. Anger played out as my major emotion, but blown away fought for a spot because this scheme was slick.

Calvin's participation was still murky, but I'd found enough documents with Granddad's signature to verify he'd run the scheme before his stroke. I sat back in my chair and worked with what I knew. I knew how Granddad and, later, Joseph laundered rent monies through the company. I knew the name of the renters. I didn't know why a company would pay exorbitant rents for broken-down warehouses.

I rounded up my three throwaway phones and stuffed them in my purse. I threw away my empty wine bottle and stared at the map over the bar. Some moments in life stole your breath and left you speechless, completely stunned at your naïve stupidity.

The first rule of real estate investment: Location—location—location.

I opened the storage closet, pulled an East Coast fishing chart out of a bin of maps, and tacked it to the wall.

I accessed Google Earth and marked the location of the first warehouse with a green pushpin, then the second. On the third, my heart skidded to a stop. I ran my finger from the first warehouse to a river and then to the ocean. I repeated the process for the second and third. All three were positioned just like Barry Island.

Barry Real Estate and Development was in business to provide the cartel with safe harbors to break down and package drugs. I slid into my chair and laid my head against the cool surface of my desk. The special reserve Chablis threatened to reappear.

My debt restructuring plan was Joseph's catalyst. My request for appraisals put his operation in jeopardy. The legal ramifications of all this boggled my mind. I inhaled a deep breath, then another, and another. I couldn't get enough air in my lungs. I tried slowing my breath. Breathe. Breathe. My gasps turned shallower and faster. My heart beat harder—paper bag. I needed a paper bag. I stuck my head between my legs.

I had to talk to Cedar. He'd know what to do. Joseph—I had to find Joseph. I no longer cared about any embezzling. All the money was dirty. But Joseph was the only person who knew I was innocent. There was no way I'd be his dupe.

I rifled through my purse for Cedar's throwaway and came up with the Walmart phone Ben warned against using. My hand stilled. If Ben was right and the Feds had satellite reconnaissance, which no longer seemed far-fetched, my office could be bugged. Could that be the reason Ben hadn't made contact?

If my office was bugged, Nathan knew I helped Beth. And Peanut would be on Nathan's radar. I ran to Joseph's office, dragged a chair to the bookshelf, found the white binder with his personal records, and stuck it under my arm. Knowledge was power, and I planned to learn every minute detail about my scumbag property manager.

But first, I needed to talk to Cedar.

I opened the safe and placed the Cecil Cummings passport inside. I had enough to explain to Parsi without adding Granddad's alias. For now, that would remain my secret. I switched off the light and hit the stairs two at a time.

I made a right out of the parking lot and checked the rearview mirror for the Explorer lights. I wanted to bolt straight to Cedar's and figure out the mud level I waded in. But hanging out with my lawyer this late at night screamed guilty. I had to call him, at least.

I passed the Montgomery County sign five minutes from home and glanced in the rearview mirror. A car resembling an Explorer had kept a textbook distance from my Hummer for ten miles. If I used the burner to call Cedar and the vehicle behind was a tail, would the driver pick up my conversation? I chewed on the problem for another mile and admitted I didn't watch enough detective shows to know the answer.

If the car's driver was a federal marshal, he probably had a bag of spy tools at his disposal—at least binoculars with a telescopic lens. My intuition said Parsi already had satellite surveillance on Spartina. I had to risk calling Cedar before I got home.

## CHAPTER SIXTEEN

*Katelyn*

I TOOK THE LAST exit off the interstate before home and stopped at the corner Citgo station. I swung in as close to the entrance as possible and hustled past the jumbo-sized candy bars and racks of potato chips. A bathroom sign hanging over a beer cooler featured a fisted hand with a finger pointing down a hallway stacked with boxes.

Slipping into the single-serve bathroom, I fumbled with the lock. My hands were shaky, and I tried three tries before the bolt slid into place. I slumped against the wall. Fear rolled through every cell in my body. I dialed Cedar's home number and whispered a two-minute rundown of my hellish day's discoveries.

He gurgled a wet phlegmy cough. "Why are you whispering?"

"Someone's following me." The hiss in my voice mimicked a pissed-off snake.

"Speak up. I can't hear you."

I stomped across the five-by-eight room, turned on the cold faucet full blast, and risked a semi-normal tone. "I'm being followed." I wedged my butt between a rust-stained sink and a graffiti-covered wall.

"Where are you?"

"In a service station bathroom." I rushed through my go-directly-to-jail discovery again. "I need your help."

"We'll talk this through in the morning."

"Cedar, I've signed three years of fraudulent financials. Before I go to the Feds with what I found, I have to go to the banks and straighten this out. This can't wait."

"Hold on a minute." The rustling of bed sheets, a mattress spring creak, and a couple more strangled coughs lasted ten seconds. Then silence.

"Cedar, are you still there?" I looked at the screen on the burner and verified the coverage bars. I had plenty. "Cedar?"

"I have early court in the morning, or I'd meet you sooner. Eleven's the best I can do." He heaved a sigh. "Come at ten-thirty. I'll try and wrap my case early."

I slid down the wall. Halfway to the floor, I looked over at the toilet and pushed back to standing. "I need to go to First National and Nations Banks. Convince them that I didn't know our financials were fabricated. I'm not sure how I'll pull off claiming ignorance. It's not like I don't understand how financial reports work." My pissed-off snake voice made another appearance.

"Calm down. Don't get ahead of yourself. You've done nothing wrong." Cedar's tone worked like aloe on sunburn soothing my anxiety. Except this was more of a blazing inferno. I didn't need a balm—I needed a Boeing 747 drowning me in chemical flame retardant.

"We can work this out." Self-confidence oozed from his voice. "We'll meet in the morning and work through the quagmire," he said.

Quagmire—a superb description of my current state. Walking on a dark boggy surface, slowly giving way. Little black dots floated in front of my eyes. The room swirled. I slid all the way to the floor.

"Kate, we'll work this out. Take a deep breath and listen to me now, because this is important. Don't talk to

Erica or Parsi before we meet tomorrow. Not one word."

Three raps on the door sent a current of electricity over my skin. I eyed the door. The knob twisted. Held. "It's occupied," I yelled. Surely the Explorer guy wouldn't pick the door lock on the woman's bathroom.

"Did you hear me?" Cedar said. "Don't talk to the Feds."

"Might be a problem since they're living on my property." My voice sounded strong, but fear swam in my stomach like three goldfish in a brandy glass. I rested my head against the wall.

"Weather," he said. "What?"

"If you have to say anything, talk about the weather. In a pinch, gardening."

"Gardening?" That was his advice? "I don't know anything about gardening."

"Fake it." He pushed a long-suffering breath through his nose. I pictured his condescending eye roll to the ceiling. "And remember Nathan Parsi can read your body language. Did you study the book?"

"You just gave it to me this afternoon. My day's been a little busy." Studying Cedar's hocus-pocus manual sat firmly on the not-gonna-happen-today line of my to-do list.

---

Thirty minutes later, I tiptoed through the kitchen without running into Parsi or his team of ninjas. Thankful I had no need to test my compelling knowledge of weather or gardening. Spartina was cemetery quiet.

I took a scalding shower, pulled on my favorite purple silk pajamas, and forced my eyes closed at two fifteen. One question after another whirled. Where were Calvin and Ben? Was my office bugged? Had I hurt more than helped Beth? My lids popped open. Would Parsi go after Peanut? Maybe. But Beth wasn't a criminal, and Pea selling Beth a car wasn't illegal.

Cedar would convince Parsi I was innocent, work a deal for Calvin. I turned on the lamp. Fifty percent of Cedar's caseload was pro bono work. Keeping miscreants out of jail, according to Granddad, was Cedar's penance for overcharging his wealthy clients. I climbed out of bed.

My wine party for one caught up with me, and I craved water like a hibiscus after a two-week drought. One of the many over-the-top luxuries in the master suite was a small refrigerator disguised as an antique chest. I kept it stocked with water. I grabbed one and chugged a full bottle, opened a second, and sat cross-legged on my bed. Even if the company didn't sell for the current book value, the family would survive financially, but the Barry name would never recover. A sudden relief washed over me: Owen and I were Landerses not Barrys.

I'd have to go back to work. Would I be bondable after the story hit the papers? Who was I kidding—my family's business was money laundering for the cartel. No matter my last name, my banking career was over.

And if the company didn't sell for the proposed value, I wouldn't be able to afford the upkeep on Spartina. Owen was just getting used to this house as his home. My chest constricted. I forgot to call, and I'd promised Owen we'd talk every day.

*You're analytical, Kate, born without the mothering gene.* I sat for a moment with my ex's reminder of my many maternal shortcomings. *Just because he said it, doesn't make it true,* my heart countered.

Any chance of sleep tonight would require calming my swirling thoughts. Think of something calming, better yet, read a boring book. I remembered Cedar's directive and located his BA Bible in my briefcase, Mastering the Secrets of Nonverbal Communication.

I thumbed through the first half. Turned back to the section on spotting a liar and started reading. In my world, scanning a person's body while conversing would be considered leering. Not exactly a page out of the How to Win Friends and Influence People manual. I plunked Cedar's book on top of another one headed for the trash, Ten Zen Seconds, an instructional guide to finding your purpose, power, and calm.

Finding my Zen wasn't going to help me convince a judge and jury I knew nothing about the money laundering business managed by my grandfather, the modern-day gangster who'd masqueraded as an upstanding businessman. And I was fairly certain a higher Zen state would fail to impress Marshal Parsi when I owned up to the scam currently being conducted under my nose by my low-life property manager, a guy who'd evidently taken Al Pacino's Godfather term 'go to the mattresses' to heart. And finding my Zen sure as heck wasn't going to help my slimeball cousin who'd left me holding the proverbial bag. I was screwed, and no amount of Zen was coming to my rescue.

I grabbed my laptop off the dresser and clicked on Ben's email account. Nothing. Not one word. The niggling soft voice of reason residing in my head was flashing a screeching alarm. Something was very wrong.

Calvin's preliminary report was still in the inbox, along with two more reports I had yet to read. One file was labeled Sanchez, which was a surprise. Ben didn't know Erica. Maybe I mentioned her in one of our conversations, and he assumed I'd want dirt on someone practically living under my roof.

I skimmed her summary page and read through her ten-year service record, her three promotions, and six service accolades and found no surprises until the final paragraph. Subject spent six weeks in rehab on three occasions in the last five years. I rechecked the dates. Her last rehab visit, a three-month stay, had been nine months ago. Her drug of choice, the report stated, was alcohol. Erica going into rehab knocked me back. But I squelched the snippet of guilt worming its way into my head. She was no longer a part of my life.

I opened the next report on Nathan Parsi, a file ten pages long. Two pages in I needed coffee, but it was already five thirty, and if I hurried, I could slip out of the house before sunup, before Parsi's men started their day of spying.

I threw on a navy pin-striped pencil skirt and a crisp white blouse with a mandarin collar. Stepped into three-inch Manolo Blahnik croc heels, and ran a brush through my hair before slapping on a little makeup. I studied my reflection in the mirror and considered my upcoming bank meetings. Adding concealer to hide the black circles, I swiped peach blush across my cheeks and chose a darker lipstick. It'd have to do.

At six o'clock, I unlocked the door connecting the house to the kitchen and faced Marshal Parsi sitting at the bar dunking an Oreo in a half-full glass of milk. My plan to sneak in, fill my to-go cup, and hide out in Savannah until my meeting with Cedar hit the skids and rolled into the danger zone. "Morning." I grabbed my travel mug from the top drawer of the coffee bar.

He grunted a greeting. The clock over the stove read 6:12. The pile of crumbs gathered on the counter by his glass indicated he'd been up awhile.

My coffee brewed, and I contemplated taking Cedar's advice, but no gardening tips came to mind. And really, weather? Better to rush out using the excuse of a morning meeting.

"Where are you going so early?" Parsi leveled his hooded brown eyes on me.

My gut turned into a jumbled guilty blob. "I have an appointment." At six forty-five? As impromptu excuses go, that one sucked. "It's supposed to rain today."

His forehead creased, his gaze lingered on me, then he turned his attention to the window.

A bright summer sun peeked over the horizon. Bold slashes of red and tangerine painted a cloudless morning sky. "Weatherman said we'd get hit with an afternoon rainstorm."

"Why don't you join me?" he patted the adjacent barstool.

I swallowed. "I need to get to the office and review a couple of files before my meeting."

"Won't take long. I have a few questions." His voice was soothing. Like elevator music or a soft summer rain or Vicodin.

Cedar's warning looped in my head. Weather.

Gardening.

"I'm really pushed this morning," I said.

## CHAPTER SEVENTEEN

*Nathan*

EVEN IN NATHAN'S sleep-deprived state, he recognized Kate's nervous energy. She danced from foot to foot while her coffee brewed, then stirred the lump of sugar in her cup long enough to churn butter.

"If you're too busy now," he said. "I can stop by your office later."

All her nerve actions ceased. She glanced at the clock over the stove. "I guess I can spare a few minutes." She made a production of rearranging a barstool against the wall as far from Nathan as possible.

He half stood and dragged his stool closer. "Was your trip to Charleston interesting?"

Her only tell was the color of her eyes—a vivid emerald melding into an intense mossy green. She swung her long hair down her back. "My appointment was canceled. I spent the day in the office." She propped a foot on the rim of her stool and relaxed against the wall. Except for the balled fist at her side, she almost exuded calm and composed.

"How about you? You arrest any bad guys?"

"Not yet."

Kate managed to look shifty and innocent at the same time. Like a kid with an empty hand, but cookie crumbs around her mouth.

"What did you want to ask me?" she prompted.

"Have you heard from your cousin?"

She relaxed, fear abated. "No."

"How about his wife?"

Her pupils dilated. The sound of the ice maker dropping another load broke the silence.

She sipped her coffee. "I'm guessing you want to play your version of twenty questions."

"My version?"

"You remember—that game where you ask the questions, and only I have to answer."

He ran his finger over the rim of his milk glass. "It's my favorite."

"So it seems." She shifted her weight, crossed then uncrossed her lean runner legs.

A jolt of heat slid from his throat to his abdomen. He leaned back and put space between them.

Her fisted hand moved over her breastbone. A nervous habit he'd picked up on and wasn't sure she was aware of.

"Will you go back into banking when you sell the family business?" he asked.

"Did I mention Cal and I were selling out?" Her fingertips drummed a rapid staccato on the bar's granite.

He waited.

She leaned forward. "I thought if I decided to sell out, I'd take up fortune telling, palm reading, that sort of thing." Her voice defined blasé. She tapped the middle of her forehead. "I've always been a touch clairvoyant."

Nathan laughed deep and long.

She let slip the barest hint of a smile. "You know anything about reading minds, Marshal?"

"Nope, not a thing. I read bodies." If he hadn't been quite so enamored with her mesmerizing almond eyes, he might have missed the color as it faded from dazzling to just shy of flat. A current ran over his skin and sizzled the air between them.

"And you're good at this body-reading thing?" she said in a voice hovering just on the edge of a nervous whisper.

His gaze moved from her eyes and meandered down, hesitated briefly on her mouth before landing on her clenched hand. He rested his forearms on the bar. "I am." His voice as smooth as his father's eighteen-year-old scotch.

Kate swallowed. "Any chance you're planning to practice on mine?"

Three inches separated his forearm and her fingertips. Fire, like tendrils of liquid heat, slid through his body. "Oh, I'm past practicing, Kate. I'm all the way up to expert."

She stared into his face with an intensity usually displayed by surgeons with a scalpel in hand.

"Must be yours," he said.

"Pardon?"

He tapped the hem of her jacket.

After a beat, her eyelids fluttered, and understanding spread over her face. She jerked the phone from her pocket and jumped to her feet. Her barstool hit the wall. "I need to take this."

By the time Nathan heard the slam of her office door, he had no doubt reading Kate Landers would be the career challenge of his life.

# CHAPTER EIGHTEEN

*Katelyn*

HALFWAY DOWN THE long hall connecting the kitchen to my office, I slowed enough to catch my breath. I vowed the next time I was forced to converse with Marshal Parsi—weather only. Not even a debate on roses versus gardenias was safe. I shut and locked my office door and read Ben's text.

—Go 2: chat-avenue.com, adult, nn-snooker—

I considered a glass of wine to calm my nerves but imbibing before breakfast wasn't likely to help me decode this cryptic message. I sat behind my desk and opened my laptop. I entered the chat room and clicked on the button marked adult. I quickly figured out nn was an acronym for nickname; I retrieved a two-line message addressed to Snooker.

—Go 2: hideyourass.com, msg brd; nn Clara—

I accessed the website featuring a donkey's behind logo with a mantra plastered across the top of the screen—Messages sent from this site will bounce your ass from Bangkok to Dubai.

I really wanted that glass of wine.

I found Clara's name. Her one-line message consisted of a link to another chat room, but this time the primary language appeared to be Middle Eastern. I couldn't read squat, but I clicked the blinking green tab, and a list popped up. Scrolling down, Ben's name was the third option from the bottom. I clicked on the adjacent button.

—Today, Shorty's n Midpoint Bluff. 11 AM. DON'T BE FOLLOWED!!!—

Ben must've found Calvin. Relief slid up my spine with a ration of trepidation hard on its heels. I'd never been to Shorty's, and my only view of Midpoint Bluff had been from a boat on the Chantilly River. Finding the restaurant shouldn't be difficult, but not being followed meant evading a marshal, a DEA superstar, and the six-ninja entourage.

I weighed the risk of texting Cedar, but if Nathan had satellite surveillance on Spartina a text message would blow any chance of sneaking away. If Cedar joined us in Midpoint Bluff, we could return to Spartina, meet with Nathan, and put this whole nightmare to rest by tonight. I said a please-keep-me-out-of-jail prayer and sent Cedar a text.

I debated going to the office, but there were only two roads from Savannah to Midpoint Bluff and both were busy highways. Slipping away from Spartina seemed the easier choice.

I played spot the lawman out of the back window and waited for Cedar's callback. I also tried to call Owen, but Uncle Stanley said he'd already left for his riding lesson.

I searched a couple of sites online, found a photo of a beautiful white stallion with red ribbons braided into his mane, and texted the picture to Owen.

—My dream horse! What's yours? Miss you! Call me!!!—

At ten o'clock I gave up on Cedar texting me back, grabbed my wallet and a burner phone, and hightailed it to the garage. Just in case Nathan's men were around, I killed a few minutes searching for an elusive something in my Hummer.

I worked my way around to the garage's main door and peeked outside. No bodies milling around. A hedge of twelve-foot oleanders ran the length of the building. I stepped through the door, slid behind the hedge, and beelined for the barn.

The old red farm truck, a rattletrap parked in one of the bays, turned over on the first try. Thank goodness my caretaker was a maintenance hound, and Granddad never bothered to install security cameras in the barn. Patting the dash, I gave the old girl gas.

I used the cow pens as a buffer, drove over a cattle grid and down a one-lane path leading to a back road. I made it off Spartina land, drove twenty miles of back roads, and blew past the sign welcoming me to Midpoint Bluff—population two hundred and fifty.

The tiny fishing village located halfway between Savannah consisted of ramshackle doublewides and fishing shacks along the riverbank. I parked beside an empty boat trailer at the Midpoint Bluff Marina and followed a clay road to the restaurant.

Shorty's was a dive, a run-down fishing shack with their proximity to the river being the only salvaging point. There were two clunkers parked by the back door and no other vehicles in the lot. Either Ben was late, or he'd arrived by boat. A flats skiff was moored to the adjacent dock, but the dinghy didn't look capable of maneuvering out of the river without sinking.

I opened Shorty's screened door, crossed a sagging porch, and walked to the bar. One whiff of stale cigarette smoke and rancid fried food, and I backtracked to the screened porch.

I had my pick of tables and chose one against the wall to give myself a clear view of the dock, and the front door.

"What can I get you?" The waitress wore a pink t-shirt

and Daisy Duke shorts that barely covered her privates but did a great job showing off her killer legs.

"I'll take anything diet."

"We've got Bud Light."

"Something soft."

Her forehead creased.

"A Diet Coke or Pepsi."

She laughed. "Oh, that kind of soft." She put down a beverage napkin.

"What time does your kitchen open?"

"It's open. We only have appetizers, but everything's made fresh." She handed me a piece of paper with a handwritten list of options, all priced at ten dollars. "Our specialty's the fried pickles."

"I'm expecting friends." I set the menu aside. "I'll wait for them before ordering."

She stuck a pencil behind her ear. "You just come from a funeral or something?"

"Pardon?"

"Your suit."

I was still in my bank meeting business attire, including three-inch croc heels, a bit overdressed for Shorty's. I started to explain, then reconsidered. "Yes."

"Sorry for your loss. Let me know if you change your mind about the fried pickles. Name's Tori."

By twenty past noon, I'd shredded my napkin, and my drinking straw had chew holes running down the side. I shot no-show Ben a text and ordered another Diet Coke. By one-fifteen, I'd finished off a heaping plate of fried dills, and a dull ache trod across my forehead like an army of ants building a new sand bed. I texted Cedar and postponed our meeting for two hours. At 1:40, I called Ben a wash, along with a few other names.

I trudged back down the road nursing a blister. Manolo Blahnik's weren't exactly walking shoes. I spotted Ben's yellow sports car nestled between my farm truck and the empty boat trailer. No one was in the Corvette, so I limped to the marina's front door in search of Ben.

The marina office consisted of a cash register, two coolers, and an ice maker. A brunette, with a braid hanging to the top of her jeans, sat on a barstool in the corner. She threaded yellow and brown beads onto a string and hummed along with Bonnie Raitt's Something to Talk About.

"Excuse me. Have you seen the owner of that car?" I pointed to the Corvette.

"Nope." She rifled through the bead box and didn't bother to look up.

"You didn't see him park? Notice which way he went?"

"Nope."

Kind of hard to believe she'd missed a bright yellow roadster. I kept my voice light and conversational. "How long's the car been parked in your lot?"

She inhaled a long-suffering breath and dropped a bead back into the box. Her gaze moved over the length of my body, hesitated on my three-inch heels, and raised her eyes back to mine. She was clearly unimpressed with my fishing attire. "About an hour and a half ago, I put a boat in the water. When I got back inside, a clunker and a shiny little two-seater had made themselves at home in my lot." Her eyes squinted into thin slits. "This here's a private establishment, and my lot's for paying customers."

I glanced through the window at her fifteen unused spaces, mumbled a disingenuous apology, and left the marina lady to her love beads.

I peered through the Corvette windows. The door locks weren't engaged, and a white envelope with my name printed in bold black ink lay on the passenger seat. A foreboding tingling slid down my spine and lit up every cell in my body.

I opened the passenger door, and a smell rivaling rotting mackerel kicked me back a step. I cupped my hand over my nose and grabbed the envelope, then slammed the door and backed up ten feet. I raised the flap and pulled out a picture of Owen and me on Barry Island. My heart skipped its own beat, ground to a stop, then kicked into triple time.

There was no plausible reason Ben would have a picture of Owen and me standing in the middle of the cow path staring down the airboat. The scream in my head silenced midhowl as if someone pushed my pause button. I couldn't make sense of the photograph.

A cold slice of fear ripped through me, and I had an overwhelming need to leave for Florida. I stuck my hand inside the envelope searching for something to give a reasonable explanation for Ben's absence and pulled out a piece of paper.

Let sleeping dogs lie, or your son will pay the price. You came close to losing him once.

Will you chance it again? This time for good.

Sending him to Florida won't protect him. Proof in the trunk.

A tsunami wave of panic slammed my body and forced air from my lungs.

Owen.

I keeled over as if someone had thrust a battering ram into my solar plexus. My baby. Someone was threatening to hurt Owen. I didn't understand anything that was happening.

Let sleeping dogs lie, or your son will pay.

I called my mother on my cell. Didn't breathe until I heard her voice. "Are you all right?" My tone was harsh, and I forced myself to swallow. Blood rushed in my ears as loud as waves breaking on a stormy day. "Is Owen okay?"

"You're worse than a mother hen with a new brood."

My mother's laughter assuaged my deepest fear. "He's fine."

I stared at the note I couldn't tell her about over the phone.

"Can I talk to Owen?" I had to hear his voice, satisfy myself he was really okay.

"Sure." She called Owen to the phone.

"Hey, Mom. When are you coming?"

I glanced at the note in my hand. "Tonight. I'll be there right after dinner." I listened as he described his morning. I murmured and made all the "I'm interested" sounds, relieved to hear about the nothingness of his day. "I'll see you in a few hours. I promise." I disconnected.

Proof in the trunk.

I fumbled with the car door and located the trunk release. The lid popped open. The stench rolled out thick and foul.

# CHAPTER NINETEEN

*Katelyn*

FIVE POLICE CRUISERS surrounded the Midpoint Bluff Marina's parking lot, lights blazing, sirens muted. Nathan clipped on his badge and ducked under the yellow crime scene tape. He scanned the lot and spotted Kate, still dressed in the same business suit as this morning, sitting on the tailgate of an old red Ford truck he recognized from Spartina's barn. Willie stood by her side, his arm wrapped around her shoulders.

A tall lanky woman with braided hair stepped from a door marked office. She hailed the first cop in her path, which happened to be Erica.

Nathan kept walking. Ten feet from the Corvette, he instinctively switched to mouth breathing. A uniformed officer handed him a container of Vicks, and he smeared salve on his upper lip. Then he peered into the trunk and assessed Calvin Thompson. Fetal position, hands tied, no cuts, no abrasions. No visible marks to the face or neck. A single bullet hole pierced the forehead. Clean shot. Close range.

Erica angled in Kate's direction, stopping across the blacktop as if the asphalt under her feet pissed her off.

He sprinted to catch up.

Erica planted her feet in front of Kate and jerked her

thumb over her shoulder toward the Corvette. "I want to talk to your private dick."

Kate's gaze skimmed past Erica and locked on Nathan. "Me, too." A light sheen of perspiration covered her face and neck.

Erica leaned in. "Where is he?"

Kate raised her palms five inches and dropped them to her thighs as if she held twenty-pound weights in each hand. "I don't know."

Nathan nudged Erica aside and stood in front of Kate. "Sorry for your loss."

Kate's eyes filled. Phony tears were as easy as wiping on a mentholated rub under the bottom lashes. But Kate wore no sunglasses, and with a cloudless sky, the afternoon sun bore down in full force. A pupil the size of an eraser's tip was impossible to fake in bright sunlight.

"Were you supposed to meet your cousin here?" Nathan asked.

Kate hesitated, shook her head. "I came to meet Ben." The cadence of her voice was off, whether it was the irregular breathing or from fatigue, he couldn't be sure. But either was symptomatic of shock.

"Ben Snider?"

She crossed her arms over her waist and rocked in place. "Yes."

Rocking was a natural self-soothing response. "He's the private investigator you hired?"

Her eyelids fluttered. "Yes." She continued to sway.

A dark blue Chevrolet with sirens blaring cruised to a stop. A man wearing jeans and Western boots stepped from the car. He possessed a lawman's swagger, and Nathan pegged him as Sheriff Jim Nelson. The sheriff, six-two by Nathan's estimation, could easily tip the scales over the two-hundred mark. He surveyed the surroundings, zeroed in on Willie, then Nathan. Nathan needed no special training to ascertain the sheriff wasn't pleased to have federal officers on his turf, usurping his power.

Nathan turned to Erica. "Give Sheriff Nelson a run down on our case while I talk to Kate."

Erica shot Kate one last scathing glare and strode away wearing the burr-up-her-butt expression she'd donned since receiving Willie's call.

One of the three forensic officers called for Willie and saved Nathan from sending him on a nonsense errand.

Willie raised a just-a-minute finger, then patted Kate's arm. "I'll be back in just a minute."

Her eyes followed her friend like a puppy with separation issues.

The forensic team gathered evidence. Bagging and logging and working around a police photographer snapping a continuous stream of pictures aimed at the Corvette's trunk.

Nathan caught a fume of vomit by the front tire that he suspected was Kate's. "You thirsty?"

Kate looked up with vacant eyes, managed a nod.

He walked to Willie's car, removed a bottle of water from a cooler on the back seat. Kate chugged the liquid like a drunk on a binge.

An ambulance swung into the lot; two attendants piled from the vehicle. Nathan did a quick head count; they were up to twenty-two. He turned his attention back to Kate. "Why'd you hire Mr. Snider?"

Her gaze flitted from left to right and landed on Erica and Sheriff Nelson.

Nathan slid sideways and blocked her view. "Is Mr. Snider a friend?"

"Yes." She searched the lot and found Willie working with the forensic crew. "No. Not really a friend. He's done work for me in the past."

"Who asked for the meeting?" Nathan kept his voice low and soothing.

"Ben." She'd hesitated a few seconds before giving her answer, but he didn't get the impression it was an evasion tactic, more an inability to focus.

"How'd he contact you?"

She ran a hand down her throat. "Text."

Snider must've called her on a burner, but he'd hold that for later. "Why did Snider ask for a meeting?"

"I'm not sure." Kate pointed at the bar on the corner. "He never came."

"What made you look in Snider's trunk?"

She buried her head in her hands. "I'm dizzy. The smell."

Nathan wasn't sure how much longer she'd be able to keep it together.

"Kate."

She raised her head; he waited for her eyes to refocus. "What made you look in the trunk?"

She covered her trembling mouth with her hand. "I saw Ben's car and went to look for him."

Erica walked across the lot and rejoined them.

Nathan leaned against the tailgate. "Seems odd you'd look in the trunk."

"Car wasn't locked." She had the cadence and tone of a sleepwalker.

He let her answer rest.

She raised the water bottle as if she wondered where it came from. "The car smelled like dead fish."

He caught the hitch in her voice. A normal reaction under the circumstances. He waited.

Erica stepped forward. "Why'd you hire an investigator?"

Kate folded her arms and hugged her middle. "To find Calvin. "

"Did he?" Erica asked.

"Don't know." Kate lifted her shoulder as if it were an

afterthought. "Until the text this morning, I hadn't heard from Ben since yesterday."

Her cognitive skills were improving. "Which phone?" Nathan asked.

"What?"

"Snider didn't call your cell." Kate's forehead creased.

Nathan stared unblinking into her eyes.

She cut her gaze left, then right, like a hunted animal looking for an open space to run. "I have more than one phone."

Erica pointed her notebook at Kate. "What reason would you have to use a burner if you weren't hiding your cousin?"

"I'm not." Kate looked at the Corvette. "I wasn't."

Nathan didn't buy it, and based on Erica's bite-me look, neither did she. He'd let Erica have a go. Maybe she could rile Kate enough to get to the truth.

"If you weren't involved in Cal's disappearance, why'd you need a burner?" Erica asked.

Kate's coloring rose, but she made no effort to answer.

"Two kinds of people use throwaways." Erica made a show of thumping her notebook on her palm. "People without credit and people who have secret conversations. First option doesn't fit." Erica's cop stare was identical to her bite-me gaze.

"Your man in the gray Explorer follows me everywhere." Kate rubbed her forehead as if a headache were brewing. "I assumed you'd have a tap on my phone." She looked at Nathan. "I'm not a criminal. My privacy's a civil right."

"No one's sitting on you," Erica said.

"Your man in the Explorer followed me from Charleston to Savannah. And last night he stalked me back to Spartina." Her voice jumped higher with each word. Two forensic cops glanced in their direction.

"Erica's right." Nathan brought their conversing volume down a few rungs. "We don't have an agent assigned to you."

"You tapped my phone." Kate glared at Erica. "I had a right to know."

Erica didn't rise to the bait.

"No." Nathan pushed off the tailgate. "You don't have the right to know."

Kate's attention swung back to the Corvette. Two attendants loaded Calvin's body on the stretcher.

"We're done here," Nathan said to Erica, then motioned Willie over. "Appreciate it if you'd ask Sheriff Nelson to forward his preliminary report to my email as soon as it's available."

Erica pocketed her notebook. "Can one of your men drive Kate's truck back to Spartina?"

Kate slid off the tailgate. "I'll drive my truck."

"You'll ride with us," Erica said.

Kate's gaze swiveled from Nathan to Erica to Willie. "Am I under arrest?"

"Not yet," Erica said. If Kate were slow and dimwitted, she might've missed the challenge in Erica's voice.

Nathan stepped between them. "I'll drive Kate's truck." He motioned Kate to the passenger side, passed Erica and lowered his voice. "Restrain yourself, Agent."

Willie gave a hand signal to one of his officers and the yellow tape dropped to the ground. Nathan started the engine and rolled out of the lot. The twenty-minute drive should be enough time to secure Beth Thompson's current location.

"I've got to call Beth," Kate said as if Nathan had spoken his intentions out loud. "She'll have to fly back to Savannah."

"Where is she?"

She reached under the seat and fished a phone from her purse. Thumbing through a couple of screens, she placed a call and left a message for a callback. "Can you find Beth with her phone's GPS?"

"Her cell's dead."

"I gave her another phone. If I give you the number, can you locate her?"

"Won't even require a warrant."

Kate nodded. Then, as if registering his words, she slowly rotated her neck and eyed him with the intensity of a cobra. "Why wouldn't a warrant be required?"

"It's a burner phone in a drug case. Beth's also the widow and deserves notification of her husband's death."

"I want to be the one to tell Beth about Calvin."

Nathan made a left turn onto the interstate. "Not a job any cop covets. Even Erica shouldn't argue."

Kate leaned her head against the seat rest. "Don't bet on it."

"Why'd you give Beth a throwaway?"

Kate punched another number on her phone. She asked to speak to Cedar. Her voice remained in control until she described her cousin's body stuffed inside the trunk. She asked Cedar to meet her at Spartina. Then she stopped talking and focused on whatever the attorney said. "Are you serious?"

Kate shook her head in disgust as if Nathan had just farted at a fancy dinner party. "Okay. Yes. Okay, I hear you. No. I'm driving to Florida tonight to tell her in person."

The rumble of Cedar's answer drifted from the phone, but Nathan couldn't decipher the words.

Kate grunted. "Why would they do that?" She listened.

"Too bad. Stalking liars don't always get what they want."

Nathan would bet his next paycheck Cedar just told Kate that the airboat was registered to the DEA.

## CHAPTER TWENTY

*Katelyn*

CEDAR EXPLODED INTO the library as if propelled by a tornado and pulled me into his arms. "I'm sorry you were the one to find Calvin's body." He held me at arm's length and sighed. "You bend or break in this life, sweetheart."

The image of Cal stuffed inside Ben's trunk slammed into my head, then disappeared like a game of hide-and-seek.

"You need to leave for Florida as soon as possible." Cedar nodded as he spoke. "Break the news to Roslyn." His take-charge attitude, a demeanor I'd found condescending in the past, enveloped me like a comforting cloud.

The dike trapping my emotions burst. One tear escaped, then another; after the third tear, I turned into a sobbing mess. "You should have seen him. They jammed him inside a trunk not big enough to hold a set of golf clubs." Words jumbled and twisted on my tongue. "And Cal's eyes were open." A hazy image of Cal's face swam in front of me. "But they reminded me of a cheap doll's faded rubber eyes." I swiped at my tears.

Cedar guided me to the bar, reached for the brandy,

and filled a glass. I hated brandy. He shoved the snifter into my hand. "Drink."

I set the drink aside and washed my hands in the bar sink. I couldn't get the smell of death out of my nostrils.

Cedar picked up the brandy. "Drink. It'll help clear your head."

I sipped and breathed through the burn.

He grabbed a Coke from the refrigerator and led me to the sofa. He pointed to the brandy. "Finish. You'll need the fortification. The marshal wants to talk to you."

"He already questioned me at the marina."

"That was round one," Cedar said in his version of a conspiratorial whisper. The words came out slightly lower than an announcement over a loudspeaker.

I glanced at the closed door, and my heart bumped against my rib cage. "There was something else in Ben's car." I retrieved a message from my wallet and handed it to Cedar.

He put on his readers and scanned the note. "Where did you find this?"

"On the passenger seat of Ben's car. In a white envelope addressed to me." My hands shook so violently that I had to place my glass on the table. "I called Mom. Owen's fine. And Parsi still has his security detail at Uncle Stanley's."

"Your shakes are a delayed reaction to shock." He placed his arm across the back of the sofa and rubbed my shoulder. "The brandy will help."

"I can't drink anymore." I wrapped a throw around my shoulders. "There was a picture of Owen and me on Barry Island in the envelope."

He held out his hand and wiggled his fingers. "Let me see."

"I stowed the envelope with the photo under the passenger seat of the farm truck. But Parsi insisted on driving me back to Spartina, and with the let sleeping dogs lie warning, I assumed that included not blubbering to a US marshal. Until we talked, I didn't want to bring the envelope to anyone's attention." My head pounded like a woodpecker foraging for food. I went in search of aspirin, poured a glass of water, and swallowed three.

Cedar's fingernail tapped his coke can. "Describe the picture."

"Owen and I were on the island. In a stand-off with the airboat. Based on the angle of the shot, the photographer had to be sitting in a tree."

I returned to the sofa, kicked off my shoes, and wrapped the blanket around my shoulders. "If you're right about the boat being registered to DEA, who do you think took the photo?"

"Oh, I'm right about the DEA. Printed out a copy of the boat registration as proof." Cedar sipped his drink. "Don't let it slip that you know about the airboat. At the right time, we'll use it as leverage and snatch the punchbowl before their party starts."

Cedar gripped the threatening note between his forefinger and thumb. "I think the Cabral boys sent you this message."

"Boys?"

"My sources say Juan Cabral retired six months back. His nephews run the show now."

"Your sources?"

"Some of my clients have checkered pasts—a couple are still connected."

Alarm cinched my throat, and I couldn't sit still. I jumped to my feet, shed the throw, and paced. Hearing the worst possible option spoken out loud made the unbelievable real. My family was and is still linked to a drug cartel, and now thugs were giving me ultimatums. "The sleeping dog reference is the warehouse scam. They want me to bury what I've found and are fortifying their demand by threatening Owen. Did you review the spreadsheet I emailed you?"

"Haven't had a free minute."

"It's important, Cedar. Millions of dollars important." Thirty years of washing dirty money drilled down to a one-page report. I waited for him to answer. "Cedar."

He finally nodded and picked up the note again. "This reference to losing Owen again." He ran his finger over the second line. "They're talking about your custody case."

"Or Adam's accident. Owen could have been killed." The tremors began in my heart and spread down my arms, tingling my fingers.

"I hadn't thought of that." He rubbed his temples as if stress had finally penetrated his cool façade. "Either way, they know a lot about your past."

"I can't reach Beth. Do you think the cartel threatened her?" My stomach burned as if the brandy mixed with the aspirin had ignited a flambé. "The threat against Owen, Calvin's death, the warehouses, Barry Island—it's all tied together." I walked back and sat on the arm of the sofa. "You closed all the company's real estate deals. You never suspected any discrepancies in the values?"

His fatherly concern mutated into a mask of irritation. "I'm not a property appraiser. I prepared and filed legal documents. And Noah wouldn't have appreciated me meddling in his business."

True. Granddad had no patience with meddling. And an attorney working as a closing agent would have no reason to visit the real property. "Hard to believe something didn't jump out as suspicious in thirty years."

"Could say the same about you." Cedar eyed me over his reading glasses. "You've been intimately involved in the company for three years. Did you suspect?"

I yielded with a dip of my head. "You're right."

He dropped the note on the cushion between us. "Tuck that away for now."

Six lines, written in neat black print and designed to create panic. It worked. I folded the paper into quarters and stuck it in my wallet. "I should have listened to Erica and sent Mom and Owen to a safe house with a full team watching them." It wasn't the first time I'd ignored Erica's advice and regretted my decision.

The worst days of my life replayed in my head like the scene snippets of a movie in fast forward. The agonizing month when Adam and Owen had disappeared. Weeks of searching.

Adam, Owen, and Erica stepping off the plane. Police hauling a handcuffed Adam away.

Owen screaming for his dad.

Erica pleading for me to be reasonable. My stubborn refusal. Owen clinging to Erica. Refusing my comfort.

Owen's face when we buried his father a year later. Begging me to promise I would never, ever leave him. Ever.

And here I was, a hundred miles away, skirting the law and facing arrest.

A phone buzzed. It had to be Ben. I rushed to my desk, but the ringing didn't come from a burner. My iPhone flashed.

—Come 2 kitchen. ES—

A message from Erica. I slipped into my shoes and answered.

—in 5—

I had three text messages from Owen. I skimmed through them. A picture of a black stallion racing across an open field gripped my heart. I would buy Owen a horse as soon as I found a way out of this mess.

I texted back a thumbs up, a smiley face, and a big red heart.

Cedar sat, hands crossed and as quiet as a kid in the principal's office.

"I have one more thing to tell you," I said. "Do you know Cecil Lucifer Cummings?"

"No. Who's he?"

"An alias. I found old passports in Cummings's name with Granddad's photograph."

Cedar reared back, mouth agape. I would have expected less reaction if I had said my grandfather had been a resident of Mars. "Where'd he use the passport?"

"Central and South America."

Cedar removed his glasses and rubbed his eyes. "That stays in this room. Do not mention Cummings to anyone. Even in your sleep."

"I'm sure it's connected to the money laundering scheme for the Cabrals." My heartbeat danced like the barrel of monkeys had escaped the nursery rhyme and landed in my chest. "There's no way to explain away thirty years of washing dirty money. Calvin's dead, and Parsi has a murder to investigate." Realization filtered from my brain into every pore of my body. "Cal owned half the company. Barry Real Estate and Development will be one of the first places Parsi will look for his killer."

The room faded, and a floating sensation filled my body. I slid to the sofa, inhaled to a five count, and slowly expelled the air from the bottom of my diaphragm. "I have no choice but to be honest and show Parsi the note. Then ask for his help."

Cedar shook my knee. "Are you all right?"

I rested my head against the cushion and closed my eyes. "Just give me a minute."

"You need to forget about asking Parsi for help. Word on the street is the DEA has a snitch. Two agents were killed in Charleston. One was undercover. It's why they sent a US marshal to take over Erica's DEA team. Parsi's a trained behaviorist. His primary job's to find the snitch."

I opened my eyes and raised my head. My brain felt as if it'd been marinated in mud. "What did you say?"

"One of Parsi's men is a Cabral snitch. There's no such thing as a safe DEA house for your family. If the cartel's behind Calvin's murder, and they're threatening your son…" He gave me a sage nod.

My thoughts spun. I was a law-abiding citizen in the middle of a family of crooks who did business with the freaking cartel. And I remembered from eighth-grade civics: ignorance would be no excuse. Panic gripped my chest and squeezed. I switched to timed breathing to let my heart settle.

Cedar removed his phone from his jacket pocket. "If you want your family in a safe house, we'll create one. Of course, you'll go, too. But you can't up and disappear and still expect the authorities to believe you're not involved with the Cabrals."

"I can leave the spreadsheet for Parsi to find."

"You secure your family's safety before giving a tell-all to the Feds." Cedar's fingers flew over the keys of his phone. "I have a friend with properties on the West Coast." He walked to the bar, propped his phone against the wall, and poured the rest of his coke into a glass of ice.

His phone buzzed. "I've pulled in a favor. Found a friend who'll rent you her house in California. It'll take a few hours to work out the details, but you should be able to leave by tomorrow."

"What will we tell Parsi and Erica?"

"Nothing." Cedar paced the room with his drink. "You're not remanded, and I'll make sure we keep it that way. You're free to leave, and we'll tell them you're going to visit with Roslyn to give her the news about

Cal in person. Parsi has security there, so he should be okay with that arrangement."

He rejoined me on the sofa. "When you and your family disappear, my story will be that you were exhausted and are recouping in an unnamed health spa." He patted my knee. "While you're gone, I'll contact the banks and smooth things over."

I didn't think even Cedar could smooth away bank fraud, but that was tomorrow's problem.

"I'll handle it, sweetheart. Just stay calm."

For the first time since I opened the trunk of Ben's car, I felt a modicum of peace, like an elixir of calm pouring into my veins.

I went to my desk, unlocked the bottom drawer, and removed a copy of the spreadsheet. I folded it in thirds and placed it in my purse. "Maybe I should email a copy of the spreadsheet to Parsi once we arrive in California. Ben showed me how to send anonymous messages. I could walk Parsi through the ins and outs of the money trail. Prove I planned to cooperate."

"Don't email anything to the Feds until I give you the okay." Cedar handed me a tissue.

I hadn't realized I was crying.

I tried registering the emotions sliding through my body, sadness, relief, fear, but a relentless aching heart trumped them all. "Once Mom and Owen are settled, I'll return and face the consequences."

"Don't leave California without talking to me first." He pulled me into his arms. "I'll see you through this. You may be worse for wear, but you'll survive."

"Without going to jail?" My voice broke, and I let go, sobbing into his neck like a five-year-old who'd fallen off her bike.

"Do as I say, and there'll be no jail." He gave me his handkerchief.

I wiped my face, tucked my blouse into my skirt, and attempted composure. "I'm afraid something's happened to Ben."

"If the cartel's behind Cal's murder and Erica's team has a snitch…" Cedar's voice lowered to a true whisper. "No telling what happened to your investigator. You want to be very careful in this meeting with Parsi. Letting sleeping dogs lie could mean no confiding to the cops."

"They're living in my house." I hiccupped and glanced around for my water.

"Don't admit anything. Get your family safe first."

I opened my mouth to argue, but Cedar's hand shot into the air. "Just consider leaving for a week. That's all I'm saying. Spend time with your son; if you still want to confess, I'll stand beside you."

It didn't quite sit straight on my shoulders, but murderers had threatened Owen. "The sooner I admit to what I know, the better." I was sure withholding information from federal agents had to be an enormous risk.

"No disrespect to your highfalutin' morals, young lady." Cedar's tone seethed with impatience. "Keeping your mouth shut a few days is an understandable response to your cousin's murder and a threat to your boy." He placed both hands on my shoulders and gave me a wake-up-fool shake. "You or your mother could be next. You have no choice, Katelyn."

"Joseph manages the warehouses," I said. "He knows I'm not involved with the cartel. He can attest to my innocence."

"Considering Joseph must be on the cartel's payroll, I'd say he's not much of an insurance policy." Cedar sighed, expelling enough carbon dioxide to keep the rainforest alive for a month. "I'm the one who'll keep you out of jail. And I can defend your actions to a judge all day long."

"You assumed control over the business when your grandfather had a debilitating stroke." He strode across the library in grandstanding courtroom fashion. "You focused on restructuring the company. Left running the warehouses to your property manager, Joseph Lafferty." Three sharp raps interrupted Cedar's defense of my honor. He placed his forefinger to his lips and cracked the door.

Erica stuck her head inside and caught my eye. "We need to talk."

"We're in a conference," Cedar said. "Shouldn't take much longer, another ten minutes or so." He pushed the door.

She blocked the bottom with the toe of her boot. "Now." Erica's tone left no room for rebuttal.

My eyes locked with hers, and raw guilt seized my heart. How could I stand on the opposite side of the law? It went against every rule I'd ever lived by. "I'm ready."

"We're in the kitchen." Erica turned and then looked back. "You're not under arrest. You won't need your attorney."

Cedar flashed his winning, mega-watt-courtroom smile. "Oh, I think I'll tag along."

# CHAPTER TWENTY-ONE

## *Katelyn*

CEDAR AND I followed Erica down Spartina's main hall. My feet grew heavier with each step, like a condemned criminal taking her last walk as a free woman.

"I need to get something from my car." Cedar winked at me, then half sprinted past Erica and disappeared through the atrium that connected the house with the kitchen.

A cold sweat worked its way over my skin. I had no idea what Cedar's twinkling eye meant or why he'd chosen to abandon me. We entered the atrium, and even at five o'clock in the afternoon, the glass ceiling bathed the room in sunlight.

The space was cozy and cheery with yellow chintz cushions and white wicker furniture, but no manufactured comfort could dispel the wave of trepidation washing over me. My knees buckled, and I slid into the closest chair.

I was trapped in a circle of deception. Evading and postponing the truth about my family's past was a lie, no matter how I wrapped it. A wave of maternal yearning penetrated so deep it caught my heart. Owen had to be kept safe. Nothing else mattered.

Erica glanced over her shoulder and stopped. "Are you okay?" I motioned for her to go on, but she backtracked and stood in front of me. Her olive skin seemed to give off refracted light; her eyes were serious and watchful but held no worry or concern. "You need a glass of water or something?"

"I'm fine." I rose and forced my feet forward. My world was compressed into three words: get to Owen.

Parsi was the only person in the kitchen and had made himself comfortable at the breakfast table. His briefcase lay open on one of the chairs, and he studied his small, ever-present notebook. He looked up.

I stood paralyzed. I weighed my instinct to beg his help and regurgitate my deepest secrets—the threatening note, the money laundering, the alias passport—against the bombshell a cartel mole had embedded himself or herself in Nathan's group. If Cedar was right about the snitch, my safest option was to wait until Owen and Mom were safely harbored in California.

Finding resolve, I slid onto the bench seat opposite Nathan.

Erica checked something on her phone and pulled on her earlobe, a nervous habit I remembered her having in high school. Whatever she was reading made her uneasy, or maybe it was what was to come.

Nathan leaned forward. "We'd like to review a few things. Let's start with why you hired Ben Snider." His tone came across as easy, almost friendly.

But I wasn't Nathan Parsi's friend. "I told you why."

He scanned my face as if he planned to run the results through his list of known felons, searching for a hit.

I stared back.

Cedar practically danced into the kitchen, placed his briefcase beside the table, and joined me. He looked animated, eyes sparkling with expectation, like butting heads with the Feds was a favored pastime.

Fury swept like a dust storm through my body. I

crammed every ounce of my irritation into a seething look and directed it at Cedar.

Nathan flipped through the pages of his notebook. "Earlier, at the marina, you said you hired Mr. Snider to find Calvin."

"Yes, that's right."

Nathan clicked his pen open, closed, open. "But that's not accurate." Cedar opened his mouth to speak, and Nathan wagged an index finger without looking away from me. "What difference does it make why she hired Ben Snider?" Cedar said.

It'd take more than a wagging finger to shut Cedar up.

"How is the reason pertinent?" he added.

"Snider summoned Kate," Nathan said. "Then didn't show up for the appointment." He raised a brow, "But he left her dead cousin in his trunk."

Tears filled my eyes, surprising me, and from Nathan's expression, a surprise to him as well. "Ben didn't kill Calvin. He didn't even know him." An unadulterated sureness engulfed my voice.

"You think your cousin's killer just happened to steal Snider's car?"

"I don't know," I said. "But I can't reach Ben. Maybe they've hurt him, too."

Erica blew a scoffing breath worthy of a politician caught in a lie.

Nathan referred to his notes. "You called Snider late Sunday evening. But Calvin wasn't missing on Sunday. You met with him Monday morning. Locating Calvin couldn't have been the initial reason you contacted Snider."

"Kate has lost a close family member."

"Not all that close," Erica chimed in.

Cedar shot Erica a scathing glare. "Berating Kate over details that have nothing to do with his death is counterproductive." Cedar's rebuttal shot forward like machine gun fire.

Stone-faced, Nathan didn't bother to acknowledge my attorney. It was as if his roaring tirade held no more importance than a two-year-old's temper tantrum.

I hadn't anticipated the timing discrepancy of hiring Ben, but I should have. A couple of plausible excuses ran through my head, and I decided to go with the truth. "I didn't say the original reason I'd hired Ben was to find Calvin, just that I asked him to find my cousin after he disappeared."

Erica perked up. "Then why did you originally hire Snider?"

Nathan sat back and crossed his arms, reminding me of Owen when his mind was made up, and nothing I said would change it.

"Sunday, after the airboat stalked Owen and me, I returned to Spartina." I hoped the edge in my voice would be taken as steel, not the nervous jitters spiking inside me. "A dive boat, which I later learned was Calvin's, blocked my lift." I glanced at the paper in front of Erica. Even upside down, I recognized my Orlando address. I slid my hand to the sheet and swiveled it to face me.

She slapped a palm over the paper and pulled it back.

I made a show of rolling my eyes and shaking my head. Checking into my life in Orlando was a waste of time, but knowing they were digging into my past pushed my anxiety up a few degrees. Their next logical step would be to dig into the family business.

Nathan studied me. There was too much weight in his stare to believe he'd accept my innocence without proof, and I had none until I located Joseph Lafferty. I had to buy time, be smarter, calmer, and more calculating than my nemesis.

I reiterated a brief recount of my altercation with Calvin's skiff and gave the impression, without actually saying so, the run-in was the impetus for hiring Ben.

"You couldn't just ask your cousin about his boat?" Nathan's delivery was smooth as if he were truly perplexed.

"I could, and I did." I shut my mouth, remembering my old accountant's advice to refrain from offering the IRS anything not specifically requested. I figured the same rule applied to federal marshals.

Nathan pulled out a red file that I recognized from our first meeting. "Yesterday afternoon Beth Thompson visited you. You had coffee at Starbucks and then went to a boutique. Twenty minutes later, you returned to your office. Beth disappeared."

"You're blaming Kate for Beth Thompson's disappearance?" Cedar wrapped a protective arm around my shoulder.

"Have you found Beth?"

"No," Erica said. "And we would appreciate you providing her whereabouts."

Nathan flipped through his red file and didn't look up.

"Beth didn't disappear," I said.

Nathan considered me through hooded lids. "Then why'd she leave through the back door and need a disposable phone?"

My face heated, but I kept quiet until my rush of emotion stilled. "She didn't want to be followed. I gave you her number. Track her down, and ask her these questions. I need to get on the road. I want to see my son and tell my mother of Cal's death."

Erica shook her head. "Not happening."

"Kate's a free woman. You can't keep her from her family. She has every right to go to Florida." Cedar spoke at a reasonable conversational level, but his tone held a bucket of provocation.

Erica's head moved back and forth like an old-fashioned oscillating fan. "No way. It's called obstruction of justice, Counselor."

Nathan's deadpanned expression held no promise that Erica's response was an overstated knee-jerk reaction. The realization they might hold me here, not let me leave, came as a backhanded slap of surprise.

"Surely you can understand Kate's desire to be with her family after such a shock. Seeing her cousin murdered and stuffed into the trunk of a car…" Cedar squeezed me to his side. "She's devastated."

Nathan slid his laptop around to face me. Pushed play and started a video of Beth and me entering the Twisty Sisters boutique, browsing, then pushing through the back door and into the alley. Me rubbing Beth's back, then our walk to the gray SUV. Finding keys. Beth driving away. The SUV's tag number. Me walking alone down the alley. A close-up of my hands as I threw her phone receiver into the ice bucket.

"Stores have security cameras," Nathan said. "Inside and out."

I drew a deep breath.

Cedar bolted upright, even his hair looked an inch taller. I could feel his attempt to throw furtive glances my way.

Nathan removed a stack of photos from his notorious red file. The last time he'd pulled eight-by-tens from that folder, a black hole had opened, sucked me down, and destroyed my new post-divorce picture-perfect life.

He lined seven photos side by side on the table.

# CHAPTER TWENTY-TWO

*Nathan*

NATHAN SENSED KATE'S angst as soon as he played the video. He pulled out the photos, and the color drained from her face. Then she rubbed her hand over her chest, a subtle gesture used to soothe a quickening heartbeat.

He picked up the first photograph in the line of seven. "Do you recognize this man?" He pointed at a guy bellied up to a bar surrounded by his buddies.

Kate leaned across the table and studied the face, taking her time. "I don't think so." Her face remained neutral. No change in pupil size. No shortness of breath. No flicker of recognition.

Nathan switched to another image of the same man. "How about him?" The photographer had snapped the same tall stringy-haired guy striding down a sidewalk.

Kate compared the two photographs. She pointed to the second shot, then tapped the middle guy in the group photo. "These two seem to be the same guy. He resembles the man that drove Cal's boat."

Erica adopted an amiable expression that she didn't completely pull off. "Yeah, they're brothers. The deadbeat straddling the barstool's the oldest."

Kate's eyes rounded. "Did he kill Calvin?"

"Doubt it. He was a weekend blow user, but not in

the Cabral army." Erica reverted to her deadpan cop cadence. Nathan assumed she'd tried on her nice voice, and it pinched.

"What do you mean, was?" Kate said. "Is he dead, too?"

Nathan removed a photograph from the bottom of his red file and placed it before Kate.

Revulsion rolled over her face and turned her skin a putrid green. She raised her hand to her mouth, motioned Cedar off the bench seat, and ran to the kitchen sink. She spat, then washed her mouth with water. She grabbed a Diet Coke from the fridge and swallowed a tentative sip.

Nathan, accustomed to viewing all the sordid and inventive ways man used to murder, had no physical reaction to the partial face and one-armed torso he'd just shown Kate, a repercussion of twelve years witnessing the remains of Taliban and ISIS captives.

Four dead bodies had surfaced in the last forty-eight hours: Calvin in the trunk of a sports car, another gunshot victim left in the bed of a pickup on Sapelo Island, a male drowning victim with suspect wounds to the head, and a drug overdose dumped in the ocean, all washing ashore within a mile of one another. The fish had only left two fingers on one of the DB's hands, but two fingers had been enough to run prints. "Do you know him?" Nathan held up the photo.

"How am I supposed to tell?" Kate leaned against the counter, gripped her Coke with both hands, and downed a healthy sip.

"This is a ridiculous, sadistic lack of concern for my client's mental welfare." Cedar waved a hand toward the photos. "She's been through enough trauma today." He walked to Kate and mumbled close to her ear. She held his gaze and nodded.

Nathan would agree with the attorney if Kate were an ordinary citizen. But he had to know if she were cold blooded enough to have ordered the hit on this guy. If so, her visceral signs would be close to nil. They weren't.

Nathan opened his laptop and scrolled through screens until he landed on a driver's license headshot. He joined Kate and Cedar at the counter and positioned the screen so he'd have a clear view of Kate's face when she looked. "Was this the man you observed diving under your dock?"

Her forehead creased, then a rapid blink. Her confusion appeared genuine. "I can't say for sure." She encircled her skull with her hands. "The guy wore head gear—like a miner's light." She drew the computer closer. "But I know this guy."

"How?" Nathan asked.

"It's Jacob." Her gaze found Cedar. "Joseph Lafferty's son."

Kate dropped back a step. "Is this the dead man with half a face?" She turned the sickly gray color of three-day-old snow, stumbled to a barstool, and sat.

"Joseph Lafferty?" Erica's pupils shrunk to pinpoints. "Isn't he your property manager? The old guy that's on a two-month leave of absence?"

"Four weeks." Kate's eyes had the medicated haze worn by the very confused, too many stimuli, too fast. Jacob Lafferty's death had come as a shock.

"You saw Jacob Lafferty, in the flesh, in the dive boat on Sunday," Nathan prompted.

Kate snapped to attention as if his statement rebooted her brain. "I didn't recognize him then."

"He didn't say anything to you?" he asked.

"No. And he was careful to keep his back turned. Even when Owen asked him a question." Her delivery wasn't smooth enough to be a well-thought-out lie. But she was a trained dealmaker and mentally agile enough to deflect.

Cedar squeezed Kate's shoulder. Nathan couldn't tell if the gesture was a comfort or an unspoken message to keep quiet.

She met Nathan's gaze straight on. Her jaw was relaxed, her fist open, but the subtle eye shimmer was a giveaway. Or not. Hard to tell. She was what he referred to as a grand master. Kate had an innate ability to mask inner turmoil and was a challenge to read. Nathan admired the skill. He'd spent years honing his own to near perfection, but in his case, it had meant life or death.

"Was Jacob a friend?" he asked.

"I didn't know him well. The last time I saw him, we were kids." As soon as the statement left her lips, trembling fingers covered her mouth. Her calm dissolved into walleyed panic. "I need to leave for Florida." She turned to Cedar. "I want to go now."

Why had knowing Jacob as a child caused the sudden frenzy? Kate was a conflicted pain in his neck. One minute he was certain she knew more than she was telling, the next, he was convinced she was an innocent pawn in someone's elaborate game.

Erica shook her head. "You're not going to Florida."

"I want to see my son." Fear rolled off Kate's body and settled like a rancid meat stink. She faced Erica. "You remember Jacob?"

"Yeah," Erica said. "I remember the little snot-nose."

That was news to Nathan. "Were Jacob Lafferty and Calvin friends?"

Kate inhaled a long, lingering breath—a stall tactic.

Nathan could almost feel the heat searing Kate's brain as she scrambled over one answer, then another, searching for the perfect response.

"When they were kids," she said. "I'm not sure about recently."

Erica studied the photo like an art student slobbering over an Ansel Adams original. "They were thick as thieves through high school."

Cedar laid his hand on Kate's shoulders, but she shrugged him off and walked to the window.

Erica tapped her phone. "Need you to look at one more DB."

"DB?"

"Dead body." Erica handed Kate her phone.

"I'm not looking at another gruesome photograph." Kate kept her back turned.

Erica shoved the phone closer. "Just tell me if you know this person. He didn't drown, so the fish didn't gnaw on him."

Gripping the sink with one hand, Kate accepted the phone. 'No. I've never seen him."

"You sure about that?" Erica raised a doubting eyebrow.

Kate looked from Parsi to Erica. "He wasn't on the dive boat."

"How about yesterday in Savannah?" Erica said.

"If I'd seen him yesterday, your guy in the gray Explorer would have put it in his report."

Silence enveloped the room like an invisible shield.

Erica locked her jaw and tapped the counter with a fingernail as if counting to a predetermined number that might keep her from blowing an internal fuse.

Nathan closed his computer. "If you've got a tail, the guy's not one of ours. But we'll check it out." An uneasy feeling slithered up his back. If Kate was under someone's watch, he'd missed something. He needed to reassign two men at the evening briefing.

Kate stepped toward the door leading to her private residence. "I want to get on the road."

Nathan gathered the photos and stuffed them in his file. "I'm requesting you remain in the area until we wrap the case."

Kate stopped midstride. The little bit of color in her face drained away, and for a moment, she reminded Nathan of a marble statue.

If hostility had a sound, Cedar would've crackled. "Your request is ludicrous. What possible reason do you have to detain her?"

Erica snorted a laugh. "How about she's paramount to our case."

Kate and Cedar turned, their eyes met, and Kate shifted into her calm façade.

Heat engulfed Nathan's neck. Kate was hiding something, and he was determined to question her without her attorney. "Kate's remanded to this county for the duration of our investigation."

"Paramount how?" Cedar boomed. Undoubtedly, the counselor believed the loudest voice won the battle. "She has nothing to do with your drug investigation." Cedar locked eyes with Nathan. "The man you needed was Calvin, and he's dead."

"In case you haven't noticed, bodies are stacking up like cordwood," Erica said.

"What's that have to do with Kate?" Cedar spat a disbelieving scoff that only a defense attorney would attempt to pull off. "She hasn't murdered anyone. And she wants to see her son."

Nathan snapped his briefcase closed. "Your client's remanded to a one-hundred-mile radius of Savannah. And, Counselor, this matter is not open for discussion."

"Kate." Nathan pulled out his final ace. "You said you looked in the trunk of your investigator's car because of an unpleasant odor. But the lady who works at the marina told Erica you removed something from Snider's car. An envelope you looked in before you opened the trunk. Where's that envelope now?"

Cedar opened his case and handed Nathan a photograph.

Nathan glanced at the image. His heart skipped. Evidence was rarely linear, and sometimes information surfaced in unexpected ways. He passed the picture to Erica and focused back on Kate. "Why would that photograph cause you to open the trunk?"

Kate blew a worn-out breath. "The smell. The photo. Ben was missing. I just opened the trunk. Nothing more."

Her answer sounded so reasonable. But Nathan didn't buy it. "Either give me a straight answer, or I'm placing you under arrest for the death of Calvin Thompson."

Kate's lips lost color. Her eyes rolled.

Nathan jumped forward and caught her in his arms.

# CHAPTER TWENTY-THREE

*Nathan*

NATHAN CLOSED THE guesthouse sliding doors overlooking the river. The temperature hovered at ninety, and someone had left the sliders open. Inside the apartment, the temperature had to be close to eighty.

Erica stomped up the stairs and slammed the front door. "It's a sauna outside."

"Not much different in here." He set the ceiling fan on high and punched seventy on the air controller. "How was Kate when you left her?" It was his fault she'd fainted. He'd successfully pushed past her aloof boundary but intended to knock her off her stoic perch, not lay her flat.

"She tossed Cedar and me out." Erica walked to the sliding glass doors and peered through a slit in the curtains.

The feeling of Kate in his arms haunted Nathan like the phantom sensitivity of an amputee. He shook his arms and slapped them around his waist like a boxer readying for his bout. Nathan had allowed himself to get too close to Kate. Bunking at Spartina, seeing her every day, he'd lost his perception. That was all it was.

Erica snatched up the highly suspicious photo of Kate and Owen on Barry Island. "Who took this shot? Only one of our guys was on that island Sunday, and he's driving the boat in the photo."

And there was the crux. Access to Barry Island required an airboat to ride over the marsh grass or navigation through one of the three entry creeks. His team controlled the airboat and had live feeds on all three waterways.

Nathan had to figure out how to break the news to his boss that their worst fear looked to be fact. "We might have a rat." The words seared his throat like kerosene charcoal set afire.

Erica stalked the eight-hundred-square-foot living area like a wary feral cat. "I'd trust every one of my agents with my life. No way I have a snitch." She paused at the front window and tipped the blind.

"You on surveillance?"

"Just making sure that skank of an attorney doesn't double back and slip Kate out."

"She's formally remanded. Haynes won't risk jail, even for Kate." Nathan opened his laptop and read the preliminary autopsy report on Calvin. "You need to check the duty logs for Sunday. Find out which agents were off."

"Travis already did. Everyone's accounted for."

"Put your eyes on it. Travis could've missed something."

Nathan scanned the preliminary work-up on Calvin's murder file.

Erica tossed the photo back on the counter and headed to a space roughly the size of a walk-in closet that Kate called a galley kitchen and peered into the fridge. "That photograph could be nothing more than a lucky Google Earth shot."

"Came with a dead body."

"Point taken." She shut the fridge a little harder than necessary.

"There was a photographer planted in a tree, or drones are monitoring Barry Island." It was a draw which option was worse for their case.

"I vote for the drone." She ripped into a pack of Chips Ahoy.

"A ghost photographer not showing up on one of our feeds means they know how to circumvent the cameras, and we have a snitch," he said. "But if there's a drone, the increased visual range means our position at Spartina is compromised."

"I had Travis looking for a warm body," Erica said. "He might've missed a UAV. I'll go back over the feeds after I eat. Where's the dinner tray?"

"Not six o'clock." He scanned the ballistics report. Inconclusive, but Nathan's guess was a nine millimeter. Erica tilted the kitchen blinds and looked out.

"Kate's got a migraine, and she's lying."

"Is one connected to the other?"

"Got no stomach for lying—puts her down for twenty-four hours, minimum."

Interesting. But based on his analysis, Kate had been less than truthful for the past two days and continued to function upright. "She take any knock-out meds?"

"No. Said she'd already sucked down eight aspirin. Cedar wanted her to take something stronger, but she threw us out. Claimed she needed an hour of quiet. Asked for privacy to call her mom and Owen and tell them she wouldn't be coming to the beach tonight." Erica slowly chewed a cookie. "Today at the marina, Kate was scared."

"Finding your cousin dead in the trunk of a car can do that to a person."

"Scared and shocked aren't the same." She took another four cookies from the package.

Nathan pointed at the bag.

She passed him the cookies and dropped into a chair.

"If you're right, and Cedar told Kate the airboat was DEA, why didn't she use that when you threatened to arrest her? She's clutching to something, but I can't figure out what." Erica wiggled a cookie at him. "You need to push her."

"I plan on it." He boosted himself off the sofa in search of caffeine. He removed two Cokes from the fridge and threw one to Erica. "Speaking of holding back, why didn't you say you knew Jacob Lafferty?"

"Didn't connect the name to the face. Only met him once or twice when we were kids." She held the cold drink to her forehead. "God, it's hot." She sipped and belched. "Calvin and Jacob's murder changes things."

"Like me being skewered on a spit?" Nathan debated whether to tell his supervisor about the newest evidence of a snitch before or after he told him that their prime suspect had been snuffed and stuffed in a yellow Corvette.

"Better your backside in the fire than mine," Erica said. "Kate will hide behind her attorney. And by tomorrow, she'll throw us off her property."

He couldn't argue with Kate hiding behind Cedar Haynes, and if they had a drone, leaving Spartina was inevitable. He had two hours of paperwork, and maybe more depending on what Erica did or didn't find on the creek feeds.

Erica perched on the edge of her chair. "Go." He waved her away. "I have work."

She scowled, but there wasn't much behind it. "I think you should put two more agents in Florida."

His stomach rumbled, if he was going to spitball theories, he might as well eat. He went to the fridge, removed a leftover pizza from lunch, spread a napkin on the bar, and slid a piece from the box. "No additional agents are necessary. The whole family, including Kate, will be in a safe house by tomorrow night."

Erica leaned over the counter, plucked a pepperoni, and popped it in her mouth. "Now, there's a pipe dream. Katie'll never agree." She peeled off another pepperoni.

"She'll agree if a safe house is the only way she'll see her son." Nathan slid the remaining full piece to his napkin.

Erica opened the pantry and found an unopened Lay's potato chips bag.

"Where did you get those?"

"Stashed them behind the flour canister." She shook a few chips onto Nathan's napkin. "With Cal dead, if Kate gets the vibe the danger has tentacles, she'll grab Owen and Roslyn and bolt. Make sure our Florida team understands she has the means to spirit her family from under their noses and disappear."

"Nobody disappears with my guys sitting on them."

"Really?" Erica gave him a look that could pierce titanium.

Her not-so-subtle poke aimed at Hartley, the female agent he'd assigned to Beth Thompson, reminded him to check his inbox. He scanned his cell, threw the phone on the bar, and returned to his pizza. "The number Kate gave us for Beth Thompson's a wash. Phone's out of commission. Probably removed the battery."

Erica stuffed a handful of chips in her mouth. Chewed and swallowed. "How would a nurse know to remove a battery?"

He finished the second slice and considered eating the piece Erica had raided, but the pepperoni was the best part of a cold pizza. He swiped his hands down his jeans and grabbed the chip bag out of her hand. "Beth's Calvin's wife. Not a big stretch she'd know how to go off-grid."

"Call the Colorado employer," Erica said. "See if she's checked in."

"Kate didn't get the name of the clinic."

There was a short rap on the door. Agent Hartley walked in with eyes cast to the floor. She placed a sandwich platter on the counter.

"What'd you bring us, Hart?" Erica looked over the tray.

"The usual. Turkey, ham, tuna, and chicken salad."

Hart cut her eyes at Nathan.

He acknowledged her with a quick nod, and she slunk out the door. She'd been moping around since Beth gave her the slip. It was a hefty screwup, and Nathan gave her a ration of grief.

"Can't be that many clinics in Boulder hiring a new manager." Erica stood over the sink and scarfed down half a tuna on rye. She couldn't weigh over a hundred and ten, but she ate with the gusto of a sumo wrestler. "Put Hartley on it," Erica said between bites. "Give her a shot at saving face."

Nathan thought Erica's idea had merit.

"Beth was jumpy yesterday," Erica said. "Girl acted as if she were an hour late for a fix."

Nathan had tried getting a clear read on Beth during their interview, but obtaining a baseline with Erica grilling her on Calvin's whereabouts had been impossible.

"Maybe Beth already knew Calvin was dead," Erica said. "Could be she played Kate."

"You think Kate's that gullible?"

"Just saying we shouldn't count on Beth being in Colorado. I couldn't locate Joseph Lafferty, so I ran him—no credit card usage for five days. Last hit was Albuquerque. Kate says he has a daughter in the area." Erica finished off her sandwich and put the top back on the tray. She swept crumbs from the counter into her hand; half of them fell on the floor. "I put the daughter's contact information in the file."

"Okay, that'll be my next call." Nathan tossed his empty coke can in the trash. "Go. I need to work."

Erica grabbed her laptop and the chip bag off the counter, but Nathan gave her a stink-eye and stopped her from snagging the chocolate chip cookies.

"I'll tag Hartley," she said. "Get her started on the clinic calls."

"Do that."

Erica had been right about one thing—dead bodies were stacking up. Nathan's hypothesis was the Cabral's were sweeping their house clean. If Kate was an innocent caught up in a family of criminals, no surprise she'd be spooked.

Nathan studied the island photo with a fresh eye. The kid's hands covered his ears, and he appeared agitated, most likely from the sound of the airboat engine. Kate stood with one hand stretched in front of her body as if daring the boat to move closer; her other arm hugged her son to her side. The wind from the propeller blew hair across her face and prevented Nathan from seeing her expression.

He bought that the island confrontation would be a bad memory and finding Calvin's body traumatic. Still, Nathan found Kate's confusion level and inability to converse coherently within an hour's time leaned more to fear. Reminiscent of a soldier after a close call in the field. Suddenly, he felt like a dunce that it had taken him this long to realize this two plus two equaled five. The photo hadn't been the only item inside the envelope.

Six thirty in Georgia would be four thirty in Albuquerque. Nathan called the number Erica had left for Lafferty's daughter Jessica. He spoke with Jacob's mother, Kathleen, and gave her the sad news of her son's death. Then he spoke with Jessica. Then he called Kate.

She answered on the second ring. "I just spoke to Kathleen Lafferty."

"How did she take the news?" Kate asked.

He thought he caught a hesitation. "As well as can be

expected. Difficult to get the news of your son's death over the phone."

"How did Joseph hold up?"

"That's why I'm calling. Something's come up I'd like to discuss."

This time he heard a definite intake of breath. "Can't it wait until morning?"

"I don't think so."

"Okay." Her tone indicated it was anything but. "I'm in the kitchen eating a bowl of soup."

---

Kate was standing at the bar when he arrived, freshly showered and wearing a silk shirt and jeans. He recognized her sandalwood scent from the bath gel in the guesthouse. He'd used the subtle, clean fragrance during his morning shower. It smelled better on her.

"Appreciate you agreeing to meet this late," he said.

Something akin to guilt coiled into an inflexible stone and lodged in Nathan's throat. Kate looked exhausted, faint purple rimmed her eyes. Her lips were pale and thin. If eyes were the windows to a soul, lips were the gateway to human emotion.

Their eyes met, and Kate smoothed a hand over her hair. Her fingers fluttered over her collar, then ran over her midsection.

Two agents were eating at the small table by the window, and she waved Nathan through the door. "We'll be more comfortable in the atrium."

It was a glass room, even the ceiling. Based on the books and magazines stacked in every available space, he assumed the area was used for casual reading. The furniture and pillows were different shades of yellow as if someone had gathered ten gourmet mustards together for a color match.

Kate switched on a floor lamp in the corner, and along

with the night stars overhead, the room had a cozy glow.

He sank into one of two wicker sofas.

She waffled between the sofa and a nearby chair; he patted the cushion, and she eased beside him.

"I spoke with Lafferty's daughter," he said.

"Jessica?"

"You know her?"

"Yes. But I haven't seen her since we were teenagers." Kate perched on the edge of her seat, her fingers locked in her lap.

He realized she wasn't going to say anything else. He'd invited her to the party, and initiating their dance was up to him. "Kathleen Lafferty's visiting her daughter. Joseph's not."

"Where's Joseph?" The slight eyebrow raise and narrow separation of her lips were conducive to surprise.

"Wife says she doesn't know. Joseph hasn't called in three days."

"I've left several messages on his cell. He hasn't returned any of my calls."

Nathan counted to five. "Mrs. Lafferty says that she called you today and left two messages with your assistant."

Kate massaged the area between her eyes. She usually made the gesture right before swallowing aspirin. "I haven't checked in with my office today."

Considering her day, that sounded reasonable. "Don't you think it's odd that a wife doesn't know where her husband's gone?"

Kate tugged her bottom lip. "Very strange."

"Joseph received a phone call at three o'clock Monday morning." He let his statement rest, but Kate showed no signs she knew what would come. "The wife claims the call was from you. She claims you sent Joseph on an urgent errand."

"Me?" Her colorless lips ringed white. "I haven't spoken to Joseph since he left Savannah."

A prickle on the back of Nathan's neck stopped him from commenting. A person's brain can notice details much quicker than conscious awareness, sometimes in as little as one-twenty-fifth of a second, literally in a blink of an eye. The phenomenon was known as thin slices. Nathan's ability to register and react to his slices was one of his strongest assets. Kate's fear now tilted close to petrified. He'd witnessed similar expressions on videos—on the faces of prisoners of war right before the Taliban beheaded them.

"Kathleen said Joseph was doing something for me?" It wasn't that she sounded angry, more shocked and confused.

"A person who learns of their child's untimely passing rarely has the mental faculties to fabricate a lie."

Kate raised her right palm. "Hand to God, I don't know where Joseph is or why he'd lie about his trip." She leaned forward. "There's something else you should know." She rushed her words, reached across the cushion as if she planned to touch him, then reconsidered and rested her hand on her knee. "Joseph's office computer has been wiped clean."

An itch crawled between Nathan's shoulders. "Who has access to Lafferty's computer?"

"Other than Joseph, only me."

Getting a warrant for Barry Real Estate would take at least forty-eight hours. "I want a look at Lafferty's computer. There's a good chance his data is retrievable."

Kate nodded. "Of course."

He picked up the landline on the side table and handed her the receiver. "Call your assistant, ask her to meet my agent at the office, and allow us access."

She made the call, articulated precise instructions, and stood.

He rose and gripped Kate's hand. Her icy fingers caught him off guard. He squashed an urge to warm them between his own. "Right now, I'm still on your side. But if you're hiding something, anything I should know—now's the time to come clean. Otherwise, this isn't going to end well."

"I promise you. I have no idea where Joseph's gone or why."

Nathan didn't get the lying buzz. She looked straight into his face, no quick glance over his shoulder, no fluttering eyelids.

"What did you find besides the photo of you and your son in Ben Snider's car?"

Kate inhaled a sucker-punch breath. "Nothing." She tilted back and glanced away.

He got the lying buzz. Didn't make sense to close him out. With Calvin dead, she should want federal protection—unless telling him the truth was more dangerous.

"Kate, help me understand why Joseph would lie to his wife about you being behind his sudden trip, why you were summoned to find Calvin's body, why your private investigator has suddenly gone missing. And why the phone you gave Beth Thompson is now out of commission? If you want me to believe you're innocent, you've got to give me something."

Kate shook her head. "I can't."

# CHAPTER TWENTY-FOUR

*Katelyn*

I CLOSED MY BEDROOM door and slid into a chair. A murderer threatened my son, and someone working for that enemy presently lived under my roof and watched my every move.

Cold fear crystallized in my core like water slowly freezing over a pond. My grandfather and Calvin were dead, and Joseph had vanished. I had no one left. No one to testify that I was innocent and had no connection to the Cabral family or any part in the money laundering.

Everything Nathan had said in the atrium was true.

Ben was missing.

Calvin was dead.

Kathleen claimed I had sent Joseph on a trip in the middle of the night.

The white notebook from his office sat on the bedside table, a vivid reminder of the secrets Nathan and his team would soon uncover. The possibility of jail and being forced to abandon my son paralyzed me.

Accessing my shambled life brought agony in waves—stronger, weaker, and stronger again. All my hard work—the company debt restructuring, the Atlanta construction projects, the enormous amount of time required to turn those properties into substantial profit centers, all wasted efforts.

But a kernel of hope simmered, then caught and blazed.

During my tenure at the bank, I'd scaled the corporate ladder to vice president, busted the symbolic glass ceiling at thirty, and negotiated five multimillion-dollar deals using one philosophy.

If you know yourself but not the enemy, for every victory gained, you will also suffer a defeat. If you know neither the enemy nor yourself, you will succumb in every battle.—Sun Tzu

I had lived by that tattoo-worthy philosophy in my business life. And I had to do that now.

I grabbed Joseph's notebook and flipped to his bank statements. If my lying property manager had slithered underground, he'd still need money.

I sat cross-legged on the bed, opened my laptop, and created a spreadsheet listing his liquid accounts. His checking and savings were joint accounts with Kathleen; the combined balances were just over fifteen thousand. An investment portfolio at Morgan Stanley, solely in Joseph's name, had a value of forty-seven thousand. But the bulk of his holdings were housed in Surinvest Bank located in Uruguay, in a town called Montevideo.

In banking circles, Montevideo was known as the Switzerland of the Americas. According to the Surinvest monthly statements, Joseph's offshore account had over ten million dollars. All deposited since Granddad's stroke.

The last section in the notebook was labeled Additional Funds and held another Surinvest bank statement and a copy of the initial application that opened the twenty-year-old account. My hands stilled. I flipped back a page and reviewed the paragraph on account types and beneficiaries; Right of Survivorship had a check mark.

I rested my hands on my knees and sucked in some very necessary oxygen. I must be hallucinating—the names and numbers couldn't be right. I read somewhere that the human brain, an amazing instrument no computer could duplicate, processed millions of stimuli in hundredths of a second. Mine went into a deep freeze. Seconds passed, or I suppose it was seconds, then my brain raced forward.

Granddad had laundered millions of dollars over the past twenty years. And according to this record, he had stashed his money in Montevideo.

The beneficiaries listed on Granddad's account were Katelyn Landers and Calvin Thompson. The check beside the Right of Survivorship box meant the entire balance transferred to me with Calvin's death: all twenty-nine million, nine hundred sixty thousand, twenty-seven dollars, and seven cents.

Based on my limited knowledge, all deriving from television police dramas, in a murder investigation, the police assumed family first, then business associates, then anyone who benefitted financially. Me. Me. And me.

A stampeding hysteria swamped me. Nothing I could do would change what Granddad put in motion twenty years ago. Even if I disowned the Surinvest account, with all the evidence weighing against me, especially Calvin's death, Nathan would never believe I didn't know this money existed.

My world had just bent and broken in two. I'd never be whole again.

Joseph's plan was ingenious.

When I ordered the warehouse appraisals, Joseph knew I would discover the embezzlement scheme. Logically, I'd search his office and find this notebook he'd planted. If Calvin and I screamed fraud, we'd have to give up almost thirty million dollars. Joseph thought he'd jammed Cal and me against a moral wall—but Joseph had overplayed his hand. Cal was dead, someone was threatening to kill my son, and within a few hours, Nathan Parsi would reconstruct Joseph's emptied hard drive and discover his money-washing scheme. My grandfather's Montevideo money held not one smidgen of interest to me.

But if I stayed holed up in my room, immersed in the injustice of my situation, and gave Nathan time to fit the final pieces together, my future home would have bars. I couldn't let that happen without a fight. I needed time to ferret Joseph from his hiding place. And there was no way I'd leave Owen unprotected. My thoughts scurried with one idea after another, like a squirrel searching for the perfect place to hide an acorn.

I fixated on a marsh-view landscape hanging over the sofa in my sitting area. Behind the artwork was the key to slipping away from Spartina undetected. I plugged the Montevideo account information into the spreadsheet, hit save, and emailed myself a copy.

I removed my cell phone from my purse and placed it on my bedside table. Pulled on a pair of black jeans, a black t-shirt, and a black blazer, then laced up my black Nikes. I swung my purse over my shoulder and swung the marsh painting to the side. Running the tips of my fingers over the cypress paneling, I pushed a brown button hidden in the wood's natural grooves. A section of the wall slid open. I stepped into a secret passage that connected the master suite to my grandfather's office, a narrow musty hall Calvin and I had played in as kids.

---

I crouched under the bay window in Granddad's office and peeked over the window ledge. Parsi's sentry ninja marched by. I had fifteen minutes before he made another sweep of the perimeter.

I opened the safe, picked up two tightly packed bundles of hundred-dollar bills, and stuffed the fifty grand in my purse. I considered taking the Glock on the second shelf before locking and turning the tumbler. In my frame of mind, it'd be safer to forgo a deadly weapon.

Nathan's remand to remain on the grounds of Spartina hovered over my head like a thunderous black cloud. I knew from experience the only way through despair, heartbreak, or treacherous fear was to dive straight through. Just breathe, block out everything but Owen's face.

Cedar said Joseph wouldn't be anxious to stick his neck out on my behalf lest the Cabrals chop it off. But my plan didn't include convincing Joseph to cooperate, only to find out where he was hiding. Then I'd turn the spineless jellyfish over to the authorities and beg Nathan for clemency.

I had to leave Spartina and get Mom and Owen to safety. Then I'd use my banking connections to follow the money trail and find Joseph. I didn't buy Kathleen's story that her husband had disappeared in the middle of the night. She was Joseph's wife; she'd cover for him. And Nathan didn't know what I knew—Joseph had ten million dollars stashed in Uruguay.

I refused to let the only person who could attest to my innocence slip away with millions in dirty money without a fight. But before I'd risk working with Parsi to find Joseph, I wanted Owen and Mom safely hidden from the snitch on Parsi's team. And I had no idea if the Cabral snitch was one of the men here at Spartina or one of the agents assigned to the security detail on Mom and Owen.

I found the extra key for the caretaker's cottage in Granddad's desk drawer. I pushed against the end of the bookshelf and stepped back into the passageway. I stopped halfway down the dimly lit hall and studied the door impersonating a ceiling-to-floor window—the only Spartina exit not connected to the alarm system. It took four tries and a broken fingernail to pry the rarely used latch open. I stepped through the passage and into the side garden, then quietly pushed the door back in place.

I hugged a five-foot hedge covered in pink blooms and slipped down the walkway. The jet-black sky had no moon, so I leaned against the garden gate and searched for the flashlight app on my burner phone. The smell of tobacco smoke didn't register until the unmistakable rumble of speech echoed to my right. I stepped back and melded into the bushes.

The end of two burning cigarettes ghost-walked past me and continued down the path that led to our koi pond.

I remained in place, nestled inside the hedge, and attempted to calm my racing heart. I hadn't factored smoke breaks into my timeline. If I waited until the agents finished their cigarettes, the next security sweep would bring the sentry ninja within feet of where I stood.

I peeked around the cottage wall. The cigarette guys walked along the viewing deck. I assumed the destination would be one of three benches on the pond's bank.

Dropping to a crouch, I crawled towards my caretaker's cottage. The hedges surrounding his place weren't tall enough to hide me, so using a flashlight wasn't an option. I had five yards between the end of the garden and the cottage. I rose to a running stance and shot across the open space. Reaching the back steps, I placed my back against the wall, tuned into the night sounds, and waited—an owl's hoot and frogs croaking, but no footsteps.

I tried lining the key with the lock, but my fingers were slick with sweat, and the key slipped. The ping of the aluminum hitting concrete sounded as loud as a tree branch tumbling to the ground.

James's Ford Fusion was the only vehicle on Spartina property not monitored by the security cameras. I assumed if his car were here, he had left his keys in the cottage, or at the very least, he'd have a spare set in the cottage. But first, I had to make it inside. I ran my hand over the steps. My knee pressed against something sharp—the door key.

I risked turning the flashlight on, unlocked the door, and slipped into the kitchen. A man who insisted on changing smoke alarm batteries every three months would keep his spare car key by the back door—the most logical place. A pegboard for hats and coats hung to my right. I plucked the ring with a silver Ford medallion off the hook.

My hand was on the Fusion's door handle when I realized the dome light would come on as soon as I opened the car. A quick check on the smokers verified they were still at the pond. I hurriedly slipped inside and turned the engine over, the rumble of the hybrid as soft as an electric golf cart.

I turned right and drove without headlights through the back pasture, risking a collision at any minute. An empty hayrack loomed in my path. I swerved right and left, coming within inches of the water trough. I kept my speed at fifteen miles an hour, bordering treacherous in a bumpy, pot-holed pasture with no headlights.

I drove over the cow grate and headed for the highway. The farther I drove from Spartina, the crazier my plan seemed. I had a better chance of winning the Boston Marathon than finding Joseph.

I thought of Owen, the custody battle, the divorce, Adam's death, and everything Owen had been through over the past three years. My baby having a felon for a mother was incomprehensible. I would do anything, legal or otherwise, to protect Owen and prove my innocence.

I wouldn't stop until I found my scumbag property manager. But first, I had to relocate Owen and Mom to a safe place.

# CHAPTER TWENTY-FIVE

*Katelyn*

THE FLORIDA LINE loomed another twenty-five minutes down the road before my mind settled enough to call my mother. "Mom." My pent-up anxiety rolled into sobs, and I pulled to the shoulder of the highway.

"Kate, what's happened?"

Words padlocked in my memory wouldn't budge, as though the left side of my brain dared the right to articulate the impossible truth of today.

"Take a breath, sweetheart. Just say the words one at a time." My mother's intuition had always been uncanny. I was in my teens before realizing she wasn't psychic. She couldn't see beyond the veil, view the past, or predict the future—she just knew me.

"Someone murdered Calvin."

Her mournful, wounded-animal whimper pierced my heart. "Who killed him?"

"Cabral. At least, that's what Cedar thinks. I have no idea what the police think; they don't confide in me."

She struggled to catch a breath. "Cedar's wrong. Juan wouldn't kill Calvin."

"I didn't say he pulled the trigger. But Cedar thinks the drug cartel is responsible, and Nathan's convinced Cal was part of the Cabral drug cartel."

"Not every wealthy man of Mexican descent is a drug lord. Juan was a friend of your grandfather's. He'd never hurt anyone in our family." Not a trace of doubt entered her declaration.

I agreed with her in theory. It was like a splinter my mind kept getting stuck on. Whoever killed Calvin threatened to hurt Owen if I went to the police. But if the Cabrals had a snitch on Nathan's team, they knew the island and the warehouses were compromised. So why would they care if I told the police? Something didn't add up. "Cedar thinks we should go into hiding until Nathan closes his case."

"We can't leave. We have to bury Calvin." Pragmatism—Mom's undying strength. "Owen and I will leave for Savannah in the morning."

I ached to see Owen. Touch him. Hold him. *You came close to losing him once. Will you chance it again?*

A sharp and fiery maternal anger spread. "You can't go back to Savannah. Calvin's murderer also threatened Owen."

"What?"

"There was a note with Calvin's body." I recited the words seared into my brain, but by the time I came to the last two lines, I couldn't breathe. I leaned against the steering wheel as hot pain ripped like a knife across my forehead.

"Katelyn, you must come to the island," Mom said.

I gripped the wheel and straightened my back against the seat. "That's why I'm calling. I'm on my way. But Mom—"

"Do the police believe Juan threatened Owen?"

"The threat warned me against going to the police. Only Cedar knows. I'm—"

"Have you talked to Beth?" she asked. "She shouldn't be told of her husband's death by a stranger."

"I left three messages." I was worried about Beth.

I was worried about Ben. Neither had answered my phone messages. But protecting Owen came first. "I've decided we should leave. Go out west until everything settles down. The authorities won't release Cal's body for a few days, and his burial won't be scheduled for at least another five, maybe more."

"This house is safe. Two marshals are parked in our driveway." Her tone seemed off as if half her mind still tried to process Cal's death. I didn't want to dump any more on her, like the possibility that one of the men guarding them might be working for the Cabrals.

"Cedar's working on securing us a place in California," I said. "But Parsi's issued a remand for me to remain at Spartina, and I can't risk coming to Stanley's."

"Why would the marshal do that?"

Too many reasons. "Cedar's trying to work it out, but don't tell anyone about me coming to Florida or that we're planning a trip. Can you meet me at the club in the morning? They open the restaurant for the early golfers at seven. Tell Stanley you want to introduce Owen to golf or something?"

Mom exhaled a wearied breath. "Katelyn—we need to talk."

"About what?"

"Not over the phone." Her voice broke.

"What is it?" Mom never cried. She was silent for so long my curiosity began to put down roots.

She sniffled again. "I can't talk anymore."

"Meet me at the club in the morning at eight o'clock. The marshals will follow you, so meet me in the women's locker room. There's a back door."

"Are you sure that's the best thing?"

"Mom, we have no choice but to get Owen to a safe place until this is over."

"Of course, you're right." Her voice was now resolved. "We'll be there. I have to go." She disconnected.

I stared at the phone and wanted to call back to satisfy myself she was okay. I'd dumped a lot on her. Might be better to give her a little time to process it all.

Hoping Cedar was still awake at eleven-thirty, I dialed his number. He answered and didn't wait for my greeting. "The house in California is in a town called Eureka."

A good omen, I hoped. "When will it be ready?"

"Already is."

"Did you book the plane?"

"Working on it. Can't have your name or mine on the manifest. Too easy for the Feds to trace. A hurricane is supposed to hit South Florida tomorrow. It has all the pilots skittish. There's a small airstrip thirty minutes south of Talbott Island, if I can book a plane, you should leave from there."

I laid my head against the headrest. God, I was so tired. "Parsi and Erica will claim I'm on the run from the law. Hunt me down."

"I'll handle them. Once you text me that you're in California, I'll call my Georgia Bureau of Investigation friend and float the idea that Nathan and Erica's team has a drug cartel snitch. Tell him about the threat. Explain that's why you secured a haven for your family."

Cedar would be Nathan's first call when he discovered me gone. "Mom's meeting me at the club at eight in the morning."

"No. Stay at Spartina until you hear from me." Fatherly concern rippled through his voice.

"I've already left Spartina. I'm on the way to Florida."

"You're what?"

I jerked the phone from my ear and kept the receiver a safe four inches away.

"I found evidence that Granddad socked thirty million in an offshore bank." I waited for Cedar's response. Dead silence. No doubt he was as shocked as I was. "Now that Cal's dead, I'm the sole beneficiary. Cal was found in my investigator's car. And tonight, Kathleen Lafferty told Nathan I sent Joseph on an errand, and now he's disappeared. Nathan confronted me. I know he's close to arresting me."

"For what?"

"Calvin's murder." My heart turned as dark as volcanic stone. "I will not go to jail and leave Owen unprotected."

"The marshal remanded you to Spartina." Cedar enunciated each syllable as if English wasn't my first language. "Running makes you appear guilty. You should've followed my instructions and let me handle things."

"I don't think the Cabrals are threatening Owen. If they have a snitch, they know their ring is compromised. Me going to the police would be moot. Doesn't make sense they'd threaten to kill Owen. And if the Cabrals aren't my enemy, who is? I have to find out who sent the threat. And Owen has to be safe before Nathan throws me in jail."

"The message didn't say they'd kill your boy."

Cedar's condescending tone shredded the last of my patience. "Never seeing Owen again constitutes a death threat." I dropped my voice. Arguing accomplished nothing.

He blew a frustrated breath. "I told you I'd keep you out of jail."

"Joseph's the only person who cares if I keep my mouth shut. And he knows I'm innocent. I have to find Joseph. But first, I want Owen safe. Are you going to help us get away or not?"

"I am helping you." He huffed again, but this time more anxious than mad. "This hurricane has resulted in a mass exodus from South Florida. Every plane is booked. You may have to drive. I've got another call coming in, maybe it's the pilot. I'll call you back."

I didn't know any pilots personally, but I bought annual NetJet shares through Barry Real Estate. Booking required my name or my company name on the manifest. But there was one pilot that might skirt the rules.

I found the zippered pouch holding my collection of business cards in my purse and located the card for Chuck Mitchell, a NetJet pilot who'd recently flown me to Atlanta. I called, identified myself, and apologized for the late hour. "The last time we flew, you mentioned having a partnership in a private plane."

"Yeah. A Cessna Citation XLS—sweet little ride." His voice held the wonder of a first-time father describing his newborn.

"I need to get to California tomorrow. Three people." My heart beat at the pace of a broken metronome. "Is there any way you can help me out?"

"How soon do you need to leave?"

I did a fast calculation. "We can meet you in Jacksonville by one o'clock tomorrow afternoon." I closed my eyes and said a prayer.

"Well." He stretched the word into five. "My only plans for tomorrow involve my wife and mother-in-law, so yes, I can swing it. Long flight, though. We'll have to stop and refuel halfway."

I recognized the tone; we were about to negotiate the price. I didn't have time. "How much?"

"Cross country's going to run close to seven grand."

I kept my voice light. "Cash, okay?"

"Cash?" He laughed. "Okay, but only small unmarked bills." I didn't respond, and he cleared his throat. "Yeah. Cash is fine."

"And Chuck, I don't want my name on the manifest."

# CHAPTER TWENTY-SIX

*Nathan*

ERICA WALKED INTO the Spartina kitchen, and Nathan glanced up from the three open reports on his computer. It seemed personal hygiene hadn't been on her morning to-do list. Her fatigues looked like they'd endured twenty-four hours of continuous wear, and her hair needed a comb. Her disheveled appearance tugged something deep inside his chest—it felt a lot like regret. "How long since you slept?"

"Coming up on thirty-six hours." She slipped a folded sheet from her back pocket and handed it to him. "DMV email with the property manager's Fusion tag number." She opened the Krispy Kreme box and picked up the last chocolate glazed, Nathan's favorite.

For weeks Erica had scoffed at the idea Kate and the Cabral cartel had a connection. But Beth Thompson had disappeared, and Erica's rose-colored glasses sat slightly skewed. After Calvin's murder, her tinted shades cracked. Then Kate and the Fusion went missing, and Erica stomped her pink spectacles to smithereens.

Erica's new mantra: Kate Landers—the Southeast's largest drug kingpin. No question. No debate. Based on circumstantial evidence and supposition, over the past twenty-four hours, she'd hammered a relentless campaign for Kate's indictment.

Nathan shot her down. So Erica bypassed Nathan and proposed the theory to the brass, requiring Nathan to spend two hours defending his opposing position. He had won the battle and submitted a request for Erica's reassignment, citing her previous relationship with the Barry family as a hindrance to their investigation.

He planned to give Erica the news before the replacement arrived, but she knew Kate better than anyone on the team, and until he cut her loose, he intended to hold her tether short and take advantage of her insight. "You see my last text?"

She finished off her donut and carried a Boston cream to the bar, Nathan's second favorite. "Been too busy running down flight plans." She licked cream off her finger and swiped it across the screen on her phone. "The email about the Charleston appraiser?"

"Sheriff's original observation was off the mark." Nathan considered the remaining donuts and slid a blueberry cake on a napkin. "The appraiser didn't have a heart attack, and his head trauma wasn't conducive to a fall. Coroner suspects foul play."

"Bam." Erica's fist pumped. "That guy was Noah Barry's go-to appraiser."

Nathan's espresso finished the brew cycle, and he joined Erica at the bar. "And now the guy meets his maker under questionable circumstances."

"Doesn't pass the smell test." Erica licked vanilla cream from the corner of her mouth.

He shoved his napkin across the bar. "Joseph Lafferty left Savannah the same day the guy died—now Joseph's skipped out."

"He didn't skip." Erica picked up the napkin, wiped her mouth, then savored a second bite. Cream oozed from the side and plopped on the counter. "The princess is a problem solver, always has been. Kate sent Lafferty on a trip just like the wife said.

"Now that Jacob Lafferty is dead, Kate's afraid her second-in-command will come unglued. Kate's somewhere trying to minimize the fallout. Only people who've disappeared into the wind are the private dick, Beth Thompson, and Kate."

"Kate being responsible for the disappearance of her investigator and Beth Thompson is supposition."

Erica played an air violin. "Now, who's the cheerleader?"

Heat slid down his spine and into his shoes. He blamed his flash of irritation on three hours of sleep and Erica eating his two favorite donuts. "You ran down the flights?"

"Nothing so far."

"Have you tried NetJets?"

"Yes. Nothing there. But Kate won't be far from Florida. We've got Owen."

He stuffed the last of his donut in his mouth, chewed, swallowed, and looked around for another napkin. He wiped his hands on his jeans. Nathan agreed Kate wouldn't abandon her son.

"Something caused Kate to bolt," Eric said.

He suspected it was the atrium conversation, but he kept that to himself. He finished his coffee and carried his cup to the sink.

"Once we toss Princess in jail, she'll come clean and tell us everything we want to know."

"There's no indictment, Erica."

"Would be if I were heading the team." She pursed her lips like a teen landing a zinger.

And a good reason you're not. Nathan checked his phone and pulled up his notes. "I got the impression last night that Kate was scared." He gave Erica a minute to consider his read. "She has left eight lawmen on her property with the opportunity to go through every inch of her house."

"Only if we break in," Erica said, clearly not buying it. "She left it locked tight."

"If Kate's guilty, she'd assume we'd get a warrant." He reopened a report on his laptop. "Atlanta pulled together a map tagging the commercial property owned by Barry Real Estate—the warehouses are all on the East Coast. Take a look and see if anything pops." He pushed his laptop across the bar to give her a better view.

Erica studied the map for a full minute. "These are all inland properties with direct ocean access."

"Bingo," Nathan said.

She slapped her hand on the bar. "This proves Noah Barry was head of the Cabral cartel on the East Coast."

Nathan grabbed a bottle of water out of the fridge. "Maybe he was, maybe not. But he's dead."

"He could've passed the baton."

"To Calvin?"

"Cal didn't have the smarts." Erica sat silent. Then her gaze shifted. "Kate took over for her grandfather."

"Kate worked for the past three years holding a full-time bank position. As you've repeatedly pointed out, running drugs ain't no part-time gig."

Erica gave him a suit-yourself shrug. "All I know is our team moved into Spartina and everything went quiet. Even the street's dried up."

All true. Fatigue settled deep into his pores. He scrubbed his face. His eyelids felt as if someone had coated the inside with adhesive.

Last night, Kate exhibited visceral signs of fear and guilt. Drug cartel kingpins might experience fear, but guilt wasn't in a psychopath's archetype. "I think Lafferty wiping his computer threw Kate."

"She's a number cruncher. Her primary job at the bank was to vet hedge funds."

"Your point?"

"No way Lafferty hitched a ride down a road Kate didn't check, cross reference, and map," Erica said.

"Being trusting of an employee isn't a crime." He pressed two fingers against a knot lodged in his shoulder. Nathan wanted one more shot at Kate before she lawyered up. His sixth sense, his training, and everything he put into solving a case told him Kate wasn't a cold-blooded killer.

But he couldn't discount Erica's claim he was a dupe. Or ignore that his stomach fluttered like a smitten teen whenever Kate entered the room. It was throwing off his mojo.

Erica opened the fridge and popped the top on a can of Diet Coke. "You think this appraiser's death could be a coincidence?"

"Murder has no coincidences. Calvin Thompson, Jacob Lafferty, this last kid, what's his name— Norwich, and the appraiser. And it doesn't look good for Kate's investigator, Ben Snider. The Cabrals are covering their tracks."

Erica ran a finger around her Coke can. "I don't see their reasoning for whacking the appraiser."

"I'm betting Kate's figured it out, and she's spooked. When we find her, I need her to talk. She doesn't do that when you're in the room."

Erica slid onto a stool, laid her head against the wall, and closed her eyes. "Don't bet on Katie spilling her guts with or without me in the room. She's a student of Sun-Tzu." She laughed. "Kate quotes The Art of War at dinner parties. Used to drive Adam crazy."

The Art of War—Nathan could use that. But this morning, he had another battle to win. "I'm going to Savannah. Have a talk with Cedar Haynes's staff."

Erica didn't bother to look up. "Waste of time without a warrant."

"You take four hours and get some shut-eye. Then check the destinations of every private plane that took off after nine o'clock last night." He closed his laptop.

Erica grunted.

He stood in place.

She opened one eye and raised a thumb. "Got it. Before I hit the hay, is it okay if I issue a BOLO on the Fusion?"

"Yes." He thought it'd be a waste of time. Kate was smart enough to dump the car, but busy work would keep Erica occupied.

Nathan stopped at the guesthouse and searched for slick, smooth-talking Texan clothes for his field trip to Cedar's office. His choices were limited. He pulled on a white silk shirt, removed his socks, and slipped into tasseled loafers he only wore while working undercover. He plundered under the bathroom sink and found styling gel. He greased his hair and used his fingers to spike the ends into a punk-gangster style.

Haynes had morning court. Nathan's wardrobe change was directed at Cedar's assistant Shirleen, a single mom with a reputation for late-night partying. He counted on a bit of flirtatious chitchat leading to an invitation for Shirleen to accompany him in an impromptu New York City weekend. Then he'd ask her if she knew any private pilots. Thus netting the name of Cedar's favored local pilot. But if Shirleen was a fail, Nathan had a plan B.

---

Zipping down Broughton Street, Nathan found a parking spot a half block from Cedar Haynes's law office. The office opened at nine. Five minutes later, he stepped inside an empty lobby. A good sign the attorney wasn't in residence.

Cedar's receptionist wore skin-tight white pants and a purple jacket reminiscent of those worn by Spanish bullfighters. A nameplate advertising Lizzie Idleman sat on the desk.

The young lady was twenty-one years of age, a native Savannahian, and a recent graduate of SCAD, Savannah School of Arts and Design.

Lizzie was Nathan's plan B.

She cast him a beaming smile. "Can I help you?" Based on a phone conversation with a SCAD record clerk, Lizzie had a fashion merchandising degree.

"Darlin', are you a fashion model?" Nathan matched his smile to his twang.

Lizzie shifted in her seat and preened like a pedigreed poodle in front of a pack of mutts.

"I need a few minutes with Mr. Haynes this morning," he said.

"Mr. Haynes is in court today." She flipped her jet-black Elvira hair over her shoulder in one smooth, practiced move.

Nathan shot her a deflated frown. "Now that's a shame. How about his assistant?" He closed his eyes, then snapped his fingers. "I think her name is Shirleen."

"Her son had an accident at school. She's at the emergency room. I'm not sure when she'll be back." Lizzie pushed a group of wooden bangles up her forearm, slid her notepad from the corner of the desk, and looked up expectantly. "If you leave your contact information, I can have Shirleen call you."

Nathan donned his jacket, slipped his badge from his back pocket, and held it in front of Lizzie's face. "Marshal Nathan Parsi."

Lizzie's eye widened. She studied his badge, then rolled her chair back.

"What time do you expect Mr. Haynes?"

"No idea." Lizzie's face would make a suitable substitute for a roadblock. "He's in the middle of a case. Could be today. Could be tomorrow." She swiveled and glanced down the hall.

Nathan figured he had less than ten seconds before she called for backup. "Well, Lizzie, looks like you and I will be having a private chat."

She ran her long slender fingers through her hair again and gave it a little shake. "Not without a warrant." Her hand inched toward her desk phone.

Cedar's gatekeeper was well coached. Nathan leaned in three more inches. "Our conversation won't affect client confidentialities. It'll be about you."

Her brow wrinkled.

"Chief Ellington's a friend of mine." Nathan straightened to his full height. "You were the topic of our conversation earlier this morning."

"Me?" Understanding settled over her face like a veil.

"We can talk here if you want." He raised his voice. "Makes no difference to me."

Her gaze skittered toward the hall. "Not here."

"Starbucks. Five minutes." Nathan waited until she nodded her agreement, then walked out of the office without an ounce of guilt. Lizzie Idleman was about to learn a valuable lesson. One day, if she were half as smart as she was pretty, she'd be grateful—but probably not today.

He commandeered a corner table at Starbucks across the room from the line of addicts waiting patiently for their five-dollar fixes. Not that the privacy issue concerned him, but he was sure it'd be paramount to Lizzie.

She entered, maneuvered through the crowd, and stopped at his table.

He half stood. "Thanks for agreeing to meet with me."

"Did I have a choice?"

"Sure. We could've had this conversation at the police station." Nathan waited until she sat. "This is how it works. I ask questions. You answer." The chatter around their table faded into the background. "And I'll know if you're lying."

She jerked back as if Nathan were toxic. "I'd prefer to wait until Cedar's available."

A chastised expression settled over Nathan's face. "Trust me. You don't want to make me wait."

"What happens if I refuse to talk to you?"

"You spend no less than a year in jail and have a record for the rest of your life." His gaze locked on her face. "You think the fashion industry hires many ex-cons?"

The heady scent of fear rolled off her. "Cedar said he'd talk to the judge and get the charges dropped and expunged from my record."

"Your boss is an attorney. I'm a federal marshal." Nathan tilted his head back and forth. "Who're you going to trust?"

He tried to get a clean read, but it was impossible. The girl came in scared and had moved into petrified. Her breath turned short and choppy, and her body's frame was as rigid as a tree's trunk.

She uncrossed her arms and gripped the edge of the table. "It was only a dime bag. And it wasn't even mine."

"How original," Nathan deadpanned. "You be sure to explain that to the sentencing judge."

Tears swam in her eyes.

Time to throw the lifeline. "If I'm satisfied with your answers, I'll have the charges dropped. Otherwise, you receive the maximum sentence."

Her heaving chest and a steady stream of tears had no impact. Nathan looked at his watch. "What's it going to be?"

In less than ten minutes, Lizzie coughed up all she knew. Nathan placed a call to Savannah's chief of police and gave the okay to drop the cocaine possession. He disconnected his phone and turned his attention back to the girl. "Keep our conversation to yourself. You confide to your boss or anyone in or out of your office, and I'll rescind my request to Chief Ellington." He leaned over, picked up a stack of napkins from an adjacent table, and handed one to the girl. "We understand each other?"

She wiped her tears and nodded.

He stood. "And in the future, Lizzie, don't do anything anyone can hold over your head."

Nathan hit the sidewalk, texted Hart, and gave her the airstrip and the name of the local pilot who'd called and left Cedar a message about flying a group from Florida to California. He instructed Hart to run the guy, the company, and all their registered aircraft through the system. Then he assigned two agents to the Coastal Pines Executive airport, thirty minutes south of Talbot Island.

He attempted a call to the two officers assigned to Roslyn and Owen, but his agents didn't answer. They'd complained of spotty cell service on the island for the past two days. Nathan sent a text to their backup satellite phone.

If somehow they missed Kate returning to the island, they'd pick her up at Coastal Pines. But if she managed to slip through their net, Nathan would have no alternative but to issue an arrest warrant, and he'd lose the opportunity of talking to her without Cedar Haynes glued to her side.

# CHAPTER TWENTY-SEVEN

*Katelyn*

I STOOD IN THE lobby of the Jacksonville Airport Hampton Inn, out of a misting rain while I waited for my Uber car. Seven minutes later, I climbed into the back of a black SUV and met Les, my driver.

I dialed Mom, but she didn't answer. She was usually up by six. I sent her a text.

—My ETA is 10:30, call me.—

My previous two messages and three phone calls to Mom had gone unanswered. Anxiety weighed like a cement block on my chest. Until I had Owen in my arms and safe, I couldn't relax. I reminded myself that Mom refused to carry her phone around like a security blanket. She kept her cell by her bed or sometimes in her purse and sometimes she forgot and left it on the kitchen counter. She thought it sufficient if she checked her messages periodically throughout the day. My pulse settled somewhat, but the weight tightened as if a blood pressure cuff wrapped my heart and each beat released a spurt of pressure.

The weather app on my phone showed Sebastian stalling off the coast of Miami. The map predicting the storm's path showed it colliding with another front and hurtling up the coast at a breaking twenty-three miles an hour. Gusting winds would top out at a hundred and fifteen.

I texted Cedar on my last unused burner.

—Got plane. Lvg @ 1. Need directions to house.—

Ten miles from Talbot Island, Les pulled into a rest stop. I used the restroom, grabbed a Diet Coke, and hopped back into the car. An eighteen-wheeler backed into a parking spot and blocked us from pulling out.

My cell dinged a text from Cedar.

—In court. Will send soon.—

I glanced sideways, and an intense tingle of déjà vu settled over me. The face of the man in the car beside us fired fragmented memories through my head, like a ball spinning on a roulette wheel.

Then the ball slid into a winning slot.

The SUV was a gray Explorer, the same make and model that followed me from Charleston. I studied the driver's profile—Hispanic male, in his late forties or early fifties. Nothing about him stood out, no visible scars or tattoos. But there was something. There had to be hundreds of gray Ford Explorers, the odds of this one being the guy who'd followed me was a long shot.

The driver's eyes locked on mine, held for one hot, vibrant moment before he turned his attention back to the semi. The truck moved, and Les gave the Explorer the right of way. We both merged with the northbound traffic, and the Explorer zoomed three cars ahead.

I couldn't seem to shake my unease. I wanted another look. "Les, can we pick up speed?"

He glanced at me in the rearview mirror. "Can't afford tickets in my line of work. I set my speed five miles over the limit and stay there."

Suddenly, my insides felt as though I'd swallowed broken glass. Recognition zapped my brain. I bolted upright and called my assistant Jennifer, at home.

"When you apply for a license to marry, isn't there a section to list former spouses?" I asked. Jennifer should know since she'd chalked up two marriages by the age of twenty-five and was working hard on number three.

"Yeah, I had to admit to the jackasses from my wayward youth when I married the second third bozo, why?"

"I need you to scan the picture on the middle bookshelf in Joseph's office. It's of three men, Joseph, his son, and another man standing in front of a wooden building with a sign written in Spanish." If I was right, the other man in the photo had the same features as the guy in the wedding photo stuck in the Journey book. "And there's a book on his desk, Michener's Journey. A photo's inside, scan that one, too. Text them to me." If my hunch was right, the photos were of the same man, and he had similar features as the man in the gray Explorer.

"I met the US marshal at eleven o'clock last night and turned over Joseph's computer."

"I'm sorry you had to go in so late, but it was an emergency. I also need you to locate a copy of Joseph and Kathleen's marriage license. I want to know if Kathleen was Joseph's first wife." If I was right, the photos were all the same man and another confirmation that Joseph was the one threatening Owen.

"Kate, is everything okay? The Feds hauling out a manager's hard drive can't be good. Tell me the truth, do I need to worry?" Jennifer's voice begged for reassurance.

"I'll explain everything as soon as I get back in the office." I gave her my new cell number. "Don't give the number to anyone else."

Jennifer didn't question why.

Les turned into the Marsh Coast Golf Club and stopped. A bride and groom posed in front of a group of palms outlined in tiny lights under the porte cochère, a morning wedding.

I instructed Les on where to wait and jumped out of the car. Opening the service door on the side of the building, I slipped through, turned left, and entered the women's locker room. I planned for us to sneak out the back entrance, hustle across the eighteenth green, cross a backyard that led to a side street, and meet up with Les. Simple enough. Except my hands were shaking, my knees were knocking, and I couldn't seem to take a full breath.

I roamed the locker room looking for Mom and Owen and came up empty. I sat in a chair by the sink and sent Mom a text.

—I'm here. Where r u????—

My phone vibrated, and a blank text popped onto the screen with an attachment. I recognized Mom's number. The pressure in my chest eased. Thank goodness she was finally answering her messages.

I opened the attachment.

Let the sleeping dog lie or your son will pay the price.

You came close to losing him once. Will you chance it again?

This time for good.

Sending him to Florida won't protect him.

My heart skidded, then crashed. The words were a replica of the original threat I'd found in Ben's car on Monday—except for the last line. The first note instructed me to open Ben's trunk. That sentence was substituted with a new demand.

Go straight to Spartina. Wait for further instructions.

Or you'll never see your boy again!

# CHAPTER TWENTY-EIGHT

### *Katelyn*

I STUMBLED OUT OF the locker room and punched Mom's number into my phone. Pick up. Pick up. Pick up. "Please, Mom. Answer the phone."

Panic fueled my muscles, and I ran for the parking lot. My brain stretched for a reason, a less horrifying explanation—a phone hacker. Joseph's hacker.

I darted up and down the rows of parked cars hunting for Stanley's sedan—Range Rovers, Lexus, BMWs, plenty of Mercedes, but none were chocolate brown.

Mom and Owen had to be here. Somewhere. I dashed back to the locker room and checked every stall. I searched all three seating areas in the restaurant. Then called Mom's phone again, and it went straight to voicemail. "Call me. I need to talk to you."

I called my uncle's home, then Mom's cell, back and forth. Ranting each time Stanley's number beeped busy, and Mom's calm, unruffled voice said she'd return my call. I stopped the madness and called Cedar. "Do you know where Mom is?"

"She's not with you?"

"Joseph's kidnapped Owen and Mom." The words slid from my lips, and the jarring truth sank in.

"What?"

"I got a text…"

"Don't be ridiculous. Why would Joseph kidnap Roslyn and your boy?"

I swallowed an urge to scream. "They were supposed to meet me. They're not here. She's not answering her phone."

He sighed. "You sneaking away from Spartina most likely got Parsi's nose out of joint. He's probably socked them in one of his safe houses until he finds you." A serves-you-right tone engulfed Cedar's voice. "I'll call him, find out where they are. But this wrecks the California plans."

I stood in the club's foyer and locked on to the idea that a federal marshal had forced Mom and Owen to leave my uncle's—not really that far-fetched. Unlike Joseph holding Owen and Mom hostage, which fell apart somewhere between my heart and brain. "But if Parsi has Owen and Mom, who sent the text from Mom's phone? The same text left with Calvin's body?"

"You got that message again today?"

"Except this one's ordering me back to Spartina."

"I haven't talked to Roslyn since yesterday."

Apprehension finally drifted through Cedar's tone. "When's the last time you spoke—"

I hit disconnect. Cedar didn't know anything. I redialed Stanley's home number.

Please answer. Please. Please. Please make sense of this nightmare.

"Kate." Stanley's voice broke.

Relief soared through my veins. "Thank God. I'm trying to reach Mom—"

"They're gone."

My relief plummeted. "Mom and Owen aren't there?"

"We can't find them. But she left an envelope on her bed addressed to you." New relief swept over me. Mom must've changed her mind about going to California. "What's the note say?"

Stanley read the message. The words were an exact replica of the text I'd just received.

"Do you know what the note means?" he asked.

The perimeter of the club's foyer turned fuzzy. My stomach rolled and knotted. Bile rose in my throat.

"Kate." My uncle's voice echoed from the phone. "Kate, are you there?"

Questions rushed forward. "How long have they been gone?"

"We're not sure." Stanley's voice faltered. "But we think sometime within the past two hours. I tried to call you. Left messages at your house, your office, your cell."

Two hours? Where was I two hours ago? Ten miles away eating breakfast. Joseph stole my baby while I scarfed down eggs. "Oh, God." My chest seized, then squeezed—no way to get air. I slumped into a chair. Breathe, Kate—slow breaths. Just breathe.

"My car's in the garage." Stanley's words broke through. "And Roslyn's purse is still in her bedroom."

It felt like I'd been cut, the knife so deep the wound wasn't yet painful. "The marshals guarding Mom and Owen didn't see anyone on your property?"

"We were all passed out."

The minute amount of blood remaining in my heart drained away. "Passed out?" I pushed the phone tighter against my ear.

"I couldn't sleep…" Stanley's voice cracked. He cleared his throat. "I came to the kitchen to get water, sat down with the marshals, and drank a cup of coffee with them. The coffee must've been laced with something because we all woke up on the kitchen floor. And Roslyn and Owen were gone."

My field of vision contracted to one black point, then disappeared altogether, leaving behind a bright, blinding void. "Is Owen's iPad in his room? His Ranger's cap? He doesn't go anywhere without them."

"I'll look." The telephone bumped against what sounded like wood, then Stanley's voice mixed with another and floated through the receiver.

My phone pinged with an email from Cedar.

Word on the street is Erica's gunning for your indictment. My source says there's a good chance she'll get it. Be careful.

"Kate Landers?"

I jumped and came close to dropping the phone. "Yes."

"What's your location, Ms. Landers?"

One long quiver ran up my spine. "Who's this?"

"Officer Warren Peabody. My partner and I are investigating the possible disappearance of your son and mother."

The police officer's words were muffled, drowned by the stronger and far more compelling voice in my head.

Go to Spartina

Wait for further instructions.

Or you'll never see your boy again!

I disconnected, jammed the phone in my purse, and ran out of the building. Cut through the eighteenth green, skirted a backyard fishpond, and found Les. The car door was locked, and I banged on the window.

Les disengaged the locks, and I climbed inside. "Interstate. Head north," I wheezed and pointed toward the exit.

Les drove to the front entrance of the golf club, stopped, and turned to face me. His lips moved, but the blood rushed through my ears, roaring like a fierce summer squall.

"Why are you stopping?" I pointed to the road. "Go." My brain recognized my pitching screech, but I didn't care. "This is an emergency. Drive."

"I can't go to Savannah. My daughter has a fever. I need to go back to Jacksonville."

"No. I have to go home. I live an hour south of Savannah."

"I'm sorry. I can't take you to Savannah." His soothing voice was soft and fluid, as if he were consoling a lost child.

James's car was near the airport. "Okay, you can drop me in Jacksonville. Near the airport."

Les put his SUV in gear. "Give me the address."

---

Ten minutes later, we hit the bridge connecting the island to the mainland and headed north on the interstate. Eight lanes of traffic traveled at a steady seventy-five miles an hour, and the dark clouds in the sky were as black and desolate as my thoughts.

This wasn't the first time Owen had disappeared. But his last abductor had been his father. And although I was livid, I wasn't worried about Owen's safety. I'd called Erica and begged her to find Adam. She dropped everything. Used her resources, called in favors, and found Adam six days later on a remote island in the Abacos. A voice in my head, whispered call her, call Erica now. She loves Owen, she'll find him again.

A louder voice drowned out the first.

Let sleeping dogs lie or your son will pay.

The message was clear, don't go to the police. But Erica was already at Spartina, and so were Nathan and their team. And one of them worked for Joseph.

My imagination conjured images of Owen, then blended with the horrific sight of Calvin's body stuffed into Ben's trunk, morphing back to Owen's sweet face. I pushed my ricocheting delirium to the deepest pit of my consciousness. Succumbing to frenzied hysteria wouldn't get my son back. I called Cedar.

"Have you heard from Roslyn?" he asked.

"No. The kidnapper drugged Stanley and the two marshals. The local police are investigating. Do you have a contact in the FBI?"

"I do. But the text instructed you to wait for instructions. Not saying you're wrong, but make sure you're willing to take the risk. Might be better to go home and let the kidnapper contact you. Find out what they want first." His words rushed together, a cadence he often used when convincing someone over to his side.

"Joseph is sending me back to Spartina because he has a man on Nathan's team. I can't fight this alone. You make the call to your friend."

I felt better. No, I felt less. The pain in my chest eased, the tightness in my neck dissipated, and my mind honed to laser sharp.

"You don't know for sure that Joseph is the kidnapper," Cedar said. "And it'll be quicker if Parsi calls in the Feds."

"I don't trust him."

"A US marshal isn't behind this kidnapping."

Stanley tried to ring through, but I ignored his call.

"Maybe not, but Parsi has a Cabral man on his team."

"We don't know that for sure."

"We don't know anything for sure except that Owen and Mom are gone. Call your contact. Now." I disconnected and turned the sound to vibrate. The only call I intended to answer was Joseph's.

Stanley made a second attempt to get through, but I had nothing to tell him. And if the police were still at his house, I didn't want to explain my decision to go to Spartina. I typed a text.

—Talking to FBI. Will call w/update.—

Not quite the truth, but close.

Drizzling rain turned into a steady stream. Long stretches of shiny blacktop closed in and brought new images from the dark, foreboding sky. Owen frightened and crying. Mom attempting to be strong. Oh, God, would I see them again? Blood oozed between my fingers. I unclenched my fist and ran my finger over the four half-moon cuts in my palm.

I had promised myself I'd be the world's most loving and attentive mother. And two months later, I'd failed the most basic parental responsibility—protect my son from evil.

I leaned my head against the seat rest. I didn't have the luxury of giving into panic. Owen was with Mom; I had to take comfort that she'd protect him with her life. My job was to focus on their rescue.

There were so many places Joseph could hide them. In state, out of state. Where would he take them?

Owen's iPad.

iPads had GPS locators. I kept a serial number list of all electronics. The authorities would know how to access the coordinates. I had asked Stanley to check Owen's bedroom for the iPad and Ranger's cap, but I'd hung up before he'd answered my question.

I hurriedly texted my uncle.

—Did u find Owen's iPad?—

Les pulled alongside the Fusion, and I jumped out, unlocked my car, and headed north for Spartina.

Rain rapped on the car's roof like the restless drum of fingers on a tabletop. A beep noted an incoming message, but it was from Jennifer, not Stanley. I moved to the right lane, slowed, and read her text.

—J & K married 1988—

Jacob was three years younger than me. Jacob would have been three when Joseph married Kathleen.

A picture of Owen at three years flashed in my mind. We were on the floor in the middle of the mall, playing with a litter of rescue puppies. Owen begged to take one home, but I made excuses to wait until he was older. I should've bought him the puppy. A boy should have a dog. And a horse. A dog and a horse.

I read the rest of Jennifer's text.

—J's 1st wife—Alexandria Marie Cabral Quintino, died 1986—

"Cabral?" Joseph had been married to a Cabral.

Jacob was a Cabral.

Traffic stalled. As far as I could see, a line of cars crept like maple sap tapped two weeks early—stop, start, stop, start. The wind began in earnest, blowing so fast and furious the Fusion rocked in place. I called Stanley.

"Any news from the FBI?" he asked.

"Not yet. Did you find Owen's iPad?"

"On his nightstand. But I couldn't find his Ranger's cap."

My body turned to cement, and I sank feet first into a bottomless chasm. I had no way to find Owen. I hung up. My despair was like a trough on the ocean's floor, obscure, black, and silent. It held me in place. You can't quit, Kate. The voice in my head warned. Owen needs you.

I dragged my mind out of the darkness. I had to trust the FBI had the human resources to find my baby. They'd root out the snitch on Parsi's team and force him to talk. The traitor would lead us to Joseph and ultimately to Owen and Mom. I had to get to Spartina.

An ambulance drove down the median and circumvented the stalled traffic. I pulled out, ignored the horns blaring, and followed the whirling lights. A mile down the road, the ambulance stopped. An officer directing traffic stepped to my car, peered in my window, and favored me with a chastising frown. He directed me to park behind a black SUV.

Don't argue. Take the ticket and go.

A group of four police officers huddled next to the SUV's tailgate, then parted.

Erica Sanchez stepped forward.

She stood in the beam of my headlights, hands on her hips, feet spread. I heard Cedar's warning: Erica's gunning for an indictment. She walked to the car, tapped the window, and motioned for me to step out.

I climbed out of the Fusion. Sheets of rain poured from the sky and drenched my clothes and shoes. I pushed dripping hair from my face and stared into Erica's brown eyes, caverns empty of warmth, concern, or human kindness.

"We have to go to Spartina," I said. "Joseph Lafferty's kidnapped Owen."

Erica gripped my forearm and pulled me toward her SUV. "You're wanted for questioning."

I jerked my arm away. "After we find Owen and Mom, I'll go wherever you say."

"I don't make deals." Erica removed the handcuffs from her belt. Four police officers circled us.

My heart squeezed. I couldn't fight Erica and four cops. "I demand to speak with Marshal Nathan Parsi."

"And Marshal Nathan Parsi is anxious to talk to you." Erica snapped the cuffs over my wrists. "But it doesn't matter whose shoulder you cry on, Katie. You're going to jail."

# CHAPTER TWENTY-NINE

*Nathan*

NATHAN CARRIED TWO cups into Spartina's library. An oversized mug of black coffee strong enough to raise his pulse and a cup of tea from a box with calming splashed across the front. He set the tea in front of Kate. Exhaustion rolled off her like rain from a gutter.

Her face, swollen and puffy, matched her voice, raw and hoarse as if she'd spent the entire trip from Florida sobbing.

Kate showed clear visceral signs of desperation, which could be attributed to being handcuffed and locked in a car with Erica for the past two hours.

Erica had been aloof and uncharacteristically quiet since arriving. She switched on the weather channel, muted the sound, and stood with her back to Kate.

He had a better chance of Kate opening up without Erica hovering and ready to swoop at the slightest provocation. Nathan placed his hand on Erica's shoulder. "I'd like to talk to Kate alone."

Erica nodded.

"I want her to stay."

Nathan turned to Kate, certain he'd misunderstood. If Erica was right and Kate's visceral signs were from facing her comeuppance for a crime-ridden life, perp stress and not shock, then why would she ask for her champion nemesis to remain at her side?

"No matter what's between us, Erica loves Owen. She'd never betray Owen. She's the only one on your team I trust isn't working for the Cabrals." Kate's face captured the muddled consternation of a soldier trapped behind enemy lines. "She stays, or I have nothing to say."

Erica shrugged, a poster child for unimpressed dispassion. The sound of wind whistling and whipping across the gardens filled the room. Nathan nodded his approval, and Erica turned back to the television. "They've downgraded the hurricane to a tropical storm, but it's headed this way."

He sat in the chair across from Kate and quickly texted Jonathan Wright asking for an updated ETA. He'd called in a favor and pressed his friend in the Georgia Bureau of Investigation to open a kidnapping investigation. No easy task since the alleged abduction happened across state lines, and responding officers determined the evidence pointed to a contrived disappearance, presumably orchestrated by Kate.

He sipped his coffee and studied Kate studying Erica. Kate's eyes held the remnants of defeat, the injured gaze of the wounded.

"You have the original note you claim was left in Ben Snider's car?" he asked.

She extracted her wallet from her purse, removed a slip of green ruled paper, and passed it to him.

He read the note. "We need to list people you believe have reason to abduct your family."

Kate pressed her fingers against her eyelids. "How many times do I have to say it? Joseph Lafferty abducted Owen and Mom. He's your drug kingpin." Her voice gained strength as she made her case. "He laundered millions of dollars through my company. He abducted

Owen to keep me from going to the police. And someone on your team works for Joseph."

Erica huffed, but she was smart enough to keep her back to Nathan.

Kate's gaze lingered on Erica's back, then settled on Nathan. "Joseph's the only possibility."

"GBI's going to push for a list of other prospects," Nathan said.

"Only if they open a file," Erica chewed the words, but the meaning was clear even with her back turned.

Kate leaned across the table and grabbed Nathan's hand. "You have to convince them. Your agent, who reports to Joseph, will know how to contact him. That's who told Joseph Owen was with Mom on Talbot Island."

Erica met Nathan's gaze and rolled her eyes. "Here's the latest forecast on the storm."

Wind gusts spit hail against the glass panes like BBs in rat-ta-tat-tat succession. At the same time, a forecaster reported Hurricane Sebastian, now a category three hurricane, hugged the Atlantic Coastline, gaining strength.

Erica turned to Kate. "Does your generator power the guest house?"

Kate's forehead creased. "You still have men here?"

"Six, plus Nathan and me," Erica said.

"You said the drug ring left the island. Why are your men still here?"

Nathan tapped the green paper. "If this threat is from the Cabrals, you'll be glad our team's at Spartina sitting on ready."

Kate ran her hands over her forearms, then massaged her chest, her favorite self-soothing gesture. "During the ride here, Erica said the police believe my mother and Owen left by boat. Our company warehouses have access to water, and Joseph knows the terrain better than anyone."

"We've checked the warehouses." Nathan kept his voice level and studied Kate's face. "Joseph's house in Savannah, and his son's place in Brunswick."

"Yeah," Erica said. "Even if we're manipulated and jerked around, we do our job."

Kate's head whipped in Erica's direction. She rose from her seat, her jaw set, her body humming with fury. She walked toward Erica. "I've had enough of your patronizing crap. Either take this seriously or leave."

"Me, take it seriously?" Erica met her halfway and shoved a finger in Kate's chest. "You didn't bother to go to the abduction site and talk to the police. Cut the crap about who's taking it seriously."

Kate swatted away Erica's hand. "I couldn't go to my uncle's." Her voice reverberated off the ceiling. "Joseph's message said to go to Spartina."

"You're pandering for sympathy. This hoax won't stand up," Erica said. "You're going down for murder and racketeering. You'll be behind bars for the rest of your natural life. Have you considered what your life of crime will cost Owen?"

"Erica, I haven't broken the law."

"When the GBI gets here, they'll agree with me. Roslyn and Owen are tucked away in a safe hidey-hole." She shot Kate a knowing smirk. "We know about the California house."

Nathan prayed for enough strength to keep his hands from wrapping around Erica's skinny little neck. His phone vibrated with a message. "Weather's delayed the GBI. Six o'clock is the new estimate."

"Five more hours? Why can't we answer their questions by phone?" Kate's desperation didn't seem to touch Erica. She believed Kate was hiding her family, but Nathan was certain, down to his core, that Kate was petrified for her son's safety.

"You're lucky Nathan has friends," Erica said. "Otherwise, the GBI wouldn't waste their time making the drive from Atlanta."

"Stop it, Erica." Kate slid into a chair and rocked. "I'm begging you. Joseph kidnapped Owen and Mom. You have to believe me."

"An underage minor walked away with his grandparent," Erica said. "And when the police notified his mother of a possible abduction, she hung up on the officer and headed in the opposite direction."

Kate continued to sway. Her soft sobs held the deep grief of defeat. All visceral reactions were conducive to absolute loss and impossible to fake. She believed her son and mother had been abducted.

Erica stood over Kate. "If you really found that note with Calvin's body, if the threat to Owen were real, you would've come to me. But you didn't. No way, Katie, I don't believe your claim."

Fire flashed in Kate's eyes. "I didn't believe you'd have an affair with my husband behind my back either. So, like me, perhaps you should reconsider what's believable."

Erica triple blinked but didn't look away. "When I was involved with Adam, he wasn't your husband."

Kate pushed out of her chair and lunged.

Erica stumbled back, tripped over a chair leg, and fell. She popped to standing. Nathan figured Erica had underestimated Kate's anger. Being bested by a civilian wouldn't sit well.

He rushed the pair, got in between them, and shoved each woman in opposite directions. "Enough."

Kate glared at Erica and pointed to the door. "Get out."

"Be honest, Katie. Owen isn't in any danger," Erica said. "And while you're soul-searching for the truth, admit you didn't love Adam. You hadn't cared who he was involved with for years."

Kate inhaled a deep breath. "You're right. I didn't

love Adam anymore. But I loved you, Erica. And you betrayed our friendship." She faced Nathan. "I'll contact the FBI and convince them I'm telling the truth. You better pray I find my son and mother unhurt, or when I'm through, neither of your careers will be worth saving."

"Calm down. I believe you." Nathan gripped Kate's forearm. Her body hummed beneath his fingers. "My contact at the GBI is Agent Jonathan Wright. I've made all the arrangements, and we're ready for the kidnapper's next move. Your phones are tapped, and your email accounts are being monitored—at least all the accounts we know about."

Nathan let go of her arm and grasped her shoulders. "In child abductions, a parent is always the first suspect. You have to be ruled out. Whether it was me, Agent Wright, or the FBI, this conversation will happen more than once. You'll answer questions, the same ones, over and over until we find your family."

Kate's lovely eyes, the color of green jade, glistened. She had dropped weight in the past four days, and her features appeared sculpted as if someone had carved her face with a keen and clever blade. Her chiseled cheeks gave her an intriguingly dangerous look, and her eyes, slightly sunken, appeared fearless and daunting. Her eyes. He remembered those eyes.

Recognition is a convoluted phenomenon. A nearly instantaneous connection of memories and perceptions. Variables that might never be replicated. A slight head rotation, a side view of a body, coupled with an expression. Even an instant later, it was almost impossible to pinpoint what triggered the click.

Nathan fast-forwarded through a slide show of photographs stored in his memory and pushed pause on a group shot of Juan Cabral in the mid-eighties. A critical clue slipped cleanly into place.

Then quick as a hissing snake, Kate's fingers coiled around his wrist, and she flung his hand from her shoulder. "Gather your men, Marshal. I'm tired of playing hostess. I'm tired of your pretend game of cooperation. And I'm tired of being your one and only suspect. If you were going to arrest me, you would have by now, but you haven't. So get off my property."

# CHAPTER THIRTY

*Katelyn*

PARSI CLASPED MY forearms with a cast-iron grip. "Is this tantrum worth your son's life?" Disgust covered his face.

I shoved my palms against his chest.

He pulled me within two inches of his body. "Do you realize you've just banished every available agent from your estate? There's no one left to search for your family."

My outrage slipped away as quietly as a sun's shadow. I stared into his chestnut eyes, and for an instant, his expression conjured the image of a stalking cougar. The silence expanded between us, filled with my fears and his frustration.

Parsi's colorless lips pressed razor-thin, but he dropped his hands. "Either you and I work together, or you spend the night behind bars."

His voice held not one whiff of kindness. But inexplicably, his presence centered me, and a piece of the boulder resting on my shoulders fell away. "I want you to stay. Please. Help me find Owen and Mom."

Rain poured from the sky like God had opened heaven's door to blow his wrath to earth.

"If you want my help, first—" He held up his index

finger. "No holding back. No matter what I ask, I get complete honesty."

"Same goes."

He frowned. "I've always been honest with you."

"Really?" My questioning tone raised his brow. "What about the airboat? Owen and I were stalked across Barry Island by one of your men. You never once bothered to mention that fact. Why did you expect me to be honest and forthright when you weren't?"

"Okay." His voice softened. "You're right, I should've mentioned that the airboat was ours. But Johnston was trying to get you off the island before Cabral's men showed up." He ran his hand through his hair and inhaled a breath. "Let's start over. And this time, we trust each other."

"Okay."

"And you're a walking zombie, Kate. You're no good to your son or me if you collapse."

A thunderous crack shook the house, then an earth-slamming thud. A tree limb the size of a small canoe landed on the patio, mere inches from the French door.

Parsi remained focused on only me. He pointed in the direction of the kitchen. "Eat. Drink."

My body exploded with heat. "You think I can eat? Owen could be hungry or cold. He must be scared to death."

"Kate, stop a minute and think. If you didn't coordinate this disappearance, then your mother did."

"What are you talking about?" I stumbled backward. "My mother? Are you crazy?"

"She had access to the kitchen." Parsi stretched his words as if slowing them down would make the incredible more palatable.

Indignation rode over my fear. "My mother would not put me through this nightmare."

"Traces of ketamine were in the coffee carafe and the Mountain Dew cans but in no other liquids in the kitchen. One of my agents had an affinity for gourmet coffee and the other Mountain Dew. How would an outsider know that? Your uncle was knocked out along with my men, so this wasn't his rodeo." He tilted my chin and forced our eyes to meet. "How well did your mother know Juan Cabral?"

His quiet confidence was the catalyst behind the panic clawing up my spine. I stepped away from his touch. "Mom barely knew Juan Cabral. Hadn't seen him in thirty years."

Parsi's sigh exuded exhaustion. "She knows Cabral better than she admits."

My thoughts stalled, stuck on words I couldn't reconcile. Could he be right? This wasn't a real kidnapping? Please, God, let him be right.

I bent over, tense as a coiled spring, then snapped upright and paced the room. "What reason would Mom have to run off with Owen unless someone forced her?"

His eyes followed me, assessing, measuring. "There's no evidence of physical coercion," he said. "Two sets of footprints led away from the house and down to the beach. An adult print, women's size six and a half. The other print is a child's size nine. No indication of dragging or stumbling or resisting. And no other footprints."

He grabbed his laptop and sat on the sofa. "And your mother tried to contact him."

"Who?"

"Juan Cabral. At 2200 last night, she made a call to a Cabral safe number. The call popped for us, but we didn't know it was your mother until we cross-referenced her phone number with your burner."

Mom had called Cabral after I told her Calvin was murdered. My mind scrambled for a plausible reason she would have a current phone number for Juan Cabral. "What's a safe number?"

"Contact number to leave a secure message. The number belonged to an art gallery in Mexico City. The store's a front for the Cabral syndicate."

I didn't gasp or argue. My heart simply stopped, as if a hand reached inside my chest and squeezed. Had I known when Mom's color faded at the mention of Juan's name? The jade box? The old letters? The rare and expensive jewels she never wore? Would she put me through this purgatory to cover up a long-ago affair?

I knew in the depths of my soul that this kidnapping resulted from Granddad's dirty money. "I can't explain the footprints, but Mom wouldn't fabricate a kidnapping to cover up an old love affair. This is Joseph's doing. He's laundering money, and that's why he threatened Owen. To keep me quiet."

"I'm not saying you're wrong about your property manager or his motives. Just that your son wasn't kidnapped."

"What about your GBI friend? When's he going to get here?"

Parsi checked his phone. "He had to pull over and wait out the storm. His new estimate is in the morning by ten o'clock."

I gripped the desk, my nails dug into the wood.

"I have an idea how we might locate Lafferty." He made himself comfortable on the sofa, his back against the armrest, and he began typing. His phone beeped. He swiped the screen on his cell, then returned to his keyboard.

"What are you doing?"

"I'm hunting. Your mom called Juan, but that didn't work."

"If my mother and Juan are in contact and such good friends, why wouldn't he help her?"

"Because he's dead." Parsi picked up his iPad.

"Dead?" My mind swirled with this new information. Did it impact anything? I had no idea. "When did he die?"

"Our sources say two, maybe three months."

If Mom called Juan and found out he'd died, would that cause her to run? But why? Mom and Juan seemed such an unlikely pair. But there was the jade box, the jewelry... "I've tried working out a timeline on the robbery at Mom's house, but something's off. Joseph was out of town. He couldn't be the thief. And Calvin breaking in doesn't fit."

Parsi looked up. "Why doesn't Calvin fit?"

"I went to Cal's house Monday morning, around seven o'clock. We argued, and he stormed away within fifteen minutes. You claimed your men followed him to the Abercorn diner. Even with traffic, that's a ten-minute drive." I paced between the desk and the sofa, working out the timeline. "His pal Bubba picked him up at the restaurant, and Ben confirmed with a neighbor, Cal and Bubba arrived at the condo before eight. That's another twenty-minute drive."

I continued pacing the room. "The police officer noticed the door to Mom's house open at eight. There wasn't enough time for Calvin to leave Bubba's, go to Mom's, wreck the library, and steal a box of old letters and some jewelry."

Parsi sat quiet long enough that I knew I'd surprised him. Finally, he nodded. "And take care to leave no fingerprints, but careless enough to leave his briefcase."

A tingle swept my body. "You agree the briefcase was a plant."

"I never bought the idea Calvin ran out and forgot it." He picked up his empty water bottle. "Good instincts. You might think about getting into detective work."

Detective. My missing detective. "Have you found a lead on Ben?"

Parsi shook his head. "Guy's vanished." He unfolded his body, rose from the sofa, and stretched his back. "Cedar Haynes had an interesting phone call the morning your grandfather's old appraiser died."

"The appraiser's dead?"

Nathan nodded.

"You have Cedar under investigation?"

He shrugged, "He's your attorney. Your mom's boyfriend. And best friend to your dead father." He grimaced. "Sorry, that was crass."

I waved his apology away. "Dad's been dead for twenty years." But now that Mom and Cedar were involved, maybe Mom confided she'd had an affair with Juan, and Cedar helped her fake the kidnapping. But why? I struggled with sharing this thought because the scenario didn't make sense. And Cedar had worked out the California house for me. We were within hours of leaving when Owen and Mom disappeared. "What kind of interesting call did Cedar receive?"

"I traced the call back to a burner." Parsi grabbed water from the bar refrigerator and threw one in my direction.

"Might have been one of the burners he gave me on Tuesday," I said.

"The call was last week, Wednesday, the day before Lafferty left town. My gut says it's all related, and your attorney's holding back information." He chugged his water and tossed the empty bottle in the trash.

I walked to the bookshelf, pushed, and stepped inside the hidden passage.

"Where are you going?" Parsi called.

I glanced over my shoulder. "Hunting." He followed me to the entryway. "There's something in my room I want to show you. I'll be right back." I rushed down the passage, snatched the white notebook off my nightstand, and ran back.

Back in the library, Parsi lightly pushed the shelf. The case swung silently back into place. He ran his hand over the wall. "This craftsmanship is impeccable. I would've never known."

I carried the notebook to the desk. "This notebook has Joseph's personal bills, phone records, and bank statements for the past year."

"Where'd you get them?"

"His office. Nerdy bookkeepers collect paper." I flipped to the section with Joseph's bank statements. "I believe Juan Cabral paid handsomely for my grandfather to provide safe havens for his drug ring. When he had his stroke, Joseph stepped in and continued the scheme."

"You found proof?"

"Bogus construction contracts, leases, and inflated rents for broken-down buildings, all with access to the ocean."

I walked to the corner desk, picked up my phone, swiped the screen, and handed it to Parsi. "I recently found out Joseph's first wife was a Cabral."

He read the text from Jennifer, then tapped out a text message on his phone. "And where did the money end up?"

"Offshore accounts."

"How much?" Parsi asked.

"What's left is thirty million for my grandfather. Ten million for Joseph."

He blew a low whistle.

I flipped to the back of the notebook. "These are the statements with the account numbers."

"Maybe we can put together something," Parsi said. "I've pulled Lafferty's phone records. He called the same phone number six times the day he left town. I ran the number, but this weather's slowing everything down. I should hear back soon."

My dam of emotions resting just below the surface broke. I covered my face and cried. "We have to find Joseph. I know he has Owen and Mom."

Parsi rubbed my back, made soft, soothing sounds.

After a few minutes, my crying jag slowed, the last of my energy spent, but we were no closer to finding Owen. I pushed away from Parsi and used a tissue to dry my face. "Exactly how do you plan to find Owen?"

"We have a thread leading us to Joseph, and I plan to pull that string."

"What thread?"

Parsi tore out the most recent bank statement from the notebook. His smile was more bad guy than good cop. "Montevideo. Now that is a charming coastal city large enough for a man to vanish."

My heart somersaulted. "You think Joseph would try and take Owen and Mom out of the country?"

Parsi's cell buzzed. His phone conversation lasted less than thirty seconds. "Yes, sir," his only words. He disconnected. "Erica's been summoned to Atlanta."

"I shouldn't have thrown her out." I sat in my chair and rested my head on my desk. I was so tired. "No matter what's happened between us, Erica loves Owen."

Parsi's laptop signaled an incoming message. "Got a hit on the cell number Lafferty called. The address is twenty miles from here, someplace called Hidden Cove." He rubbed the back of his neck. "Why does that sound familiar?" He grabbed his iPad and scrolled.

I rose and walked across the room. "Come to the window." Relentless rain poured from turbulent clouds casting a gloomy foreboding over the day. I pointed. "You can't see it now, but the strip of land across the river is Hidden Cove. It's a small fishing community. Thirty minutes by car, ten by boat."

Parsi looked relieved. "Okay, now we're getting somewhere. We'll check out the address as soon as Jonathan arrives."

We stayed at the window and watched the fury. "This has to be an eighty-mile-an-hour wind," I said, then whispered a prayer that Owen and Mom were safe from harm.

"We'll find them." Nathan's voice turned soft and consoling.

I searched his face for assurance and, for the first time, saw empathy and concern in his eyes.

"You have to stay strong," he said, an oddly rough note in his voice. "Your family's depending on you."

I pressed my fingers against my lids to hold back my tears, and he wrapped his arm around my waist and pulled me closer.

I leaned my head on his shoulder and accepted his warmth. I couldn't draw a full breath. But his arms were steady, and he didn't let go.

Slowly, slowly, I let myself breathe.

The hours dragged by, each longer than the last. At five o'clock, my cell phone buzzed. I raised my head off the sofa cushion, patted my pocket for my cell, and checked my email for the hundredth time. The buzz had been nothing but a weather alert.

For some reason, my emotions were under control, and my mind was engaged again. A nagging thought persisted. I rolled it around and tried to remember where I'd run across the word Hidden Cove. On a form or a report? Maybe in one of Joseph's files? No.

I returned to the desk and found my purse, shuffled through the notepad where I'd written down Joseph's scribbled notes from the Journey novel in his office. I read what I'd written.

Hidden Cove 132 Shell Landing

On my computer, I googled and found a cross-directory website, typed in the pieces of an address, and got a hit. David Norwich, 132 Shell Landing, Hidden Cove, GA.

"Does David Norwich mean anything?" I asked.

"Norwich?" Nathan raised his head. "Yeah, there's two Norwich boys. One was our third DB. The other one was Calvin's low-life dive boat captain. Why?"

I searched the DNR website, then I checked the time; we still had four hours before Nathan's GBI friend would arrive. "I think you and I should take a ride."

# CHAPTER THIRTY-ONE

### *Katelyn*

I OPENED MY GRANDDAD'S safe and removed the Glock 17 semi-automatic and two extra clips.

Nathan frowned at the gun. "What are you doing?"

I shoved the gun into the waistband of my still-damp jeans and grabbed two rain slickers from the closet. "We should be back before your friend Jonathan gets here."

"Back from where?" Nathan had stood in front of me, hands to hips, wide stance, and blocked me from the door.

I handed him a yellow rain slicker and turned to go.

He spun me, snatched my gun, and stuffed it in the waistband of his jeans. "Back from where?"

"Hidden Cove's ten minutes by boat and can't have more than ten roads. Finding Shell Landing won't be hard. But I'll need the gun."

Nathan's expression was as unwavering as a slab of concrete.

I pleaded my case. "I checked Department of Natural Resource records, and David Norwich, Cal's scary dive boat driver, has two boats registered in his name: a thirty-year-old shrimp boat and a sixteen-foot Carolina skiff. Whoever picked Mom and Owen up off the beach had to have a small skiff. And a shrimp boat would've been the perfect way to disappear."

"You think your mother knows David Norwich?"

"No. I think Mom knows Joseph, who knows David Norwich. And Norwich is our first real lead. I'm not willing to risk him disappearing."

"I'm not going anywhere until Jonathan arrives." Nathan backed me up a step. "And neither are you."

I twisted my hair into a tail, grabbed a rubber band off the desk, and snapped it in place. "If Norwich's boat is at the dock in this storm, chances are good he'll be home. I'll let you know if your theory of my mother kidnapping Owen pans out."

"You're not going alone."

Relief slid over my body. I wasn't sure how well Granddad's sixteen-foot Ranger, a flats boat that worked great for visiting the island, would navigate the river's five-foot waves. Having Nathan with me would at least ensure a call to the Coast Guard if I fell overboard.

"You think Norwich will spill his guts because you ask politely?" He ran his fingers through his hair.

I snatched my Glock back. "I'm a five-million-dollar dealmaker. I can be very persuasive." I shoved the gun deep into the slicker's front pocket.

Nathan attempted his flat cop stare. "When Jonathan arrives, we'll ride over and check out Norwich's place."

I propped open the French door with my foot. "If it were your son, would you sit here waiting?"

He exhaled a long, suffering sigh. "Okay. Fine. I'll go. You stay and wait for Jonathan. And possibly a call from Joseph." Nathan used his no-room-for-negotiation tone.

"I'm going," I countered, my tone well past the negotiating stage. "If you go alone, you'll end up stuck on a sand bar. Norwich will vanish like everyone else. I'm the best chance you've got at crossing that river in this weather."

Nathan put on the slicker. "This is probably a dead

lead. And crossing a river in a flats boat during a hurricane is ludicrous."

The wind caught the French door and slammed the frame against the brick. "It's not a hurricane anymore, Erica said they downgraded it to a tropical storm hours ago."

I hoped my levity would get him out the door.

He scanned my face as if looking for some clue I might change my mind, but then he locked his arm around my waist. Halfway down the path to the dock, a squall pushed across the rose garden. I bent, head down, and fought the wind with each step.

Nathan pulled me along, spread my fingers, and forced them around the dock's banister. "Use the railing."

I held on to the wood and pushed against a wall of wind. "I'll handle the lift. Pick me up on the floating dock."

Nathan raised his thumb and shimmied over the side of the boat. He opened the storage bin and removed two inflatable life jackets and slid one over his head.

I wedged my butt between one of the supports and the railing and hit the switch on the lift controller. The stainless steel cable unfurled at an agonizingly slow speed. A blast of wind swept across the river and pitched the boat into a support beam.

Nathan spread his legs, riding the boat like a surfer. The propeller finally sank below the water, Nathan turned the engine over, and seconds later, the boat slid off the rails.

My heart sank to my toes. "Gun the engine." My voice lost in the wind. I made a megaphone with my hands. "The seawall. Watch the seawall." I set the lift on auto, gripped the railing, and stumbled down the ramp connecting the stationary dock to the floating jetty. I crouched and waited for Nathan.

The center of the jetty buckled. I ducked my head, and

a monster wave washed over me. The boards slapped the river, and the jetty righted.

Nathan slung a rope in my direction. The white snake arched, held, and then rode a gust of wind back to Nathan. The boat slipped past the jetty. He made another full turn and inched forward for a second attempt. He pitched the rope lower this time.

I grabbed the lifeline. Fighting against the wind, I kept the rope tight. My burning palms walked up the line, pulling the boat closer. I jumped on board just as another wave hit the dock.

Nathan threw me a life jacket and spun the bow toward Hidden Cove. "Brace yourself."

A five-foot wave slammed into the boat and slung me to the floor. I gasped; cold river water filled my mouth. I gagged salt water. Crawling forward, I slid the life jacket over my head and climbed on the bench seat. "Turn down river." I waved in that direction.

Nathan threw his body against the helm and struggled to turn the boat in time to catch a mammoth wave.

I slapped at the seat, arms flailing, searching for something solid to hold. The wave hit. Water gushed the port side and slammed me starboard. My fingers wrapped around a cleat. I gripped the steel, but my foot slipped, my body heaved forward, and I lost my hold.

Nathan clutched the back of my slicker and yanked me to his side.

Marsh grass and water were all I could see in any direction. "We need to find a creek and get off the river." I waved at an orange marker stuck in the muck. "Over there."

I knew this tributary from my kayaking days. The stream, which was impossible to navigate in anything larger than a canoe, kayak, or flats boat during extremely high tides, ended a few hundred yards from Hidden Cove's public dock.

We made it to the sheltered stream and picked up speed. Nathan powered down thirty feet from the working boats parked bow to stern.

"Look for Deep Shit. That's Norwich's boat." The jerk must think he had a sense of humor.

Nathan maneuvered past Miss Denise and Papa's Girl. Nestled in between The Kelly Marie and Docked Wages sat the Deep Shit.

"We need to tie up to a dock," Nathan said.

"Keep going. There should be open docks around the next bend."

Nathan approached the first private dock. In this storm, most boat owners had moved their boats to dry land.

"Take the rope and jump." He bumped the bow into the side of the floating jetty.

I jumped, landed in a squat, and tied the rope to a cleat.

I scanned the only paved road dead ahead. "All the roads over here will intersect this road." A group of dirt roads peeled left, and we walked head down, looking up only to read the county road signs. Each dirt road led to fishing shacks, decades-old mobile homes, and occasionally a clapboard house. The fifth street sign read Shell Landing.

We turned left. Dead ahead was a white clapboard house with a rusted-out Ford truck on blocks in the front yard. A black plastic mailbox sat cockeyed out front. Someone had hand painted the number thirty-two on the side.

Nathan squeezed my hand. "Keep walking."

My heart raced. "Why? The mailbox said thirty-two. This is the house."

"Walk." He tugged me along. "Look straight ahead. I want to check out the back first."

The treeless property next door to Norwich's house offered an unobstructed view of his backyard. The rain eased to a steady drizzle, and our visibility improved.

I estimated the wind still clocked forty miles per hour.

Norwich's brown plastic trash receptacle lay on its side. It looked as if raccoons had foraged inside and scattered garbage across his sandy patch of grass. "Stay behind this bush." Nathan pointed to an azalea plant, so scraggly it wouldn't hide a three-year-old. He disappeared around the corner. Seconds later, I heard him pounding on Norwich's front door. Either Norwich wasn't around, or he slept exceptionally soundly. Either way, I wasn't leaving until I'd checked every corner of his house for Owen.

The pounding stopped, and Nathan returned. "Let's check the back door." He grabbed my hand and dashed across the yard and up the steps. He manhandled the door, but the deadbolt held. "I need a warrant to get inside."

The top half of the door was jalousie windows. I pulled out my gun and smashed the bottom pane.

Nathan wrestled the Glock from my fingers. "That stunt could cost me my job."

I stuck my hand through, turned the deadbolt, and turned the doorknob. "Broken glass on the steps. Door open. Looked suspicious to me."

"You watch too many detective shows." He glanced left, then right, and shoved me inside.

## CHAPTER THIRTY-TWO

*Nathan*

NATHAN SHOVED KATE behind him and swept Norwich's enclosed porch, then the kitchen. Even in bad lighting, he was struck by the shabbiness. Peeling paint, grease stains on faded Formica counters; the odor of days-old garbage assaulted his senses. He stopped in the middle of the kitchen and listened for sound.

Kate barreled into his back.

He held his palm in the air, gave her the universal sign to stay put, and then stepped to a closet. Sensing heat behind him, he swiveled and stared into Kate's green eyes. He put a finger to his lips and held his palm out. Even semi-trained puppies recognized a 'stay' hand signal.

He didn't think anyone was home, but putting a civilian at risk meant following protocol—although protocol had sunk into the depths of the muddy river the moment he let Kate board the flats boat.

Nathan studied a half-eaten sandwich and two empty Ranch Doritos bags littering a folding table pushed against the front window. He finger-tested the bread and then sniffed the ham. By his estimate, the meal had been prepared within the last forty-eight hours.

He checked the hall, and the bathroom before canvassing both bedrooms to verify they were unoccupied.

"All clear." He returned to the bedroom with the king-sized bed.

"This is interesting." Kate handed him a congratulations letter from Clemson Athletics for Dennis Norwich, the younger of the two brothers.

He knelt and picked up a photo on the floor. It showed a couple standing on a deserted beach. The man was David Norwich, Calvin's dive boat captain. He flipped it over and read the message scrawled on the back.

Skinny, thanks for an awesome day. Luv, Sharon.

He handed the photo to Kate. "Do you recognize him?"

"I remember the snake tattoo. He was on the dive boat. He scared Owen," she said.

Nathan knew the guy's face and the tattoos. His file included a dossier and photos. "This guy is a lowballer in Cabral's army." He slipped the photo into his jeans pocket. "Come on. Norwich isn't here."

They left the house the same way they'd entered and fast-walked down the dirt road.

"Neighbors might've seen Norwich," Kate said. "They'd know if he brought anyone here the last couple of days."

"The younger Norwich brother washed up two days ago, and his body's still at the coroner's office. I imagine the older brother's hanging close by." If this drug-running two-bit shrimper had picked up Roslyn and Owen, Nathan would roust every person in this fishing village to find him. Nathan pointed to a white and blue doublewide. "Lights were on when we passed. Let's see if they've seen Norwich."

A blonde woman, he guessed to be in her mid-forties, stood in the front window holding a coffee cup. A wraparound wood deck led to the mobile home's front door.

"Let me ask her." Kate passed him and walked to the door. "When you're focused, you're a little scary."

Nathan scrambled after her. "Don't mention I'm a marshal. Don't say anything about the kidnapping. People don't like to get involved. Nice easy chitchat."

Kate nodded and knocked.

The woman at the window opened the door and screwed her eyes into two tight lines. "You all stranded, honey?"

"No, ma'am." Kate beamed a phony smile. "Just trying to locate one of your neighbors."

"Well, come in out of the rain." The woman waved them inside. No hesitation, smooth brow, and her smile appeared genuine and open. "I'll have to get out my mop if this door stays open any longer."

Kate shed her rain slicker and left it on the porch, as did Nathan. The aroma of kerosene, cigarette smoke, and coffee filled the air of the kitchen.

The woman wore a faded blue robe and fuzzy gray flip-flop slippers. Remnants of her former beauty lingered if you didn't stare too long. She held a half-smoked cigarette between her fingers. "Who'd you say you were looking for?"

"David Norwich," Kate said.

The woman redirected smoke through her nose. "You mean Skinny?"

Kate shrugged. "Is that what people call him?"

"People call that boy a lot of things." Her gaze flicked back and forth between Nathan and Kate. She crossed an arm over her midsection, a protective gesture. Either David Norwich, or their asking about him, made this woman uneasy.

Nathan stepped forward and handed her the photograph he found in the house. "Is this Skinny?"

She studied the picture. Her eyes flashed with recognition. "Yeah, that's him." She tapped the woman in the photo. "Put that girl in the hospital. Busted a couple of ribs, broke her arm."

Kate visibly shuddered.

"Heard the girl moved back to Wisconsin." The woman took a step back. "You two cops?"

She didn't want to get involved. Probably didn't want to cross Norwich. He waited a beat for Kate to respond, and then realized she was somewhere else. "No, ma'am. My name's Nathan. And this is Kate. She lives across the river. I'm sorry, we didn't ask your name."

The woman removed her cigarette, and smiled. "Susie Campbell." She stuck the cigarette back in her mouth. "No offense, but I don't believe you aren't cops. No other reason a couple of dandies like you two would be out in this weather looking for Skinny Norwich."

Susie met his gaze straight on. She might be hesitant to get involved, but her hands moved freely, and she stood at ease. If she thought he was a cop, she didn't seem overly concerned that he'd knocked on her door.

"We need to ask Skinny a few questions is all," he said.

"Well, good luck. That boy hasn't said more than a handful of truths since he slunk back home after flunking out of college. Ever since, he's been as mean as a pissed-off moccasin."

Kate inhaled a ragged breath at the pissed moccasin comment.

He wrapped his fingers around her hand. "Your coffee smells great. Is there any way Kate could have a cup? She's wet and a little chilled."

Helping others often calmed people. And if Kate drank slow, they'd have a reason to stick around and probe for more information.

Susie removed the percolator from the camp stove, held an empty cup in Nathan's direction. "How about you?"

"That'd be great," he said.

Nathan leaned close to Kate's ear. "Drink slow, and just play along."

She nodded, ran a shaking hand over her lips. Susie handed Kate her cup, then gave Nathan his.

He sipped his coffee. "This sure hits the spot. You have any idea where we might find Skinny?"

She glanced at the clock on the stove. "Might try Jake's place in about an hour. Jake said he'd open by six unless the storm blew away his bar."

"Jake's?"

"Bar down on the bluff where I waitress. When the Norwich boys aren't shrimping, they spend most of the day and night playing pool and getting drunk."

Kate placed her full cup on the counter. "Was Skinny at the bar night before last?" Nathan heard the edge of desperation in her voice.

"Yeah," Susie said. "In the back, playing pool. I remember because he had two visitors."

Kate stepped closer. "Male or female?"

"Male," Susie said. "And both of them dandies." Nathan shook his head. "Sorry?"

"A Savannah snooty. One fellow came in wearing a suit. Don't see that every day at Jake's." She eyed Nathan. "As tall as you, maybe taller. The second fellow was more casual like. He wore jeans and a flannel shirt, but his boots gave him away."

"How so?" Nathan asked.

Susie placed her cigarette in the ashtray, picked up a dishcloth and wiped down the counter. "They weren't shrimping boots. This guy's boots were brown leather, the kind you see in fancy hunting magazines."

"Did you happen to catch a name for either one of the men?" Nathan asked.

"Sugar, I didn't ask. The first one, a tall good-looking fellow, skedaddled out with Skinny before I made it back to the table. That was about midnight."

Nathan could almost see Kate's brain working through the timeline.

"Could you be more exact about the time?" Nathan asked.

Susie picked up her pack of Benson and Hedges and considered Kate.

"Susie." Nathan waited until her eyes met his. He placed both hands on the back of the kitchen chair and leaned in her direction to establish confidence. "It's really important."

She cut her eyes at Kate, and then to Nathan. She popped the Benson and Hedges pack against her palm, drew out a cigarette, and reached for her lighter. "Well, let's see. Skinny always orders nachos on the kitchen's last call." She put a fresh cigarette in her mouth, noticed the last one burning in the ashtray and stubbed it out. "That'd be around eleven-thirty. So I'd say Mr. Elegant turned up a little past midnight, and they took off." She lit the fresh cigarette.

"You said he had two visitors," Nathan said.

"Earlier in the day, he was playing pool with a group of construction fellows on their lunch break and fancy boots came in. I asked him if he wanted a drink, he said no, and that was the extent of our talking. He and Skinny left right after."

Kate slid her cell out of her pocket. She skimmed through several screens. "Is this one of the men?"

Susie took the phone. "Yep. That's Fancy Boots." She handed the phone back to Kate.

Kate showed Nathan the photo of Joseph Lafferty on the company website.

Nathan finished his cup, walked to the sink, and rinsed it out. "I'd like to leave you my phone number and if you see Skinny, I'd appreciate a call."

Susie took a step back. "I ain't going to cross those Norwich boys."

Nathan nodded. "I understand. I appreciate your time and the information." Nathan moved to the door, held it open for Kate, picked up their rain slickers, and handed Kate hers. They slipped them on, but since the rain had all but stopped, left the hoods dangling.

Kate glanced back. "Thank you for the coffee, Susie." She turned and cleared the porch steps first. "Susie recognized Joseph's picture. He's back." Relief laced in fear reverberated through her voice.

"I want to check out Norwich's vessel," Nathan said.

They headed for the docks and located Deep Shit. The condition of the shrimp boat matched Norwich's house. Peeling paint, dirty ropes, broken gaffs scattered over the deck.

Nathan headed straight for the helm. Starting with the storage compartments, he combed through and found nothing but empty beer cans. "Let's go below." He used his phone to light the narrow passage. The skeleton smelled of fish guts and cigarette smoke.

"Check the lockers." Nathan poked through torn nets on the floor, and upended buckets.

Kate slammed through several cabinets. "There's nothing here but old candy wrappers and more beer cans." She leaned against a cabinet. "Where is he? Where did he take Owen?"

Nathan's instinct that Roslyn was a partner in this kidnapping still held; his gut said Kate's mother was in control. But what if he was wrong? Nathan wrapped his arm around Kate's shoulders. "There're too many coincidences for this guy not to be connected in some way. I'm not giving up. You can't either. Let's check the bridge again. Maybe I missed something."

Beside the helm, Nathan spotted a closet with a new lock. The door had three hinges corroded in rust. "Any shine on this boat is suspect."

He picked up a wrench and swung. The first hinge

broke. After five more pops, the remaining two hinges slipped sideways, and he pushed the door away.

Joseph Lafferty landed face up. A small, neat hole penetrated his forehead. He wore jeans, a red flannel shirt, and boots, the kind you might find in a fancy hunting magazine.

## CHAPTER THIRTY-THREE

*Katelyn*

I STARED AT JOSEPH Lafferty's lifeless body. His face, pale and dusty, was like an unfinished piece of greenware waiting for a kiln.

The symmetrical hole pierced his forehead. A sharpshooter's bull's-eye slid past hair, skin, and muscle, smashing into his brain. A brain that leaked from his skull. The pungent gagging odors of rotting meat and sweet dollar-store perfume slithered up my nose.

A wail lodged in my lungs and exited as a groan. I turned away, unable or unwilling to comprehend the scene. Then I raced over nets and ropes and broken gaffs.

"Kate, wait..." Nathan's words jumbled together as if they ran at the wrong speed.

I kicked an empty bucket, clamored to the top of a storage bin, and grabbed the bottom rung of the ladder.

Nathan encased my waist and pulled me back to the deck. "Breathe." His warm hands grasped my cheeks. "Breathe."

I couldn't breathe.

"Take a breath. You're okay."

I collapsed against him and buried my face in his neck. "Oh, God. Oh my God." My chest tightened, like a vice squeezing air from one lung, then the other.

Nathan held me at arm's length. "I have to secure the body."

"I can't go back." Nathan's face blurred into Joseph's. My body screamed flight. "I can't look again."

Nathan lowered me to the storage bin. "Sit here. I'll work fast."

I cradled my swimming head and tried blocking the image from my brain.

Skinny must've shot Joseph.

If Joseph was dead, and Skinny had Owen—

I leaped up. My head whirled. Blinding stars of light pirouetted inches from my eyes, and I slid to the floor. A flash of blue and red flickered in my periphery like a ghost playing hide-and-seek. I squeezed my eyes shut, opened them, looked again, and my heart ricocheted against the wall of my chest.

I crawled across the floor, pushed the handle of a rusted gaff away, and yanked out a ball cap. Owen's ball cap.

I screamed a guttural ache.

I pushed off the floor and jumped to the jetty. I stumbled, landed on my knees, and clambered across the rough boards. I clutched Owen's cap in my hand.

My son was here. Somewhere. My foot caught. I kicked.

"Don't kick me!" Nathan gripped my calf.

I shook the cap in his face. "It's Owen's!"

He massaged a red welt growing on his chin. "I have to call in and report Lafferty's body. I'll request an APB on Norwich." Phone in hand, he stood and turned a slow circle. "No service. Susie had a landline in her kitchen."

I ran and didn't stop until we turned up Susie's drive.

She met us at the door. "Where's the fire?"

"I need to use your landline," Nathan said.

"My what?"

Nathan sidestepped Susie, picked up her phone, and punched the numbers. "Sheriff Schroeder, please."

I stood beside him and rubbed the heel of my hand across my sternum to slow my breath.

"Can you patch me through?" Nathan said.

Susie pulled out a kitchen chair. "Sit down, sugar. You look ready to fall over. What in the world happened?"

My mind couldn't string a coherent thought.

"Ya'll tussle with Dennis? 'Cause, something's sure up that boy's craw." She walked to the refrigerator and removed a pitcher of tea. "I was just about to call your man when I saw you running up the drive. He lit out of here like there's no tomorrow."

"Who?" I asked.

Susie set three empty glasses on the counter. "Dennis, Skinny's brother."

Nathan spun around. "You saw Norwich?"

She nodded. "About ten minutes ago. He barreled down the road on his motorcycle."

Nathan's crime scene photo of Skinny's brother Dennis, the bloated torso with the missing arm, flashed in my head. "It couldn't have been Dennis because…" My reasoning stuttered to a stop. "It was Skinny."

Nathan raised his index finger, still on the phone. "Willie. I'm in Hidden Cove, and we have another DB." He opened the door and stepped outside.

A few seconds later, he stepped back into the kitchen. "Willie's ten minutes away. I need to meet him at the dock. And Jonathan texted he'll be at Spartina within the hour. I'll ask one of Willie's officers to drive you over. I'll follow as soon as I can."

I moved to his side. "We need to check Skinny's house again."

Nathan held my shoulders. "Skinny didn't bring Owen and Roslyn to Hidden Cove on a motorcycle." He released his hands and stepped off the porch. "But if it'll ease your mind, I'll walk through Norwich's house again. The best thing you can do for Owen is to meet with Jonathan and answer his questions. We need the GBI team on board as soon as possible." He sprinted down the drive.

Susie came outside with two tall glasses. "You like sweet tea?"

"Thanks." I accepted the drink, but my stomach rolled.

She sat in a rocker and removed a pack of cigarettes from her pocket. "Why are you looking for Skinny?"

I carried my tea to the other end of the porch, searched, and found the roofline of Norwich's house. I closed my eyes and tamped down my worst nightmare. Please, God, let Owen still be alive. "Someone kidnapped my son. We think Skinny's involved."

"Kidnapped?" She slapped a hand over her heart. "Sugar, you need the law. You don't want to play around with those Norwich boys."

The red-hot poker in my stomach punched another hole. "Nathan's a US marshal."

"I knew he looked like a lawman." She sat back, lit a cigarette, and then pushed the rocker into a slow sway. "How old is your boy?"

"Eight."

She clucked her tongue. "Those Norwich boys are the seed of Satan. Their daddy was just as mean." She upped the speed of her chair. "What's a DB?"

"A dead body."

Her rocker stopped. "You found a dead body?"

"Yes." I forced a sip of tea hoping to settle my stomach. "One of the men you saw with Skinny."

She gasped like an emphysema patient gulping her last breath. "Oh, no." She coughed and rubbed a fist over her chest. "Not the tall one?"

"Tall one?"

"That first dandy. He was six two, maybe three. About as tall as your man."

"Nathan's not—I mean, we're not—" I shook my

head. "No, Joseph's shorter than Nathan. Around five-nine. He was the one you called fancy boots."

"Whew." Her face pinked. "I mean, it's awful anybody's dead. But that other one was a heartstopper. Always been a sucker for cleft chins."

"Cleft chin?"

Susie's chatter faded. Pieces shifted, theories cracked, and mutated into new suppositions.

I yanked my phone from my back pocket and called Nathan. Nothing but dead air. "I need to use your phone."

I ran into the house and called Nathan, but the call went straight to voicemail. I left a message. "Call me."

Susie came inside. "What's wrong?"

"I need to use your truck."

I sent Nathan a text.

—Call me. Urgent.—

Susie's mouth firmed pencil thin. "My truck?"

I clasped her forearm and pleaded. "I have to go to Savannah. I think I know who has my son."

Her gaze roamed the room. She looked everywhere but into my eyes. "I don't know."

"Please. Skinny and the other dandy have my son."

She squinted, searched my entire face, then drilled me with a stare. It was the same trick Mom used to ferret out a lie.

She removed a set of keys from a bowl on top of the fridge and held them close to her chest. "If Skinny killed that man, you should wait for your marshal."

I clasped both her hands in mine and wheedled the keys from her fingers. "I sent him a text. He'll meet me there. But just in case, I'll leave a note. Can I borrow some paper?"

She opened a drawer and handed me a pad.

I scribbled a quick note. "A police officer will be here soon. Give the officer this note."

Susie stood in her doorway, as shell-shocked as any war-torn orphan I'd seen on television.

I flew down the porch steps and slid behind the wheel of her truck. I called Cedar—voicemail. I sent a text.

—Call me. NOW!—

Susie's description of the second dandy—a six-foot-three man with a cleft chin, wearing a suit—had to be Cedar. Why hadn't I connected the dots that my grandfather's corporate attorney would've set up the bogus construction companies? He'd been on the inside of a twenty-year money-laundering scheme. Granddad might've held the information close, but Cedar couldn't have been in the complete dark. And all of a sudden, Cedar and Mom were cozy.

I merged onto the interstate and headed north. I called Cedar again. No answer. I resent my earlier text. Waited sixty seconds. Clicked resend. After two minutes with no answer, I threw my cell across the seat. The phone fell to the floorboard out of reach. "Never mind." I pushed the gas pedal and drove.

Fifty minutes later, I cruised over the Wilmington Island bridge, fishtailed down Cedar's driveway, and skidded to a stop in front of his house. I scanned the yard and looked for Skinny's motorcycle, but it was nowhere in sight. I stuck the Glock in the waistband of my jeans and yanked my shirttail over the butt.

Cedar answered the door with his cell in one hand and a blue-striped tie in the other.

# CHAPTER THIRTY-FOUR

*Nathan*

SIREN WAILING, THE sheriff's black Silverado pulled up to the pier so close Nathan could kiss the bumper if he leaned six inches.

Willie climbed out and hitched his pants. "Dead bodies, and you are becoming a habit, Marshal."

Nathan couldn't argue. "Norwich's boat is the third one down." Nathan removed his rain slicker and threw it on the hood of Willie's cruiser. He stepped on the dock. "Anything on the APB?"

Willie followed Nathan down the ramp.

"Nothing yet. Storm's moved north, but there's hardly a road in the county that doesn't need clearing. My deputies are working traffic for the road-clearing crews. Norwich will have a hard time getting out of Montgomery County without notice."

Nathan jumped on Norwich's boat and walked to the helm.

Willie scaled the ladder and followed. He squeezed a tube of Vicks VapoRub and smeared the ointment under his nose, then passed the salve to Nathan.

Nathan lifted the corner of the blue tarp he'd used to cover Lafferty's body. Stepped back, squirted out a blob of VapoRub, and swiped his upper lip. He'd never understood the biological sense of opening nasal passages to block the decaying, sickening sweet smell of death.

Willie folded his hands against the small of his back, bent at the waist, and studied the body. "You say this guy worked for Kate?"

"And her grandfather before that."

Willie pulled the tarp back over Lafferty. He unwrapped a toothpick, stuck it in his mouth, and put his hands in his pockets.

Understanding the need to leave no additional fingerprints, Nathan stuffed his hands in his pockets.

Willie slow-chewed his wooden pacifier. "Didn't see your car by the dock."

Nathan had learned the sheriff's tendency to talk and move slow didn't extend to his observation skills. "Came by boat. We docked downriver."

"We?"

"Kate's with me. She needs a ride back to Spartina."

"Why'd you and Kate cross the river in the middle of a hurricane?" Willie's calculating eyes didn't sync with his just-two-friends-passing-the-time tone.

Nathan considered arguing the storm had downgraded to tropical before he'd boarded the boat, but that'd just be hitting a nail already in place. "I was pulling a thread on her son's kidnapping."

Surprise and concern battled for dominance on Willie's face. "I didn't hear anything about Kate's boy being kidnapped."

"Early this morning Owen and his grandmother disappeared from Talbot Island," Nathan said. "Florida police are working the case. Kidnapping's still unconfirmed, but the GBI's due at Spartina within the hour to review the case."

Willie nodded toward the blue tarp. "And you think this DB could be related to the abduction?"

"Maybe. But there's a higher probability he's linked

to the drug ring working on Barry Island. One of the DB's that washed up this week was his son."

"So the dead son would be Jacob Lafferty." Willie looked to Nathan for confirmation, then rolled his toothpick. "And how'd you come to find this DB?"

"David Norwich popped on a telephone log for this guy, and I decided to take a ride, check out Norwich's home address and his boat."

"Uh-huh." Willie gave Nathan a Sherlock Holmes glare of dubiety. "And you let Kate tag along?"

"I couldn't very well handcuff her to her house." Nathan wished he had used handcuffs to keep her at Spartina. Explaining Kate tagging along to his boss would take every ounce of finesse and imagination he could muster.

Four men and two women clamored over the deck of the boat wearing blue parkas and black ball caps with MSD on the brim.

"Water's still choppy," Willie said. "Give me a second to brief my team, and I'll run you and Kate back to Spartina."

Nathan sent Jonathan a text with a new ETA and wondered if Erica had left for Atlanta. He could use a local for the door-to-door canvassing.

Erica answered his call with a grunt hello.

"Any chance you're still in Savannah?" he asked.

"I've managed to drive twenty-five miles in five hours."

Nathan walked to the other side of the boat. "Joseph Lafferty turned up in Hidden Cove. Dead. On a shrimp boat owned by Dennis Norwich's brother, David."

"Calvin's dive boat captain?"

"Yes. I'll keep you posted, but you might want to drive slow every chance you get." He disconnected and halted the litany of questions he didn't have time to answer.

Willie returned, and he and Nathan walked up the ramp. "Where'd you leave Kate?"

Nathan pointed west. "Doublewide on the corner." Susie met them at her front door and handed Nathan a piece of paper. "She left not long after you." She waved a cigarette in the direction of the two rockers on her porch. "We were having a glass of tea, and Kate started talking crazy. Insisted she had to go see that dandy with the Kirk Douglas chin." Susie glanced at her empty driveway. "She borrowed my truck."

Nathan scanned Kate's note and turned to Willie. "With lights running, how quick can we make it to Wilmington Island?"

"Forty-five minutes, give or take."

"Let's go." Nathan thanked Susie and slid into the passenger seat of the Silverado.

"What's up?" Willie started the engine and backed into the street.

"Kate thinks her attorney's behind the kidnapping. She's on her way to confront him. Seventeen Pelican Point Drive." Nathan called Kate's cell and left a message. "I'm on my way. Don't do anything without me." He shot off a text.

Wait 4 me. Don't go 2 Cedar's house or his office. Wait 4 me.

Willie dodged a limb and wove the truck through a minefield of trash, potholes, and water. He slowed the truck to a crawl and climbed over a limb the size of Nathan's thigh. "Why would Kate's attorney kidnap her son?" Willie asked.

"Noah Barry left a sizable offshore bank account. Kate thinks Cedar knew about the money and abducted her son to gain access. The problem is that Roslyn's also missing, and she and the attorney are hitting the sheets."

"Muddies the water," Willie said. "This whole damn case is about as clear as tar and twice as sticky."

Nathan couldn't have said it better. He did a fast calculation of Kate's head start. He wasn't sure if he was naïve or just plain stupid to have left her alone. Right now, he didn't see much daylight between the two. "Can you get an update on the Norwich APB?"

Willie fiddled with the scanner. "Stacy, did we get a hit on our APB?"

"Which one, Sheriff?"

Willie heaved a weary sigh. "We only have the one outstanding."

Silence.

"No, sir. Nothing yet."

A tree large enough to build a small yacht straddled both lanes. Willie shifted into four-wheel drive and swung off-road.

Nathan tightened his seatbelt and grabbed an overhead strap. His text to Kate failed. Willie veered back on the road, and Nathan hit resend. Twenty seconds later, another failed message popped on his screen. His phone had service, which meant the towers servicing Kate's phone were down.

Willie braked hard, and the truck abruptly stopped in front of a gaping hole in the road.

Nathan surveyed miles of boggy marsh to the left. On the right, the river rushed by in a relentless pursuit of the ocean. Off-roading wasn't an option.

Willie reversed. "We'll have to take the long way around."

"How long?"

"Back to where we started, then another twelve miles across the island to the south end."

Nathan flung his cap to the dashboard. If Kate wouldn't stay at Susie's long enough for Nathan to return, she sure wouldn't wait to confront Cedar Haynes face to face.

Nathan's phone rang and displayed a familiar country code. This wasn't Nathan's first perp to flee to Montevideo, and Paco Rodriguez was the best police detective in Uruguay. "Tell me something good, Paco."

"You owe me big, Parsi. It took three hours to sift through the security tapes and find the shot of the perp who opened the account you asked about." Paco's exaggerated sigh hinted at good-natured heckling. "But it's not the man you suspected."

"No. Joseph Lafferty's dead."

"Huh." Paco's tone retained no emotion. "I'm texting the still shot of the perp now, and I'll upload the video when I get to my office. Two weeks ago, he moved in and out of Montevideo in one day. And as you suspected, tried using a power of attorney to close the account. Instructions to transfer the entire balance to a Caymans account came across an hour after he received notice the bank would accept the document."

"You froze the account?" Nathan asked.

"Yes. And for that, you owe me a drink."

"Next time you're in Atlanta," Nathan said. "And you sent a false verification that the transfer was complete?"

"Just as you requested," Paco deadpanned. "I had to promise the bank president lunch at the Carrasco Polo Club."

"Okay, a drink and a steak dinner next time you're in town," Nathan said.

"And a bottle of that fancy bourbon you drink because it took another hour of fast-talking and substantial threats to get the bank in the Caymans to agree." Paco yawned. "It's been a busy afternoon."

Paco's news confirmed what Nathan suspected. Owen's kidnapping had nothing to do with the Cabrals.

"Thanks, friend."

Paco's photo of the perp came through. Nathan chastised himself for not suspecting a man who wore seersucker suits. If Cedar believed the money had transferred, he'd bolt out of Savannah faster than a short-range scud missile. Even if Kate went to his house, Haynes wouldn't be home.

He forwarded Paco's photo of Cedar Haynes to his office and left instructions to attach the incoming video to his dossier.

Nathan turned his attention to Willie. "You think Cedar Haynes could hoodwink Roslyn Barry into faking her grandson's kidnapping, or is she brazen enough to orchestrate the entire charade?"

Willie slowed the truck, drove through three feet of water, then picked up speed. "It's hard for me to see Mrs. Roslyn putting Katie through that kind of misery." He swerved to miss another pothole. "My money's on the attorney."

Willie sped along the southern tip of Island Road and over the mainland bridge. They'd lost ten minutes backtracking over the same ground, another twenty getting off the island, and Kate had a half-hour head start. Nathan checked the map on his phone. "How long before we get to Wilmington Bridge?"

Willie merged onto the interstate and switched on his lights. "Twenty-five minutes."

Nathan called his team and scheduled a rendezvous at the bottom of the bridge, and then he called Erica. "Where are you?"

"Same place as the last time we talked. Interstate's flooded, and traffic's backed up for miles. I pulled over for food."

"We found a connection between the Hidden Cove shrimper, Lafferty, and Cedar Haynes. Witness claimed Cedar was chatting up the shrimper night before last. Kate figured out Haynes was behind the kidnapping and took off for Wilmington Island."

"What do you mean she took off?" Erica's voice scaled into high soprano range. "Without you?"

"She got a head start." His phone buzzed, and he

checked his text messages. Jonathan had arrived at Spartina, but there was no message from Kate.

"You knew Kate was slippery. How'd she manage to get by you?" Untempered disapproval encased Erica's voice.

She was still pissed at him for having her removed from the case. He couldn't blame her. "Focus on the new information. Cedar Haynes is after her grandfather's offshore money, and he snatched Owen as insurance."

"What offshore money?"

"Thirty million in Montevideo."

Erica blew a low whistle.

"I've got the team headed to Haynes's house. We'll meet on the back side of Wilmington bridge in thirty."

"Hate to whack a dying horse, but that thirty million's now Kate's. That many greenbacks can hide a lot of people for a long time. If Owen was at Cedar's, he was with his grandmother. No reason to get your panties in a wad, the whole bunch are in this together and are long gone by now."

Nathan considered ripping Erica on her inability to keep an open mind, but people who lived in glass houses...

"And if you're wrong? We've had five DBs in less than a week. You think Cedar Haynes won't hurt Kate? You think he won't use her boy as a pawn?" He stopped and gave his words time to plunge through Erica's inflexible mindset. "Our team can handle recovery, but we could use your help keeping the boy calm."

"I'm turning around."

"Run your lights. We won't wait."

"Roger that."

This was just another rescue op. Nathan had saved victims in far worse conditions. With any luck, Haynes had fled, and Kate was holding her son in her arms. Only that scenario didn't mesh with the burn in his gut.

"You need to call in SWAT," Willie said.

"Call in SWAT?" Nathan's gut flame found his neck. "My team is SWAT."

Willie slow-chewed his toothpick. "You dispatched half your team to Florida, and Erica may or may not make it in time. With all due respect, four men do not a SWAT team make."

Nathan squinted. "Six counting you and me."

And one thing Nathan was sure of—no way Erica would miss this takedown.

# CHAPTER THIRTY-FIVE

*Katelyn*

"WHERE'S MY SON?"

"He's not here." Cedar considered me as if I were the runt of the litter, and he was figuring out the quickest way to pawn me off.

I glared back. "I'm not leaving. If Owen's not here, where is he?"

Sighing, he swept his hand toward the foyer. "Come on. I'll show you."

"Show me what?" I stepped inside his house and searched for signs of my son. The only furnishings in the small foyer were two six-foot antique marble urns and a Persian rug.

Cedar stepped toward the hall and looked back. "Well, do you want to see your boy or not?" he snapped, his tone a reminder of who was in charge.

I followed him down a marble-tiled hall. Resigned to play along long enough to find out where he'd hidden Owen.

As we passed, a hallway of antique mirrors allowed a quick view of the rooms. Wingback chairs, a camelback sofa. A pedestal dining table with twin cherry servers. Nothing out of place. Nothing to give the impression an eight-year-old was in residence.

We entered a bedroom-office combination. Wall-to-wall shelving held an impressive collection of leather-bound books and a horde of mantel clocks.

Cedar walked to a king four-poster bed and put a paisley tie inside a Bric's carry-on.

I stayed by the door, kept my back to the wall, and scanned the room. "Where's my family?" A six-inch chair rail pressed the butt of my gun against my spine.

Mom's jade box sat on a small Moroccan game table across the room. My mind careened back to the day of the break-in. Mom had called Cedar and asked him to come. But why? Why would she and Cedar need to fake a robbery if she were behind the kidnapping sham? The pieces didn't fit together.

Cedar walked to an overly ornate Romanesque marble fireplace and flipped a switch. Flame stitch paneling opened to reveal a flat-screen television. He tapped a key on his laptop, and my son's beaming face claimed center stage on the television screen.

Verifying Cedar was behind Owen's abduction circled in my head like a search plane looking for a reason for the unbelievable.

Cedar tapped again, and the camera zoom receded. My thoughts swam three strokes ahead of my logic.

In the background, behind Owen...the painting on the wall, the drapes, and the chair. All familiar. Owen was inside Mom's bedroom. Relief cannonballed my heart. Owen was ten miles away. I turned for the door, but Cedar had moved to block my exit.

"Not so fast." He pushed me against the wall. "I'll take your gun now."

I looked down and verified the nudge to my ribs came from a pistol. A pistol Cedar held with his finger on the trigger. I glanced up. His smile of triumph spawned an emotion so foreign it frightened me. He'd callously used Owen for money, and I wanted Cedar dead.

"Your son's expecting you today. Play your cards right, and you won't disappoint him."

My mind twisted into an angry hard knot. This backstabber was not getting my gun until I had Owen in my arms and knew he was safe.

"You want to make your boy an orphan?" He pushed the barrel deeper into my ribs. "Raise your hands," he said. "And turn around."

I looked into Cedar's stone-cold eyes and realized he was capable of following through with his threat. Then I saw my son's pleading face. Owen's eyes brimmed with tears, asking if I would leave him, too. Go to live with the angels like Daddy. Cedar was right. I wouldn't risk making Owen an orphan. I lifted my shirttail and faced the wall.

He pulled the Glock from my waistband and walked me farther into the room. He threw my gun on the bed, well out of reach.

I'd subconsciously set aside the most obvious of sequences. If Cedar were callous enough to orchestrate the abduction of my son to steal Granddad's thirty million, nothing would keep him from his prize. Not me, not Owen, and most likely, not even Mom. I'd never considered Cedar would hold me at gunpoint. Bringing my gun inside had been more a prop than a weapon.

I had to keep him engaged until Nathan arrived. Encouraging a blowhard to brag shouldn't be hard. "Clever idea to hide Owen at Mom's house."

"Roslyn didn't want your boy upset." A nervous energy poured out of him. His eyes were too bright, his body movements too strained, as if his brain had to remind his hands, feet, and mouth to move.

A slow panic skittered across my chest, like spiders running under my skin. I coerced my mind to still. Inhaled a calming breath. Owen was safe. He was with Mom in a familiar environment. But a warning voice in my head screamed it's not that simple. "I was in agony thinking Owen and Mom were kidnapped."

He shrugged as if my pain was an insignificant detail. "Couldn't be helped. Nathan's crosshairs moved off you and onto me." His faux-genteel tone caused my blood to heat to boiling. "When Roslyn and Owen disappeared, Nathan was skeptical it was a kidnapping. But I know the way a behavioral analyst thinks. The visceral tells a person can't fake. And I knew once Nathan read your body language, he'd conclude your panic was real. Which bought me the time I needed."

His cocky explanation cooled my anger. Overconfident people were easy to manipulate. Stroke their ego—they'd brag for hours, explain every minute detail of their ingenious plan, and gloat over their superior intelligence. I nodded as if impressed. "But I'm surprised you talked Mom into drugging Uncle Stanley."

"Roslyn agreed to drug the marshals when I claimed one of them was the Cabral snitch, and Owen's life was in danger. Stanley drinking the coffee wasn't planned."

"Was the snitch guarding Owen and Mom?"

Cedar laughed a deep belly chuckle. Slid a photograph from under Mom's box and held up the picture of Owen and me on the island, the same shot that accompanied the first threatening email. "There is no snitch. I authored that theory. Even had Nathan and Erica buying in."

"Then who took that photo?"

"Cabral boys love their drones."

My stomach contracted into one single flame. I hadn't seen a drone that day, but with the airboat whizzing around, a drone wouldn't have stood out.

"Stanley drinking the coffee shook up your mother." Cedar's eyes turned as dark as molten lava. "But Roslyn will do a lot to protect her secrets."

I couldn't tell if he admired or resented Mom. "How'd you keep her from calling me?"

"The hurricane worked in my favor. Seemed reasonable that the cell towers were down. I cut her landline and switched off her power."

But the storm was over, and Mom wouldn't keep me in a state of despair unless—

"You have guards posted at her house?"

"Of course." He pressed his lips together as if he didn't intend to say more, then lifted a shoulder. "One stationed at every door."

The panic spiders scampered across my heart. "Does Skinny Norwich know Owen and Mom are at her house?" On the run after killing Joseph, Mom's well-guarded house would be the perfect hideout.

"Skinny's on a rampage to avenge his brother." Cedar veered to the bed but kept the Smith and Wesson pointed squarely at my chest. "Got the local Cabral boys scurrying like roaches hunting for cover. I need to get on the road before Skinny decides to show up here."

My mind stalled, backtracked. "Skinny's blaming you for his brother's death?"

"Skinny's an equal opportunity revenger. He's blaming everyone."

My brain argued with my heart. Should I try and overpower Cedar? What if it backfired? Better to wait for Nathan. "Where are you headed?"

He removed a stack of pressed and folded shirts from a drawer, laid them neatly in the suitcase, and then checked his gold Rolex. "I think we should toast to our final goodbye. And my good fortune."

Opening a chest-high travel trunk repurposed into a bar, he poured two neat drinks from a bottle of Glenlivet. He dropped a pill in one, swirled it around, then put the doctored glass down by my hand. He raised his drink. "To our long-standing friendship." He chugged his scotch.

I barely glanced at my drink. "Think I'll pass. So you sent the email threats." I nodded. "I get that. Slowed down Nathan and Erica's investigation. Kept everyone off balance and allowed you time to put your affairs in order."

Cedar sipped his drink and didn't comment.

"And if I ran to California, you'd have the cover to escape. When I disappeared with Owen and Mom, Nathan would assume you'd left with us. What changed your plan?"

"You." He pointed the nine-millimeter at my chest. His body swayed, he overcompensated, jerked, and stumbled forward. Not Cedar's first drink of the day.

He straightened, walked to my side, and steered me three steps to the Moroccan game table. He pulled out one of the chairs. "Sit." He pushed the doctored glass into my hand. "Drink."

His breath reeked of alcohol. I hesitated over the chair, stared at the semi-automatic, and lowered my butt into the seat. I placed the tumbler back on the table with a shaky hand.

"Erica was gunning for your indictment. If I'd left town and she'd managed to throw you in jail, I wouldn't be around to ride to your rescue. My absence would've caught Nathan's attention quicker than flies on a sugar tit."

Cedar picked up his glass, shook the ice, walked back to the bar, and poured another two fingers. "I couldn't have Nathan ordering a manhunt until I had time to square things in Montevideo."

He puffed his chest and looked down his nose in the style of a taunting schoolyard bully. "But two hours ago, the last obstacle keeping me from the grand prize…" He flicked his fingers in the air. "Poof. Vanished." He laughed too hard and for too long. He carried his drink to the game table and sat in the other chair.

Cedar was drunk.

Drunk and holding a nine-millimeter aimed at me.

He took a sip of scotch. "Won't take the Feds long to trace the shell companies back to me. My assistant will roll faster than a flopping mackerel. Roslyn and Owen's disappearance refocused Nathan's attention back on you." He glanced at my glass. "Drink your scotch, girl." His voice steeled. Cedar would be a mean drunk.

I picked up the glass. "What's in here?"

"It's harmless, knock you out for a while. Give you a headache."

I tapped the rim with my fingernail. "I'll drink if you call your guards. Tell them to release Owen and Mom."

"I'm pressed for time." A smirk played on his lips. "Got a tight schedule."

My shirt clung like a wetsuit. I rubbed a damp palm over my thigh. Where was Nathan? "Did Joseph kill Cal?"

Cedar's smirk vanished as if I'd slapped it off his face. "He panicked and was convinced Erica was out to get him."

I struggled to catch up. "Calvin or Joseph?"

"Joseph doesn't panic. He kills." Cedar's cold declaration was a jolting reminder I didn't read people as well as I once believed. "So Joseph killed Calvin?"

Cedar sipped his drink. His edgy disposition had slipped into false courage, the kind found inside a bottle. "Monday morning, Cal banged on my door, wired and jittery. It was an accident."

"Accident?"

He looked at his watch, stood, and walked to his bed. He shut the suitcase with his free hand but kept his gaze and gun on me. "Calvin assumed I'd double-crossed him, and no amount of convincing got through his thick skull. Gun just went off."

"You shot Cal?" I pushed out of my seat. Raw anger, the burning, seething, roiling kind, crept up my neck. "You stuffed Calvin in the trunk of Ben's car? For me to find?"

Cedar circled the bed. "Get back."

I stood my ground.

"I'm done messing with you." He waved the semi-automatic in my face. "Drink, or I'll pour that scotch down your throat."

I backed up to my chair. "Tell me what happened to Cal, and I'll drink."

Cedar's jaw set. I could almost hear his teeth grinding. "Joseph's son overdosed. He had Skinny dump him in a river to keep the cops from getting involved. But the kid washed ashore, and the Feds found him. Calvin was convinced the DEA was following him, and for some reason, he concluded I'd sicced Erica Sanchez on him. He was half-crazy, not making any sense."

Cedar waved the nine-millimeter in the air. "I had to use my gun to get his attention, and then your investigator knocked on the door. Calvin jumped me."

"What happened to Ben?"

"After Calvin barreled into the house that morning, I didn't lock the door. Your man walked right in."

The floor dipped and waved like a roller coaster ride. "You shot Ben?"

"No other choice. He saw Calvin bleeding on the floor."

The roller coaster ride picked up speed, then dropped fifty feet. "Ben's dead?"

"Unfortunately."

My knees turned to mush. I slid into the chair. "What'd you do with Ben's body?"

"Root cellar. Mama's deep freezer's been empty for years."

I choked back bile. Held up my hand to stave off details. Owen. Just think of Owen. Keep the psychopath talking, and jump him at the first opportunity—my only plan.

Cedar glanced through the window. "Finish your scotch. I need to leave."

"Joseph's dead."

"Smartest move Skinny's ever made." Cedar heaved his suitcase off his bed.

I searched my brain for anything to keep him talking. "How much of my grandfather's money are you planning to steal?"

He looked up and smiled. I knew he wanted to brag, could see it in his eyes. "I've transferred every last cent to an account in the Grand Caymans, then routed the funds to three separate accounts in Hong Kong, and from there—well, that's my business. Drink."

"Call your guards and tell them to release Owen and Mom, and I'll sign whatever papers you need."

"Once I'm out of the country, I'll release your boy." He lifted his gun and looked down the barrel. "Guards won't make a move without orders from me, and Cabral men are loyal. But I don't need your signature. The bank accepted your power of attorney."

"What power of attorney?"

He shrugged. "Forged." He pointed at my scotch and made a drinking gesture. "Bottoms up."

He'd already owned killing Calvin and Ben, no reason to think he'd stop now. I sipped but had to stay awake long enough to warn Nathan about the guards.

"You're going to have to chug it." He thrust the nine-millimeter toward the glass and then back to me. "I'd rather not shoot you, but don't push me."

I didn't move.

He aimed at my thigh.

I took another sip and held the liquid in my mouth. It tasted like rich single malt, made for sipping, not chugging. The liquid mixed with my saliva and grew, then trickled down my throat.

"Drink it all," he said.

I coughed and sipped.

Cedar appeared satisfied.

"How'd you find out about the Montevideo money?" I asked.

"Private codicil to the will listed an offshore account and explained how to access the money. But it made no sense. Noah insisted you'd understand. I couldn't make heads or tails of the jumbled mess."

Granddad had loved his anagrams.

I sat forward. If I planned to jump him before he left, time to get it over. It wouldn't get any easier if I waited.

"You try anything, and I'll shoot you. You'll never see your son's face again."

I shifted back in my chair.

"I figured Noah's hidden account had to be in the millions," Cedar said. "After his stroke, I nosed around Roslyn's and found a receipt from Montevideo in his wallet." He leaned against his desk as if we were two friends having an after-dinner drink. "I found a connected guy in Uruguay, and he started hunting. Took two years to grease enough palms to run down the account." He threw a key onto the table beside Mom's box. "You can take that back to your mama. I don't need the insurance."

I fit the key into the lock and opened the lid. The jewelry was inside. "Surprised you aren't selling the diamonds." I slouched lower in the chair, my energy slowly slipping away.

"Too risky. The diamond's quality is too rare."

"The diamonds were your insurance?"

His hazel eyes filled with a merriment impossible to ignore. "The letters, not the diamonds." His tongue clucked in disapproval, disappointed in my inability to grasp his grand design. "In case I needed you to get my hands on the money. But you might want to read them. Learn your true heritage."

My eyelids were as heavy as stones. "Nathan and the Cabral nephews will hunt you down." My words slurred. My vision blurred.

"I'm not stealing from a Cabral. Well, technically, I am, but not from the nephews."

Cedar's image wavered. I blinked. Tried to focus.

He pushed my shoulder forward. "Get on the floor."

# CHAPTER THIRTY-SIX

*Katelyn*

I OSCILLATED BETWEEN CONSCIOUSNESS and sleep. Incessant ringing, ringing, ringing. A doorbell. No deeper. Bong, bong, bong. A clock. I needed to move. But why?

Dueling hammers played inside my head. My brain swam in sludge. I opened an eyelid. A brilliant, painful white light seared my pupil and drilled into the back of my skull.

I rolled sideways. Rested my cheek against a slick, cold surface. Floor. Table leg. Chair. Windows. Dark blinds. Cedar's bedroom.

I clutched the edge of a chair and pulled to my knees. The room spun like a merry-go-round gone wrong. I gripped the game table and waited for the sensation to ease. Owen's laughing blue eyes and face-splitting grin splashed across the television screen on the wall.

Snatches of my conversation with Cedar filtered through my consciousness. Three guards. One at every door. A tidal wave of terror drenched my body, propelling a blind fury that cleared the last of my confusion.

I had to get to Owen.

The room turned a steady pirouette. I braced against the headboard, then bumped from the bed to the desk and out of the bedroom. Using the wall for support, I moved down the hall like a drunk on a binge and zigzagged my way into the foyer. My fingers battled with the front door's deadbolt. The lock clicked, and I pushed the handle, pitching myself over the threshold. I wrapped my arms around a porch column and gaped at four flat tires on Susie's truck.

Call Nathan.

An image of my phone sliding off the seat of Susie's truck flashed in my mind. I staggered down the stairs, opened the truck, and swept my fingers under the front seat. My fingers touched plastic, and my chest cavity oozed with relief. I palmed my lifeline and punched redial.

"Kate. Where are you?" Nathan's desperate tone skipped a quick chill up my spine.

"Go to Mom's house—"

"I'm on the causeway."

My head swam, and I grabbed the truck door. "No, go to Mom's."

"Is that where Owen is?"

Trepidation squeezed my chest. "Guards." The drumming of an oil rig pounded in my head. Slam. Slam. Slam. Words skittered across my brain and disappeared as if caught under the rig's hammer.

"Kate, are you there? Where's Cedar?"

I latched onto the solidity of Nathan's voice. "Cedar's gone. Three guards." My stomach rolled. I gagged on scotch. Spat. "Mom and Owen are at her Whitaker house. Cedar has three guards. One at each door. Go." My eyes skimmed the flat tires, and I searched the street. A blue sedan crept down the road. "I'll meet you."

"Stay where you are. Don't—"

I disconnected and lumbered down the driveway, waving my hands over my head.

The car pulled to a stop. The driver met me at the end of the drive. "Ma'am, are you okay?" He was young, not long out of high school, and wore a brown shirt with a security patch on the sleeve.

I clutched his hand. "Please, help me."

He walked me toward his vehicle. "You need to sit."

"No. I need to go to Whitaker Street." I pulled him to his open car door.

"What's your name?" He turned and glanced down Cedar's drive. "Are you visiting Mr. Haynes?"

A wave of dizziness hit, and I gripped the doorframe. "I'm Katelyn Landers. Please. Drive me. Downtown."

He eased me onto the seat.

"My son. Whitaker Street." I tried articulating details, but the muscles in my tongue battled with the brain-muddling drug Cedar dumped in my scotch.

He squatted in front of me. "I can't leave the neighborhood." His mouth molded his words slowly and distinctly as if I were a crying child or an escaped mental patient. He was gentle and kind and had no intention of driving me anywhere.

I glanced at the dangling keys in his ignition and pointed to Cedar's house. "There's an injured man."

"What happened?" His gaze turned to Cedar's house. "Is it Mr. Haynes? Did a tree fall?"

"He's hurt. Please. Check on him."

"Stay here." He jogged down the drive.

I swung my legs in and closed the car door. Shifting into drive, I headed for Whitaker Street.

---

I parked on the far side of Forsyth Park, fell in step with a group of tourists, crossed Bolton Street, and slid behind an old oak tree with limbs touching Mom's side balcony. In my teens, the branches made a perfect ladder for sneaking in and out after curfew. I plastered my back against the bark.

A hand clamped over my mouth. "What do you think

you're doing?" Erica's voice rumbled in my ear. She eased her grip on my face and slid around the tree. "Go to the park until this is over." She hugged a basket of white and yellow daisies to her chest. Three smiley-faced balloons waved cheerfully in the air.

"Cedar has three goons guarding Mom and Owen. One at each first-floor entrance." I pointed to the balcony. "They won't worry about the second floor. I can get inside."

"You're not trained." Impatience simmered through her skin as clearly as the exasperation filtering her voice. "You're not going inside."

"Owen will be petrified when he sees men with guns. I can keep him calm."

She held my gaze, a cop's stare—assessing, suspicious, wary. "No, Kate."

I balled my hands into fists. "I'm his mother." I sidestepped, determined to get inside...not about to let Erica get in my way.

She yanked my arm. "Don't risk this op. We're a trained rescue team. We'll get Owen out safe."

"I'm going in." My calm voice betrayed my racing heart. My only experience with rescue operations was from TV. Bullets flew, and people died. I had to get to Owen and protect him.

Erica looked up at the balcony, then pulled me behind the tree. "Thermal imaging shows one person in the library, another near the front door, and one on the move in the hall. It looks like Owen and Roslyn are upstairs."

I offered up what I knew. "Cedar had a video. Mom and Owen are in her bedroom." I pointed at the balcony. "Three doors down from my old room."

Erica scrunched her mouth as if chewing on ways to get rid of me. Finally, her lips pressed together. "Christ." She shoved her hand through her cropped hair.

She bent over, yanked her backup pistol out of her

ankle strap, and handed a revolver to me. "You make it inside without getting shot, head to Roslyn's room, and hide everyone. We'll clear the downstairs and come to you. We all move out together."

I nodded and didn't say anything to give her a reason to change her mind.

She held up the flower basket. "Fake delivery. Move in when the doorbell rings." Startling me, Erica grabbed my hand and squeezed, her eyes holding worry and twenty years of friendship. "Whatever this was, your mom was in on it. Don't forget that." She disappeared around the tree.

The balcony had a set of sliding doors that led to my old bedroom. They'd be locked, but I knew a simultaneous jiggle and push would release the latch.

The lowest oak limb was eight feet up. I caught the branch on my first jump, lay vertically, and inched my way forward. I pulled myself to standing and cleared the railing, praying for Owen to stay safe. I wiggled and pulled on the door. Nothing. Not now. Not this close.

Push, shake, and pull. I leaned against the door frame, jiggled the catch, and yanked. The lock gave way, and the door skated soundlessly across the tracks.

The doorbell rang—Erica's fake delivery.

I stepped into my old bedroom with Erica's revolver leading the way. The quiet hum of the air conditioning sounded turbocharged but paled in comparison to my jackhammering heart. I crept toward the bathroom that would bring me one room closer to Mom's suite.

I pushed open the door. A creak stopped me midstep. I pressed against the wall. An icy prickle slid up my neck. Owen was only ten feet away.

I inched forward. No sound.

The shower curtain rustled. A fist headed for my face.

I didn't duck.

# CHAPTER THIRTY-SEVEN

*Katelyn*

ON ANOTHER DAY, in another place, the fist might've hurt. But today, the blow had zero impact—no more than a sand gnat's annoying sting. Beyond pain, beyond caring, this low-down bastard threatened my son.

Erica's eighth-grade, how-to-knock-a-bully-on-their-ass tips kicked in. Whoever connected first won. Erica's mantra—the one she'd drummed into me at thirteen-years-old—move into the punch, tilt, and make your opponent's next hit veer off course. Then I kneed the guy in the balls. Men might be stronger, but girls fight dirtier—another Erica acumen.

His hands covered his crotch, and he folded over like the limp dick he was. The guy was short, lean, and barely over twenty. I had three inches and twenty pounds on him.

I crashed Erica's revolver into the right side of his head—a sickening thud.

One of his hands abandoned his balls and grabbed his ear. I smashed the gun into the left side of his face.

Blood spurted. His knees buckled, and he sprawled on the tile floor.

I bashed another blow into his skull.

Satisfied, he wouldn't get up, I crossed into the next room and cracked the door.

A man's voice I didn't recognize floated up the stairway. Must be another guard.

I pressed against the wall and passed the landing.

A clunk, then the sound of glass crashing. Mom's antique Murano bowl.

My heart seized.

I fast-tracked to Mom's room, slipped inside, quickly scanned her suite, and verified Mom and Owen were alone.

Owen leaned over the gaming table in the sitting area, focused on a chessboard. He had one foot on the floor, and his knee braced in the chair.

Mom sat across from him with her hand raised to move her pawn.

I placed a finger against my lips.

She released the chess piece, mimicked my finger to the lips, and pointed at me.

Owen turned, and his entire face lit. He flew into my arms and seared a thousand and one fissures in my heart.

I reveled in the warmth of his body, wrapped my arms around him, kissed his face, and drank in his little boy smell. It was as if someone had opened a window and let the air in again. I could breathe.

I leaned him back and forced an oversized smile. "Aunt Erica's here. We're playing a game. We have to be really quiet, hide, and only come out when she gives the password. If we win, she'll spring for ice cream. You want to play?"

"Sure." He laughed, and my heart exploded with love.

A calm warmth spread through my chest. "You hide in the closet. Nana and I will stand guard." I carried him to the door. He slid out of my arms, settled against the back wall, and hid behind Mom's long formal dresses.

"I'll be right outside." I touched my finger to my lips again. "Remember, not a sound."

He pushed aside a burgundy gown and peeked through.

"What's the password?" he whispered.

I blanked and then latched onto the first thing. "Black Beauty." His favorite book.

He covered his mouth and smothered a giggle.

I snapped a mental picture of his radiant face, then shut the door.

"What's happened?" Mom pounced. "Why are you hiding Owen?"

I dragged her away from the closet so Owen wouldn't hear. "Erica and Nathan are working on getting us out of the house."

"Why?"

"The men guarding you are dangerous."

"They're Cedar's men. They're protecting us."

"They're Cabral men. They can't be trusted."

She touched my forearm. "Kate, there's so much I need to explain. Juan's nephews have the misguided belief you're a threat to their inheritance." Her shoulders dropped, and bewilderment settled in the wrinkles around her eyes.

Tension swam in the air between us like motes of dust.

"I'm so sorry Juan's family threatened Owen." Mom's voice barely reached a whisper. "They've caused you so much pain. Juan promised he'd always protect you, but he died, and..."

"Why would Juan Cabral promise to protect me?" I hunted her face for an explanation.

She stepped back, her hand gripping a Louis XV commode. She swallowed and drew a short, hard breath. Color drained from her face, and her lips thinned. "I... haven't been honest." Her eyes filled with tears, but I saw love and worry in them.

I finally said the words out loud. "Juan Cabral's my biological father, isn't he?"

Tears streamed down her cheeks. "Yes."

My heart tumbled, twisted like a rag, and shredded.

Cedar's flippant taunt that he'd stolen from a Cabral, just not the nephews, echoed in my head. I was Juan Cabral's daughter. My God, my father had been a drug kingpin. My cousins ran the biggest drug cartel in the Southeast.

I had a million questions but set them aside with my shock. Owen's safety was my priority. "Being here under guard has nothing to do with Juan's nephews. That's a concocted story. Cedar's on the run."

Mom frowned, and based on the lines on her forehead, her bafflement was genuine. "What do you mean?"

"He stole thirty million dollars from Granddad's offshore accounts. This fake kidnapping plan is a diversion so Cedar can leave the country and get the money."

Erica slipped through the door. "Owen secure?"

I wiped my tears with the back of my hand. "We're good."

"I neutralized one guard, and Nathan took care of another. He's checking the rest of the second floor now."

"There are usually three guards," Mom said.

"One's in my old bathroom," I said. "I took care of him. He was unconscious when I left him." Erica gave me a thumbs-up.

Nathan came through the door. His hot focused gaze soothed my skittering heart.

"Willie spotted Skinny Norwich in the park, a half block away," he said. "Skinny's carrying and moving with a crowd of tourists in this direction. He could have recruited help and have eyes on the main doors. Our best option is the balcony."

Cedar's warning of Skinny's revenge flew through my mind. I opened the closet and tugged Owen's hand. "Come on. We have to go."

He pulled back. "Aunt Erica didn't say the password."

I knew Owen. Rules were rules. I stuck my head out of the closet and whispered to Erica, "Say, Black Beauty."

She turned and, without hesitation, said, "Black Beauty."

Owen fist-pumped. "We won." He jumped out, ran to Erica, and grabbed her around the waist. "I want chocolate sprinkles." He spotted her gun and jerked back.

I pulled him to my side. "It's okay. Just part of the game, like in one of your videos."

"We've positioned a ladder against the wall leading to the balcony." Nathan motioned us into the hallway.

I knelt and faced Owen. "We're going to sneak out of the house and down a ladder. Okay?"

His gaze cut to Erica. "This isn't a game, is it?"

Erica knelt beside me. "You can do this, Champ. "You'll be right between your mom and me." She waited until he nodded, then stood.

Nathan led the way. We crept from Mom's suite and walked follow-the-leader style down the carpeted hall, Nathan, then Mom, me, Owen, and Erica. We made it past the open staircase and into my old bedroom.

Nathan maneuvered around the desk, slid past the bed, and opened the sliding glass doors leading to the balcony. "When I give the okay, bring Owen out, and I'll take him down the ladder." He stepped outside.

I hugged Owen close and rubbed a calming hand down his back. Then I heard a squeak. I turned just as the bathroom door swung open.

# CHAPTER THIRTY-EIGHT

*Katelyn*

I PUSHED OWEN BEHIND me and blocked him with my body.

Erica thrust me, Owen, and Mom toward the balcony. "Get Owen to the ladder." She ran around the bed and faced off with a human wall.

Nathan rushed back into the bedroom, pushed Mom and Owen into a crouch, swiveled, and reached for me.

I stepped toward Erica.

"Kate, get behind me." Nathan held his finger to his ear. "Move in. Repeat. Move in."

"Kate, get down." Nathan's demand reverberated off the ceiling.

The Wall, eyes hot, teeth bared, kept his gun aimed at Erica. "Don't. Move."

"US marshal. Drop your weapon." Nathan's commanding voice filled the room.

Erica remained mute, intent, and focused on her opponent.

I stared at the Wall's gun, his arm a mass of corded muscles. He could knock Erica into unconsciousness with one backhanded slap.

Except…I held the upper hand.

I straightened my shoulders, pretended my heart still beat at a normal rhythm and slipped on my authoritative boardroom persona. "I'm Juan Cabral's daughter. This woman works for me. Drop your weapon."

Erica fast-blinked, then used my intro, and said, "Lay your weapon on the floor, and no one gets hurt."

"Jake, where the hell are you?" a man yelled. Skinny Norwich staggered into the bedroom waving a pistol, blood dripping from his shoulder. His gaze centered on me, and his face twisted. He shook his head like a rabid dog—salvia and bubbles of foam slid down his chin. "You Cabrals." He shoved his gun toward me. "You're going to pay for Dennis."

"Mom!" Owen's cry sliced my heart.

Skinny's gaze flicked in Owen's direction, and he swung his pistol.

Every cell in my body leaped. "Noooo!"

I dove, aimed for Skinny's bloody shoulder. A gun blast.

Then another. Skinny toppled.

I landed, jammed my fist against his wound, and rolled off.

I scrambled to Owen. My hands flew over his body, patting, sliding, and searching. No blood. I crushed his body to mine. Rocked him, soothed his tears from fear and not injury, thankful the blood on my hands was Skinny's and not my baby's.

Nathan pressed a finger to his earpiece. "Civilian shot. We need an ambulance. I repeat. Civilian shot."

"Oh, God." I crushed Owen to my chest, turned, and looked at Mom. Her legs were skewed at an unnatural angle as if she were a rag doll thrown aside without a care. Above her breast, a dark wet stain crept over her sky-blue Chanel blouse.

Please, God. Don't do this. I let Owen go, pulled Mom into my lap, and cradled her head. "Hold on, Mom. Look at me. Don't close your eyes. Look at me. Help's on the way."

Nathan knelt and pressed two fingers against her throat. "She has a pulse." His eyes met mine. "She stood up to shield Owen. Faced Norwich straight on."

Mom's brilliant cobalt eyes met mine, slowly fading into a dull, lifeless gray. Her body shuddered. "I'm so sorry." She gasped a short, hard breath, and her body relaxed in my arms.

"No." I rocked back and forth. "Don't give up, Mom. Please. Don't. Give. Up."

# CHAPTER THIRTY-NINE

*Katelyn*

**Seven Months Later**

A CAR DOOR SLAMMED, and I set an armload of books on the kitchen table, stepped to the window, and tipped the blind. Nathan had called this morning and asked to stop by, so seeing him striding down the sidewalk carrying his bulging briefcase wasn't a surprise. But my heart still flipped a couple of somersaults.

He paused at the door, glanced back toward the street as if surveying the neighborhood, then tapped his knuckles on the doorjamb.

I let the blind slip back and opened the door. "Hey, stranger."

He stepped inside, and I instantly understood the term pitter-patter—an inane elementary description of a racing heart. But the thing about clichés—they're usually right on.

He shrugged off his blue jacket with the gold star emblem, and I hung it on the peg by the door. "You arrest any bad guys today?"

He studied my face with an intensity that once made me think he was running my features through a known felon list. It still sent spiders scuttling over my skin, but now for a different reason.

"No arrests yet," he said. "But it's still early."

There are moments in life when everything goes quiet. Nathan and I stood in my foyer and stared into one another's eyes. There was nothing else—just us.

And then the neighbor's dog barked and shattered the magic. "I'd planned to make a pitcher of iced tea," I said. "You interested?"

He followed me into the kitchen. "Sounds perfect." He wore jeans, a navy polo shirt, and scuffed brown boots. His hair was shorter than I remembered.

"You've cut your hair."

"Shaved it for an op." He smiled. His eyes twinkled as if they held some private joke.

I didn't pry, I knew him well enough to know he'd never confide details to an uninvolved civilian. "I was surprised when you called. Didn't expect you to be in Savannah again so soon." I kept my voice casual and hoped he couldn't read my excitement. I filled a teapot with water and placed it on the stove to boil.

He leaned against the counter. "I have a month of vacation accrued and thought I'd hang out in Savannah and get to know...." He smiled. "Familiarize myself with the city and the locals."

His presence took up my entire kitchen, the space, the air. I noticed the strength of him, his chest, his shoulders. Heat flushed my skin, crept up my neck and into my cheeks. His choosing Savannah as a vacation destination didn't seem coincidental.

His gaze swept my galley kitchen. No fancy coffee machine or eight-burner stove, or Sub-Zero freezer. But his expression, cop flat, left no clue what he thought about the cozy two-bedroom, one-and-a-half-bath carriage house attached to Mom's house.

"Hear you've been busy," I said.

He raised a brow. "Yeah?"

"Willie called and said Cedar is scheduled for extradition and will be arraigned next week." I pushed a pile of Owen's schoolbooks to the end of the counter. "According to Willie, you chased Cedar for five months, as focused as a junkyard dog after a pork chop."

Nathan's chuckle didn't disguise his pride. "We found Cedar holed up in a hostel in the mountains of Machu Picchu."

"So I heard. I have to admit, I'm a little disappointed." I measured a cup of sugar, opened the cabinet, and placed two glasses on the counter. "I dreamed of the police dragging him from a ritzy hotel in Asia, or maybe Australia, never considered a hostel." I filled the glasses with ice. "How'd you find him?"

He lifted a shoulder. "He used the name, Jeddah Anderson. Jeddah was his great-grandfather's given name. Anderson a family name on his mother's side."

I considered the irony. "I guess the moral is—if you need an alias, choose one from the phone book."

My cell buzzed with a message. "It's Erica checking in with Owen. She's adopted a self-inflicted godmother devotion that's pretty heartwarming." I typed a quick reply.

Baseball practice. Ck back after—

"She mentioned you two keep in touch."

The teakettle whistled, and I rummaged through the cabinet for my stoneware pitcher, then poured hot water over the tea bags. "Our relationship will probably never be what it once was, but after Owen's kidnapping, I reassessed my priorities."

I exhaled the same way a delivery nurse tells an imminent mother to breathe and let the memory of those painful days recede. "I wasn't much of a friend to Erica. I learned from Ben, my private investigator, about her three rounds of rehab. How did I not know? I should've been there for her." I removed a tin of macadamia nut cookies and set a few on a plate. "I asked her to meet me for dinner one night and asked for forgiveness."

"How'd that go?" He reached for a cookie, a hint of a smile playing on his lips.

"Asked might be a stretch. It was more of an applied apology."

His wrinkled brow reminded me of one of the pug puppies Owen had his eye on.

"I bought her a steak, and we talked girl shop."

He finished off his cookie. "Girl shop?"

"A little college football, the sorry state of fashion footwear, whether our waiter complied with the standards of smoking hot or merely hot. You know, all those dark, serious subjects women debate when they decide to let well enough alone."

His confusion cleared, and he nodded. "Guy talk, plus the shoes." He opened his briefcase and handed me a box. "I didn't trust Fed Ex with this."

I searched a drawer, located my box cutter, and slit the tape. "Mom's jade box." I ran my hand over the top. My fingers tingled as if the memories stored inside fought to be free. "Thanks for this. I'll take it over later."

"How is she?"

"Three more weeks of physical therapy, and she'll be back on the golf course."

He laughed, twisted a key off his ring, and handed it to me. "I kept this with me."

I accepted the key. His desire to protect Mom's secrets sent me a warm rush. "I appreciate you delivering them." I couldn't help hoping the box wasn't the only reason he'd stopped by.

Nathan picked up a book from the stack I'd been sorting earlier.

"Beth had movers pack up Spartina," I said. "I guess the shipment arrived because she sent me these books from Granddad's collection." The pile included works by Mark Twain, Hemingway, Dashiell Hammett, Michener.

Nathan flipped through one written by Dashiell Hammett. "This volume is a signed first edition."

"They were gifts to Granddad from Mom and me. We'd hunt all year for first editions of his favorite authors." My heart swelled with tenderness. "Beth sending these gifts is so thoughtful."

A cigar humidor sat beside the books. I peeled off the yellow sticky note.

Remembered this was your Christmas gift to Grandfather a few years back. Thought you might want to save it for Owen.

Love, Beth

I opened the lid of the burl wood chest and flashed back to the Christmas morning that Granddad opened this present. Memories flew faster than cascading water over a running rapid.

Mom's fruitcake baking in the oven, Elvis Presley's pitch-perfect voice crooning I'll be home for Christmas, and Granddad's booming laugh filtering from behind the doors of his study. "I don't know where to put my family memories of Noah now," I said. "I feel like a divorced woman staring at her wedding dress."

Nathan touched my shoulder. "I heard someone say once that memories are like bullets. Some whiz by and only spook you. Others tear you open and leave you in pieces." He dropped his hand, and the sudden loss of his warmth was like a blast of frigid air. A full-body shiver ran through me.

He walked to the sliding glass door leading to the garden. "How do you like living back in Savannah?"

"This is home, where my roots are. I may not be a Barry, but on Mom's side, I'm still fourth-generation Savannhian."

He removed a small box from his briefcase, this one

wrapped. "I'd hoped to see Owen. I brought him something. It's a signed Braves baseball. One of the guys on my team has a brother who plays outfield."

I accepted the present. "I'm sure he'll love it. He's hoping to be the team's pitcher this season. Working hard on his curve ball."

"He's adjusting to the move. That's good." Nathan swiveled Owen's math book lying on the counter. "Erica mentioned you're homeschooling."

"Just for the first semester. I wanted him to settle into our new life, and after traveling so much over the past eight years, I have a lot to make up for. I wanted to take advantage of this time when I'm still Owen's number one girl."

Nathan nodded. "You've got about five months left." He glanced at the yellow sticky note on Granddad's humidor. "How is Beth?"

"She checks in every few weeks. She has no family left except for her baby." My voice gave away my elation. "It's a boy."

His face scrunched into a help-me-understand expression. "You seem excited."

"Thrilled. Owen and I are planning to visit her in Colorado over the Christmas holidays."

"I didn't realize you and Beth were that close."

"We weren't. But we're the only family she has left. Her mom suffered a fatal heart attack on their trip to Colorado. The night she left Savannah, Beth turned off her phone, removed the battery, and never switched it back on. When I asked her why, she said there was no one left to call." I tore a paper towel from the holder and wiped tears from my cheeks. "I'm determined to change that."

Nathan sat at the kitchen table, and I handed him his tea glass. Placed the cookies on the table.

"How'd the negotiations with the DEA end up?" he asked.

I sat in the chair across from him. "I salvaged enough money that Beth will come out okay."

"Not you?"

I shrugged and sipped my tea. "I'm not a Barry."

Disapproval came and went across his face. The sound of a leaf blower echoed through the window. The harsh sound contrasted with the quiet between us.

He tapped the edge of the table with his fingers. A steady rhythm, lost in thought. "According to Noah Barry's will, half of whatever you have left after the DEA negotiations are legally yours."

"Granddad would have never named me as trustee if he'd known I was Juan Cabral's daughter. Owen and I will start fresh. Beth and Calvin's son is the rightful Barry heir."

He bit into another cookie. "How about the house you bought from Calvin?"

"On the market. I priced it to sell."

"And you sold Spartina."

"Nope. Beth sold Spartina."

He contemplated me for an agonizing minute, and I forced myself not to fidget. He nodded. "A clean slate." I pulled the jade box closer. Each panel on the box depicted a different season. Spring, with the promise of new beginnings, was my favorite. "Mom will fully recover, and Owen's happy and healthy. Those are the most important." I reveled in the positives of my life.

Nathan's intense gaze shot something airy and light through me. He traced a knot on my kitchen table with his finger, and it seemed his touch trailed up and down my spine.

"My boss says he made an attractive offer, but you haven't committed."

I laughed then, a full-out, up-from-the-gut roll that left

me breathless. "Sorry." I waved a hand in front of my face. "The DEA confiscated a company I managed. I'm no longer bondable. I can't work in a commercial bank or hold a financial broker's license. Yet I have an attractive job offer for top-secret government work."

Nathan squinted. "You cheat a bank, you go to jail. You cheat the US Marshal Service, you disappear."

"Touché."

"But seriously, you have good instincts, and your financial background would be invaluable."

"Yeah, bad guys like their money." I stacked then restacked a pile of Hemingway books. "Joining the service is a significant commitment." I flipped the cover of The Sun Also Rises and pretended to study Hemingway's dignified signature. I stole a look at Nathan's face. "Are you advocating for me to join up?"

"Absolutely." He grinned. It hit his eyes first, then moved to his lips.

"I've promised to give my answer by Monday."

The atmosphere in the cottage turned heavy as if the air had been cut off and the oxygen was slowly vanishing. I curbed an urge to crack the kitchen window and let in the breeze.

He leaned across the table, lifted a strand of my chin-length hair, and tucked it behind my ear. "I'm not the only one who got a haircut."

My body displayed all the classic symptoms of a high-school crush. Prickling spine. Nervous hands that wouldn't still. Hairs stood on my arms when my eyes met his.

He removed a large manila envelope from his briefcase. "These are the papers to transfer the Montevideo money. It's a formality, but signing off would be appreciated. I've also included the agreement for the State of Georgia to designate Barry Island as protected land. The state agreed to your request for a perpetual clause for you and your heirs to have visiting rights ten days a year."

"Great." I reached for the envelope and peeked inside. "You include mailing instructions?"

He finished his tea and stood. "I'd hoped you'd agree to take a ride. The documents require notarization." He tilted his head. "If you're not busy, maybe we could have dinner."

I looked down at my plain t-shirt and jeans. The same outfit that had taken an hour to pick out after his phone call. But it wouldn't work for dinner. "I'll need a few minutes to freshen up." I popped out of my chair.

"Take your time." He rose, then ran a hand through his hair. A gesture I'd come to realize as his nervous tell. "Maybe you give me a tour of the hot spots around town."

My heart performed an Olympic-worthy backflip. "Let me make sure I understand." I tapped the envelope. "If I sign over thirty million to the United States government, I get a dinner date with you?"

He flashed what could only be called a conquering smile and closed the distance between us. "That about sums it up."

I stepped into his arms. "Well, Marshal, no one can call you a cheap date."

# WANT MORE?

Join Katelyn and Nathan in their next adventure—can Katelyn prove she's a good fit for the U.S. Marshal Service when a key witness vanishes on her watch? Even Nathan has his doubts.

### FIND OUT WHAT HAPPENS NEXT!
https://tinyurl.com/ReadChangingWinds

Reality Meets Fiction: The True Events Behind *Changing Tides.*

### FREE BONUS CONTENT!
https://dl.bookfunnel.com/vvowb8k3qq

# ACKNOWLEDGMENTS

Bringing my books to life is a collaborative effort, and I'm fortunate to have an incredible team by my side—my Lucky 13. These thirteen dedicated professionals and passionate readers elevate my writing in ways I can hardly express, but I'll do my best.

To my two brilliant editors, Jenn and Ann—your insights and skills transform my stories, and I'm endlessly grateful. Jenn, you wear the dual hats of editor and book mechanic, performing the technical wizardry that turns words into polished books ready for the world. My deepest thanks to you both; I know my readers are just as thankful!

A special shoutout to my ARC team, a group of eleven amazing individuals who read, comment, and review each book before it's released. Your feedback is invaluable, and I truly couldn't do this without you.

To my husband, whose unwavering support and belief in me make it possible to live out this dream—thank you from the heart of my heart.

And finally, to Fiddler, my three-year-old Labradoodle and faithful writing companion, who stays by my side during those long hours of crafting stories.

What a wonderful life you all allow me to lead!

## ABOUT THE AUTHOR

*Join My Email List For Updates On My Books!*
*www.veronicamixon.com*

VERONICA MIXON IS an Amazon chart-topper who writes suspense and contemporary book club fiction. She has authored eight books, all set in the South, except for one international thriller.

A career in marketing, twenty years of world travel, and a large and boisterous southern family supply her with ample material for the fiction novels she loves to write. She lives on the Georgia coast with her husband and two-year-old Australian Labradoodle, Fiddler.

You can find a catalog of Veronica's work on her Amazon author page or her website at: *www.veronicamixon.com*

Made in the USA
Columbia, SC
23 October 2024